D0502969

PROSPERO LOST

TOR BOOKS BY
L. JAGI LAMPLIGHTER

Prospero Lost
Prospero in Hell (forthcoming)

PROSPERO LOST

L. Jagi Lamplighter

A TOM DOHERTY ASSOCIATES BOOK
NEW YORK

This is a work of fiction. All of the characters, organizations, and events portrayed in this novel are either products of the author's imagination or are used fictitiously.

PROSPERO LOST

Edited by James Frenkel

A Tor Book
Published by Tom Doherty Associates, LLC
175 Fifth Avenue
New York, NY 10010

www.tor-forge.com

Library of Congress Cataloging-in-Publication Data

Lamplighter, L. Jagi.
Prospero lost / L. Jagi Lamplighter.—1st ed.
p. cm.—(Prospero's daughter ; bk. 1)
ISBN 978-0-7653-1929-6
1. Sisters Fiction. 2. Magicians—Fiction. I. Title.

PS3612.A547435P76 2009
813'.6—dc22

2009016708

First Edition: September 2009

Printed in the United States of America

0 9 8 7 6 5 4 3 2 1

To William Shakespeare and John C. Wright
who, between them,
invented nearly every character in this story
except for Mab Boreal, Astreus, and Caurus

ACKNOWLEDGMENTS

Thank you to:

Mark Whipple, Dave Eckstein, and Catherine Rockwood, without whose insistence this novel would have been abandoned in its infancy.

To Von Long, Erin Furby, Kirsten Edwards, Bill Burns, Dave Coffman, Elizabeth Livingston, Jeff Lyman, Melanie Florence, Jessie Harris, Donna Royston, Robin Buehler, Jane Thornley, Don Schank, and Diana Hardy for their support and advice, and to Danielle Ackley-McPhail and the Yesterday's Dreamers for all their useful ideas concerning the craft of writing.

To my editor, Jim Frenkel, for not giving up on me! And to my agent, Richard Curtis, the Knight in Shining Armor who gives me hope!

To Milton, whose title, I hope, this book honors rather than mocks.

And, most important, to my mother, Jane Lamplighter, without whose selfless devotion to her grandchildren this book literally could not have been written.

CONTENTS

PROSPERO LOST

CHAPTER ONE

Miranda

It was after midnight when I discovered Father's last message.

After a long day of work, I had been relaxing in the lesser hall of Prospero's Mansion in Oregon, flipping through one of my father's old journals, when I came across a blank page. An intuition from my Lady prompted me to hold the book up to the phoenix lamp.

With a loud crackle, red-gold sparks leapt from the burning phoenix feather housed in a glass lantern beside the hearth and crawled across the journal, scorching words into the parchment. A strong odor of burnt paper and cinnamon filled the air. I nearly dropped the book.

I had seen secrets revealed by the phoenix lamp before. Father had a habit of scribbling notes in the margins that could only be read in this way. Normally, the letters appeared slowly. This smoldering script was something new.

The blazing letters read:

My Child:
I have unwittingly unleashed powers best kept bound. If I fail to constrain them, they will destroy me and all I have wrought. If you have not seen me since the writing of this message, assume the worst and warn the family. Counsel my children to keep close the gifts I have bestowed.
Beware the Three Shadowed Ones!

Prospero,
Magus

I turned the page, but the rest of the journal was blank, even by phoenix lamp.

Was Father in trouble, or was this another of his pranks? Our family had many supernatural enemies. We had bound many malevolent creatures throughout our long lives, any number of which could have broken free of their restraints. On the other hand, in the last century or so, Father seemed to handle every difficulty that came his way with ease. This letter was most likely one of Father's many jests, set up years ago to startle any youngster unlawfully searching his books. Finding no further evidence that this message had been written recently—and not knowing any method by which he could have sent it into the book from a distance—I dismissed it and continued reading.

That night, letters of flame troubled my dreams.

The next morning, I sent one of the invisible spirits of the air who serve our family to Prospero's Island. (Father refused to keep any kind of phone. He claimed the "constant caterwauling of that new-fangled contraption" disturbed his concentration.) If Peaseblossom found him at home, she was to tell him of the laugh he might have at my expense.

Only, he was not there.

It took Peaseblossom six days to circumnavigate the globe, reach my father's island retreat, and return to Oregon. Upon returning, she reported that the Aerie Ones on Prospero's Island were agitated. Great Prospero had not returned from his most recent voyage, even though he had been expected several months ago. Nor could his servants find him anyplace upon the earth.

This news disturbed me. Never in my long life could I recall a time when the Aerie Ones had been unable to find Father. It was time to act. I sent for Mab.

I DECIDED to meet with Mab in the Everblooming Gardens, as I seldom could afford to take time from my busy workday to enjoy them. This botanical wonderland, which one reached by leaving the house through a back door, was always in bloom, no matter the season. It lay between Prospero's Mansion and a tall stone wall, beyond which stood an enclosed forest of aspens and virgin pines. At the garden's center, in the midst of the flower beds, a fountain leapt, the water rushing and gurgling.

I sat at a wrought-iron table next to the fountain, stirring my tea. My hair, so pale as to appear silver, was piled atop my head in a Grecian style that had gone out of vogue more than a century ago. My garment, a tea gown with a high lacy collar—the enchanted satin of which matched the emerald of my eyes—was also of a bygone age. Fashions change so quickly. Long ago, I had stopped bothering to keep up.

As I reached for another sugar cube, Mab, our company's head gumshoe, came slouching down the path, his hands stuck in the pockets of his gray trench coat. He was the granite-faced, hard-boiled type. Too many years of chasing supernatural perpetrators had given him an intense dislike of all things arcane. He might have passed for human himself, had he not looked so precisely like a detective from a 1940s movie.

Coming up beside me, Mab respectfully removed his fedora and gave me a nod. Mab and I had worked together on numerous occasions, though I never called on him personally unless the matter was one of particular importance. Lesser matters I left to his men.

"You wanted to see me, Ma'am?" he asked, in his Bronx accent. There was a sardonic quality to everything Mab said; even his terms of polite address, such as "Ma'am" sounded defiant.

"Mab, are you familiar with the Three Shadowed Ones? The name sounds vaguely familiar, but I can't place them."

"Don't know, Ma'am, but they sound like bad customers. If you want my opinion, you'll turn down whatever they're offering and stick to legitimate mundane business."

"This has nothing to do with me . . ." I began.

"Glad to hear it, Ma'am," Mab picked up his hat and turned to leave.

I frowned severely to express my disapproval. Secretly, I was amused. I appreciated his concern for my safety but would have preferred if his methods had bordered less upon insubordination. Still, he was a superb detective and as loyal to Prospero, Inc. as an old hound dog.

"It's about my father. I have reason to believe he may be in danger."

Mab froze in the act of returning his fedora to his head. "From these 'Three Shadowy Ones'?"

"Shadowed. It's Three Shadowed Ones."

"Sounds supernatural."

"They are."

"Too bad. Rather liked the old man."

"I didn't say he was dead!"

"Playing with fire gets you burned, Ma'am," Mab said. "Playing with the supernatural gets you dead. You gotta take my word on this. I destroyed my share of meddling humans in my youth. I know how the game is played. I told your old man he'd run afoul of one of us someday, if he kept putting his nose where it didn't belong. And the nose of a human never belongs sniffing about in the arcane."

Mab had been one of the blustery winds before he agreed to inhabit a fleshly body, and he was blustery still. When dealing with Aerie Ones, it was often quicker to let them say their piece and then nip any further impertinence in the bud rather than to try to restrain them.

Because of this, I was in the habit of allowing Mab to rattle on, but this did not mean that I allowed his doom-and-gloom speeches to ruffle me; gales may blow, but a queenly peak remains undisturbed.

Besides, what use was asking a detective for advice if one did not listen to what he advised?

"We're not here to discuss Father," I clarified in my calm and businesslike fashion, "although I want you to have your men begin searching for him. We're here because my father left a note saying that these Three Shadowed Ones might be a threat to my siblings and me. He asked that I warn the family, and so, I shall do so. However, it has been years since I've spoken with most of my brothers. I want you to help me find them."

"Your personal safety comes first, Ma'am. I suggest you rid yourself of all supernatural devices. It's a matter of security, Ma'am. When you stink of magic, it draws them like a beacon. If you rid yourself of magic, no supernatural being will be able to sniff you out." Mab tossed his hat onto the table and counted off his points on his fingers. "Quench the phoenix feather. Burn the magical tomes in the library. Empty the Vault. Unravel your enchanted gown. Dismantle the wind-slicing fan. Destroy the orrery. Pour out the Water of Life. Free us Aerie Spirits who are in service to you. Oh, and break that accursed flute. That should do it. You'll be safe then."

I smiled behind my teacup. It always came down to the flute. Not that I blamed him. If a flute controlled my free will, I would plot its destruction, too. Ignoring the rest, I limited my reprimand to his mistake of fact.

"The orrery is mechanical, Mab. It is made of clockwork."

Mab frowned. "It looks arcane. I'd destroy it to be on the safe side."

"Mab . . ." I began sternly.

"Yes, Ma'am?"

"My brothers. I want you to help me find my brothers."

"You won't be expecting me to find the dead one, too, will you?" he growled.

"Could you?" I inquired, taken aback.

Mab crossed his arms. "Hrumph! Wouldn't if I could. Same as I told your father."

A chill ran down my spine. I felt relieved not to have been privy to that conversation!

"Let's stick to my six living brothers . . . oh, and my sister."

"I don't know your brothers, Ma'am, excepting Mr. Mephistopheles and Mr. Ulysses. However, if the others are anything like them, I don't think I'd care to meet them, thank you. Might be better if you left well enough alone."

I inclined my head regally. "Ordinarily, Mab, I would quite agree with you, but as Father has specifically asked . . ." I paused and asked curiously, "When did you meet Ulysses?" I knew he had met Mephisto on one of the many occasions when my brother came by to borrow money.

"It was back when Mr. Prospero was still living here. He had a blue crystal called the Warden that he kept in the Vault. Some gizmo given to him by a two-bit gypsy."

"Oh, yes. I recall. It warned its owner if something was about to be stolen. Worked for quite some time, too."

"Catch was, if the Warden itself was the target of the theft, it didn't work. Ulysses stole the Warden, and then the jewels." Mab shook his head. "I warned him and warned him; it never does to put too much store in magic. Mr. Prospero didn't listen. You take after him a bit, Ma'am."

"Why, thank you, Mab!" I replied, flattered. Mab scowled. "We got the stolen goods back, if I remember, thanks to your good work."

"Bah," Mab spat. "How is any self-respecting detective supposed to track a teleporting thief? He let us have them back is more like it. Even then, two of the pieces we recovered turned out to be fakes."

Mab's point regarding my brothers was well taken. With the exception of Theophrastus, they had become a sorry lot nowadays. Theo . . . well, I would face that hurdle when I came to it. Normally, I would not have even considered squandering the time and resources necessary to search for them, but Father had asked it of me, and Father's requests could not be ignored, even if I disagreed with them.

"Mab . . . I want to find my brothers." I remained firm. "How would you suggest we begin?"

Mab rubbed his jaw. Like every tough guy since Bogart's Philip Marlow, he showed half a day's growth of beard. Only, bodies inhabited by Aerie Ones do not change, so it must have been put there deliberately. "I'd start by finding out what we already know, Ma'am. Do we know where any of them are?"

"We will ask." I whistled for the butler.

As we waited, I sipped my tea, savoring the strong minty flavor of the pennyroyal. A soft breeze blew through the enclosed forest that lay beyond the stone wall surrounding the gardens, causing the pine needles to whisper and the aspen leaves to make their peculiar clapping sound. I listened to the chatter of three magpies and enjoyed the soft caress of the balmy air as it mingled the delicate scents of lilac and hyacinths with the heady perfume of honeysuckle and roses, as well as the faint odor of pine.

Breathing the fragrant air, I had a hard time believing that if I were to leave the mansion by the front door, or even walk through the archway into the enclosed forest behind me, I would step into the sharp chill of early winter. Prospero's Mansion was situated in Oregon's Cascade Mountains, where December meant cold winds and near-freezing rains.

Taking a last sip of tea, I emptied the tea ball into the remaining liquid and swirled the cup. The tea leaves settled into the patterns for *tall dark man* and *long voyage*. Shrugging, I pushed the cup aside. Standard tea-leaf rhetoric, could mean anything.

Meanwhile, Mab stood beside me, frowning and fidgeting with his hat.

From somewhere in the vicinity of my shoulder, my invisible butler spoke. His voice was soft and lilting, as like a flute giving tongue to words.

"All hail, Great Mistress! Vestal Lady, hail! I come to answer your best pleasure; be it to fly, to swim, to dive into the fire, to ride on the curled clouds; to your strong bidding, require of your servant what you will."

I smiled ruefully. The butler had learned English during the reign of King Henry VIII and still spoke much as had the men of that age.

"Ariel, I must contact my brothers. What is our latest information about their whereabouts?"

"Mortals must sow to reap, even so Master Cornelius. Twice yearly, tidings of the yields from his stocks in your father's great company are sent to him in braille at his post box in faraway New York City," Ariel's voice sang.

"I'll send him a letter," I said. "What of the others?"

"The Sun in Scorpio shone when Master Mephistopheles last came weeping to your gates. He had lost that wand, curiously carved and steeped with strong enchantments, which Prospero had bestowed upon him. He claimed to have lost it during a tryst with a damsel of dubious nature; but what became of it, whether lost at sea, or upon the mountains of Tibet, or in remote Hyperborea, he knew not, nor could his addled wits recall. Pity touched even my airy heart to see him, who was once so keen of mind and so skilled of sword, so piteously reduced. Empty-headed and empty-handed he came, and empty-handed went away. You refused him audience."

I shrugged. "He was drunk."

"The cold and adverse wind, which escorted Lord Mephistopheles from the property, reported to me the words he muttered beneath his breath. He sought your noble sister, the Lady Logistilla, in some isolated isle of the Western Indies."

"He'll be lucky if she doesn't turn him into a toad. She has even less patience for his drunkenness than I have. What of the others?"

"I ride the rumor-bearing winds, and what I hear, I know. Of Lord Erasmus, word on the wind is mute. Yet, certain of your servants, mortal men made of clay, found trace of his name in print. The magazine was called *Smithsonian*; many learned men know it; but fey spiritlings do not."

"You can follow that one up, Mab," I said. Mab nodded. Pulling out a stubby blue pencil, he scribbled something in a small spiral-topped notebook.

"Of the other three, few tidings have been gathered," Ariel continued. "Of Master Titus, no word has been heard by breeze or zephyr, not for two autumns now; and yet you know his art. Our kind never could approach him."

"Probably sat down somewhere and forgot to get up," I murmured. Titus, once a great warrior, had become lazy in recent years.

"Lord Ulysses, you well know, can be everywhere and nowhere, all at once; he is swifter than the swiftest wind, and he hides his deeds. Master Theophrastus is still governed by his strange vow. He has asked the family not to seek him out."

I nodded slowly, considering Ariel's news. How little I knew of the recent doings of my siblings! Once, not so long ago, we had all worked together, back before Mephisto's madness, Gregor's death, and Theo's desertion. Now, that life seemed but a distant dream. I wondered if we would ever do anything together as a family again.

I could feel Ariel still hovering over my shoulder.

"Is there something else, Ariel?"

"Let me remember thee what thou hast promised, which is not yet performed," came the soft answer.

"Oh? And that is?" Though, I knew, of course. We had this conversation nearly every time we spoke. Poor Ariel. He had been having this conversation with Father since his days as Father's personal servant on the island, and he was still harping on the same note now that he had been promoted to running Father's entire establishment. Only when Father retired, he asked Ariel to stay with me, as there were many Aerie Ones back on Prospero's Island but few competent enough to oversee the workings of this vast and multifaceted house.

"My liberty."

"Before the time is out? No, Ariel. Neither you, nor any member of your race, will be released from your service to our family until the thousand years of the millennium you swore to serve have gone by. It has been a little over five hundred and fifty years since you swore to Father in 1458, the year of my birth. Be glad that you are finally more than halfway through."

"I pray you remember, I have done you worthy service; told you no lies, made no mistakings, served without grudge or grumbling. Your father, the great and dread magician Prospero, did promise if I accomplished these things to free me one full century early."

"Even then, you still have three and a half centuries to go, Ariel. Do you forget from what torments my father freed you? Or, would you prefer to have remained within the cloven pine where the witch Sycorax had imprisoned you?"

"No," Ariel replied sadly, "though still I dance to its tune."

Mab snorted. I shot him a quelling glance.

"That will be all, Ariel!"

Ariel departed, but Mab still stood beside me, fidgeting with his fedora and frowning. I met his gaze evenly.

"And you are waiting for . . ."

"I'm on it, Ma'am," he said quickly. "I'll let you know as soon as I find something."

THAT evening, I lit a fire in the enormous hearth of the lesser hall. The night air had a crisp coolness to it, though not enough to warrant turning on the heat. The amount of oil it took to warm this drafty old mansion could keep a small town toasty for a year.

I sat cross-legged upon a priceless Persian rug before a coffee table that had once graced the Versailles of Louis XIV. To my left, the phoenix lamp shed red-gold sparks, illuminating the reflective objects upon the mantelpiece: a black marble bust of my farther; the sapphire eyes of a little wooden figurine of an elf—a gift from my brother Mephisto; and a shiny vase of Jerusalem lilies. Nearby, amidst silk-covered pillows, my familiar, Tybalt, Prince of Cats, lay purring.

The matter of Father's letter troubled me so much that I had decided to take an evening off from company business—something I seldom did. While Peaseblossom had been at Prospero's Island, searching for my father, she had recovered more of Father's journals. Officially, I was reading one of these, looking for clues that might give me some hint as to Father's whereabouts; however, concern over Father's disappearance kept disrupting my concentration. Finally, I closed the volume and let my thoughts wander over the past.

Shakespeare wrote a well-known account of my youth. His version tells how my father, Prospero, the Duke of Milan, was betrayed by his brother Antonio and sent into exile with only his books and my infant self for company. Stranded on an island, Father freed Ariel from the cloven pine in which the witch Sycorax had imprisoned him and received in return, a promise of servitude from Ariel and his kind.

With the help of Ariel, Father called up a tremendous tempest. The storm blew to our island a ship carrying, among others, my wicked uncle Antonio, his friend the King of Naples, and the king's handsome son, Prince Ferdinand.

I was, by this time, a young maid of fifteen—innocent and dewy-eyed—who had grown up with only Father and Caliban, the vile and misshapen son of the witch Sycorax, as company. Through the machinations of Father and Ariel, as Shakespeare tells it, I fell instantly in love with the handsome prince, the true perfidiousness of my wicked Uncle Antonio was brought to light, and Father was reconciled with the king. As we prepared for our triumphant return to Milan, where we were to celebrate the marriage of myself and Prince Ferdinand, Father drowned his magical tomes and freed his spirit servants.

Only, Shakespeare did not get our story quite right. Father never drowned his books nor freed his airy servants. Nor did I marry Ferdinand, who was but a tool of Father's stratagem to reclaim Milan. When I was five, Father consecrated me to Eurynome, the Lady of Spiral Wisdom and the Bearer of the Lightning Bolt. Handmaidens of Eurynome receive many privileges—among them immortality. Yet, every blessing has its price. Eurynome's other name is Monocerus, Greek for "one horn," and unicorns only come to virgins. I was not about to trade immortality for the likes of Ferdinand, Prince of Naples!

Father finally did retire, three years ago. He turned his back on the modern world and returned to our ancient island home. (Funny how the most solitary of prisons can become a longed-for haven.) Even then, however, he did not drown his books but gave them to us, his children. He split them among the eight of us, saving the most important volumes for me. After all, I had lived with him back in the days when books and airy spirits had been our sole companions—unless one counted Caliban, which I did not. Father also signed over to me this mansion and control of our company, Prospero, Inc.

What did I do with my share of his books? The same thing I did with all arcane tomes. I scoured them from cover to cover, searching for any hint as to the nature of the Sibyl, the highest order of Eurynome's servants.

During my first few decades in Her service, I rose rapidly, climbing from Initiate, to Novice, to Vestal Maiden, to Handmaiden in record time. Only the rank of Sibyl remained beyond my reach, and I yearned to be worthy of this final honor. Days turned into weeks, however, weeks into years, and years into centuries, yet Sibylhood continued to elude me.

After five hundred years of searching, I was beginning to get discouraged.

Alas, Father's journals, my latest glimmer of hope, were also proving unenlightening. In their pages were copious notes on ancient fertility rites, drafts of a metaphysical treatise on death and rebirth, numerous renditions of Father's latest attempts at poetry, and descriptions of some horticulture project, not a word of which shed light on the mystery I pursued.

When Father retired, I fancied him enjoying centuries of relaxing study. I had even harbored the secret hope that he might spend some of his copious free time helping me track down the *Book of the Sibyl*, an ancient volume in which the secrets of the Sibylline Order were recorded. After all, it had been Father who originally set me upon this path, so I had hoped he would be inclined to help further my progress.

I certainly had not expected him to vanish, leaving behind but a single cryptic note!

Leaning back against a large silk-covered pillow, I spoke to my familiar, purposefully making light of my growing concern. "If Father must release enemies to hunt down the family, he could certainly have picked a more convenient time to do it! I wonder what these Three Shadowed Ones are. Efretes, maybe? Or brollachan? I swear I've heard the name before. Do you recognize it?"

The black cat opened one golden eye and regarded me disdainfully. Raising his head, he glanced this way and that, as if to confirm no one else was present.

"Were you talking to me?"

"I was."

"Did you not notice I was napping?"

"You always nap. If I waited for you to wake up, I could never talk to you . . . which would make you useless as a familiar."

"I will be useless as a familiar if you disturb me while I am cavorting with the Dream Gods," the cat replied.

"Were you really cavorting with the Dream Gods?" I asked, curious.

Tybalt did not answer.

"This is a very busy time of year for Prospero, Inc.," I continued. "We have nine large contracts due to be completed before the New Year, not to mention the myriad of other matters to be seen to: The Johannesburg office is being remodeled and is all in disarray, the Zurich office is in the midst of three major purchases—a real estate firm, a confectionary chain, and a watch factory, and we have warehouses all over the world working overtime to fill requests from retailers who need more stock before the final Christmas rush. Worse, five of the contracts coming due are Priority Accounts, and you know how touchy those can be!"

"How inconsiderate of your father." The cat yawned. "A more thoughtful man would have waited until after Christmas to disappear. Perhaps we should ask these Three Shadowed Ones to hold off until after the New Year before they begin attacking your family."

"Ah, if only . . ." I sighed, smiling at my own expense.

"What puzzles me," continued the cat, "is why your father asked you to warn the others. He must have known you were busy and that you don't like your siblings anyway . . . all those latecomers, born after you and Prospero returned from exile."

"It's not their birth order I object to so much as what they've done recently. When they are loyal to Father, I like them just fine—most of them, anyway," I objected. "Besides, I adore Theo."

"For all the good that will do you," Tybalt replied. "If there even is a Theophrastus anymore. How old would he be now? Sixty? Eighty?"

"Well over five hundred," I replied, deliberately ignoring the cat's point.

Unbidden, the faces of my six living half-brothers and one half-sister arose before me, few of them dear to me, but all of them familiar . . . family. I thought about Gregor, who had died in 1924. I had never cared much for Gregor, nor had I been close to him. Yet, I had genuinely grieved when he died. Father had been so distraught, he had gone into seclusion for three years.

"I don't know, Tybalt," I shook my head. "My brothers may have failed the company, and mankind for that matter, but they are still my brothers. Perhaps, Father asked me because he thought I was the only one of his children who would obey him."

"You are certainly the only one who *always* obeys him." Tybalt watched me, unblinking. "What are these Three Shadowed Ones after?"

I gazed into the fire, enjoying its warmth upon my face. The logs crackled. The flames leapt like dancing imps, casting flickering shadows against the back wall of the great hearth. Tybalt waited patiently, fixing me with his unblinking stare.

Finally, I sighed. "Our staffs."

"Oh, dear. That could be less than pleasant for you!" the cat exclaimed. "After all, what would the mighty Prosperos be without their staffs? Heaven forbid you should become perfectly ordinary humans."

I shot the black feline a sideways glance. "Ah, how very droll you are."

The cat fixed me with his golden eyes. "You do not fool me, Daughter of Prospero, with your affectation of icy disdain. I know you are terrified for your father's safety. He may be the Dread Magician Prospero, but even dread magicians can go astray, especially if they meddle with that which is even more dreadful."

With my comfortable mask of mild concern pierced, the fears besetting my heart poured out. "How could anything have happened to Father?" I cried. "I thought he had grown tired of magic. Why would he take it up again? If only he had let me know he was planning something dangerous, I could have stood by to help! He has always appreciated my help in the past!"

"Perhaps, this recent mishap was an accident—Dread Prospero was strolling in the garden and stumbled over a flower pot which contained some horror once bound up by your brother Gregor and his ring, inadvertently releasing it." My familiar tilted his head to one side, his gaze acute. "Or maybe he wished to perform some act of magic of which he feared you would disapprove?"

"Me? Disapprove?" I cried, aghast. "Why would I disapprove of anything Father thought suitable?"

"Why indeed?" the cat echoed softly.

"At the very least, he might have told his servants where he was going!"

"Now, now, Handmaiden of Eurynome, fret not." Tybalt leapt lightly onto my lap and rubbed his cheek against mine. "Would you like me to inquire among the denizens of the dreamlands and the spirits that wander afar?"

"Yes." I quickly wiped away a stray tear before he could spot it and mock me. "That would be very nice."

The cat turned about three times, kneaded my legs with his soft paws, before settling down, his black body vibrating with contentment. I stroked his sleek fur, touched that this prickly cat had felt my plight so great he was willing to put aside his eternal snideness to comfort me.

"Very well, then." His voice was a gentle purr. "Shall we see what the Guardians of Dream have heard?"

I would have responded, but when I glanced down, I saw he had fallen asleep again, his tail twitching. Smiling, I left him to his dreams. Who knows? Maybe he was cavorting with the Dream Gods.

MAB stood in the doorway of my office in the mansion, fidgeting with his hat. "It's bad, Ma'am . . . you're not going to like it."

I glanced up from behind the desk, where I had been answering company e-mail while speaking on the phone to Foxglove from Accounts Receivable. I had spent the day juggling matters at Prospero, Inc., trying to insure that service to our Priority Accounts would continue uninterrupted, should the matter of Father's message require that I leave town. In the three years since I had become the executive officer, I had not bothered to take a vacation, so no precedent had been set for how to handle matters in my absence. Thus, I was now conducting a sort of corporate triage, giving certain vice presidents my cellphone number, turning some projects over to subordinates, and putting others on hold until after the Christmas season.

Hanging up the phone, I regarded Mab as he chafed his arms against the chill. I was more fortunate; a small space heater hummed away to my left, blowing a pleasant dry heat upon me where I sat, behind my great rosewood desk.

"Yes, Mab? Go on. What am I not going to like?"

"I traced Mr. Mephistopheles to Chicago . . . that's the last known location where he's approached a Prospero, Inc. office for money. With some additional research, I located a person matching his size and description. The official I talked to described a guy with longish black hair who was wearing a poncho when he was apprehended. Oh, and he answered to 'Mephisto.' "

"Official? Apprehended?" I reached down and turned off the space heater, so as to hear better.

"Prison official, Ma'am. He's in jail."

"What was he arrested for? Drunken and disorderly conduct?"

"Apparently, he does have a previous conviction of that nature. But, this is more serious, Ma'am," Mab paused. "He has been accused of . . . of rape."

Of all crimes, rape is the one I most abhor. In my youth, my father's horrible servant Caliban had thrown me down and broken my arm in his attempt to dishonor me. The memory of his betrayal still haunted my nightmares, even centuries later, and my heart went out to all my sisters who had suffered such degradations. My relatives all knew how I felt about this heinous act. Even in their soldiering days, my brothers were careful never to mistreat women.

Were I savaged thus, my own discomfort and humiliation would be nothing compared to the harm my family would suffer. Loss of my innocence would deprive me of my station as Eurynome's Handmaiden. Since the blessings this station brought included the Water of Life that maintains my family's immortality, this crime would, in effect, murder my whole family.

Father and I differed sharply as to the proper punishment for monsters who attempt this offense. I had always held that rapists, even attempted rapists, should be killed. Father favored a more lenient sentence. Years after our rise to power, I returned to our island prison to seek my own revenge but found no sign of father's loathsome servant.

"If my brother has become a rapist, let him rot!" I thumped the rosewood desk. "Even family honor does not demand I protect him under these circumstances. Perhaps Providence will arrange that the Three Shadowed Ones get him. Modern justice is far too gentle."

"He claims he's innocent."

If Mephistopheles were guilty, he could hang for all I cared. In fact, I hoped he would. If he were innocent, however, locking him in prison would make him a helpless target. We might as well hand him over to the Three Shadowed Ones on a platter.

"Okay, Mab. Where is he?"

"Chicago, Ma'am."

"I'll have Ariel pack the usual gear, and we'll leave first thing in the morning." I rose. "But first, I need something from the Great Hall."

CHAPTER
TWO

The Great Hall

The doors of the Great Hall were vast and ornate with a large windrose, depicting the eight ordinal directions of the compass, painted upon the dark wood. A heavy iron chain bound them shut. The padlock that secured it was in the shape of a fanged serpent. I fitted the cast-iron key into the serpent's mouth and twisted. The lock sprang open.

"Always wondered what was behind these doors," Mab remarked as I unbound the chains. "Considering all the unrestrained supernatural iniquities in this house, it's hard to imagine what could be so dire that even Mr. Prospero thought it should be locked up with cold iron."

"Let's do this quickly, Mab," I said. "There is much to do before we depart."

Planting my feet, I yanked on the iron door handles. The massive oak doors parted slowly, splitting the windrose. Their hinges groaned. Beyond lay a long sunny hall of reddish stone. Alcoves set into its walls held statues carved from different shades of marble. At the far end of the hall, two thrones sat on a raised dais.

It was late afternoon and shafts of sunshine, falling from small, round windows high overhead, pierced the chamber, illuminating the statues along the right wall. Dust motes danced in the light. The effect was striking. Mab took off his hat.

"Whoa!"

Despite the brightness, the air here was cold and dank. Shivering, I walked briskly toward the far end, my footsteps ringing out against the gray and black marble checkerboard floor. Mab followed more slowly, stopping to squint at the first statue on the left: a gray marble figure of a slight young man dressed in a tuxedo and a domino mask.

"That's Mr. Ulysses . . . I never forget a perp," Mab scowled. "Nice likeness."

Smiling, I paused in a sunbeam and gestured toward the statues. The afternoon sunlight sparkled off my emerald tea gown, causing flashes of green fire to chase each other across its enchanted satin.

"Behold, the family," I announced. "From youngest to oldest: Ulysses the Gentleman Thief; Gregor the Witchhunter, who is dead; Logistilla the Sorceress; Titus the Silent, whom spirits fear; Cornelius the Cunning, who is blind; Erasmus the Enchanter, whom I abhor; Theophrastus the Demonslayer, whom I adore; and Mephistopheles, who is mad. The last two, down near the thrones, are myself and Father."

"Impressive!" Mab stalked over to the next statue, examining it closely. "I notice each statue has a round opening between the fingers and thumb of one hand, as if it were meant to hold something.

"Very perceptive of you, Mr. Detective. Long ago, Father used the most potent magic from his books to fashion staffs of immense power. He made one for each of his children but did not feel we were ready for them yet. So, Mephisto fashioned these statues to hold the staffs. They remained in the grip of the statues for many years. Eventually, a day came when Father decided we were mature enough to use them wisely, and he handed them out." I recalled those carefree days, when Father held all the magic, and only Erasmus and Logistilla showed any interest in the arcane, and sighed. "Sometimes, I wish he had kept them longer."

"I wish he'd never made 'em at all. Or better yet, that he had drowned his books like that Spearshaker fellow said," muttered Mab. "Where'd he get those accursed tomes anyway?"

"Father would never say."

"Bears looking into," Mab growled. He screwed up his face and scratched at his stubble. "I think I've been in this room before. In the old days, before Mr. Prospero put me in a body. My memory worked differently back then, though."

"You probably were," I replied. "The stones of this hall have been part of every mansion our family has owned. We had a Great Hall when we lived in Illinois, before that when our family home was in Boston, and even before that, back in Scotland. Once, long ago, these same stones were part of the great *Castello Sforzesco*, my family's ancestral home in Milan."

From the pocket of his trench coat, Mab pulled out his notepad and stubby blue pencil. He examined the statues and noted down the inscriptions above each alcove, which recorded the name of the staff once housed there.

"Must you dawdle, Mab? Time's a-wasting."

Mab tipped the brim of his hat. "Ma'am, if I am to find your siblings for you, I need to have some notion of who they are. This seems as good a place to start gathering that information as any."

I glanced around at the family statues. "True. Very well, Mab, carry on."

Mab continued taking notes, and I strode forward, seeking that which I had come to find. The click of my heels against the marble echoed through the chamber. I passed the marble likenesses of my various siblings: The statue of my dead brother Gregor, carved from red marble shot through with black, portrayed him as a Catholic cardinal; my sister Logistilla, sculpted in a deep blue stone, looked splendid in her flowing robes with their high pointed shoulders; enormous Titus, portrayed in earth tones, wore his kilt. The statue of Cornelius was of a rare type of purple marble—it pleased him tremendously that his statue was more valuable than all the rest of ours put together. His likeness bore the symbol of "the eye within the triangle" upon its chest, and bandages, carved into the stone, covered its eyes, so that he looked like a male Blind Justice.

Erasmus, who could do nothing without competing with me, had chosen for his statue a dark green marble shot through with black, as if changing the shade made it a different color. The marble of his gauntlet was pitted and dull from years of holding the *Staff of Decay*.

My brother's many cruel barbs and unprovoked abuses of me rose to mind, and a burst of wrath swept over me. I clenched my fists. It was hard to think rationally about anything related to Erasmus.

Mab came up beside me and ran his hand over the damaged stone.

"Looks deadly. How'd he wield it?"

"He has to wear a gauntlet of Urim."

"Urim! You mean that imperishable shining stuff the warrior angels wear?" Mab whistled. "That's . . ."

". . . a waste of good Urim." I glared at the statue.

"I gather you and Mr. Erasmus don't quite see eye to eye, Ma'am. How did that come about?"

"Frankly, I don't know. Erasmus is malicious and spiteful and delights in tormenting me."

Mab eyed me skeptically and raised his stubby pencil. "Can you give an example? Just in case it turns out to be important?"

I caught a strand of my hair that had come free. It gleamed like spun silver in the sunlight. "Our family is from Milan, Mab. Six of us are entirely Italian. The other three are half-Italian. With the exception of Ulysses and Mephisto, we all have Roman noses. Have you ever wondered why I am the only one in my family who is not a brunette?"

"Does seem incongruous," Mab grunted. "What's the cause?"

"Ask Erasmus," I growled, "and the *Staff of Decay.*"

Only one alcove held a statue of traditional white. A handsome youth in an armored breastplate stood with legs braced, as if attempting to restrain something unwieldy, such as a fire hose. His hair and cloak flared about him, as if he faced into a strong wind. He smiled bravely, showing his teeth. A pair of goggles covered his eyes. The inscription above the alcove read *The Staff of Devastation.*

Mab looked up from his notebook and jerked his thumb at the statue. "Any idea of his whereabouts?"

"No. Theo turned his back on us in the 1960s. He declared we'd turned into a bunch of unruly criminals and left the family. He gave up magic completely. Said he was tired of all the violence and horror. Even started aging. Must be an old man by now," I concluded sadly.

My dear brother Theo, how I missed him! The thought of him as aged and weak, or, worse yet, dead, was excruciating. I preferred to think of him as the statue had captured him: young, confident, and filled with *joie de vivre.*

"Sounds like a decent guy, Ma'am. My heart goes out to him."

"You two would get along swimmingly," I replied. "He was the only one of the youngsters with sense. If he's really put aside his magic, he might be safer left alone. It is unlikely a supernatural enemy could find him. Yet, I'm certain he'd want to know that Father is in trouble. It was Theo who nursed Father the time he became so ill, after Gregor died."

Mab glanced at the inscription above the statue. "What'd his staff do?"

"Blew things to smithereens."

"Why'd the peace lover get the war staff?" Mab asked.

"Back then, he was Theophrastus the Demonslayer, the bane of dark powers everywhere."

"Oh," Mab lowered his voice respectfully. "*That* Theophrastus!"

"He used to love his staff," I recalled. "Its blast was so hot that it would tan his skin and bleach his forelock. You should have seen his face when he fired it. Mephisto almost caught his expression on the statue, a sort of exquisite glee."

"Perhaps we should leave him alone, Ma'am. Our showing up might do him more harm than good." Mab looked across the hall, squinting. "Who's that?"

Over the years, my memory of the next statue had dimmed. Startled by the tears that unexpectedly rose to my eyes, I halted and stared. Portrayed in shiny black marble, a heartbreakingly handsome youth stood with his arms thrown wide and his head tossed back in exultant joy. A keen intelligence lit his elfin features. He wore high boots, loose pants, and long loose sleeves covered by a quartered surcoat, the livery of which depicted a unicorn, three interlocking rings, a curling grass snake, and an eye within a triangle.

"Lively fellow. I don't remember you mentioning him." Mab crossed the hall and read the inscription above the alcove. " '*Staff of Summoning*'? Hey, isn't that the one Mr. Mephistopheles lost?"

"That is Mephistopheles. Or, rather, was. . . ."

"Seriously?" Mab peered closer as I came to join him. "Doesn't look like the same fellow at all. No . . . now that you mention it, the features are the same; however, the resemblance ends there."

"He has his cheerful periods and his morose periods. He was in one of his morose periods when you met him. But this statue is from the days before he lost his wits."

"So, he wasn't always crazy? What happened?"

"No one knows. One day, he came back, and he was different."

"Did he change over a period of years? Or all at once?" Mab asked.

"We don't know."

It had been so very long since Mephisto had been sane that, even with the statue before me, I could hardly recall what he had been like. I wondered if perhaps Mab and Theo were right about the nature of magic. On the other hand, even mundane men could go mad. If it were not for magic, Mephisto would have been dead long ago. Madness was preferable to death.

"He doesn't have his staff anymore. Lost it to some woman who seduced him. I don't know why she'd keep it. She can't use it. No one can use the staffs except our family. Perhaps, without his staff, Mephisto's in no danger from the Three Shadowed Ones." I shook my head, still finding it difficult to contemplate the notion that my crazy brother could be a rapist.

"Let's hope," Mab muttered. He walked by the next column and stopped before the last alcove on the right wall.

"Mr. Prospero."

My father's statue held a tome in one hand and pointed toward the horizon with the other. Kind but penetrating eyes peered out from beneath bushy brows. A full beard framed his mouth. Mephisto had done a good job of catching Father's age and wisdom in the yellow marble. I could almost imagine he stood here before us. If only it were true!

"Nice likeness," Mab commented again. "Looks just like him."

"Mephisto did Father's statue first," I replied, "That's how Father got the idea for the others. In fact, Mephisto carved all the statues, except for Ulysses. By the time Ulysses was born, Mephisto was just too far gone. Father hired some Englishman to carve it."

"What about the inscription here?" Mab peered upward. "It says . . . '*The Staff of Eternity.*' "

"What!" I hurried to examine the inscription. "That wasn't there last time I came!"

Our nine staffs had existed, had been an intrinsic part of our experience, for so very long that the idea of a new one was more shocking than I could find words to express. Where had it come from? Why had Father never mentioned it?

"When were you last here?" Mab asked, pencil poised.

"About six years ago."

Standing on my toes, I ran a finger over the engraved letters. The stone was smooth with crisp sharp edges, with little flecks of stone dust still in the letters. "This carving seems recent. I wonder if Father added it before he retired. Or even last time he was here."

"When was that?"

"September."

"That would be about three months ago." Mab squinted at the inscription, but the mute stone revealed no secrets. He straightened. "Has Mr. Prospero been heard from since then?"

"No. The last time any of his servants saw Father was when he departed for America."

"So, this 'finding your brothers' thing isn't urgent," drawled Mab. "I mean, if your father left you a message three months ago . . ."

I cut him off. "His message was only just brought to my attention by an urging from my Lady. I am certain She would not have taken the trouble had the matter been unimportant. Therefore, until I know otherwise, I must assume some member of my family is in immediate, or at least imminent, danger."

He walked over to the red stone thrones, splashing through a shaft of sunlight as he went. His footsteps echoed loudly in the empty hall. When he reached the dais, he sat down upon the arm of Father's throne and began scribbling in his notebook.

I sat down on the arm of the second throne, the "Wife's Chair" we called it, but the stone was icy cold. Standing, I rubbed my arms and gazed at the painting that hung behind the chair. It was a portrait of my mother, whom I had never met. She had died in childbirth, bringing me into the world. Giovanni Bellini had painted her portrait upon the occasion of her engagement to my father. It showed her young and fresh and vibrant with life.

Beneath the portrait, a brass plaque held an inscription:

Portia Lucia dei Gardelli
Duchess of Milan, 1456
"*Thy mother was a piece of Virtue.*"

The last was from *The Tempest*; Shakespeare's rendition of my father's description of the only woman Father ever loved.

Beside me, Mab halted his scribbling and asked, "Hey, do you think there could there be a relation between this new staff and these Three Shadowed Ones? What does the *Staff of Eternity* do?"

"I don't know. Father never mentioned it."

"Do you think this new staff could have anything to do with Mr. Prospero's disappearance?"

I shook my head in puzzlement. "I could not tell you, Mab."

Mab straightened and scowled at me. "Begging your pardon, Ma'am, but you must know something! Think back. When did you last talk to him?"

"Early September."

He began scribbling again. "What about?"

"At the end of December, the treaty between the djinn and the efretes comes up for renewal. The djinn have great respect for Father and are more biddable in his presence. And you know how dangerous they can be when they get incensed! Last time they rioted, the resulting earthquake killed over twenty thousand people! Anyway, Father promised to come."

"Early September. Was that while he was here at Prospero's Mansion?" Mab's pencil scratched away.

"No, he was here in late September."

"You didn't speak to him then? What? The house is so big you couldn't find each other?"

I laughed. "Unfortunately, his visit coincided with Prospero, Inc.'s once-a-decade rendezvous with the *kami* of Mount Fuji, so I was in Japan at the time."

"No leads there," Mab grumbled. "Any idea what's he been working on recently?"

I sighed. "I've often asked him what he was up to since he retired, but he always replied with the same answer: 'Keeping busy.' "

"Mr. Prospero was always one to keep matters to himself," Mab grunted, "Still, bears looking into. I'd wager my hat . . ." His voice trailed off. He was staring at the remaining alcove.

Within the last alcove stood a statue of pale jade-green marble. The subject was a young woman. The high stiff collar of her Elizabethan gown framed a strikingly fair face. Her eyes gazed demurely down, but there was a proud cast to her upturned chin. Her delicate green hands were carved so as to hold a flute. Her lips were pursed as if to play. Her features were my own.

In the statue's delicate hands rested a flute, four feet in length and made of the palest wood. It had been fashioned long ago, wrought from the cloven pine in which the witch Sycorax had imprisoned the spirit Ariel. Its virtue was to command wind, weather, and the Aerie Ones, the race to which Mab and Ariel belonged. Even the lightning bolt, the symbol and servant of my Lady, bowed before its song.

Mab had drawn back his lips, exposing his teeth. "So this is where you keep it."

Reverently, I drew from the statue's grasp the gift Father had bestowed upon me. Holding the instrument close, I brushed its cool polished length against my cheek. My flute. My birthright. The key to mystery and magic, to tempests and storms, and to everything I held dear, save my Lady Herself.

Feeling the flute between my fingers brought back memories of the first time I ever heard it. I had been on the island, out by the bluff, plaiting daisies into a wreath for my hair and gathering orchids to brighten up Father's cold stone study. Caliban had followed me, as always, slinking among the shadows of the trees and ogling me, but, though his presence filled me with revulsion, I no longer feared him, for I knew he dreaded Father's wrath and dared not approach me again.

As I returned to the mansion, where it stood on the highest point of the island overlooking the vast expanse of the sea to its west and a deep ravine to its east, I heard something new. It sounded like the voices of the Aerie Ones, if the Aerie Ones were both singing and weeping simultaneously.

It was as if the wind itself had been given tongue. Its song reached into my soul and drew me out from myself, simultaneously embracing me and making me one with the sky. The wind sang, and the sky answered. My body never moved, yet my spirit was swept up into the air. As the winds chanted and the earth danced, the sea leapt from its bed. Walls of water flew up rather than down, ringing us in a fortress of storm and fury.

"Tempest," Father called it later, and the glorious sound that had drawn me from myself, he named "flute."

This was the very storm that drove the ship carrying the King of Naples, his handsome son Prince Ferdinand, and my wicked Uncle Antonio—the one responsible for exiling us to our lonely island—against our shores. That same vessel was destined to take us back to civilization.

I could not look upon the flute that had played such music without recalling the wonder of that day when I, an earthborn and duty-bound creature, first tasted freedom. Nor had the desire to return to the sky ever left me.

"My staff," I murmured, cradling the precious flute, "The *Staff of Winds*!"

"And the bane of my race." Mab stomped up beside me. "One whistle from that oversized piccolo, and we Aerie-Born start hopping like rabbits. Doesn't such a contraption violate the Thirteenth Amendment? I'm going to complain to my congressman."

I laughed. "Mab, you don't have a congressman."

Mab drew himself up as tall as his stocky stature allowed. "Oh, yes I do! I've read your constitution through and through, and nowhere does it specify that men need be born of flesh to be protected by its rights. 'Race, color, and/or previous state of servitude.' Says it right there. In my case, it's previous state of servitude."

"But Mab, you're not just another race, you're another species."

"Are you certain?" Mab's gaze was fierce. "Haven't you heard it said that we Aerie Ones are the shades of men who escaped from limbo when the High God broke open the doors of Hell to rescue his son?"

"Really? I thought your people were much older than that."

"Perhaps we are," Mab shrugged. "Or perhaps, by the High God, the story meant Odin."

I looked down the immense hall that held the statues of my brothers and sister. Ghosts of ages past seemed to walk its marble floors, dancing before my mind's eye. I saw the family gathering to hear Father's latest tasks for us; Mephisto practicing sword stances; Theo patiently teaching Logistilla to waltz; Titus practicing his golf swing (to Father's dismay); Erasmus leaning casually against the wall, his arms crossed, throwing me a supercilious sneer;

grim and pious Gregor and blind Cornelius playing chess while Ulysses filled them in on the latest gossip of the Ton.

Once, all the power, all our staffs, had been under Father's control. Working together at his behest, we freed mankind from the tyranny of the supernatural. Then, Father put the staffs into our separate hands, and, one by one, each of my siblings deserted our cause. Now, they roamed across the planet, wasting their strength and squandering the gifts Father had granted them. Only Father and I remained at our posts, and now, Father was missing.

With the setting sun, darkness was gathering, obscuring the faces of the statues. I sat down on the arm of the Wife's Chair again, icy chill and all. My fingers curled about the polished shaft of my long flute.

"Never mind, Mab. Go on back to the office and finish following up whatever petty larceny case you're working on. I'm not going to warn my family. They just don't deserve it."

"Wise decision," Mab stuck his notebook back in his trench coat. "You'll only increase your own danger by traipsing around trying to locate these goons. My suggestion is that you hire a lawyer to check out Mr. Mephistopheles's situation, drop Mr. Cornelius a letter in braille, and hire a few mundane detectives to locate that Theo chap, to give him the warning just in case. I'll do the initial legwork myself, if you prefer."

I nodded. "Yes, I guess that would be best. Maybe you could put Gooseberry in charge of looking for Father."

Mab scowled, "Ma'am, Gooseberry's been dead for eighty years."

"Has it been that long?" I felt a pang of sorrow as I recalled. Gooseberry had been a helpful spirit, adventurous and brave. Whenever I went boating, he had been the Aerie One I called to blow into my sails, and when I was but a child, he had taken me flying over the beaches of Father's island. We swooped through the air like gulls, racing over the shore, and then soared upward, the earth falling away beneath us until the island appeared to be but a sandcastle in the midst of the tide. Father put a stop to those expeditions, fearing the danger to his darling little angel, but the memory of them shall remain with me so long as I live. The joy of those flights has seldom been paralleled in my long life. It was that joy the music of that first flute concert brought back so vividly.

Back in the early twentieth century, when Father conceived the idea of putting the Aerie Ones into fleshly bodies, Gooseberry had been the first Aerie One to volunteer. He had done a fine job as a fleshly servant. He was never as intelligent as Mab, but he had been loyal and diligent. Then, while out on a case for Father, a thug shot him repeatedly, killing his fleshly body instantly. When the body died, Gooseberry perished, too. This was a shock to Father and me. We had not known Aerie Ones could die.

I sighed. "Well, pick someone else then, someone you trust. Mab . . . Mab?"

Mab was not listening. He stared into the darkening hall, a strange and inhuman alertness on his craggy features.

"Mistress," his voice rang oddly. "Beware!"

"People with congressmen don't have mistresses, Mab."

"The darkness . . ."

"The sun is setting, Mab. Those little windows don't light the room all that well."

"No," Mab cried. "Look up!"

High above, sunlight streamed through the tiny round windows. Yet, the sunbeams no longer reached the statues. Instead, they were being dispersed by a gathering gloom. The hall before us was thickening with shadows.

"Shadows . . . the Three Shadowed Ones!"

Mab grabbed my arm, and we ducked behind the two massive stone thrones.

Darkness billowed through the Great Hall, spreading like ink through water. Silent as shadow it came, wafting toward where Mab and I crouched upon the cold stone behind the thrones and bringing with it the scent of newly-struck matches.

"It can't be!" I whispered.

"Can't be what?"

"This billowing darkness. That smell!" I whispered. "I'd swear it came from Gregor's staff! But it can't be. We buried the *Staff of Darkness* with my brother's body. I was there for the funeral. I saw it go into the coffin!"

"Shh," Mab cut me off. "Something's moving!"

We gazed silently into the murk. Something flitted from alcove to alcove, pausing momentarily to peer at each statue. A shiver, like a finger of ice, slid down my spine. Our staffs! It was after our staffs! Silently, I thanked my Lady that I had come and claimed my flute before the intruder arrived!

Whoever it was drew closer, until I could make him out through the clouds of darkness: a black figure in a billowing opera cape, carrying a length of ebony traced with angular red runes.

"That *is* Gregor's staff!" I hissed. "If this is one of the Three Shadowed Ones, and they can use our staffs, no wonder Father wanted me to warn the others! What is that thing?"

Mab squinted. I knew he was taking in the creature's silhouette, motion and gait, and other characteristics a thaumaturge uses to identify his supernatural quarry. "Can't tell for sure from here. Either cacodemon or incubus."

A demon! A knot formed in the pit of my stomach. I had been certain he would say shade or, at the worst, djinn. My family had no truck with the denizens of Hell! We were solely devoted to the Forces of Good. Ordinarily, this protected us from the Powers of Darkness. What could have gone wrong? How had this one slipped past the wards that guarded the house?

The demon stepped from the shadows, his footsteps ringing against the marble. His hands, his short spiral horns, and his perfectly chiseled face were smooth and sable-dark, as if the night itself had coalesced into the shape of a man. I stifled a gasp. This creature was unlike any demon I had ever beheld. Despite eyes as red as newly pooled blood, he was handsome enough to beguile the moon, possibly the second handsomest male I had encountered in all my long life.

"Definitely an incubus," mouthed Mab.

"Do you think he saw us?"

"Only if he can see through the darkness your brother's staff produces."

"Not likely then," I whispered back.

Coming to my statue, the incubus swore softly. A cold shiver trickled down my spine. He had been expecting my flute! Who had told him it would be here?

And why did he continue to stand there, staring in such rapt fascination at the stone likeness of me?

After an uncomfortably long pause, during which chills traveled up my spine, our sable intruder turned away, heading for the center of the hall. From under his opera cape, he drew a crystal bottle. Unstopping it, he released something bright and sparkling. Then, shadows billowed from Gregor's staff, embracing him, and he was gone.

Immediately, shafts of sunlight from above pierced the gloom. I began to rise, but Mab grabbed my arm, yanking me down.

"That thing he dropped, it's a star spark!" he barked. "As soon as it realizes it's no longer constrained, it will attempt to return to its proper place."

"Which is?"

"In the Sphere of the Fixed Stars!"

"Which means?"

"This whole place is about to blow!"

"We can't lose the Great Hall!"

I raised my flute to my lips and began to play. Music issued forth, swelling and filling the hall with a marvelous noise. The flute's eerie and lilting voice still sounded to my ear like the lamentation of the air, and perhaps rightly so, for with it I could compel the Aerie Ones to sing, but I could not forbid them from weeping for their lost freedom.

Through the music, I called to the Aerie Ones, commanding them to carry the spark to one of the high round windows, so that it might return to its proper sphere unimpeded. My servants obliged me, and the shimmering ball of orange and red sparks was whisked upward toward the windows by a billowing breeze.

The star spark expanded quickly, showering golden and crimson about the hall as it wafted upwards, shedding a fragrance like sweet ozone.

Fearing it would not reach the window in time, I changed my song, altering my instructions as I ordered some of the Aerie Ones to form an airy cushion between the spark and the rest of the hall, to protect us from the impact of any explosion.

A shuffling *gacking* noise to my right drew my attention. Mab had left the protective cover of Father's throne and now moved toward the center of the hall, dancing and jerking like a puppet. His trench coat whipped about him. One hand grasped his hat, holding it in place.

I was contemplating scolding him for endangering us with foolishness when the horrible truth of his situation dawned upon me. The music was compelling his obedience! Yet, an explosion would destroy his fleshly body. Given time, I could have remedied the situation, but time I did not have. I would have to sacrifice Mab's fleshly body, which was a shame because, without Father, I did not know how to replace it. I hoped being blown apart would not hurt him much.

Then I remembered Gooseberry.

I could protect the Great Hall, or I could save Mab. This hall had been part of my family for over five hundred years, and I was not going to let it and everything it represented be destroyed by a demon! What a shame. I had liked Mab. I was going to miss him.

As I glanced up to wish him a silent good-bye, Mab looked back at me, his eyes wild and beseeching. When he saw me glancing his way, his face lit up with tremendous hope. Then, quick as it had come, despair followed. He knew. He knew I was about to let him die.

Unexpectedly, this troubled me. If I were in Mab's place, it occurred to me, I would not wish to die.

Blowing sharply on the flute as if it were a whistle, I recalled the Aerie Ones to me. The desires of Mab's spirit united with those of his flesh, and he leapt toward the safety of the heavy stone thrones.

With a deafening bang, the star spark exploded into a bloom of fireworks. Mab flew toward me, silhouetted by dazzling red-and-gold light. He plummeted down upon me, and we clutched each other until the brightness dimmed. For a moment, all was silent, except for the ringing in my ears. Then, came the terrible sound of stone grinding against stone, followed by an ear-rending crash. The hall shook.

"Mab?" I whispered, when the shaking finally ended.

"Here, Ma'am . . . Thanks to you," he replied. "Are you whole?"

"Yes." I rose and regarded the Great Hall. "Oh my, Mab, oh my!"

Large chunks of red stone lay about the hall. Above, clouds sailed across a blue sky. To the left, flickering tongues of flame licked at the gaping hole in what had once been the wall between the Great Hall and the library. The air was thick with rock dust.

"Mab! The library's on fire!" I cried, "Father's books!"

"Let 'em burn. About time we got rid of them," Mab growled from where he rose to his feet, rubbing his shoulder.

"Some of those volumes are bound with the Seal of Solomon. Who knows what might escape if the seals break!"

"Merciful Setebos!" Mab leapt up, bellowing for the rest of the household to attend him.

My flute had come through the disaster intact. Raising it to my lips, I played a favorite passage from *The Rite of Spring*. The music soared and moaned, echoing my shock and sorrow and yet lifting me above it. Overhead, clouds gathered rapidly, and a downpour quickly quenched the flames. Once the fire was out, I switched to a pastoral movement from Beethoven's Sixth. Its gentle soothing strains dispersed the clouds, allowing the early winter sun to shine upon the damp library.

By this time, Ariel had arrived to direct the clean-up effort. Dry books were moved to the far side of the library; damp ones hurried off to the bindery. It pained my heart to see six-hundred-year-old volumes drip with water, but better damp books than burnt ones.

THE sky was growing dark, and the first stars of the evening could be seen above the Great Hall. The steady drip-drip of water, still falling from the edges of the rent, echoed throughout the hall, pattering down upon the great chunks of red stone scattered across the floor. This hall had stood remarkably unchanged, despite its several moves, for over five hundred years. Seeing it thus nearly moved me to tears.

The biggest question on my mind, however, was: how had the demon breached Father's wards? We had fought supernatural monstrosities, even—upon a rare occasion—demons, for half a millennium, but none of them had ever attacked us in Father's house. It was a safe refuge, inviolate! To have an intruder, and an infernal one at that, break into my house and violate our refuge made me feel simultaneously helpless and furious.

Worse, why had the demon been able to use Gregor's staff? And why was the staff not in Elgin, Illinois, in my brother's grave?

I made my way across the rock-strewn floor, splashing through puddles as I walked. About halfway down the hall, I found Mab sitting on a chunk of broken stone. Water sluiced off his trench coat. He held his wet hat in his hand.

"Ma'am," he said wearily, "I realize you will not listen to me, but I'd like to respectfully suggest you get away from this house. You're not safe here. The perpetrator could return any time."

"Are you all right, Mab?" I asked, ignoring him.

"Yeah. I'm all right," Mab rubbed his shoulder. "If you won't flee, Ma'am, may I, at least, have your permission to refresh the wards that protect the house, so this won't happen again?"

"Of course!" I paused. "Thank goodness we were in the hall when this happened!"

"You can say that again!" Mab nodded. "North Wind only knows what might have been released if that fire had been allowed to burn unattended. I've heard stories about some of the forbidden powers Mr. Prospero, in his foolishness, keeps bound—stories that would scare your socks off."

"That is not all." My fingers flexed about my flute protectively. "If we had arrived a few moments later, my staff would still have been in the hands of my statue when the incubus came."

Mab scowled and put on his hat. "Forgive me, Ma'am, if I don't dance a jig over the preservation of your precious little flute, but I think I've done enough dancing to its tune today."

"You don't understand, that's . . ." I began.

"You can say that again," Mab interrupted.

"That's what the demon was after," I finished, "He was looking for my flute!"

"Shame he didn't get all the staffs. World would be better off with those atrocious pieces of kindling in the hands of people who can't use them," Mab grumbled. Then, his head snapped up. "That black staff! You said it was Mr. Gregor's . . . the demon was using it!" An expression of supernatural horror came over his features. "Holy Croesus! Are you telling me that if we'd arrived a few minutes later, some minion of Hell would now be in command of my entire race?"

"Yes."

Mab's craggy face froze in a grimace of terror. Then, he stood and reached out his hand.

"Tell you what. Hand me the damned thing. I'll solve the problem once and forever."

"Luckily for us both, it's not damned yet." I added, "Not that I would give it to you under any circumstance, but just to satisfy my intellectual curiosity, what, specifically, would you do with it?"

Mab shuffled his feet and scratched his head. He stuck his hands into the pockets of his trench coat. "Take it down to the wood shop and saw it into a thousand tiny pieces. Then, I'd give a piece to each of us Aerie Ones, as a perverse kind of memento."

"Kind thought, Mab, but no."

I ran my fingers down the polished grain of the flute and imagined its soulful voice singing out amidst the smoke and moaning in the flaming pits of Hell, its gentle beauty perverted to nefarious ends. The thought of losing it—of being stuck in the mundane world without its voice to remind me of higher things—disturbed me tremendously, perhaps even more than it disturbed Mab.

"Huh!"

"What's that, Mab?"

"See those designs on the back of the door, Ma'am?" He jabbed his finger toward the far end of the hall, where the oak doors stood open. "Those faces carved into the four corners? They are guardians. Together, they form a word. I don't think it was a coincidence the incubus showed up while we were here. Mr. Prospero had those doors chained with cold iron for a reason. Between the chains and the enchantments woven into the doors themselves, the demon could not have entered this hall any more than I could have. It had to wait until we opened the way for it. Must have had some kind of spirit servant waiting around to inform it if the doors ever opened. The thing could have been hanging around for weeks, months even. When we entered and left the doors ajar . . ." Mab hung his head. "Should have thought of that and insisted we lock it up from the inside. Guess I'd gotten lazy, too used to the outer wards of the house doing their job."

"Don't blame yourself, Mab. You had no way of knowing what was in here."

"On the contrary. I knew it was important enough that Mr. Prospero, who thinks nothing of leaving phoenix feathers and unicorn horns lying around in the open, thought it should be locked up." He shook his head again. "Still wish I knew how the incubus or its servant got through the outer wards and into the mansion to begin with!"

I frowned. "So do I!"

Mab stared at the door a moment longer and then sat down glumly. "Sure is a shame about those nice statues."

"Our statues!"

I leapt up and began running up and down the length of the hall, dodging large chunks of fallen debris, trying to see the statues. Those along the right wall, Ulysses, Titus, Cornelius, Mephisto, and my father, were undisturbed, save that the outstretched arm of my father's statue had broken off and fallen to the floor. The left wall, however, had not fared as well. The reddish marble, which had once portrayed my dead brother Gregor, lay in several large pieces. The statues of Logistilla and Erasmus had been reduced to blue and green rubble, respectively.

I felt as if I had been kicked in the stomach. Most of these statues were older than the United States of America. The statue of Erasmus predated the birth of the younger siblings: Cornelius, Titus, Logistilla, Gregor and Ulysses. It had always stood in some Great Hall, here, or in England, or, long before, in Italy. The statues had seemed eternal, inviolate—like my brothers.

Tears of fury filled my eyes.

"How dare he!" I cried, my fists clenched. "Does he think he can attack Miranda Prospero, immortal Handmaiden of Eurynome, and escape unscathed?"

"Ma'am, not a good idea to challenge the powers of Hell . . ." Mab began warily, but I was running again.

Theo! Theo's statue!

An enormous chunk of reddish stone that had once been part of the roof blocked his alcove. The Water of Life that keeps us young also makes us more than human. Putting my shoulder against the stone, I drew upon this supernatural strength and shoved the obstacle aside. It grated loudly, then slid.

Beyond, the green head and torso of my statue lay sprawled at the foot of the Wife's Chair. The delicate hands, so painstakingly fashioned, had shattered. My statue's fingers lay scattered across the gray-and-black floor like so many shards of jade. It was disconcerting to see myself broken in pieces upon the floor. I suddenly felt frightened.

With my heart beating loudly in my ears, I ran to Theo's alcove. If the statue of Theophrastus were destroyed, then it would be as if the young knight who had taken such joy from the power he wielded were lost forever. The old man Theo, if he even lived, would never be that boy again. It would be as if the incubus had murdered the brother I had so loved.

Rounding the edge of the alcove, I saw the white body of Theo's statue standing tall upon its pedestal. Giddy with relief, I laughed and sagged against the wall. Trust Theophrastus the Demonslayer not to let a demon disturb him. I lurched forward and hugged the statue.

I missed Theo so much! As I embraced his marble facsimile, I recalled a cold November day, more than half a century ago. My family stood gathered about Gregor's grave on the twenty-fifth anniversary of his death. The tools of Father's spell, which had gone so sorrowfully awry, lay scattered about the chalk pentacle at our feet. Theo had stepped forward and announced in short angry words that he was turning his back on magic and rejoining the human race. I had laughed, reminding him of other resolutions he had made and broken in years past. Once, he had vowed to join the Jesuits, and he had forsworn wine and women more times than I could count. None of his other resolutions had lasted long. I predicted a similar fate for this one. How wrong time had proven me.

As I pressed my cheek against the cool marble, I noticed something white lying in the corner of the alcove. It looked disturbingly like a head. I glanced up.

The statue was headless, sheared off at the neck.

Cautiously, I approached the fallen head, unnerved by the sight of the likeness of my brother Theo lying decapitated on the floor. At least it seemed undamaged. An oread, a spirit of earth and rock, summoned properly, might be able fuse this clean break, and the statue would be as good as new. I seldom performed such sorcery myself, but Father could do it easily. Or, worse comes to worst, I could humble my pride and ask Erasmus. I knelt and lifted the head.

Where the face had struck the floor, white chips of eye, cheek, and mouth rained down onto the black marble. I turned it over. The left side of the face was whole, but the right side was sheer and smooth. The expression I had loved so dearly was irreparably damaged, lost forever.

MUCH later, when I finally rose from among the shattered likenesses of my siblings, Mab stood leaning against the edge of the alcove, his hands stuffed into the pockets of his trench coat. He tipped up the brim of his fedora.

"So which one of these scoundrels who pass for relatives of yours do we track down first?"

CHAPTER
THREE

Mephistopheles

We barreled towards the rear bumper of a deep-green Chevrolet at seventy-five miles an hour. The car loomed in our windshield, its brake lights flashed. Yet we neither slowed nor swerved. At the very last possible moment, as I was commending my soul to my Lady, Mab veered away, missing the other vehicle by a hair's width.

Relief flooded through me. I leaned back against the seat, trying to catch my breath.

I had not slept well after the attack on Prospero's Mansion and had risen in the wee hours to face a busy morning. After solving two last-minute, work-related emergencies, I had joined Mab at SeaTac well before the sun rose. Using speeds only available to a souped-up jet with an Aerie One pilot, with the *Staff of the Winds* to quiet wind resistance, we flew the Lear to Illinois, landing at Wilhelmi Field in record time, far faster than any commercial flight. Now, as we drove our rental car to the correctional center, I would have liked a few moments of peace in which to marshal my thoughts.

"We have to go back, Mab," I murmured. "I left my stomach around that last turn."

"Very glib, Ma'am." Mab was only half paying attention to me as he spun the steering wheel.

"Must you drive so wildly? In the air, you're an ace. On the road, you're a terror!"

"Don't worry, Ma'am. I've been darting in and about things longer than men have drawn breath. It's second nature to me."

"As a wind, certainly. But you're not a wind at the moment! You're a fleshly body driving his employer in a car! If you're not more careful, someone's going to report us to the police!" My voice rose as Mab performed another near miss. "How can you be sure the car can take this kind of abuse?"

"Nothing to worry about, Ma'am. Back at the rental place, before we left the airport, I had a chat with the oreads making up this car and the salamanders manning the engine. They won't let us down," Mab replied, jerking the steering wheel hard to the left.

"It's not the oreads I'm worried about!" I clung to the armrest and squeezed my eyes shut.

"I thought you said we were in a hurry?" Mab's voice continued calmly. "A matter of life and death and all that."

"True, but it won't help my family if I am killed in a car crash while trying to warn them." I opened my eyes again and sighed. "In the old days, this would have been so much easier! Father would have used the *Staff of Transportation*, and—*voilà*—we would all be standing in the company warehouse nearest to our destination."

"A crummy way for humans to behave," Mab muttered. "How come Mr. Prospero gave it up? He's never struck me as the self-controlled type."

"Ulysses has the *Staff of Transportation* now."

"Ever strike you as something strange there?" Mab glanced at me without really turning his head. "Mr. Prospero used his magic books to make the staffs, right? So, why can't he just use the books to cast the same spells again? Why can't he make two transportation staffs, or a dozen?"

"I don't know, but it's irritating. In the old days, Prospero, Incorporated had a reputation for delivering all orders by the next day, which was a real feat in the days before trucks and planes! Once Ulysses got his staff, he refused to participate. He just wanted to play. I complained, but Father just smiled and said Ulysses would come around."

"Did he?"

"No. Instead, the others went the way of Ulysses," I said, "which is terribly annoying, as not having my family's aid anymore leads to all sorts of difficulties."

"Difficulties?" Mab asked. "What kind?"

"Contracts that need to be renegotiated," I replied. "Over the centuries, some of our agreements have gotten out of kilter, resulting in fluctuating weather patterns, rising water levels, and other dangers." I sighed. "If my brothers—or, more importantly, their staffs—were available to help, we could have the weather back on an even keel."

Mab grunted. "Much as I hate to see magic in the hands of humans, I felt a damn bit more comfortable back when those human hands were Mr. Prospero's. Whatever possessed him to give the stuff to his kids?"

"I don't know, Mab," I gazed sadly out the window. "Poor Father. I miss him. I hope he's not in too much trouble."

Mab turned to look at me, ignoring the road. "Miss Miranda, why don't we go look for Mr. Prospero? Why are we going after your good-for-nothing brother when the old man might be in danger? We'll send the amateurs and the mundanes to warn your brothers. Meanwhile, we can handle what really matters."

"Mab . . . the road!"

"Er? Oh, yeah."

Personally, I was inclined to agree with Mab. It still galled me that my brothers—well, with the exception of Cornelius—had deserted Prospero, Inc. By leaving, they had failed Father, which was almost the same as saying they had failed the human race. Father, on the other hand, had never hesitated to put his principles first and his personal desires second.

"Those were not his instructions, Mab," I resolved. I had been obedient to my father's wishes for five hundred years. It would be impertinent for me to start second-guessing him now.

"All right," Mab raised his hands in a brief posture of surrender, before returning them to the wheel "It's no skin off my nose. Though, about these instructions . . . how did you find out about them if you haven't heard from Mr. Prospero since September?"

"Father left a message." I described my experience with Father's journals and the phoenix lamp.

"Huh!" murmured Mab. "Didn't know he could do that. So, as long as we're committed, Ma'am, what's our plan concerning your brother?"

"We go in and question him. If he's guilty, we leave him. If he's innocent, we break him out," I replied firmly.

"This may come as a surprise to you, Ma'am," drawled Mab, "but breaking people out of prison is against the law. Wouldn't it be better to hire him a good lawyer?"

"My family has had the opportunity to observe a great deal of human justice. Its practice fluctuates widely and is seldom just. I don't mind abandoning the guilty to its whims, but no innocent relative of mine is going to be left to the ravages of mortals. Our eternal lives are too valuable to risk!"

"Your eternal lives," Mab spat. "You're kept eternal by the Water of Life. Without it, you'd be no different from the rest of humanity. With it, they'd be no different from you. How come you don't hold all lives as priceless as yours, since all mortals have the same potential to live forever?"

"They're not members of my family," I replied haughtily, rebuking his impertinence.

As I spoke, I glanced out the window. Through the tinted glass, I caught a glimpse of an old woman crossing a pedestrian overpass with small hesitant steps. Her wrinkled face was careworn and tired. For a moment, I felt as if it were I and not she who tottered along, alone and worn.

There, but for the grace of my Lady, went I.

Meanwhile, Mab was saying, ". . . a fair trial. If the jury finds him guilty, and you still think he's innocent, there will be time enough to decide what to do."

"We'll worry about it after we talk with him," I said absently, absorbed by this extraordinary experience. In my long life, I could not recall ever having confused myself with someone else.

Besides, if I found Mephisto guilty, the cretin, it would not matter what the mortals decided.

The car screeched to a halt in the middle of the road. Car horns honked raucously. A silver Ford loomed in our rear window, with no apparent intention of stopping.

"Ma'am, I beg to differ with you, but I think we should settle it now. As I explained yesterday, I consider myself an American citizen, and I do not intend to dishonor Her laws. If you wait until after the trial, and you still think he's innocent, I'll do whatever you want. But if you intend to break him out before the trial, I refuse to help. I might even turn you in myself."

"For God's sake, Mab," I cried. "Drive!"

Mab did as he was told, barely avoiding several accidents. My heart still in my throat, my hands sought my flute. It felt warm and solid in my grasp.

"Mab, you cannot disobey me."

Mab shot a dark glance toward the flute. He growled. "I can damned well try. You might be able to move my limbs with that thing, but you can't make me think. It can only force me to do tasks that are common to Aerie Ones. My knowledge and my expertise are my own, and I am not going to use them against the United States of America! We're approaching the turnoff for the jail. What's your decision, Ma'am?"

I examined my flute curiously. Was Mab right? Could I not command those parts of him that behaved like a man? What a fascinating concept! I doubted he was correct. Father would never have put him in a fleshly body if that were the case. On the other hand, one could never tell with Father.

I made a mental note to investigate Mab's claims of free will when I had some spare time. At the moment, I just wanted to see my brother and be done with it—without losing my life to traffic.

"Okay, Mab," I said. "It hardly matters to me. If I think he's innocent, I'll wait until after the trial. But I'm going to hold you responsible for his safety. And woe to you if I believe him innocent and the Three Shadowed Ones reach him before the American courts do."

"So be it, Ma'am," Mab swore. "Let it be upon my head."

THE prison facilities were as impressive as any walled medieval city, except the great walls were meant to keep men in instead of out. Entering, we were conducted through a lengthy security procedure, made more difficult because the guard found it hard to believe someone as youthful-looking as I had been born in the 1950s. I probably would have been refused entrance altogether had he not mistaken my silvery hair for a sign of age. It was time to update my identification.

Of course, doing so would not be so easy this time, due to computers and modern security measures. As they finally waved us by, it occurred to me that it was a good thing Father had experimented with incarnating Aerie Ones back in the first half of the twentieth century. If he had produced a group of grown men out of nothing today, it would be tremendously difficult to acquire the necessary ID. Back when Mab got started, a letter of reference was sufficient.

We arrived so early that we had to wait until the visitor facilities opened. Eventually, a guard led us to a place where we could look through a window into a large room where they promised to bring my brother. There were phones on both sides of the glass, separated by slim walls that formed shallow booths. To either side of us, another prisoner spoke with his visitors. Mab and I stood silently, neither of us eager to talk as we awaited Mephisto's entrance.

The door opened, and two guards dragged in the prisoner in his bright orange jumpsuit. He gazed fixedly at the floor, long black curls covering much of his face. I tried to get his attention, but he did not look up.

Too embarrassed to face me? This was not a good sign.

I sat down in the chair, facing the window, and picked up the phone on my side. The guards handed the other phone to their prisoner. I spoke to him sternly in Italian, asking if he were guilty of the crime of which he was accused. Instead of answering, he began to chant in a breathy singsong, babbling about how he was the alpha and the omega, the Archangel Gabriel and

Mephistopheles. As he chanted, he raised his arms over his head. His hair fell away from his face, revealing wide cheeks, a crooked nose, and a heavy dark brow.

This man was not my brother!

OUTSIDE the prison, we walked silently to our car. As we reached our vehicle, Mab hung his head. "Oh, Ma'am! I hope you can forgive me for leading you on a wild goose chase."

I glanced his way, intending a stern rebuke, but he looked so woebegone I could not help smiling. Suddenly, the experience seemed inexpressibly amusing. I started giggling.

Mab frowned, hurt. Then, a grin began tugging at the corner of his mouth. He too began to chuckle, and then we were both laughing uncontrollably. As soon as one of us would stop, a glance at the other would set us off again.

"By the North Wind, it's a good thing we didn't break him out without talking to him first!" Mab chuckled as we climbed into our car. "Would have been downright embarrassing, breaking out the wrong man!"

"Very true! Remind me of this event, should the issue ever arise again," I replied. "You made an understandable mistake; the prisoner claimed to be Mephistopheles, and he did look Italian."

"Mr. Mephistopheles's trail still leads to Chicago, Ma'am. He's here somewhere, or, at least, he was here recently. Perhaps we should take a day or two to investigate. Clues might come to light here that I'd miss if I were back home in Oregon."

I closed my eyes and prayed to my Lady. She had brought this matter to my attention, I had no doubt She would help me carry out my duties. A sense of urgency, of growing danger, had begun nagging at my thoughts, and yet, as I prayed, I felt enveloped by Her calm constant presence. This feeling of peace came with no specific instructions. My Lady was gracious, all-wise, and a very present help in trouble; however, She only spoke to Her Handmaidens when it suited Her divine purpose. After pondering, I interpreted this to mean that we should stay here in Illinois.

Of course, had I been a Sibyl, I could have just asked Her directly and received a clear, unambiguous answer.

"Time is of the essence, Mab," I said, opening my eyes. "There's no point in our wasting time returning to Oregon, just to rush back again as soon as another clue turns up. Let's go to our Chicago offices and have the—whatever they are calling clerks nowadays—arrange a hotel for us. Then, you can continue searching for my brothers while I check in with the head office."

LEAVING the prison, we drove into Chicago, a city of wonders! Long ago, in Milan, I lived in a castle with a clock tower seventy yards tall. Even today, no building in Milan rivals that tower. Yet, seventy yards was like a child's toy compared to the soaring marvels of glass and steel in downtown Chicago. The Sears Tower reached over 1,450 feet. While it dwarfed the buildings around it, the shorter ones also reached heights unimaginable to the men of my childhood. I never tired of gazing up at them.

But, it was not just the buildings. I've lived in many cities during my long life: Milan, London, Edinburgh, Amsterdam, St. Petersburg, Alexandria, to name just a few. Despite their various marvels, they had one thing in common—they stank. The inhabitants routinely dumped their chamber pots and rotting garbage into streets already buried under piles of horse manure. One could not walk in these cities without ruining one's shoes—sometimes, one's entire outfit.

Today's tall looming skyscrapers rose over firm dry streets, clean except for occasional mud or litter. And the color! Ancient cities were bright on festival days, but flags and banners soon faded. Not so the brilliant signs and eye-boggling billboards of this modern age. The difference between the stinking towns of old and the glorious metallic expanses of today staggers the mind! I would never have believed men could produce such magic if I had not lived to see it with my own eyes.

And to think that none of it would have been possible without Father and Prospero, Inc.!

I ARRIVED at our Chicago office just after ten. My next hour was swallowed by company business. I commandeered the Branch Director's office and dealt with problems that had arisen since the morning. Many of our business concerns were unusually busy due to the Christmas season, and half our branches claimed to have emergencies only the CEO could resolve. Finally, I gave instructions to have all mundane troubles dealt with by the appropriate vice president and to forward to me only issues involving the five Priority Accounts.

Our company offices had been in a fashionable district when we opened them in 1910, but times change. Now, the area was so dilapidated, I hesitated to walk the eight blocks to the hotel; however, I felt a sudden intuition that I should walk the distance. After arranging for our bags to be sent ahead, Mab and I set out on foot.

We strolled through the windy streets of downtown Chicago, past delicatessens and small stores selling jewelry or cameras. Winter was nearly upon us, and the weather here was true to the season. Mab pulled up the collar of his gray trench coat and lowered the brim of his black fedora, hoping to protect the back of his neck from the icy cold. I wondered how much protection an Aerie Spirit or, in particular, the carnal manifestation of the Nor'easterlies, actually needed from the wind.

The cold was not particularly disturbing to me either. Among the many charms woven into the emerald satin of my enchanted tea gown was a protection against the chill brought by any wind. However, a high-necked Edwardian gown tended to draw odd looks these days, especially if worn unadorned in frigid weather. So, I had added a white trench coat and a matching fedora, which fit snuggly over the Grecian twist into which I had pinned my silver-blond hair. Catching our reflections in a plate glass window as we walked along in our trench coats and hats, I thought Mab and I made a jaunty pair.

The morning rush hour had ended. A few well-dressed citizens bustled past, but the majority of our fellow pedestrians were unkempt and shivering. Almost every unattended alley or doorway had an occupant sleeping in it, huddled beneath newspaper or an old blanket. Across the road, a man in a bright fez and a brown overcoat stood in an archway. His placid face could have belonged to anyone—a short-order cook, an accountant, a department-store clerk, or a stock broker—except that one eye was significantly smaller than the other. As he met my gaze, something about his expression reminded me of the past, of many people I had met over the long years: people who worked for me, both aerie and human; people I had known in my childhood and long forgotten. Disturbed, I averted my gaze and pressed on.

Others, more adventurous, dared the cold to panhandle for their dinner. A lone woman with a red kerchief over her head and earrings the size of my palm sang beside a radio. An open cardboard box on the ground before her held a scattering of coins. Her voice was eerie and lilting. Mab tossed a bill into her box and another into the instrument case of a slim figure in a blue poncho and a sombrero, who sat on an old tomato crate, playing the lute.

As we approached the door of the hotel, the lute player began a new tune, singing in a high tenor:

"The master, the swabber, the boatswain and I,
The gunner and his mate
Lov'd Mall, Meg and Marian and Margery,
But none of us cared for Kate;
For she has a tongue with a tang,
Would cry to a sailor, Go hang!
She lov'd not the savor of tar nor of pitch,
Yet a tailor might scratch her where'er she did itch:
Then to sea, boys, and let her go hang!
Then come kiss me, sweet and twenty,
Youth's a stuff will not endure."

The song brought a smile to my lips, despite its lewd nature. Many years had passed since I last heard it, outside performances of *The Tempest.* By Shakespeare's grace, it had outlasted many of its more deserving contemporaries. Yet, it seemed oddly charming to hear an old familiar tune, even a bawdy one, on the streets of modern Chicago. I walked back to listen.

The lutenist's head rose. A slim pale hand pushed stringy black hair from large brown eyes that slowly grew round with fear.

"Miranda?" My brother Mephisto peered out from beneath the sombrero. "What are you doing here?"

"Why I . . . I'm looking for you!" I replied.

Mephistopheles was slight and lithe with warm brown eyes. He was also filthy. Dirt and oily grime coated his poncho. His matted stringy black hair had not been washed, or perhaps even combed, in months. His cheap sneakers were riddled with holes. Through one hole protruded the big toe of his left foot, the nail of which was rotten and caked with pus. And he stank, abominably.

He sat on the tomato crate gazing at me fearfully. Then, a glint of comprehension sparked behind the emptiness in his eyes. He leapt to his feet and flung out his arms to embrace me, whooping with joy. The lute he had been playing flew from his hands and crashed upon the cement sidewalk, shattering into several pieces.

"You found it!" Mephisto cried, oblivious of the lute. He grabbed my shoulders and shook me. "You found it!"

"Found what?" I threw up my hands to ward him away as he tried to kiss me. The stench was unbearable. Still, I was happy to see he was in one of his cheerful periods. Mephisto stared at me in wonder, as if amazed anyone could be thinking of a subject other than what was on his mind.

My initial shock at encountering my long-lost brother on a random side street faded the instant I recalled that my Lady had prompted me to walk in this direction. That was how the Lady of Spiral Wisdom worked, subtly and indirectly, yet leading me always onward to my goal.

"My staff, Miranda! You found my staff?" His voice rose to end on a hopeful note.

"No."

"Oh."

Mephisto stepped back and hung his head. I brushed at the grime that now clung to my white coat with a handkerchief I found in my pocket. Several passers-by stopped to look at the shattered lute where it lay upon the concrete, a tangle of splinters and strings. Their attention drew my brother's.

An unarticulated moan came from Mephisto's lips. He rushed over and scooped up the broken lute, cradling the pieces in his arms and keening softly. He looked back despairingly toward me, his pathetic face streaked with tears.

"Not my lute! Not my lovely lute, too," he cried. Laying his cheek against the broken neck of the instrument, he whispered, "Who did this, my lovely? Who did this to you?"

Big wet tears rolled slowly over his hollow cheeks. Watching the pathetic figure of my weeping brother, I contrasted him in my mind's eye with the handsome statue of his youthful self.

Mab stepped up beside me and spoke in a low voice. "The poor sucker doesn't even remember that he threw it."

"It breaks my heart, Mab."

"Didn't know you had one, Ma'am."

I stepped forward and put my hand on Mephisto's grime-caked arm. "It's all right, Mephisto. I'll buy you another one."

"I don't want another lute. This was my lute," he began.

"The next one will be yours too."

". . . I've had my lute almost my whole life." A haunted look came into his eye. "It's the one my mother gave me; my mother's been dead over four hundred years. It's the lute I played for Queen Elizabeth."

I stepped away, back to where Mab stood. He was squinting at the fragments of lute.

"Was that really a fifteenth-century lute?" Mab asked.

"Most likely he lost that one long ago and forgot he'd replaced it." I shrugged. "But it is possible."

Mephisto began walking. He wound his way through the pedestrians until he came to a trash can. There, he unstrung the strings from the neck and body and ceremoniously lowered the broken remains into the wire bin. Wandering back to the tomato crate, he sat with his hands over his face.

In a tired and ragged voice, he said, "Breaks. Stolen. Falls apart. Everything I love gets destroyed. My staff is gone. I can't find my Bully Boy. My friends don't recognize me. A woman killed my cat with a car. She said she was sorry afterwards. Does that make it okay? All the things I love get destroyed, and there is nothing I can do. There's nothing I can do to protect them."

Mab spoke softly in my ear. "I think he's forgotten us."

I nodded.

Mab lowered the brim of his hat. "He's not going to hear any warning you give him, Ma'am, and he's in no position to respond if he did." When I did not answer, Mab continued, "Mr. Prospero told me nothing could be done for him. He said Mephisto resisted every attempt your family made to help him."

"It's true. Every time Mephisto seemed to improve, he would suddenly grow obstinate and refuse to continue his treatment. We tried locking him up, but sooner or later he'd escape or one of his supernatural beast friends would show up to break him out. Eventually, Father washed his hands of the matter and said we had to let him go his own way."

"Let's go then," said Mab, "There's nothing else we can do."

I started to turn away, then hesitated.

"There's one big difference between the past and now."

"What's that, Ma'am?"

"Normally, Mephisto has all sorts of supernatural friends to help him. When he has his staff, no number of ordinary thugs could overwhelm him. Without it? He may be faster and stronger than a normal mortal, but in his current condition, he could be taken out by a bum with a knife." Frowning, I contrasted in my mind once more the picture of my brother, broken and dirty on the sidewalk, with the intelligent young man portrayed by his statue. "We can't leave him like this, Mab!"

"We can't do anything for him here," Mab gestured at the sidewalk. He waved his hand in front of his face to dissipate the awful stink.

Walking over to Mephisto I grabbed his arm and dragged him to his feet.

"Come on," I said. "Let's get you cleaned up."

I HAD just finished my soup and was beginning on my salad when the door into the men's bedroom finally opened. A wet and bedraggled Mab came slouching into the parlor of our suite. Mab had been saddled with the unpleasant job of stripping Mephisto down and piling him into the shower, while I went out to purchase a new wardrobe for my brother. On the way back, I had stopped at a theater costume shop, where I had found a royal blue surcoat emblazoned with the fleur-de-lis, left over from a performance of *The Lion in Winter*. It was my hope Mephisto would accept it as a replacement for the ghastly poncho. As best I understood, he had started wearing ponchos to begin with as a replacement for his royal tabard.

"Where is he?" I asked.

"Admiring his new duds in the mirror," Mab growled. "He'll be out here soon enough, once he smells the food."

As Mab pulled the silver dome off his lunch, the door opened again to admit my brother.

Mephisto looked like a different man. He was clean. His newly-cut hair formed a halo of wavy dark curls around his head. He wore a loose, black, Russian shirt and black trousers with high black-leather boots. Over the black clothes, he had thrown the royal blue surcoat emblazoned with the fleur-de-lis in silver. When he came forward and embraced me, he smelled pleasantly of Old Spice aftershave. I had not seen him look so neatly turned out in many, many years.

Mephisto leapt back. He spread his arms and threw back his head, assuming the pose he had immortalized in his statue of himself.

"Don't you recognize me?" he cried happily.

"Of course, I recognize you, Mephisto." I looked him over once, and then gestured toward the food cart. "Ah . . . why don't you pull up a chair and eat your lunch? You look famished."

He really did, too. He was thin, almost emaciated. I wondered if he had eaten in days.

Mephisto pulled up a straight-backed chair to the serving cart of food room service had provided and began devouring the fare. He inhaled whole slices of pizza and devoured sandwich halves in a single bite. His eyes, however, remained fixed fondly, though warily, on my face.

"So?" he asked happily, his mouth full.

"I believe something may have happened to Father," I began. "He sent me a note that suggests he ran afoul of powers he could not control. His message asked that I warn the family if I did not hear from him. When I found the message, I sent Aerie Ones to his house on the island, but he hadn't been back since he left to come to America in September. So, I'm warning the family. Beware the Three Shadowed Ones."

"They're after our staffs!" Mephisto exclaimed.

"How did you know?"

"They took mine, didn't they?"

"I thought yours was stolen by some strumpet you took home for the night."

"That's because you didn't stick around to hear the whole story," Mephisto shot back accusingly.

"You were drunk."

"You were rude."

This was getting us nowhere.

"Someone broke into the house and . . . did some damage," I said, returning to the earlier topic. It was too soon after the lute fiasco to tell Mephistopheles about the shattered statues. "I believe it was one of these Three Shadowed Ones, and he was after our staffs."

"I told you!" Mephisto turned to Mab. "Didn't I tell her?"

"That's not all, Mephisto," I continued. "The creature that broke into the mansion . . . it was an incubus."

"What?" exclaimed Mephisto

"A Power of Hell!"

"Oh, them." He reached for a biscuit.

A shiver ran down my spine. Was Mephisto so far gone he no longer feared the servants of Hell? If so, he was not just out of it, he was dangerous to be near! Either way, it was time to do what I came to do and go.

"Look, I've given you Father's warning. Now, you know. Father said to 'keep close the gifts he had given.' In your case, the warning came too late. All the same. I thought you should know."

"Who else have you warned?"

"No one yet. You're the first."

Mephisto wiped his mouth with one of the napkins provided. "What a good move! Now you'll have me to help you find the others."

"Great comfort that is," muttered Mab, from where he sat hunched over his lunch. Apparently, he was still disgruntled from the drenching he had taken bathing my brother. Mephisto regarded Mab, and then turned back to me, cocking his head.

"Where'd you chase up this one? He looks like something out of the movies. Is he your bodyguard?"

I laughed, and Mab snorted.

"A body would have to be crazy to guard the likes of her. Always rushing in where angels fear to tread."

I stood to perform the proper introductions. "Mephisto, this is Mab Boreal, one of the Incarnated Northerlies. He heads our company detectives. Mab, this is my brother Mephisto."

"Detective?" Mephisto's eyes shone brightly. "As in 'finds lost things'?"

I nodded.

"And he's traveling with you? . . . And you're going where now? To warn the others? The others who have staffs these Three Shadowy Ones might be hunting down as we speak?"

"Yes, that's right."

Mephisto glanced back and forth between Mab and myself. Then, he gave us his brightest smile. "When do we leave?"

"No. Absolutely not." Mab rose to his feet and stalked over to stand in front of me. "There is no way, Ma'am, that I am going to help this kook find his magical glorified kindling."

" 'Kook'? Who you calling a kook? Mr. Sam Spade wannabe?" Mephisto turned to me. "Tell him how great it will be, Miranda. Just like old times! We'll travel together, and I'll help you. And if we just happen upon my staff? Well, that's fine, too."

His mention of old times evoked memories of countless treks, some pleasant, some disastrous. I recalled one time Father, Mephisto, and I had gone to Switzerland to meet with a yeti and discuss avalanches. Taking Mephisto, the Beast Tamer, instead of one of the enforcers—Theo, Titus, or Gregor—had turned out to be a mistake. Mephisto did gain a new shaggy friend he could summon up with a tap of his staff; however, nothing was ever done to improve the avalanche situation.

"No, Mephisto," I said firmly as I pictured Mephisto's well-meaning antics resulting in my being buried under ten feet of snow again.

"At last, she shows some sense," muttered Mab.

"But, you'll need help. What if the Three Shadowed Ones attack?" Mephisto said.

Mab snorted. "What help would you be?"

"I could hit them with my lute," Mephisto offered helpfully, evidently forgetting the instrument he had broken. Or perhaps he was envisioning a fate for the one I had promised to buy him.

"No. I'll leave you a little money. You won't be destitute." I made a mental note to dispatch an Aerie One to keep an eye on him.

"But I could help. I know I could," he continued plaintively. "I knew how to use a sword . . . once."

"No."

"Please! Don't leave me behind, Miranda. I'm afraid to be on my own without my staff. Please?"

I hated to hear him beg. He sounded so pathetic. Yet, I was certain if I brought him along, it would lead to another calamity such as our encounter with the yeti, or the time Theo and I were nearly drowned by his mermaid friends. We were facing the Powers of Hell, and even a slight mistake could lead to a fate far worse than frostbite.

"Come on, Mab," I said, "We need to keep going. Lives could be at stake."

MAB and I gathered our hats and coats. Mephisto retreated into the corner, where he sat with his arms crossed, sulking. I offered him some money, but he just threw it on the floor. I shrugged and returned to Mab.

"Do you have any more leads?" I asked, "Or must we return to Oregon?"

A crafty look came into Mephisto's eyes. He leapt up and stepped in front of us to stand in the doorway.

"And, of course, you know where you're going. So, you don't need me to lead you around. But perhaps I'll see you at Theo's? Or maybe at Cornelius's? Got to be going, now. Bye."

He waved good-bye and started out the door. Mab and I exchanged glances.

"Mephisto! Wait!"

"Yes?" Part way down the hall, Mephisto froze as if in mid-step. He turned and leaned back toward us, cupping a hand about his ear. "You called?"

"You know where Theo is?"

"And Cornelius! And Logistilla!"

"I don't suppose you'll tell us?" I asked sadly.

"What do you take me for? A fool?" he asked, throwing up his hands. "But of course, I would be willing to lead you there, if . . ."

"If . . . what?"

"If you make your detective help me find my staff," he said.

I looked at Mab. He was scowling.

"Could be a matter of life or death for some of my brothers, Mab. What if we hadn't heard of the Three Shadowed Ones when the darkness started forming in the Great Hall?"

Mab stared at me hard for quite some time. Finally, he nodded glumly.

"Okay, Mephisto," I said. "You have yourself a deal."

"Yippee," yelled Mephisto, punching the air as he leapt.

The phone rang in the room behind us.

"Could you get that Mab? It could be from our Chicago branch," I said.

"While you're at it," called Mephisto. "Could you pick up the money Miranda left on the floor? I have a feeling I might want it after all."

"Pick up your own damned money," grumbled Mab, answering the phone. He spoke into it for a moment. Then, he picked up the money and came out, shutting the door behind him.

"It was for you, Ma'am. Front desk says there's someone waiting downstairs to see you." He handed me the money. I handed it to Mephisto, who wadded it up and stuck it into his pocket. Mab continued, "She hung up before I could ask any questions. I don't like it."

"Who could possibly know I was here, except someone from our Chicago office?" I asked. "Come on, let's go downstairs."

"What was it I said about 'angels fear to tread'?" growled Mab. "Never listens to me. Okay, Ma'am, risk your neck. But I'm sticking with you. Just in case."

"Me too!" exclaimed Mephisto.

"Great, just great," I murmured. "You two have to promise me that if it's a mundane business associate, you'll both vamoose."

"Let's take the elevator to the second floor, then walk down the fire stairs to the lobby," Mab said. "Just to be safe. That way we can approach from an unexpected angle and catch any assailants unaware."

I sighed but obliged him. We took the elevator to the second floor and then found the nearest door marked EXIT. The fire stairs opened into a plush lobby covered by a maroon carpet. In the center stood a fountain surrounded by tall fronds.

Ahead, a man leaned casually against the counter. The clerk behind the counter, a pretty little brunette, blushed under his attentions. Then I saw his face.

Without hesitating, I turned and fled.

CHAPTER FOUR

Secrets from the Past

Memory is a funny thing.

We think of it as pictures in a row, like a motion picture recording of the past, but it is not. When we visit a place we once lived or hear a long forgotten song, we suddenly recall not only images but also sounds, smells, feelings. If we were victorious when we last walked the cobblestone streets of Firenze, the ringing of those cobblestones beneath our feet will bring a swell of confidence. If we were sad when we last heard Beethoven's Sixth, then upon hearing the orchestra playing the opening swell of its notes, we will find our hearts inexplicably filled with sorrow.

And, to my great shame, if we were an awkward lovesick girl of sixteen when last we encountered a certain man, meeting him again makes us feel clumsy and sick to our stomachs—no matter how many centuries have passed in the interlude.

I WAS across the lobby and through the glass doors leading to the street before Mab and Mephisto caught up with me. Grabbing their arms, I hustled them along rapidly. Mab followed without complaint, but Mephisto hung back, trying to get a good look at the man we were leaving behind. He leaned away from my grip at a precarious angle, hopping on one foot and shading his eyes with his free hand. He could not have been more conspicuous if he had yodeled. In disgust, I released my grip. He lost his balance, collapsing gently to the pavement.

Mephisto leapt up quickly and hurried after me as I strode briskly, covering the blocks back to the office parking garage without pause or comment. My heart was pounding. My cheeks felt sunburnt. By the time we reached the car, my fingers were trembling so badly I could not hold my keys. I dropped them twice before finally managing to open the door.

I climbed into the car. Mephisto went obediently to the back door, waving cheerfully to a couple walking between the cement pillars of the underground complex. They waved back, puzzled. Mab strapped himself into the front passenger seat, then watched, bemused, as I struggled to get the right key into the ignition.

"You seem distraught, Ma'am. Sure you don't want me to drive?"

"Better me driving distraught than either of you behind the wheel," I replied hoarsely. "I would like to arrive alive, thank you."

"So would I," muttered Mab.

Ignoring his cheekiness, I drove out of the garage and began weaving my way through traffic, heading back toward Wilhelmi Field, where we had left our Lear. The rush of vehicles around me seemed a distant whir. Cars honked, perhaps at me; I did not care. I held my breath and waited for my innate sense of reason to offer some rational explanation as to what had just occurred.

None came.

Having given up on getting any information out of me, Mab had turned to Mephisto. ". . . must be some explanation," he was saying. "Wonder if it has anything to do with the good-looking mug on that chap."

"I didn't know they made real people who looked like that," Mephisto replied enthusiastically. "Do you think he was an actor or a movie star? Maybe he does toothpaste commercials."

"Have you ever seen him before?" asked Mab.

"Nope. Must be after my time," said Mephisto. By which he meant, of course, that I must have met the gentleman recently, since our family had gone its separate ways. He was mistaken. I felt compelled to correct him.

"Before your time, actually," I said as I cut across two lanes of traffic to merge onto Interstate 80.

"Before? But how could that be? Unless, you mean he's . . ." Mephisto did a double-take back toward the direction of the hotel that would have done Cary Grant proud. "He couldn't be!"

"Could not be who?" asked Mab, scowling.

"Ferdinand de Napoli!" Mephisto exclaimed eagerly.

"Who?" Mab asked again.

No point in delaying the inevitable.

"You read Shakespeare didn't you, Mab? *The Tempest*?"

"Sure. That and *Midsummer Night's Dream* are the only histories of Shakespeare where anyone of importance appears," replied Mab.

"That was Ferdinand," I sighed. "Prince Ferdinand of Naples."

"Impossible! He should have been dead for some five centuries!" Mab paused. "Are you certain it was him? Maybe this guy at the hotel was a look-alike."

Behind him, in the rearview mirror, I could see Mephisto nodding sagely.

"You saw him," I muttered. My fingers were gripping the steering wheel so tightly I feared I might break it. "Do you think I could forget that man's face?"

Mephisto and Mab both shook their heads.

Mab growled, "Bet he made off with one of Prospero's books, back when he was on that island. Used it to make himself immortal, which would explain why he still looks as good as he did five hundred-plus years ago. Whatever he's up to, it can't be good!"

"Miranda," Mephisto called from the back seat, "If that's Ferdie, why are we running away?"

Ay, there's the rub.

Why were we running away? What could I possibly say to my brother? I opened my mouth to tell him the truth, but after so many years of pretending, the words would not come to my lips.

"I have nothing to say to him," I replied flatly.

Intrigued, Mephisto leaned forward, his dark eyes sparkling. "So, what's the story, Miranda? Embarrassed to see him after you used him and abused him? Afraid to face him after you made him a pawn in your revenge against Uncle Antonio for exiling Daddy to that island?"

"Ah, yes . . . our great revenge," I muttered. My mouth was unnaturally dry. What a tangled web I had woven. Now, I must bear the burden of unraveling it.

In my long life, there had been only one matter about which I had constantly been less than straightforward. I do not know when the line between fantasy and reality blurred, but I had repeated the fabrication so many times, I had forgotten the real version. Only, when I stepped into the hotel lobby and found the subject of my fabrications staring me in the face did I recall the truth . . . and my terrible shame.

If Ferdinand were really alive, the truth would come out. My brother might as well hear it from me.

"About the whole revenge thing . . ." The heat in my cheeks rose to the level of a second-degree burn. "The truth is . . ." I spoke the three hardest words of my long life in one rapid rush. "Ferdinand jilted me."

Silence fell like a lead curtain. Stomach churning, I glanced sideways and then at my rearview mirror, trying to gauge the reactions of my passengers. Mab had pulled his fedora down over his face. Mephisto's jaw hung open in astonishment. As I was turning away, Mephisto reached up and pushed his jaw shut with his hand. It closed with a snap.

"Jilted?" he squeaked. "As in 'did not marry'? You? Marry? What about the Unicorn?"

I shifted uncomfortably in my seat, wishing I had let Mab drive after all.

"I-I was young, six-sixteen," I faltered. "You gentlemen saw him. Can you imagine any young girl who wouldn't want to marry such a man? He was the only man I'd ever seen, except for Caliban. I thought . . ." My voice dropped. "At the time, I thought I'd given the Unicorn her due."

"You were going to leave the Unicorn to marry him, and he left you for another woman?" Mephisto asked. "Had you already bought your dress?"

"Had it handmade, you mean . . . one did not buy dresses back then. And yes, it had been made. I was wearing it. I was . . . at the altar." My voice seemed to have dropped out of my throat. In a hoarse whisper I finished, "He never showed up."

Amazing how a mere memory could shame me to the point of tears.

"He left you standing alone at the altar? Oh, poor Miranda!" cried Mephisto. "What was his explanation?"

"I don't know. I never saw him again. He just . . . disappeared."

"And now he's here," Mephisto said happily. "How romantic. The two of you can get back together."

"Not a chance." I stepped on the accelerator. The car leapt forward. I changed lanes, shooting between two other vehicles. This time I was certain the honking was meant for me.

We drove in silence, the other two afraid to speak. The roads flashed by, and soon we were at the exit, heading back toward Wilhelmi Field.

"That's odd," I said suddenly. "I was thinking about Ferdinand just today, right before we found Mephisto. I wonder what reminded me of him? I haven't thought of him in years."

"Maybe it was the song your brother was playing on his lute," suggested Mab.

"I doubt it. That was a sixteenth-century English song. I knew Ferdinand in 1473, in Italy. Hardly the same, at least to me."

"But it was from *The Tempest,*" Mephisto piped in knowingly. "It must have been the song!"

"Perhaps," I murmured, unconvinced.

"The real question," growled Mab, "is what's he doing here? And how did he know Miss Miranda was at that hotel? That's what I wanna know!"

WE arrived at the airport just after two, returned the rental car, and headed across the field to the Lear.

"So, where does Mr. Theophrastus live?" Mab asked as he readied the plane, a custom-designed Lear jet modified to Aerie One piloting specs. He stood on a ladder wiping the windshield with a soft cloth. Below him, Mephisto had bent himself almost halfway backwards in order to walk under the wing and examine the flanges.

"So, where's my staff?" asked Mephisto, from under the wing.

"Can't we talk on the way?" I asked impatiently, folding my cell phone with a snap. I had been standing to one side, conversing with Mustardseed, my vice president of Priority Accounts, while I waited for Mab to ready the jet. "Theo could be dead by the time you two stop bickering."

"Would like to oblige you, Ma'am, but I can't deduce anything without facts. I can't keep track of facts without notes, and I can't write notes while I'm piloting the plane. If either of you two want to fly the plane, then I'll talk about the staff while we go. Otherwise, no dice."

"I'll fly the plane," Mephisto offered helpfully, emerging. Mab and I both ignored him.

"It's your call, Ma'am. You're the one who would like to keep your family from the jaws of Hell. Mephisto, here," Mab jabbed his thumb at my brother, "and I couldn't care less if the whole kit and caboodle spontaneously combusted."

"Hey! Don't include me in that. I love my family," said Mephisto. He threw his arm about my shoulder. "Those members who don't irk me, anyway."

I gave him a cursory squeeze, then shrugged free. "This is getting ridiculous. How close is Theo's house to the nearest airport?" I asked.

"About two hours," said Mephisto.

"Why don't you tell us where to fly the plane. We'll land at the airport and rent another car. Then I can drive while you tell Mab about your staff. If Mab stops taking notes, you can stop telling me where to go."

Mephisto narrowed his eyes. He struck a pose with one hand on his hip, staring at us suspiciously. Mab and I waited.

"I'll tell him where to go," Mab muttered under his breath.

"All right. I'll agree," Mephisto threw up his hands. "Fly your silly plane to New Hampshire."

THE flight was relatively uneventful. Mephisto sat in the co-pilot's seat making comments about how the land features below resembled smiling or leering faces with long ears or enormous noses. I sat in the passenger section with my laptop open, forgoing the delight of gazing out at the sky in order to review the inventory situation for our upcoming Priority Accounts.

Yet, my thoughts kept slipping away from work and back to Ferdinand. I tried to recall Ferdinand as he had been when we first met, but his voice, his smile, his laugh, were lost in the mists of time. The real events were all tumbled with Shakespeare's version in my mind. After all, I had only lived my life once, but I had seen *The Tempest* performed hundreds of times down the centuries. It was a family favorite.

Shakespeare must have been closer to the truth than I remembered. Maybe Father really had forgiven Uncle Antonio, and I had only invented the idea we had been seeking revenge to soothe my broken heart and hurt pride. Or, had Father been as eager for revenge as I later recalled? Exactly what kind of man had Father been when I was young? I shook my head, but the mists of time refused to dispel. I wished Father were around so I could ask him. He was already an old man in those days, while I had been a mere child. Undoubtedly, he would remember what really happened.

Only, Father was missing. . . .

OUTSIDE the plane, a storm moved in suddenly—great black thunderheads looming ominously before us. Normally, Mab and I would have flown into the tempest for the joy of it; however, we were in a hurry. Mab took the plane above the clouds, while I prepared a song to play on my flute that would disperse the storm without dispersing Mab, in case the weather worsened.

As we pulled above the writhing clouds, a lightning bolt snaked across the storm-darkened sky. Smiling, I pressed my cheek against the cool glass of the window and waved. As if in answer, the lightning bolt formed, for an instant, the outline of a horned equine rearing up on its hind legs. From the cockpit, I heard Mab's exclamation of wonder, and Mephisto's yelp of surprise. They had seen it, too!

As the dark clouds fell away below us, I stared out, the afterimage of the unicorn still visible to my eye, and a feeling of joy replaced the heaviness which had overtaken my heart.

AFTER landing at Manchester Airport, we rented another car. I drove, following Mephisto's directions. We passed briefly through the city of Manchester, then found ourselves driving through beautiful rustic New Hampshire on our way to Vermont. My sense of urgency growing, I barreled down the road at well over the speed limit. Mab muttered a snide comment, but I ignored him. In Chicago, he had been speeding in busy traffic. The roads I was racing down were empty.

Once we were underway, Mab pulled out his notebook and his stubby pencil. There followed some snorting and shuffling as he arranged them on his lap to his satisfaction. Once done, he jerked out his arm so that he could glance at his watch without his sleeve blocking the view.

Noting my glance, he said, "Keeping track of the time, Ma'am. I'm expecting to get paid double my normal rate for this. Okay, Mr. Mephistopheles Prospero, fire away."

"Where should I start?" asked Mephisto. In the rearview mirror, I could see him spreading his arms. "There's so much to say."

"When did you realize the staff had been stolen?" Mab began.

"In the morning when I woke up. I reached for it to summon up a maenad or a harpy to cook me breakfast, but it was gone."

"You are certain that it was there the night before?"

"Yup. I summoned up the Archangel Uriel just before Chalandra arrived."

"The Archangel Uriel," breathed Mab in amazement. "Holy Croesus! What can't this staff do?"

"It can only call beings or beasts with whom Mephisto has properly prepared covenants, the creatures whose images are carved into the length of the staff," I offered from the driver's seat. "I believe Erasmus summoned Uriel for him the first time."

"Have you ever seen it?" Mephisto bounced in his seat enthusiastically, "I wouldn't want you not to recognize it if you came upon it. It's about six feet long. It's made of dozens of little wooden figurines with jeweled eyes, all attached together."

"Six feet! Hardly, Mephisto! Five feet at the longest," I said, picturing the staff resting in the hand of Mephisto's self-portrait statue.

"It used to be," he spoke rapidly. "I . . . uh . . . made it longer."

"How?" I demanded. "Father never mentioned anything."

Mephisto shifted uneasily in the back seat.

"Uh, I had more compacts made, so I had to add more figurines," he answered offhandedly, then continued with more animation. "But let me finish describing what it looks like. The very top has a winged lion head, then comes Uriel and celestial beings, like Pegasus and those guys. The celestial guys are all carved out of light-colored woods, like pine and birch. After that comes normal animals: cats and hounds and boars. These guys are carved from brown woods, like maple and beech. The bottom part had magical beasts: chimera, cockatrice, Nessie, my Bully Boy, seven hoods from D. C., you know, that kind of thing. They're made of darker woods, like mahogany. The last figurine at the bottom is ebony. It's a Horror of the Deep Abyss that Father met once in his travels. But I don't call him up often. He smells."

"Surprised you would notice," Mab muttered.

"I'll pretend I didn't hear that," Mephisto replied cheerfully, rushing on. "As I said, I had used it the night before. When I woke up, the staff was gone, and so was Chalandra. So I figured they had to have gone together. Bright of me, wasn't it, Miranda?"

"Brilliant," I muttered noncommittally. This was a discussion into which I did not wish to be drawn.

"Which reminds me," Mephisto chirped. "What happened to Daddy? I mean, you said something happened to him, right? So, where is he? Is he better now? Why isn't he here helping us? Or, are we on assignment for him, just like in the old days? That would be fun, I miss those days when we'd all go rushing off together to wrestle some recalcitrant rock troll that was shaking boulders onto the town at the foot of his mountain, or to mug some dopey sorcerer who had sicced an old hag on some pathetic rival."

"I wish," I said sadly. "Unfortunately, I don't know where he is."

"Well . . . what was he up to? I mean, you must know! You're Miranda. You know everything! And besides, wherever Daddy goes, you go."

"Not since he retired."

"Oh." Mephisto shrugged. "Oh well. What a shame. I'm sure he'll turn up. After all, he's Daddy. He knows everything even more than you do."

I considered pointing out to Mephisto that his comment made no sense, but Mab interrupted.

"Just a moment." Mab raised his hand. "I . . . I got to ask. Why—I mean for what awful and occult purpose—could you possibly have needed to summon the Archangel Uriel, Potentate of Heaven, Lord of the West Quadrant?"

"I wanted to look good for my date."

"You summoned up an Archangel of Heaven—an angel of the Choir of the Seraphim—to help you prepare for a date?" Mab asked, an incredulous expression on his usually stolid face.

"Yeah, angels are very good at decking people out in impressive raiment," said Mephisto. "I recommend them to anyone who needs a valet."

"North Wind blow this madness from me," muttered Mab.

He shook his grizzled head in mingled disgust and awe. I chuckled at his expression, but my sympathies were entirely with Mab. Angels were the Breath of God, living Words whose presence made one aware of the majesty of Heaven and the shabbiness of mortal things. Summoning them for any reason made me uneasy, much less for frivolous purposes! The only forces more awesomely destructive than our enemies, the Powers of Hell, were the Powers of Heaven.

Mephisto was saying, "Anyway, so when I found out it was missing, I went over to the hotel where Chalandra was staying."

"This woman you had the date with. I assume she was someone important, if you felt you needed an archangel to dress you. You were planning to propose or something, right? How long had you known her?" Mab snapped.

"Oh, a long time," Mephisto assured him earnestly. "Almost three days!"

"Three days? You summoned one of the Seraphim of High Heaven to dress you for a date with a dame you'd known for three days! By Setebos and Titania! You'd checked her out, I assume? Tell me something about her."

"Checked her out? For a date? If I had to check out every girl I went on a date with, I'd never have time to do anything else, including going on dates with pretty women!"

"Surely you could take the time for a few precautions. How many women do you date a month?"

"Twenty or thirty."

"He's exaggerating, isn't he?" Mab asked turning to me. "He's bragging, right?"

I shook my head. "No. For some reason I have never understood, women seem to like him."

"I see," Mab said grimly.

"Anyway," Mephisto rushed on, "I caught sight of her as she was heading across the lobby, carrying my staff. Then, she caught sight of me and ducked into the ladies' room. I waited a little while, but she didn't come out. So, I decided I wasn't about to let the ladies' room stop me. A bunch of ladies screamed when I looked in the stalls. But none of them were Chalandra, so I ignored them.

"The back window was broken, and the curtains were flapping. I leapt out the window and saw a man running down the back alley carrying my staff."

"Was there any sign of this Chalandra character in the back alley?" Mab asked.

Mephisto frowned at the interruption. "What does that have to do with anything? Anyway, I ran after my staff, but the guy climbed into a truck."

"Was this in Chicago?" Mab asked. "What did the man look like?"

Mephisto stamped his foot against the car floor. "Will you stop interrupting my story!"

"Do you want my help or not?" Mab flipped his notebook shut. "Never mind, Ma'am. I suggest we give up. I can't help this brother. And, if the others are anything like him, I don't think I want to help them either, if it's all the same to you."

"You help me find my staff or I'll . . . I'll have Miranda fire you!" Mephisto exploded.

"I'm shaking in my boots," Mab purred.

"Mab!" I began reluctantly.

Mab cut me off. "He's the one who won't answer questions, Ma'am. Got to proceed in an orderly fashion, or we'll get nowhere."

I caught my brother's gaze in the rearview mirror and said gently. "Mephisto, if you want his help, you must answer his questions."

Mephisto pouted and crossed his arms.

"Very well." I stepped on the brake. "We'll turn around and give up. Mab won't help you. We won't help Theo."

We were driving through miles of national forest. Dark pines flanked the narrow road. To the right, a dirt road led to a camping area. I pulled off the road here and began turning the vehicle around, my seat rising and falling as the car bumped over the deep ruts.

"Okay, okay!" Mephisto cried, as the tires spun on the sand. "I'll put up with his rude interruptions for the sake of progress. After all, my staff is more important than my vanity."

"Glad something is," Mab muttered under his breath. I shot him a warning glance.

Turning the car about again, I drove back onto the highway and continued in the direction we had been going. The forest parted to reveal craggy gray cliffs. Half visible in the distance, white-capped mountains hovered like dark ghosts.

"What were the questions again?" Mephisto asked cheerfully.

"Did this happen in Chicago?" Mab replied through clenched teeth.

"No."

Mab waited, but Mephisto did not elaborate. Sighing, he asked, "Where did it happen?"

"Washington—D. C."

"I see," Mab made a note. "What did the guy look like? The one you saw running with your staff?"

"Oh, I don't know. Stocky guy in a gray pinstripe suit, with bright red hair."

"Ever seen him before?"

Mephisto hesitated, brows furrowed, then he shrugged and shook his head.

"Go on," Mab encouraged.

"As I was saying, the guy climbed into a truck. I hailed a cab, and we chased him. It was just like in the movies. We were careening left and right, cutting off congressmen and buses! Just like James Bond or Knight Rider!"

"Did you catch him?"

The animated expression on Mephisto's face died. "No. We had to stop for a light. That never happens in the movies!"

He shot an accusing glance at Mab, who sank back in the seat. Reaching up, Mab tilted his hat over his face and muttered, "I wouldn't know."

Mephisto continued to glare.

Mab sighed. "So then what? You left D. C. and came to Chicago. Why? Because the light was better in Chicago?"

Mephisto snorted impatiently and forged ahead. "I was heartbroken! And after I'd had such faith in the cab driver! But, he was worthy after all. You see, he had noted the truck's license plate and its licensing number. You know, those numbers trucks have painted on their doors? The cab driver called a friend of his, who found the address of the company that owned the truck. We went there. It was a big warehouse in Maryland. Just as we arrived, I saw my staff going in the door. I rushed in after it, but I couldn't find the staff or the man. They threw me out, but I went back after dark."

Mephisto launched into a convoluted story that described how he snuck back in the dead of night and broke into the warehouse, but which also included what he had had for dinner that night, and the process he went through to have his fancy clothes dry-cleaned now that he no longer had his angel valet. His meandering tale was punctuated regularly by brisk questions from Mab.

The rhythm of the road and the constant scratching of Mab's pencil lulled me into allowing my thoughts to drift. We had passed the state line and were now in Vermont. Thickly forested hills rolled away in all directions, dotted here and there with patches of snow. High overhead, turkey vultures circled, their ragged wingtips silhouetted against the winter sky. Closer at hand, the liquid eyes of deer watched our progress from beneath overhanging boughs of pine and spruce.

As I gazed out at the gorgeous vista, contemplating Mephisto's story, I began to wonder, again, what had happened to him. He had always been athletic, but he had been nimble of mind as well. Back in his youth, whenever a puzzle confronted the family, Mephistopheles would invariably be the first to solve it. Things came naturally to him that others had to work hard to achieve. Erasmus might currently be the best magician in the family—other than Father, of course—but that was only because Mephisto had dropped out of the running. Nor was magic the only area where Mephistopheles had excelled. He had also been a master with a paintbrush and with a blade, at one point earning himself the sobriquet of "the best swordsman in Christendom."

When Mephisto's condition became apparent, Father devoted a century to searching for a cure. Then, one day, he ceased pursuing the matter. I questioned him about this more than once, but Father could be extremely cagey when he wished. To this day, I did not know if he had discovered something that caused him to back off or if he merely decided the matter was no longer worth pursuing.

IN the back seat, Mephisto was finishing his story. ". . . had to run, but that was okay, because by then I'd broken open every object big enough to possibly hold my staff. I think . . . I might have made a mess."

"Let me guess," Mab drawled slowly, "You didn't find it?"

Mephisto shook his head sadly. "It wasn't in there, and no one carried it out. Between the cab driver and me, we watched all the doors. But one truck left between when I arrived and when I got inside."

"And . . . ?"

"That truck went to Chicago. So, that's where I went!"

"Did you pay the cabby for his considerable investment of time?" I asked curiously.

Mephisto nodded. "I gave him my wallet."

"Was there anything in it?"

"No, but it was a really expensive wallet, studded with diamonds! My brother Ulysses gave it to me. The cab driver was happy."

"So, you followed the truck to Chicago?" Mab asked.

"Well, I started with the address the truck had been delivering to. I had found it in the office of the warehouse in Maryland. That's how I knew where it had gone. But the place was empty when I arrived. It must have been a fake address!" He frowned and shrugged. "Or maybe I remembered it wrong."

"How long between when the truck left Maryland and when you arrived in Chicago?"

Mephisto hesitated while he figured it out, counting on his fingers. Finally, he said. "Eleven."

"Eleven hours?"

"No, eleven weeks," Mephisto said. When Mab groaned, he added defensively. "It took me a while to get there. I visited Theo, Miranda, and Logistilla first. Oh, and I went by Cornelius's to borrow money."

Mab sighed. "One last question. What were you doing in Chicago when we found you?"

Mephisto answered cheerfully, "Oh, that's easy. I was on my way to Daddy's local office to borrow money. Only I'd been there to hit them up for dough already a few days ago—when I first arrived—so I didn't know if they'd help me again. So, I was trying to make a little on my own." Mephisto turned toward me. "Clever of you to come walking down the very road where I sat singing, Miranda!"

"Cleverness had nothing to do with it," I replied, "My Lady directed me to walk that way."

"What a good egg that Unicorn is!" Mephisto exclaimed. He put his chin on his palm. "She really knows her stuff!"

I cringed but did not rebuke him; calling my Lady a "good egg" was not, technically, disrespectful.

Mab took his hat off and ran his fingers through his hair. "Not much I can do here unless you want to give up the other matter, Miss Miranda. Trail's a little old."

"Wouldn't hurt to investigate the workers at that warehouse and the Chicago address. Could you find the warehouse again, Mephisto?" I asked.

"Sure!" my brother chirped, "It's right in the spot that I left it!"

"One would hope," muttered Mab.

CHAPTER
FIVE

The Chameleon Cloak

The fuel gauge was only barely below the half line and I was impatient to get to Theo's, but an intuition from my Lady suggested I should refill before going any further, so I turned onto a local road.

"Hey, where are we going? This looks familiar. Are we there yet?" Mephisto peered out the window.

I sighed. "We're stopping for gas. As for whether or not we're there yet . . . you are directing us, remember?"

"Oops! Sorry."

"You do know where you're taking us, don't you?" Mab turned in his seat. "Because if this turns out to be a wild goose chase, I'll wring your scrawny neck."

Mephisto cried plaintively, "Miranda, don't let him talk to me like that!"

I forced my voice to remain calm. "Do you know where we are going?"

"Yes. Of course. I just got confused. Everyone gets confused sometimes. Even sane people." Mephisto spoke with mock resentfulness, but there was an undertone of genuine bitterness, as if he hated his lack of sanity. Neither Mab nor I answered, and an uncomfortable silence followed.

As we arrived at a service station, however, I happened to glance at my brother in the rearview mirror, and a strange thing happened. For an instant, I had such sympathy for his plight that it was as if I were the one who had lost my sanity, who had felt slip from me my intelligence, my memory, and everything that made me myself. For the first time, I contemplated how the brilliant and talented youthful Mephisto would have felt about his foolish older self. He would have been appalled—much as I might feel were I to come upon an older version of myself who was an imbecile or who had lost the favor of Eurynome.

The experience left me shaken.

* * *

SURROUNDED by forest, the service station stood by itself except for a squat thrift shop across the road. Next to the thrift shop was a huge, sprawling, gravel parking lot, far larger than a store of its type would ever need. Perhaps the building had once been a restaurant.

As Mab pumped the gas, Mephisto rolled down his window and scrambled up until he was sitting in the window of the car door. Crossing his arms, he leaned on the roof, looking around.

"Miranda? Did you ever notice that every gas station off every highway looks like every other gas station off a highway? And, every small town thrift shop is called The Elephant's Trunk?"

"No," I murmured.

He was right about the name of the thrift shop. A gray wooden cutout of an elephant hung above the sign. The glass bay windows showed plastic mannequins with painted hair. They were dressed in outfits from the twenties through the fifties. One of the mannequins was missing a hand.

The soft voice of my Lady spoke in my heart.

Go into the store.

Immediately, I left the car and crossed the road to the thrift shop. Behind me, Mephisto had climbed out of his window and leapt down to the pavement. His footsteps echoed behind mine. He caught up with me as I reached the door, and we walked into the tiny shop together.

The musty smell of old clothes nearly caused me to retreat. I stood blinking, my hand over my nose, waiting for my eyes to adjust to the dim lighting. As my vision cleared, the clerk came toward us, smiling simperingly at Mephisto. She was a thin woman in a red knit dress.

"Oops, got to go!" Mephisto spun on his heels. He wrinkled his nose as he left, calling, "Icky smell!"

The clerk hesitated, frowning, before coming to serve me. I refrained from smirking. Middle-aged women pursuing my daffy brother always amused me, though how he managed to impress this one so quickly was mystifying.

"Can I help you? We're having a special on sequined gowns and flapper hats." An eager look came over her face as, with her trained eye, she took in my dress, examining its shimmering emerald satin, its high lace collar, its narrow fitted waist, and its puffed shoulders. "That's a lovely tea gown you're wearing. A reproduction of a Worth gown, perhaps? Circa 1894? It's amazingly well preserved! What extraordinary fabric! I've never seen anything quite like it. Is it for sale?"

I considered saying: "Actually, it's a Logistilla Original, circa 1910, and as for selling it, can you afford to offer me, oh, say, the moon?" But that would have been impolite. Instead, I settled for the more civil: "No. It was a gift from my sister."

"A pity. Maybe you came for this?" she asked. She gave the door through which Mephisto had disappeared one last puzzled glance before gesturing toward a display at the center of the shop.

Just in front of the cash register stood a large papier-mâché elephant. An iron rail snaked around the elephant's feet, and two mannequins moved along the rail with a slow mechanical whirl, revolving around the display like toy trains circling a Christmas tree. The mannequins rotated as they traveled, showing the apparel they displayed to best advantage. An Edwardian wedding gown adorned one of the mannequins. A shapeless poncho or smock covered the other. The smock was the exact shade of gray as the papier-mâché elephant behind it.

I gave the display a cursory examination, wondering bemusedly if my attire had led the clerk to assume I was a collector of vintage Edwardian paraphernalia. As I watched, the mannequin wearing the shapeless garment moved beyond the elephant. As the iron rail curved to the back, the poncho passed a rack holding a fluffy blue and green sweater. Tints of blue and green appeared in the plain smock, spreading rapidly until the entire poncho bore the same blue and green pattern as the sweater.

Was the smock transparent? I leaned closer, watching as the mannequin moved by a red raincoat. Slowly, the red spread through the blue-and-green smock. The smock was changing its color, like a chameleon.

A chameleon . . . a cloak . . .

A cold paralysis gripped my limbs, and the small shop with its musty garments began to spin. I retreated rapidly, seeking fresher air.

OUTSIDE, I leaned against the drab side of the thrift shop, trembling like the rail of a trestle when a train passes. Calling to Mab, I shakily drew my wallet from my coat pocket. Mab hurried toward me, looking both ways before he crossed the road. When he reached my side, I thrust the wallet into his hands and managed to speak.

"There's a chameleon cloak in there. Buy the abomination."

"A chameleon cloak? As in Unicorn Hunters?" he screwed up his face in disgust. "Thought they were all destroyed long ago?"

"Nonetheless."

Mab stalked into the store while I crossed the gravel parking lot to sit down on a fallen tree trunk. Breathing deeply, I waited for the wave of fear to ebb. It was a strange sensation, suffering another's panic, but I felt it worth the price. After all, my Lady calmed my fears daily, while I seldom had an opportunity to calm Hers. Very few things frightened the Bearer of the Lightning Bolt . . . but Unicorn Hunters were one of them.

THE Unicorn Hunters began as a band of the nastiest knights in Christendom. Who sponsored them and why I never learned, but they clearly had a supernatural patron. They would appear from time to time bearing magical swords or riding unnaturally swift chargers. They slew Her Handmaidens and put Sibyls to the sword. They kidnapped virgins and staked them out, then laid in wait, hoping to trap Eurynome Herself.

Once, they wounded Her. The blood spilled that day became the source of a kingdom's woe and eventually brought about its destruction. That is another tale, however, and from before my time. Eventually, the Unicorn Hunters died out or were exterminated.

Then, during the reign of Queen Elizabeth I, they appeared again. Perhaps the same patron made another attempt. Or, perhaps some of the young bloods learned of the existence of the earlier band and wished to imitate them. At first, it was all posturing and show. A few hunts were held, but nothing of substance was accomplished.

Then, Edward Kelly, the young assistant to the royal magician John Dee, became involved, and everything changed. The magical weapons reappeared, and something new: chameleon cloaks. Concealed in chameleon cloaks, the new Unicorn Hunters began to stalk Eurynome. Something about the cloaks, something more than their blending color, kept her from noticing them. With these cloaks and their supernatural weapons, the Unicorn Hunters were able to surprise her. Twice, they wounded her.

At a dance at court, one of them noticed the unicorns embroidered on my dress and remarked upon it. Naïvely, I said too much. After that, they hunted me.

They captured me as I was leaving a royal ball. I had attended without my flute. Bringing me into the country by carriage, they kept me a prisoner in a rustic cottage until the next thunderstorm. When the first lightning bolt arced across the sky, they staked me down spread-eagled on a stone bier in the rain. After the second bolt, Eurynome herself came to free me.

They struck her through with enchanted spears of copper and glass. She killed four men before they subdued her, but there were too many of them. They bound her with a rope made from the breath of fishes, the roots of mountains, and the beards of women, and dragged her into a deep dark pit, where they tied her to a stone slab. They would have killed her, sacrificing her to some dark entity, had it not been for my brothers. Mephisto, Theophrastus, and Erasmus crashed their party and set her free.

My brothers slew the Unicorn Hunters and destroyed their enchanted gear. I thought all the chameleon cloaks were destroyed that night, until today.

I GLANCED back across the gravel parking lot toward the squat gray shop. Tiny flecks of white danced in the intervening air. Shivering, I was turning up my collar as Mab emerged from the thrift shop. He came crunching across the gravel toward me, carrying a shiny brown paper bag. Mephisto reappeared as well, from wherever he had gotten to, and began hovering about Mab, trying to look in the bag.

Mab gave Mephisto a long look. My brother went pale and threw his hands up in front of him as if warding off an attack.

"I didn't do it!" he cried.

"Relax, Mephisto. No one is accusing you of anything."

"They're not?" He glanced from Mab to me in surprise.

How pathetic my brother's life had become. He lived in a world where lutes broke for no reason, where people accused him of transgressions he had no recollection of committing. The idea of a son of my father starting with fear because a servant glared at him for looking in a bag! It shamed me to see him reduced to this.

I threw him an encouraging smile, but he had become distracted and was gazing curiously back toward the thrift shop.

The snow began falling more quickly. Mab crossed to stand beside the fallen tree trunk. I stood and pulled my coat closer about me.

"Did you get it?" I asked, my voice low.

"Yeah, I got it," Mab replied glumly. "I'd like to find out where it came from, but the clerk would not answer any questions. Apparently, they have a policy against saying anything about who drops off what."

Mab hesitated, then continued, "Look, Ma'am, I know you never listen to me, but I'm begging you, listen now. Just this once. We are being hunted by the Powers of Hell. They can sniff out the stuff of the arcane like a bloodhound sniffs out fresh blood. It's bad enough us carrying the accursed flute around with us. Not to mention your green dress and whatever else you carry in your purse. I'd guess, at the very least, the razor fan of Amatsumaru, your crystal vial of the Water of Life, and a chip of unicorn horn. Am I right?"

I inclined my head. Mab knew my habits well. The vial of Water and the chip of horn were mine by right of my station of Handmaiden. The war fan had been forged by the Japanese smith god himself and given to me during our first visit to Japan in 1792, when we sneaked into the country to bind up the *oni* responsible for the eruption of Mt. Unzen. The fan was a gift of thanks from the *tengu* who serve my Lady in Her aspect as the *Kirin*. Its razor edge had been folded and refolded over a thousand times, like a katana. The blade was sharp enough to slice through sheet metal.

Mab continued. "I don't know what plans you have for this god-awful garment. But I'm begging you. Cast it aside and let me destroy it. It's our only hope. If you want to warn your family, we've got to get to them before the Three Shadowed Ones get to us. That won't happen if we carry around enough magic to alert even a deaf and toothless demi-sprite with cataracts and one bum leg. Please. I'm begging you, Ma'am."

"Very well, Mab. You may destroy it."

Mab's jaw dropped. He glanced hurriedly back and forth between me and the bag, then held it up before me and made the throat-slitting gesture. I nodded. Certain now that he had heard me correctly, Mab grinned with vicious delight. He began rummaging through his pockets as quickly as he could, drawing out the chalk and holy water he needed to unmake the horrible thing, as if he were afraid I might suddenly change my mind. As he did so, he chuckled to himself and shook his head in wonder.

Suddenly, he froze, eyeing me suspiciously. "Exactly what were you planning to do with the thing when you asked me to buy it?"

"Have you destroy it," I admitted.

"Ah. I see. Should have known it was too good to be true," he said, deflated. He continued to pull the bag of chalk from his pocket, but his actions had lost their enthusiastic bounce.

"Don't you want to destroy it?" I asked innocently.

"Sure . . . it's just that for one sweet moment, I suffered from the cruel delusion that for the first time in our nearly seventy years of association, you had actually listened to me," Mab grumbled.

I chuckled, "Oh, Mab. You poor, unappreciated soul."

* * *

MAB chose a place in the wide parking lot and began tracing the lines for his warding circles. The gravel crunched as he pushed it with his booted toe. The delay reaching Theo's worried me, but my impatience was tempered by my discomfort at the thought of traveling with the chameleon cloak in the car. Besides, Theo, who had renounced magic, would hardly welcome us if we showed up carrying an accursed talisman.

The snow was coming more quickly now, its soft flakes melting against my face. The air had grown quite cold. A little cloud formed every time I exhaled. Behind us, the bag crinkled. Swirling about, I saw Mephisto leaning over the paper bag, pulling out the chameleon cloak. It rippled and shifted, its weave revealing black birch trunks and powdery flurries of snow.

Mephisto's lips parted, forming a perfect "O."

"Oh, Miranda, this is pretty! Please don't destroy it. Please? Let me have it," He tilted his head and smiled at me. As he held the garment against his chest, it shifted to show the embroidery of his black Russian shirt and the brilliant blue of his surcoat.

"Cur! Put that back in the bag!" Mab shouted, "Do you want to send off a beacon to alert every supernatural creature this side of the Mississippi? If a Walker-Behind jumps out of the bushes and devours your sister whole, pausing only to spit out her bones, it will be on your head!"

At that very moment, a rustle came from the bushes. Mephisto jumped with fright and thrust the chameleon cloak back into the brown paper bag, wrapping it up tightly. Taking a careful step backwards, he bent and gathered up a handful of gravel. Mab pulled out the trusty length of lead pipe he carried as a weapon. I ran back to the car, returning moments later with my flute; my other hand crept toward the handle of the Japanese fighting fan that lay nestled in my coat pocket. Thus armed, the three of us warily faced the rustling laurel bushes.

The snow-sprinkled leaves trembled and parted. A black nose emerged followed by a long red snout. Then, an Irish Setter came bursting out of the laurel bushes. His long pink tongue hung out, his plume-like tail was wagging.

"Awh," muttered Mab.

He mopped his brow and returned to drawing his circles. Mephisto's face had gone slack with fear. Now, a high, weak giggle escaped his lips. Feeling almost queasy with relief, I smiled and dropped to sit upon the tree trunk, stretching my hand out toward the dog, who trotted toward me, panting happily, little white flecks of snow caught in his thick red coat.

Mephisto cocked his head and watched the animal as it stopped to smell an old cardboard box someone had discarded by the side of the parking lot.

"Remember that guy who took my staff—the one you wanted to know what he looked like? His hair was exactly the color of this dog."

Without hesitating, Mab drew his lead pipe from his trench coat and threw it at the dog. The spinning length of lead grazed its head. The big red setter yelped and leapt backwards, cowering down with its tail between its legs.

"Mab! How could you!" I cried, hurrying over to comfort the cowering creature, "You might have hurt him!"

"Get back, Ma'am! That's no ordinary dog," Mab warned, but his voice wavered.

The dog whined and licked my hand.

"You're losing your touch, Mab," I laughed. "You've gotten so you think everything is a threat. It's just a dog."

Mab frowned uncertainly as if not quite able to credit what he saw.

"Yeah, I guess so," he grumbled finally.

Reluctantly, he returned to his preparations while I squatted down and petted the animal, feeling its thick damp fur. It licked my hand, its tongue warm and wet against my skin. Its big brown eyes gazed up at me as it pushed against me in friendly exuberance, wagging its tail fiercely.

A strange cold chill traveled down the back of my neck. Turning, I saw the dog's parted white fangs gently closing over the polished haft of my flute.

I grabbed the flute, shouting. The dog leapt into the air, its teeth closing on my arm. There was a sharp ripping as the white canvas of my trench coat tore, followed by a slithering sound as its teeth slid along the enchanted material of my dress, unable to penetrate it. Losing its grip, the creature dropped back to the ground.

Mab stared helplessly from the growling dog to his lead pipe, which lay behind the dog, resting against a snowy rock.

"Dang!" he said.

"Bodyguard, do something," Mephisto yelled at Mab. He scattered his handful of gravel randomly, pelting the dog, who cringed, but then leapt again. His paws struck me full on the chest, and we tumbled backwards.

I managed to twist so as to land with my body covering my flute but without damaging it. The setter growled and snapped, its teeth still unable to penetrate the fabric of my enchanted gown. It was only a matter of time before it realized that my head and hands were unprotected.

As the dog attempted to maul me, Mab used the opportunity to retrieve his pipe. He brought it down hard on the creature's head. The dog cried out with a horrible yowl. Blood matted the fur by its left ear. It cowered back, snarling at Mab. Mab swung again.

The Irish Setter shivered and shrank, its body twisting and changing. Its fur grew feathery and deepened to a true red. Mab's pipe swung through empty air. Near his right elbow hovered a red cardinal, which quickly flew up and away.

"Holy Croesus! A blasted shapechanger!" Mab swore, swinging at the red bird and missing. "More than one shape too! That rules out skin-changer." He swung his pipe back and forth rapidly where the dog had been. "Can't be just fairy glamour, or the perp would still be here for me to pound. No, that sucker flew away for real!"

"Pooka?" asked Mephisto. "Some of them can do more than one shape."

"Maybe, but they're usually black in color. There are a lot of spirits native to the Americas that change shape . . . but an Irish Setter?" Mab shrugged, his hand shading his eyes as he surveyed the sky overhead for any sign of our assailant. "My call is cacodemon, or maybe a lesser deity. Deities change shape big time, but most of them wouldn't bother with subtlety now that the jig is up . . . they'd just blast us."

While the two men talked, I scrambled to my feet and pulled the fighting fan from my coat. The silver segments slid open silently, reflecting the falling snow like a gleaming mirror.

Mab stood silently, head half-cocked, as if listening. Mephisto stood on his tiptoes staring up into the sky. Both hands were pressed against his face, cupping his eyes like blinders. I looked up as well. All was a vast whirling whiteness.

Out of the whiteness, a rapid red speck approached. It flew toward Mab, who attempted to swat it with his pipe. Just above Mab's head, the creature swelled immensely, becoming an ugly gray rhinoceros with tiny russet eyes. Mab looked up, mouth gaping. The rhino fell heavily to the ground, its descent broken only by the mass of Mab's body.

"Mab!" I cried, stricken. "Mephisto! You said you would help! Do something!"

My cry broke Mephisto out of some kind of reverie. He lurched forward and seized the other end of my flute. Startled, I let go. With my heart in my mouth, I watched him run away, waving my precious instrument before the rhino's tiny red eyes.

"Hey, you big old beast," he cried out, flinging his arms wide. His head was flung back. The sunlight shimmered off the flute in his outstretched hand. "Don't you recognize me?"

The rhino lowered its head and charged at Mephisto, thundering across the wide gravel parking lot. Unlike the Irish Setter, I could never have mistaken this beast for the real thing. It was hideous, lacking the beauty and symmetry of its natural counterpart. An aura of malice surrounded it, something sinister and seething that turned my stomach.

As it thundered forward, Mab's crumpled and flat form emerged, sprawled upon the ground. I gasped in horror, running to his side. As I did so, Mab's lead pipe rose into the air, accompanied by a loud whooshing noise.

"It's all right, Ma'am. I'm here." To my great relief, Mab's voice spoke from somewhere above my ear. His voice sounded reedy, as if an oboe gave voice. "Saw the thing was going to squash me and abandoned my body before the rhino landed on it. If I'd waited a second longer to bail, I'd have been a goner! Body looks pretty crumpled. Hope you'll be willing to spare a drop or two of Water of Life, Ma'am, so we can fix it up."

As the rhino charged, Mab's lead pipe flew toward it. Mab reached the rhino just as the rhino reached Mephisto. The lead pipe, seemingly on its own, slammed down on the beast's head . . . and bounced off. The foul creature was not even distracted.

As I circled the rhino, desperately searching for an opening to strike, the monster lowered its head to gore my brother. Mephisto was not the least dismayed. Leaping into the air, he vaulted one-handedly across its back as lithe as any gymnast, still holding my flute in his other hand. Twisting in mid-air, he landed on his feet behind the rhino, facing his foe with his arms spread victoriously. From the air above, Mab whistled in appreciation.

"Come on, boy! Try it again!" Mephisto called, waving my flute wildly above his head. It whistled as the air whipped through it. I bit my lip. If my brother kept that up, he might accidentally call up a tornado. The beast charged again, bellowing a horrible noise reminiscent of a manic bull.

After the third time Mephisto leapt over the creature's back, it slowed and pawed the ground, swinging its great head from side to side. A gleam came into its tiny red eye. Lowering its horn, it charged. Mephisto smiled cockily. He bowed, sweeping his arms to either side, and vaulted. As Mephisto flew through the air, the beast shivered and shrank, transforming into a hideous porcupine with bright red eyes. Instead of leathery hide, Mephisto's hand came down on needle-like quills.

Mephisto yelped in pain and fell sideways. He tossed the flute into the air and hit the ground with a roll. Sitting up again, he began pulling at the barbed quills stuck in his hand.

My precious flute spun end over end, twirling like a parade marshal's baton. It arced through the snow-specked sky, and then stopped, dangling, frozen in mid-air.

I stood, gawking, and then hurried forward to grab it, thanking the invisible Mab loudly. No point in tempting him beyond his means. Reluctantly, the air released the flute to my grasp. I hugged it to me.

From behind me, Mephisto shouted, "No! Get back!"

He had jumped to his feet, his face a mask of horror. Coiled about his arm was a deadly copperhead. Its slitted gray eyes stared hypnotically into his. Its tongue flickered rapidly. It hissed. Before Mab or I could act, the vile creature struck, sinking sharp fangs into the soft flesh of Mephisto's inner wrist.

Horrified, I ran to my brother. The snake's slitted eyes fixed upon me. Slithering to the ground, it expanded into the rhino again. The great malformed beast lowered its head and charged toward me.

I had never seen a real rhino up close. The creature was enormous, a living tank with gray armored hide covering four tons of meat and muscle. It came thundering toward me, moving astonishingly swiftly despite its short stubby legs. Its loud bellow formed a white cloud in the frosty air. Its curving gray-brown horn, a mockery of my Lady's graceful spiral, pointed at my heart. The earth beneath my feet shook.

Terrified, I longed to break and flee, but that would mean abandoning Mephisto. Taking a stand for my brother, my flute, and my beloved Aerie Ones, I gripped the engraved handle of the moon-silver fan and faced the monster. Surrendering my will to my Lady, I waited for Her to tell me when to strike. As the beast bore down upon me at the speed of an automobile, the answer came like a soft breath on the back of my neck.

Now.

Stepping nimbly aside, I swung my war fan, severing the rhinoceros's horn from the creature's snout as cleanly as a kitchen knife slices butter. Apparently the shapechanger had nerves where a real rhino would not because it roared in pain. Its gray hide rippled, became reddish and furry as it reared back, and I found myself confronting an enormous grizzly bear.

The rust-colored bear was as ugly and unnatural as the rhino had been, yet as large and powerful as a real grizzly! Its monstrous head alone was broader than my shoulders. Sticky black ichor streamed down its jaws from its missing nose. The fetid smell of the ooze was overpowering as it mingled with the pungent bear musk emanating from the creature's thick, matted fur. The repulsive beast towered over me, a good eight feet tall, eager to crush me in its embrace of death.

I swung the fan, but the beast's looming bulk closed with me too quickly. The slats of the fan folded, collapsing harmlessly and doing no damage. I leapt backwards, hoping to escape the bear's embrace. With a jerk of its enormous paw, the bear swatted me, sending me sprawling. Its sharp claws slashed through my trench coat as if it were wet paper but scraped harmlessly against my enchanted gown.

Flying through the air, I hugged my flute, hoping to cushion its fall. Only the ground never approached. Instead, a wind buoyed me upward, and the earth fell away beneath me. I felt myself yanked toward where Mephisto lay crumpled on the gravel. Mab's human body hung in the air beside me, motionless and empty.

"Can't believe I'm saying this," Mab's reedy voice blew in my ear, "but you might want to play that accursed instrument. We've got to get out of here. Your brother has been poisoned. I don't think I can carry the two of you and my body without some help."

As Mab swooped to grab my brother, I raised my precious flute to my lips and played "The Daring Young Man on the Flying Trapeze." The music swelled around us, buoying us upward, and cold yet friendly winds whistled about our ears. Quick as swallows, we soared away from the grizzly, who roared with anger.

As we circled through the white flurries of falling snow, Mab's oboe-like voice sang in my ear.

"He'll probably turn into a condor next or a golden eagle. He might even try a raven and swoop at our eyes. Might want to have a few songs ready."

I nodded tensely, watching the grizzly and anticipating another metamorphosis at any moment. None came. Turning, the beast lumbered though the falling snow toward the road, growling menacingly. In the distance, I could hear the dim roar of an engine.

"What's he doing? Giving up? Seems strange, since we know he can do birds," Mab muttered. "Oh, no! Miss Miranda! He's after the car!"

Sure enough, the giant bear crossed the road, heading toward the gas station. The thin teenager behind the counter must have had a view of our entire battle. He hurried to lock the door of the convenience store. The grizzly never so much as glanced in his direction. It headed directly for the far side of the station where our rental car was parked.

Still playing, I increased the tempo, requesting more speed. We were heavily weighed down, however, by myself, my listless brother, and Mab's fleshly body. We moved rapidly across the distance, but not rapidly enough. The beast would reach our vehicle first.

Looming over our car, the horrifying bear raised its great paw with five razor-sharp claws. Just then, a white pickup truck rounded the bend in the road. A loud crack rang out across the countryside. The terrible grizzly bear fell silently backwards, ichor spurting from its left eye, and lay as if dead.

The pickup truck drew up beside us and slowed to a stop. A man in a buff coat climbed from the passenger side and came slowly around the car toward us, carrying his still-smoking Winchester. He was an older man with white hair and a neatly trimmed beard. His brown eyes were keen and deeply set. He had a strong Roman nose. I knew his face almost as well as my own.

"Father!" I shouted with joy. He looked older than I had remembered. This fight with the Three Shadowed Ones must be sapping his strength. "You trimmed your beard."

From under Mab's other arm, Mephisto said weakly, "That's not Father. That's Theo."

CHAPTER
SIX

Theophrastus

"You can stay long enough to fix up Mephisto. Then, you go," my brother Theophrastus announced.

We had driven out to Theo's house, which stood in an apple orchard in the wilds of Vermont. The road to the house led through acre upon acre of apple trees: Red Delicious, Rome, Macintosh. The apples had all been harvested, save for those that had fallen to the ground. The leafless trees stood like gnarled ghosts in the swirling flurries.

Theo lived in an old white farmhouse. Behind the main building was a large red barn. Near the barn, black-and-white cows roamed through a snowy paddock enclosed by an old split-rail fence.

Before leaving the gas station, Theo had shot the bear through the braincase, then fired repeatedly into the creature's chest. He and his driver had tried to lift the carcass into Theo's truck. They failed the first time, but with my help, we were able to heave the thing into the open back. Upon arriving, Theo had called to two farmhands, who were maneuvering a tractor between the open doors of the barn, and asked them to come help build a bonfire and burn the carcass. Twice, he seemed to think better of this plan and started off toward the farmhouse. Both times, however, he restrained himself.

He left them and strode purposefully to our car, his buff coat whipping in the wind. Mephisto lay stretched across the back seat. During the short ride from the gas station to the house, Mephisto had been writhing and twisting, muttering about starfish and his staff. Now, he lay silent and still. It was as Theo leaned over Mephisto and drew his limp body onto his shoulder that Theo had uttered his pronouncement.

This was not the greeting I had expected. Whoops of joy and a warm embrace were the more usual greeting from my favorite brother. Something was terribly wrong with the Theophrastus Prospero I had known.

Theo began carrying Mephisto toward the house. After only a few paces, his face became pale, and he began staggering. Mab got out of the car and hurried toward him. He was back in his body again, which I had restored with a drop of Water of Life—the damage was not as bad as it first looked—though he still twisted and twitched, striving to get properly situated within it.

"Let me give you a hand." He approached Theo.

"You'll stay here," Theo replied sharply. His words came in breathy spurts. "I'll have no spirits contaminating my house." Mab grasped the brim of his hat, which the brisk winds threatened to tug from his head. He raised an eyebrow and examined the staggering and puffing Theo.

"What of Miss Miranda's dress and the Water of Life she put on Mephisto's lips in the car? Can they enter your hallowed house?"

Theo glanced back and forth between the house and myself, where I stood near the car, drawing closed the belt of my tattered coat. He was panting now, and his face was flushed entirely red beneath his gray beard.

"Take his feet then," he gasped. "We'll take him to the barn."

The barn contained no bed or couch; however, there was a kitchen in the back. Entering it, Theo and Mab ducked under hanging brass pans and stretched Mephisto out on the long butcher-block table. I went immediately to the sink and began to fill a brass teakettle.

"I'll need hot water, a cup, and a mortar and pestle," I said.

"There's mugs in the first cabinet, but I don't keep mortars and pestles on my property." Theo leaned on the table regaining his breath. "Will an ordinary hammer do?"

"It will have to."

ONCE the kettle was heating, I examined Mephisto. His face was pale and damp, his breathing shallow. The wrist where the snake had bitten him was swollen and blue. As Theo came back with the hammer, I saw him look at Mephisto. His throat constricted, and he turned away.

I laid the hammer on the counter next to a blue Garfield mug I had taken from the cabinet. From under my coat, I drew forth a heart-shaped locket I wore around my neck on a velvet ribbon. It was fashioned of silver and inlaid with mother-of-pearl. Of all my antique and aged belongings, it was the oldest, having been passed from my grandmother to my mother to me, half a millennium ago. My mother wears it in the portrait of her that hangs in the Great Hall. My father had often described to me how Lady

Portia pressed it into his hand as she died, and how he, in turn, pressed it into my infant hand the first time he held me. Within it, I kept a thin twist of white ivory, a tiny sliver of the horn so eagerly sought by knights of old for its ability to cure poison.

With the hammer, I crushed a tiny chip of ivory no longer than the nail of my pinky finger. Grinding it into powder, I brushed the result into the cup and poured in hot water. The pulverized white ivory swirled in the water, giving the liquid a pearly gleam. Carrying the mug to where Mephisto lay, I carefully dribbled the concoction down his throat, swabbing the last bit onto his swollen wrist with a paper towel from a rack over the sink. From the small, pear-shaped crystal vial I carried in my pocket, I gave him a drop of Water of Life. In addition to mending his current wounds, the Water would also help heal his infected toe and any other lingering damage that neglect or malnutrition had caused. While I did this, Mab sat on a stool on the far side of the table, where he held Mephisto's other hand, carefully working the porcupine quills out of the flesh.

I leaned against the counter and prayed to my Lady. Curing poisons was one of the prerogatives of the Unicorn, and one of the six Gifts She granted to Her Sibyls. Were I a Sibyl, I could have cured my brother in an instant. I prayed to my Lady for Mephisto's health and asked, for the hundred millionth time, that She might reveal to me what I needed to know to be granted entrance into the ranks of Her most cherished servants.

As I prayed silently to my Lady for Mephisto's deliverance, a morning long ago on the windy moors of Scotland rose from my memory. I had been standing atop Grantham Tor watching for my brothers—a runner from the village, a youth paid by Father to bring his mail, brought the news that they had been spotted returning from the war. Which war, I do not recall, but it must have been an English war since we were in Scotland at the time. It might have been King James's war against Spain, or, perhaps, it was the English Civil War, where we fought with the Cavaliers against the Roundheads and lost—though probably not that war, as, after that defeat, we fled Scotland for the Netherlands in a hurry.

The six of them came riding along the old dirt track: Mephistopheles, Theophrastus, Erasmus, Cornelius, Titus, and Gregor. They rode tired, gaunt mounts, and their once-fine garments were encrusted with mud. However, the horses had new ribbons of green and yellow woven into their manes and tails, probably put there by Theo for my benefit.

I waved and waved from atop the tor. The wind blew my plaid skirts through the heather. It blew my hair, too, which was still as black as a raven's wing then, whipping it across my face and out behind my head like streamers on a Maypole. My brothers waved back as they rode by on their way toward the manor, Mephisto and Titus rising in their seats to wave more enthusiastically. Theo, however, broke away from them and galloped his charger up the tor.

Reaching me, he dismounted. He wore a heavy coat that had once been red, scuffed black boots, and a pair of patched breeches. In his hand, he carried a posy of irises and primroses. He must have just picked them, for the blossoms were fresh and sweet. Theo handed them to me, bowing stiffly, and blushed when I kissed his cheek.

Taking my hands in his, he spoke to me in the overly stern manner he assumed when he was serious, which I always found pompous yet endearing.

"I thought of you often while we were separated and was troubled on your behalf. Without a husband, you have only your family to protect you. I want you to be assured that if you should ever have need, you may call upon me. Whatever I am about, I will put it aside to come protect you or avenge your honor. I give you my solemn and eternal vow."

At the time, I laughed gaily and kissed him again, then leapt upon his horse, allowing him to lead me back through the heather to the manor. But I never forgot his words. When times were darkest, the memory of Theo's vow always brought me comfort. Yet now, Theo was an old man, weaker than Father, and no longer immortal.

Where was my champion now?

"HOW long is this going to take?" Theo drew up an armchair next to the door and sat down heavily. Leaning back, he closed his eyes, breathing laboredly.

"Theo, be patient. Your brother may be dying," I said.

"I have no brother. I left your family over fifty years ago," Theophrastus replied.

His words shocked me. I did not know what to say.

Theo may have intended to continue talking, but a coughing fit seized him. His hacking grew stronger until his body shook with wracking spasms. From the pocket of his buff coat, he pulled a medicine bottle, shook out two pills into his hand, and swallowed them, washing them down with water from a mug resting on the counter. Then, he placed both elbows on the counter and leaned forward, waiting for his coughing to subside. I stepped up next to him and placed my hand on his arm. Drawing out the crystal vial from my pocket, I offered it to him.

Theo's reaction was quick and violent. He slapped the vial from my hand so that it flew across the kitchen. Quick as the wind, Mab leapt from his stool and snatched the vial from the air. Mab shoved the crystal vial into the pocket of his trench coat and resumed his work on Mephisto's hand.

I turned on Theo.

"Darn it, Theo! You don't have to take it, but don't waste it! Don't you know how difficult it is to get Water of Life? You can't take a bus or a plane to the end of the world, you know!"

"I don't think you want to spill that stuff, Mr. Theophrastus," Mab drawled sardonically. "Every spirit in a thousand miles would be swarming into your barn, eager to lap it up."

"I don't know why you came to Vermont, but I want you to leave, now," said Theo. "You've done enough damage already."

"Damage?" I asked, taken aback. "What damage?"

"First, you led that wretched Osae the Red practically to my doorstep. Now, you're contaminating the place with the unnatural. Isn't that enough?" Theo asked bitterly.

Theophrastus had recognized our shapechanger. The name Osae the Red was familiar, but it floated in the haze of my memory, just out of reach. This was hardly a time for questions, so I filed the information away for later.

Theo growled. "It has taken me decades to cleanse myself of the filth of the supernatural. I have no intention of losing my chance at salvation now, after all I've sacrificed."

"You're willing to prolong your life with those little pills. How is the Water any different? If you fear Hell, one would think that you would wish to avoid death at all costs," I replied, annoyed.

What was making Theo so antagonistic? To find out what was wrong with my brother, I would need an opportunity to speak with him at length.

"A man never knows when his day of reckoning will come. Gregor's death showed us that. I just want to make sure that when I die, my soul is clean of the stink of the dark arts." Theo paused. "I would like you to leave now."

"We came here to warn you," I said wearily. "The Three Shadowed Ones are after our staffs. I've given you the warning; now we'll go away . . . but not until Mephisto is well enough to move. If you don't like it, you can leave, or you can shoot us."

"He won't be shooting anybody," Mab growled. "Not while I'm here. Though I must say, for a mortal, his aim was excellent. Nice shot back there with the bear."

"Thank you," Theo replied brusquely.

Mab continued. "Now, I hate to break up this touching family reunion, but there's a chameleon cloak in the car out there. And as stinking of the dark arts goes, it ranks up there with the *Necronomicon*. So, perhaps one of you could bind up the kid's hand while I go out and put a ward of protection around the accursed thing."

"A chameleon cloak?" Theo whispered, aghast. "Miranda? Have you lost your wits? You, most of all, should know the depth of the villainy of those garments. Just the presence of such an object acts as consent to allow demons to devour your soul!"

"I am aware of that," I replied flatly.

Theo gazed at us, torn with the agony of indecision. Then, he stood and extended his hand stiffly. "Bring it. I will buy it from you."

"What use do you have for it?" Mab's voice was gruff with confusion.

"I'll destroy it. Obliterate it from the face of the earth."

"You don't understand, we were about to . . ." Mab started to object, but I caught his eye and shook my head. Mab shut up. This was the opportunity for which I had been waiting.

"It's a very powerful talisman, Theo. There are few objects so accursed upon the face of the earth. A person might not wish to relinquish such an object lightly," I murmured.

Mab was staring at me from under the brim of his hat as if I had suddenly sprouted horns. Whether he was appalled or amused, I could not tell. For myself, I felt sullied even mouthing such words, but I needed a chance to sit down with my brother, give him Father's message, and see if I could not change his mind about growing old. If Theo would not grant this graciously, I would have to wrestle it from him.

"I will offer whatever it takes," Theo replied.

"Very well. I'll let you destroy the cloak. In return, you let us stay here until Mephisto is well enough to travel, and you have to answer Mab's questions."

"Questions? About what?"

"Whatever he decides to ask."

cle around me, filling it in with the crystalline rock salt. Then, dropping the bag of salt beside the newly drawn circle, he began tracing out the rest of his wards, scratching the dirt with his stick.

When he had traced all the wards, Mab hefted the bag of rock salt and began pouring its contents into the grooves he had prepared in the dirt. First, he filled the two larger circles Theo had paced out around the entire clearing. Then, he continued inward, filling in his designs. Meanwhile, Theo continued to patrol the clearing, walking always between the concentric white lines.

I sat on my rock patiently, waiting. The wind rustled the few dead leaves still hanging from the denuded apple trees. Snow continued to fall, though more lightly. The crisp fresh scent of newly fallen snow hung in the air. Seated there, watching my brother pace and Mab draw circles in the snowy leaves with his boot, I was reminded of the day we lost Milan—not so much of the actual loss as of the morning before the battle, when we still harbored delusions of victory.

That morning, we had cast a spell laid out much like this one. Funny to recall Mephisto carefully drawing wards while Erasmus lounged lazily against one of the walls of brown stone, eating an apple. It was such a reverse of the way things were now.

Nowadays, Erasmus was the studious magician in the family. Back then, he had been a gangly seventeen-year-old with no more interest in sorcery than he had in what we then called the womanly arts. Enamored of the scintillating court of my Uncle Ludovico, my father's youngest brother, Erasmus hoped to follow in the footsteps of Uncle's favorite artist, Leonardo da Vinci. He spent his time painting or designing ridiculous contraptions that never functioned as predicted—even though Mephisto's paintings were always more attractive and his contraptions always worked. Nonetheless, Erasmus continued undaunted.

Eventually, he did improve. His portraits of such worthies as Queen Elizabeth and Sir Francis Drake, painted nearly a century later, hang today in museums around the world. I searched the haze of my memory but could not recall what had prompted Erasmus to abandon art for sorcery.

Theo at twenty-two, on the other hand, had already developed a dislike of magic. Being a good second son, he expected to be a soldier or perhaps to join the church. Soldiers did not care for sorcery, as it interfered with their work, and the churchmen thought it unholy. On that fateful day, he had stood to one side, his arms crossed, glowering his disapproval, much as he was doing now.

MAB straightened and brushed the snow off his fedora. "I'm about to begin, so no one had better say anything until we're done, or all Hell could break loose—perhaps literally. Remember, wards only protect you from uninvited spirits. You invite 'em in, or just speak to 'em, and the ward goes down. At that point, you're on your own. Everybody ready?" Theo and I nodded. "Okay, here goes."

Onto the large rock at the center of Theo's circle, Mab placed a pocketknife, a stick of applewood, a penny, and the blue Garfield mug in which I had mixed the unicorn horn. Next, he took out my tiny crystal vial from his trench coat and let a drop of the liquid within fall onto the rock. I wanted to cry out and stop him—replenishing my supply of Water of Life requires a journey of a year and a day, not to mention the other dangers that might be attracted by the exposed Water—but I bit my tongue. Once, I had seen a man carried off screaming into the air after he spoke out of turn during a magic ritual. That was the last I—or anyone—ever saw of that man.

Each of the four objects Mab touched to the place on the rock where the drop of the Water of Life had fallen. He then placed each item within predrawn triangles and poured crystalline salt into the lines, careful never to step across a line of salt himself.

Next, Mab pulled the chameleon cloak out of the bag and dropped it into a previously prepared triangle within the central circle. The material shimmered. It turned gray and snow-flecked, then brown as the earth with touches of dead grass. He poured rock salt into the lines of the triangle, sealing the chameleon cloak within.

Lastly, he poured the salt into the center circle in which he himself stood. By now, he was sweating. He took off his hat and laid it on top of the bag from which the salt came.

"Spirits of the world attend me!" he called. "Behold my works and obey my commands. I am one of your number and know all your tricks. Don't try 'em."

Mab took two steps and stood at the edge of his central circle facing the northward circle and the triangle within which contained the knife.

He spoke again, "The heavens of men are orderly heavens. To enforce this order, I call upon the spirit of Copernicus."

Moving around to the east, where the mug lay, he chanted, "The waters of man are orderly waters. To enforce this order, I call upon the spirit of Lavoisier."

To the south, where the penny sat, he said, "The earth of man is an orderly earth. To enforce this order, I call upon the spirit of Newton."

To the west, where the sun sets, he said over the apple twig, "The fire of man is an all-consuming fire. To enforce this, I call upon the spirit of Oppenheimer.

"Here before me, I have a cloak. It dwells in the world of men. Let it be bound by the laws of the world of men. Let its air be an orderly air. Let its water be an orderly water. Let its earth be an orderly earth. Copernicus, Lavoisier, Newton: I summon and compel you. Let any spirit who disobeys be burned in the fires of Oppenheimer and let its name and nature be consumed forever."

As Mab spoke, Theo squinted at him in stark disbelief, clearly expecting Mab's unorthodox methods to fail. Having watched Mab work before, I knew better. Mab held that if human wizards called upon spirits, it only followed that spirits who performed magic should call upon humans. To the best of my knowledge, the shades of dead men did not rise to perform tasks at Mab's bidding, yet he achieved his desired results. Erasmus, the true magician in the family, could probably have explained the phenomenon, but I was hardly about to ask him and voluntarily give my arrogant, obnoxious brother yet another opportunity to insult me.

Mab stood silently now, head cocked. A wind blew through the orchard, swaying the leafless branches. Leaves rustled and skirled across the ground. In the center circle, the chameleon cloak shivered under the caress of the passing wind. Its weave was a putty gray now, like the sky. Oddly, not a single scurrying leaf crossed one of Mab's white salt wards.

In the west triangle, the apple twig suddenly burst into flames.

Out of the air above the burning twig, a voice of inhuman beauty spoke. "Foolish fayling, by what authority do you challenge my lord, a Prince of Hell?"

When the stick burst into flames, Mab had gone entirely still. The hair on the nape of his neck had risen like that on the neck of a wolf. His hand had shot to his coat, and his fingers had curled about the haft of his trusty lead pipe. Now he bent, took up a handful of the crystalline salt and held it ready in his closed fist.

"By the authority of the magician Prospero, in whose house I dwell," Mab growled back.

"Prospero's blood has already condoned our work. He is our prisoner now, a living man held captive in the fiery bowels of Hell. His wards and charms will not stand before the might of my lord. By what authority?"

Above, on the hill, Theo tensed, alarmed, but then he scowled and turned away. He clearly did not believe the dark angel—such spirits often lie—but then he did not know about Father's message and the Three Shadowed Ones.

A terrible chill touched my heart. Could this infernal spirit be speaking the truth? Had the Three Shadowed Ones captured Father? It would explain how the incubus passed through the wards protecting Father's mansion.

Suddenly, I feared for my Father. Demons were tremendously cunning when it came to torture. Could any man survive such an experience without losing his immortal soul? I hugged my knees to my chest and sat silently on my rock, trembling.

Mab had drawn back in distress at the dark angel's words, but he knew better than to let a denizen of Hell distract him from his goal. He stood now, scratching his stubble and glancing around. In the outer circle, Theo's gaze was focused above the west circle. His weapon stood ready in his hand.

Mab turned back to the fiery twig. "By the Lady Miranda, whom I serve, I compel you go, and by her Lady, the Holy Eurynome!"

When Mab spoke my Lady's name, lightning snaked across the snowy sky. The branches of the surrounding apple trees trembled. And the knife in the north triangle spun in a circle, then lay rattling on the stony earth. In the west triangle, the flame from the apple twig sputtered and died down. Then, it leapt back, brighter than before.

"Twice wrong, spiritling. Of all powers and places, she-whom-we-dare-not-name is weakest when brought near that over which you wish dominion. Thrice we ask, but thrice only. Three times unanswered, and, by ancient law, we may exact what price we please."

Mab gazed warily about him, weighing his options. I wondered if he would call upon one of his deities, perhaps Setebos or Titania. If he chose a power with insufficient authority, something dreadful would happen.

That the authority of the Unicorn was insufficient to drive off the guardian of the chameleon cloak did not surprise me. It had been created to confound Her.

Over by the stone wall, Theo drew a handful of rock salt from his pocket and loaded it into his gun as if it were buckshot. Kneeling, he aimed directly over the top of the burning twig.

Mab stood indecisively. The flame of the apple twig burned brighter.

The inhuman voice spoke, "Speak, little spirit. Time grows short."

Mab looked toward me, a helpless plea in his eyes. I stared back at him, unable to offer him any advice. Silently, I prayed to my Lady.

Mab's eyes suddenly focused on something beyond me. As if galvanized, he faced the west circle and called:

"In the name of Theophrastus the Demonslayer, whose fire is hotter than hell itself, I bid thee go."

At that same moment, Theo fired.

The thunder of his report shook the countryside. An unearthly scream rent the air. A dozen small fountains of golden ichor sprayed onto the cold earth, the ichor gleaming and burning like liquid fire. Not a drop of it, however, fell outside the charmed wards of the western circle.

There was a rustle, then a silence. The apple twig sputtered and burned low.

"Thou hast mastered us, we concede." The inhuman voice was almost inaudible.

Mab grinned and sprang forward to the edge of the center circle. With sweat running down his brow, he brought the tips of all five fingers together and pointed the beak his hand made toward the western triangle. Speaking rapidly, before the fire of the burning twig could die entirely away, Mab called:

"Thou has questioned when I commanded. Now, I exact your punishment as I please. I banish thee, I banish thee, I banish thee. Go to the ends of the earth and do not come back until you have counted every grain on every beach on every world that flies about a sun."

When the fire had entirely died away, and Mab had performed the Sigil of Ultimate Closing in the four directions, he added, "That should keep the surly sucker busy for a while!"

"Huzzah!" I shouted, giddy with relief. I leapt up and threw my white fedora into the air. Theo lowered his gun and stared down at Mab, an unreadable expression on his face. Mab, for his part, leaned over and looked at the chameleon cloak. It was gray now, and of ordinary cloth. He wiped his brow and waved at us.

"All done," he called.

"Good work," Theo growled back. "Let's get back to the barn and check on Mephisto. I'll send my men out here later to take up the salt and bury the dark angel's blood."

Mab picked up his hat, along with the leftover road salt. He walked to the edge of his circle of salt and stopped, scowling down at his spirit-stopping ward.

"Hey," he called to us. "Could one of you come down and let me out of here?"

CHAPTER
SEVEN

Our Father Which Art In Hell

The three of us trudged back though the falling snow, the soft powder underfoot muffling the crunch of our footsteps. Theo shrugged off with a grunt every attempt I made to speak to him, so we continued in silence, each of us wrapped in our own thoughts, as if they could cloak us against the cold and the deepening twilight. Mab was right. We should be hurrying on to warn the others, and yet I could not abandon Theo without attempting to get through to him, to urge him to embrace life again.

"We should never have broken with the Catholic Church," my brother growled, glancing behind us as we put more ground between us and the fallen-angel blood.

"Excuse me?" I asked, taken aback. This was a very old argument in our family, but I seldom took part in it. "Why bring this up now?"

"Exorcists." He grunted. "Goodness and love are all very well, but these modern churches have no teeth. No way to drive back demons."

"You don't need a church to drive back demons. You're Theo the Demonslayer," I reminded him. "Besides, I can't see how you can still defend the Church. Think of the thousands of heretics and witches they killed."

Theo shrugged. "Many of those people were witches."

"But historical documents show that many innocent people . . . oh." I faltered.

"They would, wouldn't they?" Theo snorted. "The *Orbis Suleimani* would never leave evidence of real witches for laymen to find. Historical documents only tell us what the Circle of Solomon wants us to think. But I do agree the church erred when they let laymen get involved with witch hunting. They should have left the matter to experts, such as Gregor and me."

"Begging your pardon, Mr. Theophrastus, but I don't think you and

Mr. Gregor were born yet during that period," Mab interjected from where he tramped along beside us, hauling the remaining rock salt.

"Exactly!" I agreed. "I'll remind you, I myself was nearly burned as a witch."

Theo shrugged again, his rifle bouncing on his shoulder. "Gregor saved you."

"Not every practitioner of the White Arts is so lucky as to have a brother who happens to be Pope," I countered.

Theo glowered. "There are no White Arts."

I stopped in the snow and drew myself up to my full height. "And Eurynome?"

"She serves the Almighty, does she not?" he responded quickly. I was relieved to see that he was not so far gone as to show disrespect to my Lady. Then, he frowned. "But even that would be easier were I still a Catholic. Then, I could have thought of her as a saint or an angel or something. As Protestants, aren't we supposed to look askance at that kind of thing?"

"Theo, this is getting us nowhere!" I objected.

"True," he sighed. "It's not really an argument meant for you, anyhow."

"I wish you would come back," I blurted out with less grace than I had hoped. "You've upset Father. He relies on you. Prospero, Inc. relies on you! I rely on you! How can you desert us?"

Theo's features took on that pained, weary look that often accompanied the dredging up of past arguments. "I don't enjoy arguing with Father, but I served him for nearly five hundred years. The time came for me to make my own decisions."

"Have you spoken to Father? What does he say?" I asked.

"Last time we spoke, Father declared if he could not convince me with words, he would have to demonstrate the foolishness of my position. But that was decades ago."

We trudged on in silence, my mind working rapidly. What had Father meant about demonstrating the foolishness of Theo's position? Whatever it was, his plan must have failed. Unless—a shiver traveled through me that had nothing to do with the cold—unless Father's disappearance and the release of the Three Shadowed Ones had something to do with saving Theo!

As I walked through the orchards my brother had cultivated over the last half century, I thought about him, comparing the man he was now with the man he had once been. The contrast was marked and disturbing. When had this change taken place? I tried to recall if this new taciturn Theo had already begun to emerge the last time I had seen him, back in 1965.

We had met that day on the grounds of Father's estate in Illinois. It was the day our mansion was being demolished to make way for a university. Because Gregor's death had changed many things, I only lived in this mansion a short while. I would have liked to stay longer—I had a lovely room overlooking the river, with irises growing beneath my window—however, the thought of Father grieving for Gregor all alone out in Oregon had troubled me. When I asked him how he would manage, he had stroked his long gray beard and replied congenially, "If you are so worried, you may come with me." And so, I had done so.

Theo had come walking up the tree-lined driveway just as the dining room fell before the bulldozers. When he caught sight of me, he waved and quickened his step. Coming up beside me, he gazed without expression as a wall crashed down noisily. Then, turning, he proffered me a bouquet of flowers, his eyes aglow with familiar warmth.

"You look beautiful, Miranda, as always. Like an untouched blossom preserved in crystal."

"You look older." I accepted the bouquet graciously. "You've been to see Erasmus?"

"No. I've stopped taking the Water. That's why I'm here. I've come to give you this." He thrust into my free hand a tiny oval crystal vial, about the size of a plum.

"Are you serious?" I nearly dropped the priceless container. "Theo! You'll grow old and weak! You'll . . . die!"

"Exactly," he replied.

"But . . . why?"

"Because I want to go to Heaven, or more specifically, I don't want to make my bed in Hell."

"Heaven? Theo, what are you talking about?"

"For five centuries, I served as a champion of Heaven, Miranda. At Father's bidding, I sent back to Hell every man who held a black mass or uncorked, to evil purposes, the jar of a renegade djinn. I've seen more of the ravages of Hell than any man should see. I've seen families poisoned by each other's hands; mothers who have burnt their children alive to gain some horrid imitation of youth; towns rotting from a plague let loose by some careless thaumaturge, or worse, by a necromancer wishing to placate his bloodthirsty deity. I've seen men possessed by demons eat their own eyes. . . ." Theo shuddered at some unspoken memory. "You need not hear any more. Sufficient to say, I have more enemies than most in Hell. I have no intention of winding up with Gregor's fate."

"Gregor's fate? Struck down by a stray bullet while running whiskey?"

"The day Father summoned up the Archangel Gabriel before Gregor's grave and the angel told us he could not deliver our message because Gregor was neither in Purgatory nor in Heaven . . . I knew what that meant, Miranda, where Gregor must be. Gregor was a good man, at least as good as I."

"Theo, be practical! Gregor had been Pope twice," I objected. "He hardly had clean hands."

"They were no dirtier than mine," growled Theo.

"You think people who run out on their families and their duties go to Heaven?"

"God only asks us to live good lives. Serving Him is good, but not if we have to artificially extend our lives with witchcraft to do it."

"Water of Life isn't witchcraft! It comes from the Well at the World's End."

"It's not natural."

The bulldozers knocked over another wall, the noise of it temporarily ruled out further conversation. As I watched the parlor fall, I saw in my mind's eye—like a ghostly image superimposed over the present demolitions—the groundbreaking ceremony, half a century earlier. I recalled where each of us had been standing as Erasmus stepped forward and crumbled a handful of earth from our Scottish estate into the first hole, which Titus had just dug with a shiny new shovel. Father was smiling, Logistilla wore an extravagantly enormous hat, and Mephisto splashed us all with champagne, ruining Gregor's priestly habit. Cornelius sat on a yellow lawn chair, and Theo stood beside him, describing the proceedings for his benefit. Even Ulysses was present, though he disappeared in a flash of white light immediately after the ceremony. I doubted that any of us imagined this would be the last time we would all be together.

"What about your work?" I asked when the rumble of the bulldozer finally paused. A sweet-smelling breeze blew up from the river, causing the willows to sway, and the plaintive call of a whippoorwill could be heard in the lull. "So much is still not done! We've hardly even touched the Far East! Do you know how many people are killed each year by monsoons? And who's going to put down the Dag Tsog? They're killing Vietnamese refugees fleeing their civil war. Who is going to stop them?"

Theo looked troubled. I could see the natural hero in him stirring, struggling to act. Then, his eyes dulled.

"Not my problem." His voice sounded flat and lifeless. "If I could do something without trafficking with magic, I would. As it is . . ."

"What about that Scottish lake monster? The one that magician—the fellow who gave you so much trouble some years back?—drew out of the past into the loch by his house?"

"Crowley? Thank God, that's over! I've never had so much trouble with a mortal in all my years! Cleaning up after him . . ." Theo shivered. "That's one of the reasons I want out. I never want to deal with that kind of black magic again!"

"And the monster?"

Theo shrugged. "It seems harmless. Let Mephisto take care of it. Really more his kind of thing anyway."

BACK in the present, I considered this encounter from a new angle. At the time, I had thought Theo seemed like his normal self, only moody. I had not dwelt on the subject because I had assumed he would change his mind and repent his vow, as he always had done in the past. In retrospect, I found the memory disturbing. His giving up the use of magic I understood; Theo had always objected to sorcery and enchantments. But walking away from people in need? Leaving human beings at the mercy of supernatural predators? That did not sound like the brother I knew. Theo never did go put down the Dab Tsog. Father eventually had to send Titus.

What had caused this change in my brother? Regret for Gregor? Fear of Hell? He had never feared Hell before, hence the appellation "Demonslayer." Could he have become convinced that if he died he would become the victim of all the demons he had slain? Even that would not have daunted the brave knight I recalled from my youth.

All this time, while I had been lonely without Theo's company, I had trusted, I now realized, that Father would rescue him from his foolish vow before any real harm was done. But now Father was missing—a prisoner in Hell, were the dark angel to be believed—and Theo was old, dying.

The dire facts of his situation struck me anew. If the real Theo—the Theo who loved life and loved our family—did not awaken soon, we would lose him, most likely before I could contrive another visit. Then, I would be left living an eternal life bereft of the brother I most loved.

I could not wait for Father. If anyone was going to save Theo, it would have to be me, and—since his health might not hold out long enough for me to find another opportunity to return—I was going to have to save him tonight!

RETURNING to the barn, we found no sign of Mephisto. After a futile search of the barn, Theo checked on the bonfire, where the bear carcass was burning merrily despite the snow, the flames a flickering beacon against the darkening sky. Then, he stomped off to his house, to call more farmhands. The short winter's day would soon be at an end, and he felt assistance would be needed to find Mephisto before nightfall. Moments later, however, he came stomping out again.

"Mephisto's in here, watching my television." Theo stood in his threshold, framed by golden light, and jerked his thumb toward the doorway behind him. Above, the upper windows of the house were blind eyes reflecting the falling snow.

From within the farmhouse, Mephisto's voice rang out, "Hi, guys. You weren't around, so I made myself at home. Your nice housekeeper made me some sandwiches, Theo. I've got an extra one. It's ham and cheese. Want a bite?"

"No. I do not want a bite," Theo said wearily. "I am glad to see that you are feeling fit, Mephisto. It's time for you all to leave now."

We could not leave yet. Walking out on Theo now would be the same as pulling out a gun and shooting him in the heart myself. Shivering in my ripped trench coat, I called, "What about our agreement? You promised you would answer Mab's questions."

Theo nodded stiffly. "Come in. No point standing in the cold."

He walked inside, stamped his feet, and brushed powdery snow from his coat. I followed him and did the same. As I stepped into the pleasantly warm living room, an old basset hound came trotting over to investigate the strangers invading his house, his nails clicking loudly against the bare wood. He nuzzled Theo's knee and then sniffed my coat enthusiastically.

"What about me?" Mab stood on the walkway, his hands in his pocket and his shoulders hunched against the cold.

Theo gave him a long, veiled look before finally relenting. "You might as well come in too."

"Yeah, I know," Mab muttered. "Just don't touch anything."

He entered quickly, as if he feared Theo would change his mind, and moved to stand in front of the old white radiator, warming his hands. The dog approached him slowly on stiff legs. When Mab offered him a piece of muffin from his pockets, the hound quickly forgot his suspicions and gulped down the treat. As he watched Mab scratch the dog behind his ears, Theo seemed mollified.

My brother's living room was filled with wooden furniture upholstered in fiery red and orange wool. Mephisto lay sprawled across the couch, watching an old faux-wood television. A mahogany writing desk stood to the right of the kitchen door, and a large army trunk covered with a patchwork quilt had been pushed against the wall between the radiator and the stairs. The room smelled of warm bread, with a faint aroma of canine emanating from the flannel dog bed in one corner, near the cold hearth.

It was all cozy and welcoming . . . but wrong.

Where were Theo's treasures: his breastplate of shining Urim and his sword of Toledo steel? Where was the tick of the cuckoo clock Titus made for him, back when cuckoo clocks were a novelty? And, most important, where was the coat of arms I embroidered for him as a thank-you for a time when he stood up for me against Erasmus? Theo had displayed it in every house he had owned since I presented it to him. Yet, it hung nowhere among the many samplers bearing quotes from Psalms and Proverbs that decorated the cedar walls. Nor was there a single photograph of our family. Pictures crowded the mantelpiece and the writing desk, but all featured droopy-eyed hounds or an unidentified woman. I could have been in the living room of a stranger.

Shaken, I moved closer to Mab, sinking to sit on the army trunk beside the radiator.

Theo barked a harsh laugh. "You would sit on that!"

I looked down but could see nothing special about the trunk nor about the pattern in the patchwork quilt covering it. I smoothed a wrinkle in the cloth and considered my strategy. I needed to introduce a topic that would revive the real Theo, the bold and fierce young knight who had been dormant this last half century. It had to be something Theo really cared about.

What better than the other issue that weighed so heavily upon me?

"Theo," I asked, "How are we going to rescue Father?"

"Father?" Theo sat down in an armchair. Leaving Mab, the hound lay down beside him and put his head on my brother's feet. "Rescue him from what?"

"I'm guessing she means the part about his being in Hell and all that," Mab said dryly. "Most ordinary people get a bit distressed when they learn their father's been dragged bodily into the underworld."

"Duped by the dark angel, were you?" Theo chuckled. "I wouldn't worry about that. Dark angels lie. You should know that, being a spirit."

"I do know that. Being a spirit." Mab regarded Theo coldly. "But, in this case, it fits the facts, being that Mr. Prospero has disappeared and all."

"Father's missing?" Theo turned to me. "Disappeared how? When?"

"He came to America in September and never returned home to Prospero's Island," I said. "He visited the mansion, though I was out at the time. After that, we know only that he accidentally released the Three Shadowed Ones and asked me to warn the family that they were after our staffs."

"All three of them!" Theo half rose in his seat. "Merciful Mary!" He took a step forward, disturbing the dog, then paused and glared at me for some reason. "Dam . . . er, darn! That is unwelcome news! And you say Father's mixed up in all this? Our father?"

"Apparently," I murmured.

"We don't know that the dark angel was telling the truth," Mab offered. "But demons are not averse to using a bit of truth if it will forward their goals. Makes people more likely to believe them the next time. So, we have to at least consider the possibility that Mr. Prospero is a prisoner in that horrific location. Would explain how a demon got past the wards of Prospero's Mansion. As to what we should do about it?" Mab shrugged. "Well, let me put it this way: he was a nice fella, but you won't see me going down there to rescue him!"

"Afraid to storm Hell, are you?" Theo stood and put his fist into his hand and grinned fiercely, the old light rekindling in his eyes. "Not me! Remind them what the Demonslayer stands for in 'Theophrastus the Demonslayer'!"

I nearly laughed aloud. Theo was ready to storm the gates of Hell. My work was done. Could that have been Father's plan, to get captured and stir Theo to rescue him? It seemed mighty foolish on the surface, but with Father, one never knew.

Mephisto spoke up from where he lay upon the couch, the back of which was toward me. His voice was muffled, as if his mouth were still full of sandwich.

"That sounds great! We can all go together and rescue Daddy!" he laughed happily. "What a dopey-head you are, Theo. All this time you've been carrying on with this whole 'Oh, I'm afraid of damnation, I've got to suffer and get old!' routine, and the moment the chips are down, you volunteer to charge into Hell *on purpose*!"

Theo looked shocked. The gleam of joy died out of his eyes, and he dropped abruptly in his chair.

"You're right," he muttered. "I'm far too old." He rubbed his wrinkled, veined hands and frowned. "How could have I forgotten?"

"Oops," whispered Mephisto. From the creaking sound, I guessed he was trying to sink farther into the cushions.

A flash of anger towards Mephisto swept through me, but the chagrin with which he had whispered "oops" made it clear that dampening Theo's newfound enthusiasm had not been his intention.

Frankly, I doubted we could harrow Hell and survive. The idea was ridiculous. Charge into the maw of Hell, with only our staffs and perhaps a few magical talismans, and face the combined wrath of all the Powers of Hell? We would be dead or worse before we passed the First Circle. No, if Father were in Hell, our only chance of recovering him lay in negotiation.

Even if we wanted to dare it, how would we get there? None of us knew how to reach the Gate to Hell . . . alive, that is. Still, if the thought of marching through Hell, devastating demons while demanding that they return our Father, inspired Theo, far be it from me to point out the impracticality of such a plan.

"We can fix that, you know," I offered quickly, hoping to stoke Theo's enthusiasm. I continued, "A drop or two of Water and a visit to Erasmus, and you would be fit to harrow Hell and free Father!" Theo just scowled and shook his head.

Mab had flipped open his notebook and lifted his stubby blue pencil. Now, he asked, "This *Staff of Withering*, it can work in reverse, too?"

"Yep! Saw Erasmus turn a mugger into a baby once. Nasty attack . . . but the baby was cute," Mephisto offered.

Theo reached up and rubbed his temples, as if his head ached. "Enough chatter. Ask your questions, Spirit, and go!"

"And Father?" I asked.

"I wish you luck rescuing him, but you're going to have to solve your own problems once I'm gone. You might as well start now."

"But you're still here!" I insisted. "And this is *our father*! Do you think we would have a chance in Hell without the Demonslayer?"

"Maybe with Gregor's . . ." Theo faltered. "No. Without Gregor or myself, the rest of you would never make it. We are the warhorses, so to speak. Erasmus is deadly, even terrifying at times, but his staff is less potent against eternal things."

"Do you think God will welcome you into Heaven after you abandoned your father?" I asked sternly.

Theo did not answer, but he looked troubled. That was promising, at least.

"So, about these Three Shadowed Ones, Mr. Theophrastus," Mab asked, pencil poised. "What can you tell us?"

Theo regarded Mab, frowning. "You're not like any spirit of the air I've seen before."

"I'm of a special cynical variety," Mab drawled back.

"Ah, well . . . What was the question?"

"Tell Mab about Osae the Red," I suggested. "I gather you've heard of him before?"

"Heard of him?" Theo massaged the muscles of his right thigh. This attracted the attention of the old hound, who rose and laid his muzzle across my brother's leg. "Osae the Red made my life a living hell for twelve years. Probably would have killed me, too, had Gregor not trapped him behind Solomon's Seal long enough for me to send him back where he came from. He's one of three guardians whom the Devil sends to get back his own: the Three Shadowed Ones."

"And they are?"

"Osae the Red, Baelor of the Baleful Eye, and Seir of the Shadows."

"Oh! *That* shapechanger!" I exclaimed.

The memories came rushing back. In retrospect, I felt ashamed that I had not recognized the names "Osae" and the "Three Shadowed Ones," but in my defense, I had not heard them in nearly three hundred years. Human minds were not designed to hold five hundred-plus years of memories. Over time, our memories blurred. Whole decades of my life have fallen into the mists of time. Those events I believed I recalled correctly often disagreed with the recollections of my siblings. Logistilla still swears we first encountered Peter the Great of Russia on the banks of a canal in Venice, while I recall quite clearly meeting him on a bridge over the Danube in Vienna. To this day, we do not know which of us is right.

As Father was fond of saying: "*Faulty memories are part of the price we pay for immortality.*"

"So, all three of them are demons?" Mab grimaced. "Darn. I was hoping . . . well, never mind. Tell me more about this Red chap."

Theo leaned back and stroked the dog's droopy ears absentmindedly as he spoke. "He's a cacodemon, a demon of the appetites. His particular forte is shapechange. He can impersonate any beast or man. Once you catch on, however, he's easy to spot. He's not a good actor, and he's nearly always colored gray and red. Even in his more subtle disguises, some part of him—eyes, fur, claws—is always reddish."

"Is?" asked Mab. "Don't you mean was? You drilled nearly a dozen bullets into that thing."

Theo shrugged. "Demons are eternal. They always return eventually. As to the others, Baelor is a duke of the Fourth Circle. His sphere of influence is the mind. He can see the thoughts of others. Seir is an incubus, with all the usual incubus tricks. He is called 'of the Shadows' because he can walk through shadows."

"Walk through shadows?" Mab raised an eyebrow. "You mean like step into a shadow in Hawaii and come out of a totally different shadow in Timbuktu?"

"Exactly." Theo nodded his grizzled head. "For all intents and purposes, he can teleport. The other two depend on him to move around. Neither Baelor nor Osae have a special method of travel. Without Seir, they would be stranded in the mortal world, unable to return to Hell . . . except by the method any of us could take, of course." Theo pantomimed the gesture for having one's throat cut and made an *ack* noise.

"Is there any relationship between the shadow in 'Three Shadowed Ones' and the shadow in 'of the Shadows'?" Mab circled something on his page and underlined something else twice.

Theo shrugged and stroked the dog under his chin. "Indirectly. The term 'shadowed' refers to the Styx. A demon that is allowed to cross the Styx and leave Hell can use the title 'Shadowed.' The way it usually goes, when the demon escapes from Hell, he is granted the title 'Shadowed,' and given permission to wreak havoc upon the earth. He does this until some priest or virtuous knight sends him back from whence he came. Then, he's stuck in Hell again.

"As to the connection between 'Shadowed' and ordinary shade," Theo concluded, "shadows are never seen by the sun. This gives them some kind of sympathetic relationship to the river Styx—the river that divides the world of the living from the world of the dead. Seir's power to move through shadows is derived from this thaumaturgic principle."

"So, if we kill these Three Shadowed Ones, they can't come back again the next day?" asked Mab.

"Right!" Theo replied. "Not unless they are released from Hell anew—which is apparently what just happened. Titus, Erasmus, Mephisto, and I slew them the first time. As far as I know, they remained trapped below some three hundred years, until Father released them recently."

Mephisto bounced upon the couch. "I helped kill them? Really? How exciting! Don't recall a thing. Are you sure it was me? I'd hate to think you were mistaking me for someone else. That would be embarrassing."

"It was you." Theo frowned at Mephisto and then turned to me. "What was Father up to, Miranda, freeing the Three Shadowed Ones? Father knows how wicked they are."

"I don't know, Theo," I admitted. "I have no idea."

Mab rubbed the back of his neck. "How'd these Three Shadowy Blockheads come to be following you, Mr. Theophrastus? Back in the sixteen hundreds, you and your brothers fought them for the first time?"

"They had been sent to retrieve the Spear of Joseph of Arimathea, after I rescued it from the Vatican." For some reason, Theo gestured towards me as he spoke. "Maybe Father rescued some other holy talisman, and the Powers of Darkness sent the Three Shadowed Ones after it. Miranda, what was he doing before his recent trip?"

"I don't know that either." I rested my forehead in my hand. "I've asked him dozens of times what he was about, but you know Father. . . ."

"He never gives a straight answer," Theo agreed.

"I thought he was writing poetry and working on some horticulture project," I cried, "but he must have been doing something else, too. People seldom accidentally free demons while gardening." Tybalt's theories of bound demons left lying in flowerpots notwithstanding.

"Of course, with Daddy, you never know," chimed in Mephisto. "Isn't that how he found Ariel? Just sitting around, trapped in a tree? Probably knocked that old pine with his shovel as he was puttering around the island, gardening. Bet it scared the willies out of him when the tree started moaning and wailing." Mephisto rose up on the couch wiggling his arms and making "ooh ooh" noises, his personal impersonation of a specter.

"Nothing scares the willies out of Father," Theo replied sardonically.

Mephisto gave a last "ooh" and dropped backwards, hands still held at arm's length before him. The cushions of the old couch compressed beneath his weight with a loud *poof*.

"Even he might find being tortured in Hell a bit daunting," I said, thinking this would evoke Theo's previous sympathy for Father's plight. But he just scowled. Talk of Osae the Red and his cohorts had not had the desired effect either. I would have to try a new tack. If Theo's all-consuming hatred of demons had atrophied, maybe I could appeal to his curiosity.

"We do know one other thing Father was up to: we found a new inscription over his alcove in the Great Hall that read *The Staff of Eternity*. Does that mean anything to either of you?" I looked from Theo toward the back of the couch, beyond which lay Mephisto.

"Nope! Not a thing!" Mephisto declared. The springs groaned as he continued to bounce up and down.

"Cut it out, Mephisto!" Theo snapped. "That couch has been through enough." The springs groaned once more, then fell quiet.

"Maybe he stole this *Staff of Eternity*," Mab suggested, "and that's why those three demons are chasing him."

"Could be." Theo stroked his beard. "*Staff of Eternity*? Now, why does that ring a bell?" Theo tipped back his head, then slapped his knee. "I know! I once asked Father if he missed having a staff of his own. He said he did not, but if he ever felt nostalgic, he had an idea for another one. I questioned him about it further, but he just chuckled and made the cryptic reply that he had all eternity to think about it."

I was not certain what to make of this. Referring obliquely to his subject with a cryptic quip did sound like Father's sense of humor. Had he been planning this for years? Suddenly, I found myself much more curious about this unknown staff.

Theo rose stiffly from his chair. He groaned and pressed his hands against his lower back, his face pale with pain. "Enough. I answered your questions. Now it's time for you to go . . . before you do any more harm."

"Harm? Did I break something?" Mephisto sat up and looked around quickly.

"You brought Osae the Red."

"Actually, Sir," Mab lowered the brim of his hat, "that wasn't us."

Theo squinted at Mab. "What do you mean?"

"Well, it's just that I've been thinking about it, Mr. Theophrastus, and I couldn't help noticing . . . that shapechanger? He showed up pretty quick after your brother here pulled the Chameleon Cloak out of the bag. Granted, that's a pretty big beacon as supernatural draws go, but if this Osae character can't fly super fast or something, how come we didn't see any sign of his teleporting friend? If this Seir of the Shadows guy had been around, wouldn't he have put in an appearance after you shot the bear, to grab the body before we took it away to be burned? I mean being a shapechanger and a demon, Osae can probably regenerate, even from a chest full of lead, given time, right?"

Theo nodded. "Yes, that is their normal pattern of behavior, Seir pulling them out when the situation gets too dangerous. They escaped me that way, oh, dozens of times. Almost enough to make me wish I had Titus's staff! Nice staff, the *Staff of Silence*, though I prefer mine. Er, preferred." He finished, flustered. "Seir must not have been about."

"In that case, I must conclude Osae the Red was in the vicinity of the thrift shop before we arrived—which can only mean one thing." Mab leaned forward and pointed a finger at Theo. "They were onto you, Mr. Theophrastus. Osae the Red knew you and your staff were in the area, and he was here hunting for you!"

Theo drew back, reaching out to the wall to steady himself. Mephisto sat up and peered over the couch, his eyes wide. For myself, my heart was pounding with fear and relief!

So, this was why my Lady had pressed me to hurry to Theo's! Without Her urging, I would never have turned off at that exit for gas either, nor gone into the thrift shop. Had we not found the Chameleon Cloak, we would not have discovered Osae the Red was nearby. I bowed my head and thanked Her for keeping watch over my little brother.

Theo frowned apprehensively. "Osae is easy to spot, but only when I'm on my guard. If he had come when I wasn't expecting him, when I didn't have my rifle . . ." His face paled. "He could have approached me as anything, a cow or a squirrel!"

"Or an Irish Setter." Mab gestured at the old hound with the elbow of his writing hand. "That's what he looked like when we first saw him. Good shape to lure a dog lover."

"In that case, I owe you an apology," Theo admitted haltingly.

"Nothing to worry about. After all, you rescued us from the shapechanger," Mab replied gruffly. "Dang lucky you happened to go out for gas when you did!"

"An angel sent him," Mephisto piped.

"How's that?" asked Mab.

"Nothing," Mephisto ducked down behind the couch again. "Just a hunch."

Theo gave Mephisto a long look while Mab flipped through his notebook. Raising his head, the latter asked, "Any advice on how we could find out more?"

"I'm not a magician," Theo said flatly.

"In that case, I think—" Mab began, but he was interrupted by Theo, who was still speaking.

"A magician," Theo continued, "would probably counsel you to hold a séance. Lesser spirits, such as the ones who talk to mediums, are impressed with demons like the Three Shadowed Ones and track their movements. That newfangled device popular during Queen Victoria's time would be even better. What was it called? Oh, yes . . . the Ouija board. Ouija boards give clear and understandable answers, if used correctly. Wednesdays are best, if you can't wait for a high holy day. Not that I would know, of course," he finished brusquely, aware the three of us were watching him. "Oh, and make certain that the axis of the board is aligned with the north."

The old hound whined hopefully beside his master. When Theo lowered his head to look at his dog, Mephisto gave me a thumbs up. We smirked at each other over the back of the couch. Not a magician, my foot!

"But take care!" Theo raked a hand through his gray hair. "Demons are not to be trifled with! They like nothing more than to breed deceit and mistrust, turning brother upon brother and friend upon friend. Do not trust them, no matter what they promise!"

So fierce and fervent did he look, it was as if the Theo of old had returned. My heart leapt.

Theo's next comment was cut short by a bout of coughing that bent him nearly double. Tremulously, he pulled his medicine bottle from the pocket of his buff coat and opened the brown plastic container. Upon consulting his watch, however, he changed his mind and slowly put the cap back on without removing any of the pills. Apparently, it had not been long enough since the last one. Setting the container aside, he grabbed the armchair, waiting for the coughing fit to end. The old dog whined softly, gazing up at his master with concern.

CHAPTER
EIGHT

The Circle of Solomon

I sat there watching my brother coughing his life away, my heart heavy with sorrow. If five decades of facing life as a mortal had not softened his resolve, what hope had I of saving him?

From the shifting mists of time rose a memory of my first conversation with Theo, back in 1482, some eight years after Father and I returned to Milan from Prospero's Island. I stood in the cupola at the top of our Filarete Tower, the highest point in Milan, some forty yards above the roof of the two corner towers, and over seventy yards above the courtyard below. Facing inward toward the parade grounds, the vast edifice of *Castello Sforzesco* stretched out before me, a sprawling rectangular shape in the dark. The fortified *Roccetta* was barely distinguishable, a dark bulk in the left of the rectangle. To the right, however, the windows overlooking the Ducal Courtyard shone with life, and strains of music winged their way up through the cold night to where I stood.

The gaiety and lights poured out from yet another festivity, the third this week. My Uncle Antonio was visiting from Naples, and my stepmother used his visit as an excuse to throw a series of parties. The fact that this same uncle once betrayed my father in no way dimmed her enthusiasm, though, to her credit, she put her charm to good use, winning the admiration of many of Antonio's supporters.

As I stood gazing into the dark, praying to my Lady, footsteps came echoing up the stairs. Sometimes, servants were sent to fetch me, should I be wanted at the festivities. The degli Gardelli, my relatives from my mother's side, still took an interest in me. When they were in attendance, I would be paraded so they might admire my beauty and reminisce about my lovely, talented mother. Sighing, I smoothed my skirts and waited for the servant to reach the top, savoring my last moments alone with the night.

Only, it was not a servant who came tentatively into the cupola, but a little child with a head of black curls. He was a solid fellow with lithe brown limbs and dark eyes like clear pools under a midnight sky. I saw so little of my brothers that it took me a moment to recall which boy this must be. Erasmus was still a babe in arms, born the previous Christmas, while I was journeying back from the World's End, and I vaguely recalled that Mephistopheles was taller and slenderer. So, this had to be the quieter and more stalwart Theophrastus.

"Sistah," he asked, gazing up with his great dark eyes, "Mephto told me we can see whole world from up here. Is it true?"

"Not the whole world," I said, smiling. As I let him admire the view, I pointed to some of the landmarks. Then, I showed him the sky. "You see those three stars in a row? That is Orion's Belt. Now, behind Orion, you see that star and there? That is the constellation of Monoceros Unicornus, put in the sky by the Persian astronomer Abd al-Rahman al-Sufi, to honor my Lady Eurynome. It is a secret constellation, known only to Father's people, which they use in their astrological predictions."

This was true in those days. Not until over a century later, in 1612, did the Dutch astronomer Plancius leak the existence of Monoceros and several other *Orbis Suleimani* constellations to the general public.

"Your-ri-no-may," my child brother repeated dutifully, gazing wide-eyed at the blanket of stars above us. "Father Julius did not tell me about Lady Yourrinomay. What is she? Saint? Angel? Or demon?"

"Do you think angels and men are the only children of God?" I replied, laughing. "The Almighty has more orders of servants than are known to mortal clergy. My Lady is one of these."

"Father says you were con-consecated into her service when you were little, like me?"

"Consecrated," I corrected him, recalling the ceremony and the smell of the spring rain as it splashed over the wet rocks of the chapel. "It is true. I was five."

"Can I be consecated?" My little brother gazed up at me earnestly.

I shook my head. "No, only women can serve in this fashion."

"What can men do?"

"A man may take a vow to serve Eurynome as her loyal knight, righting wrongs in her name."

My tiny brother put his hand solemnly over his heart. "I so vow it!"

My heart softened, and, for the first time, I felt a chord of sympathy with a human being other than Father or Ferdinand. That evening stands out in my memory as the single note of warmth amidst the arctic waste of my years in Milan.

THEO recovered from his coughing bout and went to stand by the hearth, staring into the dark fireplace. As I watched him, it occurred to me that reminiscing might remind my brother of his younger, happier self. Fearing that if I took time to search for a suitable topic Theo would notice the lull in the conversation and send us on our way, I blurted out the first memory that came to mind.

"The spell today reminded me of watching Father and Mephisto set the wards before the French arrived. Do you remember the day we lost Milan?"

Theo uttered a short laugh. "What a disaster that was!"

"What went wrong? Did some unsuspecting mortal get his liver ripped out?" Mab moved over to the chair at the writing desk.

"The day, I meant," Theo clarified. "The spell went well enough."

"What happened?"

"We were betrayed."

Mab leaned forward, his interest perked. "Betrayed? By whom?"

From the couch, Mephisto interrupted, "It wasn't betrayal that did us in, it was Charlemagne's Brood. Darn those sexy French sorceresses!"

"Take it from the top," said Mab, pencil poised. "What exactly happened?"

"To begin with, we were overconfident." Theo leaned back against the brick of the hearth and crossed his arms. "When we discovered the French were coming, we weren't unduly concerned because we'd just beaten them five years before, under Charles VIII. It never occurred to us that this new king might pose more of a threat. After all, Milan had risen up and repulsed the Holy Roman Emperor when he attacked some centuries before. If Milan could defeat Barbarossa himself on their own, then how could we, with our magic, fail to defeat Louis XII?"

I recalled the event vividly. "The French came sweeping down from the north, just before noon on September 10, 1499. We rode out confidently to meet them. Back then, Milan was the home of the Missaglia family, the foremost armor makers in Europe, so our men glimmered like silver coins as they marched forward into battle. Between our soldiers and our magic, we were convinced we were invincible." I smiled sadly. "Only the French brought magic, too."

"Move back a step," Mab interrupted. "How did you come to be involved in this battle to begin with?"

"Father was Duke of Milan," I said.

Mab raised an eyebrow. "That really happened? I thought that Spear-shaker fellow invented it."

"Shakespeare got his story straight from Father, though Father changed or omitted certain details, presumably to protect the play from the *Orbis Suleimani*." I glanced at Theo, who nodded.

"As to how Father came to be duke . . . " Theo stroked his neatly trimmed beard. "Our family is descended from the great Visconti family that ruled the duchy of Milan for centuries. Our father's father was a commoner who married the daughter of the last Visconti duke and rose to become duke himself. Father was his eldest son and heir."

Mab raised an eyebrow. "Married the duke's daughter and got the duchy! That doesn't happen too often. Lucky guy!"

"Our grandfather had the backing of a secret organization, to which Father and my brothers also belong," I said, despite warning glances from Theo and Mephisto. "They picked him out as a likely candidate and maneuvered him into position."

"Interesting . . ." Mab frowned, then flipped a page in his notebook. "Back to that later. So, about this battle . . . you were defeated by a mixture of overconfidence, French magic, and treachery. Let's focus on the treachery. Who betrayed who?"

"Who else? Uncle Antonio betrayed us . . . for the second time." I pulled my feet up so that I was seated cross-legged on the trunk.

"Antonio? The name sounds familiar," Mab scratched at his stubble. "Isn't he the guy who was responsible for you and Mr. Prospero getting stranded on that island in the first place?"

"Yes, that was he!"

"That dastardly Antonio," swore Mephisto. "And after he had gone out of his way to be so nice to me. He's the one who taught me how to play cards and to ride drunk!"

"Still to this day, I have trouble believing his betrayal," Theo sighed. "It may have been the French magic that destroyed us, but it was Uncle Antonio who found the sorcerers for the French king."

"What happened?" Mab asked.

"We fled." Theo closed his eyes. "Retreated to Switzerland."

"Ran away like mangy dogs!" Mephisto chimed in enthusiastically.

As my brothers spoke, a scene from the past, long forgotten, presented itself to my memory. *A figure in armor of shining steel inset with filigree of gold on the back of a splendid chestnut charger galloped across the plains that surrounded Milan. Beside me, my father groaned, for he recognized the suit of armor, said to be the finest the family Missaglia ever wrought. As the armored figure rode forward, the enemy troops parted to let him pass. When he reached the place where we sat upon our horses, he lifted his face plate, laughing.*

"Uncle Antonio!" I gasped.

My brothers, who admired their uncle, cried out in anger and anguish, but Father merely frowned grimly.

"Ah! Prospero!" my uncle cried, "How do you like my new allies? They are the bastard children of the great king Charlemagne and the fairy Morgana le Fey. I found them in some of the old records you left behind in your haste to rob us of our sacred library. In return for my rousing them from their tower in the vale of Orgagna, King Louis has promised to reward me with the duchy of Milan."

"We shall see," was my father's sole reply.

We called up our magic, but it was a sorry second to the splendor of the French. Mephisto, not I, played the Flute of Winds that day, and while Father's keen blue eyes shone with pride to see his eldest son perform a tempest, its song did not sing in his blood as it sang in mine. Nor could the flute yet call upon the other six Lords of the Wind Father later bound to it; only Ariel and Caurus bowed to its tune.

Desperate, I sought out Father and begged him to bring out his Great Tomes, the eight volumes he had kept locked away during my childhood, consulting them only in the most dire of circumstances.

"I cannot," he replied gravely. "I do not have them. Or rather, they have been put to a greater purpose from which they cannot now be retrieved."

"But, Father, we shall be killed!"

"Not killed, my dear, just routed. We shall withdraw to fight another day."

HE had been right, of course, though at the time, fleeing Milan had seemed inconceivable. Yet, many things changed that day. Years after the battle, I asked Father about Antonio's "secret library." He fixed his keen gaze upon me and asked whom I thought more likely to be in possession of a library not his own, himself or Antonio? I never reopened the topic, but to this day, I remain curious as to what actually transpired between my father and Antonio in their youth, and the fate of Father's great tomes. I made a mental note to request that Mab add this subject to our list of questions.

Meanwhile, Mab asked, "Did this uncle of yours become the duke?"

"No. He died like the dog he was!" Apparently, Mephisto had already forgotten that, moments before, it was we whom he had likened to dogs.

"Who were these French jokers again?" Mab asked suspiciously.

"The sons of Charlemagne: the sorcerer Malagigi who could call up the dead, Eliaures the enchanter—his art was much like Cornelius's—the devious, serpent-tailed Melusine on her chariot pulled by lions, the incomparable Alcina, who could sing men's wits away . . . " Theo paused, sighing. "And the sweet, charitable Falerina. Weapons blessed by her never broke or misfired."

"You're going too fast," Mab growled. "Describe them in more detail."

As Theo answered Mab's question, I recalled how it had been that day. The sorcerer Malagigi had ridden an enchanted charger, before whom none could stand. He called up spirits and colored them to resemble the great heroes of his land: Rinaldo, Astolpho, Turpin, and the Invincible Orlando. Our soldiers could not wound these phantoms, yet a mere touch of the spirits' illusory blades caused them to clutch their chests and fall dead from fear.

Horses with fangs and scaled hides drew the war carriage of Malagigi's brother Eliaures. As our soldiers fled before these demon beasts, Eliaures threw handfuls of twigs into their midst. Wherever they struck our men, the twigs were transformed into serpents that latched onto their limbs and could not be shaken off. I saw a soldier chop off his own leg in an attempt to rid himself of the serpent that had sunk its poisoned fangs into his flesh.

The vile enchantress Melusine, her serpentine tail protruding from beneath her richly embroidered robes, resembled a goddess of the classical age as she charged across the battlefield in a chariot pulled by lions. She summoned up the evil spirit Ashtaroth and sent him to rip out the hearts of our generals. Elsewhere, surrounded by a phalanx of guards, their younger sister, the incomparable Alcina, beguiled men with her sweet voice, singing away their wits and leaving them wandering aimlessly, believing themselves to be trees, birds, or beasts. And, finally, behind the French ranks, the last of them, the charitable Falerina, enchanted our enemy's weapons so their blades could not break nor their muskets misfire.

"In later years," Theo finished, "they could never have stood up to us, for their tricks depended predominantly upon hypnotism. With a wave of his staff, Cornelius could have protected the minds of any man within sound of his voice. The *Staff of Silence* would have banished Ashtaroth and the other spirits serving Malagigi. As to Falerina, while none of our magics would counter hers directly, her blessings would not have been powerful enough to protect the French weapons from my staff. Back then, however, we had no staffs."

"Nowadays, we'd a creamed 'em!" Mephisto bounced enthusiastically.

"How funny life is." Theo gave a faint, ironic smile. "How we hated Charlemagne's brood! For decades, I plotted my revenge. But time really does heal all wounds. Only two centuries later, when we met at the Centennial Ball—where the world's immortals gather once a century to dance and swap stories—we were all the best of friends." Theo sighed again, perhaps recalling the lovely Alcina, whom he once had loved.

"Logistilla even married Malagigi!" Mephisto declared gleefully. Then, he paused and tapped his finger against his cheek. "Or was it Eliaures?"

"Both," I laughed, adding, when I saw Mab's outraged expression, "Not at the same time, of course."

"Both matches ending badly," Theo said stiffly.

"Which means?" Mab leaned forward inquiringly.

"The gentlemen in question spent time as a boar or a goat," I replied. "All Logistilla's paramours end up that way.

"I thought Theo was going to marry his beloved Alcina," Mephisto sighed dreamily. "But it was not to be."

"Why? What happened?" asked Mab.

"They were French aristocrats." Theo's voice became grave. "One morning in 1793, the entire family was taken by surprise by Robespierre's fanatics. They were dragged from their home before they could gather the tools necessary to practice their art.

"They lost their heads to Madame La Guillotine—the men, the women, even the half-sister with the serpent tail." He shook his head in disgust. "A thousand years they lived secretly among men, and they were all killed in a single day, slain by envy and spite."

"Weren't they great magicians?" Mab asked. "Why didn't they save themselves with magic? Not that I recommend that course of action, mind you. I'm just surprised they would show restraint under the circumstances."

"The problem with sorcery," Mephisto announced from the couch, "is that it's no good unless you're prepared! If they catch you without your staff, you're just like anybody else—a dweeb."

"Is that what you are, Harebrain?" Mab drawled. "A dweeb?"

"Yes, and I hate being a dweeb!" Mephisto replied fiercely. More cheerfully, he added, "Which is why I want you to find my staff!"

"Then you had best get underway," Theo said stiffly. "You don't want it to fall into the hands of the Three Shadowed Ones. Where are you going next?"

When I did not respond immediately, Theo asked curiously, "Who else have you warned?"

"So far, we've reached Mephisto and yourself," I replied, "and we sent a letter to Cornelius. I'm assuming Cornelius knows where to find Erasmus."

"If he doesn't, the *Orbis Suleimani* will know," Theo said, adding, "Cornelius is their leader."

"*Orbis Suleimani?*" Mab flipped through his notes. "Did you mention them before? Who are they?"

Theo ran a finger along his mantelpiece, checking for dust. "The Circle of Solomon, the secret society founded by King Solomon, from which the Freemasons were later derived."

"Holy Setebos!" Mab's face went pale. "I've heard of those guys, and they aren't nice to the likes of me. Used to have a—well, you'd call it a cousin. Poor sucker got caught by those bastards one night, and they put him in a jar. Far as I know, he's still in there, and it has been over a millennium!" Mab turned to me. "Have you mentioned these guys before, Ma'am?"

"I don't know much about them." My eyes narrowed. "Women are not allowed to join, but our family has been involved with them since before I was born. They're the organization I mentioned earlier, the one that backed my grandfather's bid to become duke of Milan. They have tasked themselves with keeping all mention of magic out of official records."

I did not add that it was thanks to the *Orbis Suleimani* that Father and I did not appear in history books. All record of our exploits had been removed, and the period of Father's reign credited to his father and younger brothers. The *Orbis Suleimani* did not bother eradicating *The Tempest*, given that it was generally regarded as fiction.

"Shhh!" Mephisto whispered loudly from the couch, "Ix-nay on illing-spay our ecrets-say, ench-way!"

I raised my eyebrow imperiously, then whispered back just as loudly. "This is Mab we're talking to, Mephisto. He's one of our employees, and he's trying to help us. What's the point of keeping secrets from him?"

"So, these Orbis guys go around changing the history books and messing with public records?" Mab asked. When Theo and Mephisto both nodded, Mab asked bluntly, "Why?"

"It's part of their duty as guardians of the legacy of King Solomon." Theo came to lean against the back of the armchair in which he had previously sat.

His dog trotted over as well and sat beside him, gazing up soulfully at his master. "When men believed in the supernatural, they were victims. They tried to solve their problems by appealing to supernatural entities for help. Many of these beings demanded worship in return. Few of them were worthy of the honor human beings paid them, and some of them were downright evil.

"As soon as men stopped believing that pagan gods and spirits could help them, they began solving their own problems," Theo continued. "Notice the Renaissance and the Industrial Revolution started in Europe. This was not because the Europeans were wiser than other peoples, but because that was where the *Orbis Suleimani* was most active. The idea that we lived in an orderly, scientific world caught on, and men began studying nature and benefited from it accordingly.

"Of course, it's just a deception created by Solomon's heirs and maintained, nowadays, by the *Orbis Suleimani* and Prospero, Inc.—what scientists call 'physical matter' only behaves consistently because King Solomon captured the four kings of the elements and bound them to the service of mankind. But it is a deception that is useful to the dignity and well-being of men," Theo explained. He added piously, "Also, people are more likely to turn to God Almighty for their solace when they do not believe in lesser supernatural entities."

Mab scribbled away for a time and then muttered, "Got it. Thanks." He turned to me. "Anything else noteworthy about them, Ma'am?"

"Back in Milan," I replied, "my father was a member of the *Orbis Suleimani.* Soon after he joined, there was a division in their ranks. Father was loyal to one faction. Uncle Antonio and King Alfonso of Naples, Ferdinand's father, belonged to the other. Their falling out led to the treachery that ended with Father and my infant self being exiled to Prospero's Island."

"And the second betrayal?" Mab asked.

It had never occurred to me to wonder if the opposing side of the *Orbis Suleimani* was involved in bringing the French to Milan. I replied hesitantly, "As far as I know, that was fueled by personal ambition."

"And you're sure this Uncle Antonio isn't behind your current problems?" asked Mab.

I laughed. "He's been dead a long time."

"Did anyone actually see the body?" Mab asked.

"We all did," Theo confirmed. "One of his old supporters turned on him when he realized that Antonio had betrayed Milan to the French. Erasmus found Antonio lying in the mud, dying, and made his last few minutes comfortable."

"Erasmus sent a runner to fetch Father," I said, "but by the time Father arrived, Antonio was gone."

Only three times had I ever seen my father weep. The death of Antonio was the first. That was when I learned that Father and Antonio had been the best of friends as children, before power and Milan had come between them.

"His death has always troubled me." Theo frowned. "Antonio was a bad man, and he died unshriven. I fear he may be burning in Hell."

"Er . . . right," muttered Mab. He reviewed what he had just written. "Which faction of the *Orbis Suleimani* is Cornelius loyal to, Ma'am? Your father's or Dead Antonio's?"

"I don't know. I never paid much attention, myself—too much mumbo jumbo for my taste." Theo squatted beside the armchair and let the dog lick his face.

"Bears looking into." Mab scribbled furiously.

Mephisto, who had slumped down again, popped his head up over the back of the couch. "Oh, Cornelius is loyal to Daddy. No doubt about that!"

"That covers Cornelius and Erasmus, then," Theo said. "What about Logistilla?"

"Mephisto knows where she is, but he's not talking." Mab turned toward the couch. "Hey? How did a harebrain like you manage to track down so many family members anyway, when my detectives can't find hide nor hair of them?"

"What's to track down?" Mephisto folded his arms across the back of the couch and beamed at Mab. "I'm not a head-in-my-shell, like Miranda and Theo here. I never lost track of them. Well, except for Titus. He just dropped off the face of the earth about two years ago—hopefully not literally. And Ulysses, of course, but who could track him? I mean I know where he was when I last saw him, but who knows if he'll ever go back there again? He's less rooted than thistledown! I like his staff." He considered this for a moment before concluding, "But I like mine better!"

"Hardly admirable that you've kept track of your relatives when your motive is to hit them up for money," Mab observed.

"Oh, and you know so much about my motives, Mr. Bodyguard!" Mephisto replied hotly. He stuck out his tongue.

"Last I heard, Logistilla was living on an island in the East Indies," I offered. "She also has a place near the Okefenokee Swamp and another on the Russian Steppe. She loves the Steppe," I said, turning to Mab. "She's a superb horsewoman. Horses were her greatest passion before she became a sorceress."

"What changed her? Getting her staff?" Mab asked.

"No, being left out of our most famous undertaking." Theo chuckled, smiling in reminiscence. "While the rest of us risked danger and gained glory, Logistilla was stuck holding the horses. She wanted to make certain we'd never have an excuse to leave her behind again, so she took up the study of magic."

"Which most famous undertaking would this be?" Mab asked.

"The stealing of the artifacts of power from the popes of Rome," all three of us Prosperos said in unison.

"Whoa! I thought all those Catholic artifacts were hoaxes," said Mab. "Didn't they recently debunk the Shroud of Turin?"

I smiled. "Of course, the shroud the Church has is a fake. The original is in the tapestry room in Father's mansion."

Mab scowled and spat. "No wonder that demon got past the wards. That house is even more polluted than I thought. How did you Prosperos know where these artifacts were?"

Rising, Theo glowered and took a step toward Mab. "You will not use the word 'pollute' in reference to the shroud of Our Lord in my house!"

Mab lowered the brim of his hat. "My apologies, sir."

"As to how we knew . . ." Theo leaned against the wall again and scratched the dog behind the ear. "Gregor was pope at the time. But, back to Father. What of Father himself? What efforts have you made to find him? Have you at least traced him to wherever he was when he disappeared?"

"We sent detectives after Father as soon as we knew he was not at home," I replied.

"Why didn't you go looking for him yourself?" Theo asked, his voice suddenly accusatory. He jerked his thumb toward Mab. "If he's the best detective Prospero, Inc. has, why is he here, instead of looking for Father?"

"Those weren't Father's instructions," I replied simply.

Theo stared very hard at me and then sat down in his armchair and put his face in his hands. After a time, he spoke without looking up. "There's something I've been meaning to ask you for some time now, Miranda. When you were growing up on that island, did Father spend a lot of time looking after you?"

"No," I replied slowly, puzzled by this dramatic change of subject. "He was usually studying, at least until I came to be of tutoring age. Ariel kept me out of trouble."

"Ariel? Mab, you must know Ariel well. How good, would you say, is Ariel's judgment of what is good or bad for humans?" Theo sat back.

"Lousy," murmured Mab. "Take it from me."

"What's this about, Theo?" I asked.

"You were left alone a lot as a child, yet unlike every other child in the world, you never got in trouble, and you never got into Father's hair."

"I was obedient," I replied, adding under my breath, "unlike some people." Theo had been a dutiful boy, but I would not say the same for my other brothers.

Theo continued, "On an island, where every living creature—the Aerie Ones, Caliban, and even the flowers—were bound to Father's will . . . hasn't it ever occurred to you, Miranda, to wonder if he might have bound yours as well?"

"No." I dismissed the idea.

"Well, it's occurred to me many times, and I'll tell you something else. I don't think he ever got around to releasing you either. Here it is, over fifty-five decades later, and you still can't help but obey his every command, even when disobeying might save his life," Theo said bitterly.

"That is insane. Ridiculous," I objected. "You have absolutely no evidence."

"Then why don't you give up looking for the others and go find Father?" Theo asked persistently.

"Those weren't his instructions."

A deep, trembling growl came from over by the writing desk. Mab stalked slowly forward, his eyes smoldering.

"Mr. Prospero wouldn't have done that, would he?" he asked. "By Setebos and the Four Quarters! If I find that he enchanted Miss Miranda, there will be hell to pay!"

"Relax, Mab. No one has enchanted me. If you care about Father so much, Theo, why don't you go save him, rather than accusing other people of being bewitched?" I snapped back.

Theo rose, and my heart leapt, for he looked as if he planned to take up his staff and head out to save Father there and then. If he would only leave his farm and return to the world, I was certain he could find the strength of will to throw off this malady of the spirit, whatever it was that had poisoned him and made him turn his back on the family and on life.

Theo's gaze dulled. The sense of purpose left his body, and he slouched back in the chair again.

"I'm certain Father can take care of himself," he said flatly. "He can't be in Hell. That's ridiculous. No, this is about you. You just don't face up to facts. You know, Miranda, sometimes I think Erasmus is right about you. Nothing has touched you in five hundred years. You're the same now as you were at sixteen." He coughed briefly and then stood up. "Excuse me, I am going to get myself a glass of water."

Theo headed for the kitchen with the old hound following him, its nails clicking loudly against the broad boards of the floor. As they disappeared through the door leading to the kitchen, an older woman's voice rang out cheerfully, inquiring what she could get him and whether he wanted refreshments for his guests. From her tone of address, she sounded more like an employee than the mistress of the house.

As my brother stomped off, I stared after him, stung. Was this really Theophrastus, my loyal brother who had defended me unfailingly against Erasmus's cool and acerbic humor? How bitter he had grown in his old age! Even so, I found it hard to stomach his siding with Erasmus. If Theo had fallen this far, what hope had I of rousing him?

Rage toward my malicious brother swept over me. Intellectually, I knew Theo's new attitude was not Erasmus's fault, but I could not quite get myself to believe it.

The door of the kitchen, which had been propped open, banged shut behind my brother, and I forgave Theo for all his rudeness.

On the back of the door hung a shield-shaped embroidery frame. The dark walnut frame held an embroidery of an elegant unicorn rampant upon a field of royal blue. The unicorn had a silver horn and silver hooves. Tiny pale flowers of light blue and lavender grew at her feet. The piece had faded over time, the unicorn's graceful deer-like body yellowing to a creamy beige. Yet I felt it had aged well.

The sight of the faded embroidery brought back a flood of memories. Long ago, Erasmus claimed my lack of skill at womanly arts resulted from some want in my person. In truth, it was my upbringing among spirits rather than civilization that was to blame. Theo had stood up for me and told Erasmus that if he repeated his slanders, he would have to answer to Theo and his Toledo steel. And when Erasmus refused to be silent, Theo had beaten him soundly.

To show my thanks, I secretly learned the very arts Erasmus had mocked me for lacking. The first thing I made with my new skills was this embroidery of Theo's livery, for Theo had kept the vow he made in the Filarete Tower at the age of five. He had taken the Unicorn as his device and had devoted his long life to righting wrongs in her name. That my embroidery hung here, when even his beloved sword and clock were not in evidence, meant that, despite his gruff words, he had not forgotten his affection for me.

THEO came back with a tray of fresh-baked cookies and a mug of hot chocolate for each of us. He carried the tray around and handed out the cocoa before settling back in his armchair with a cookie and his glass of water. The dog scampered back as well, and laid its grizzled muzzle across his feet.

The sight of the embroidery had warmed me, and the cookie was sweet and fresh from the oven. As I sipped my cocoa, however, I felt a dull emptiness spreading through my heart. Out in the snow, I had felt so confident that a few encouraging words were all that would be needed to rouse Theo out of his lethargy. I had not counted on the debilitating effects of the physical ills from which he suffered. These ills were hardly a barrier, of course. A drop or two of Water of Life and he would be good as new again. However, they sapped his spirit, keeping him from rallying against the reaper whose dry fleshless hands clawed at his door. I had tried Father's plight. I had tried reminiscing. I had tried righteous anger against the demons, I had even tried family duty, from which the Theo of old never shirked. Nothing had worked.

I did not know what to do.

Silently, I bowed my head and prayed to my Lady, asking for Her aid, begging Her not to let my brother die.

Mephisto, who had been watching a soap opera, switched off the TV. His mouth full of cookie, he peeked over the edge of the couch and blurted. "Hey, Theo, you'll never guess who we saw at the hotel today! Prince Ferdinand. You remember him . . . the supposed sap? Did you know he jilted our sister? At the altar, even? Left her standing there in her wedding dress! I bet you didn't know that." He waggled his index finger at Theo. "Somehow, Miranda neglected to mention this down through the centuries."

"Don't be foolish, Mephisto," Theo began, then he caught sight of the blush upon my cheeks. "Miranda . . . is he telling the truth?"

I stared into my mug, my appetite suddenly gone. When I finally spoke, it may have been the most difficult single word I ever pronounced.

"Yes."

Theo looked so shocked and so hurt that, for a moment, the young man he had once been was visible through the wrinkles and the short gray beard. I would have been overjoyed had I not been wishing so very hard that I could turn invisible. The humiliation of watching the pain and doubt that warred upon my brother's features was so great, I thought I should die. Tears of shame stung my eyes.

Theo did not even attempt to maintain his pretense of gruff aloofness. He cried, "B-but, he must be dead, some five hundred years now! Are you certain the man you saw was not a look-alike?"

"I don't understand it either," I mouthed. I had intended to speak, but no breath came. "But he asked for me by name. I suppose it could have been Osae," I added more clearly. The thought cheered me, obscurely. "I didn't get close enough to check for telltale red spots."

"He abandoned you at the altar?" The muscle in Theo's jaw began contracting. "How did he justify breaking his sacred engagement vow?"

"She doesn't know. She ran away and wouldn't talk to him," Mephisto chimed in. He now had a mustache of chocolate foam. "Too chicken to face the man who wronged her and warped her for life."

My face burned like a furnace, and I feared I might faint; something that had not happened to me since the 1800s, when the dictates of fashion required that I wear a corset too tight to allow for proper breathing. Theo, who had always adored me, regarded me with something akin to pity on his face.

I was saved from further indignity by a knock at the door. The three farmhands—a hefty, bearded man and two wiry fellows in flannel jackets—returned from the bonfire to report "the weirdest thing." The bear carcass split open in the midst of the flames, and a small red bird had flown out. Theo asked a few questions and then sent them away, shaking his head.

"God's teeth!" He reverted to the swear words of an earlier age. "He escaped me that way once before! I should have told my men to keep their guns ready and shoot anything that came out." My brother shot a long angry look at the trunk upon which I was sitting.

Mab closed his notebook and adjusted his hat. "Look, it's been nice visiting, Mr. Theophrastus, and I admire your philosophy. But we've got to be going, if we're going to warn the rest of your relatives. Oh," he snapped open the notebook. “There was one other question I wanted to ask Mr. Mephistopheles.” Mab turned to Mephisto. “What color was Chalandra’s hair?”

“Oh, the most pretty auburn, just like a Titian. And she had the most lovely pearly gray eyes . . . Oh!” Mephisto trailed off. His mouth fell open. Then he screwed up his face as he began to spit and sputter.

“Eew, gross! Yuck! Phewwy!”

“Teach you to be more careful about your bedmates,” Mab said. “You’re lucky she didn’t make off with both your staves.”

Mephisto drew his knees together. Theo shook his head in disgust, though he chuckled dryly in spite of himself.

“Well, we’re off then,” I said softly. The room seemed stiflingly hot, and I found myself short of breath. I had failed. Theo would die, and I would be left, bereft.

Theo stood, suddenly awkward. “Take care of yourself. If I don’t see you again . . .”

“Oh, don’t be such a sourpuss,” Mephisto stood and slapped him on the back. “We’ll be back to bug you before you know it.”

“I would prefer if you did not return,” Theo replied stiffly.

While my brothers talked, I went to Mab and took back the crystal vial. When Theo’s head was turned, I slipped it onto the writing desk, next to the brown medicine container. I was probably wasting two ounces of the precious Water. But, some risks were worth it.

Moving across the room, I embraced Theo and kissed his bristly cheek. He squeezed me tightly to his chest.

“It has been good to see you again, Sister,” he said lamely, as he let me go. “You are as beautiful as ever. . . .” His hand rose as if to touch my cheek, then fell away. “Untouched by the passage of time.”

In light of his previous comment regarding Erasmus, his words pained my heart and nearly caused me to cry. I managed an appreciative smile and squeezed his hand, but he only stood frowning at me. Dropping my eyes, I turned to go.

That was when it struck me. One last desperate idea. Perhaps it was in my power to save my brother after all.

“Theo, do you recall the day atop Grantham Tor?” I stood in the doorway, framed by darkness and softly swirling snow.

“We were both children then,” Theo replied brusquely.

“So, your promises meant nothing?” I whispered, hurt. Maybe the Theo

I loved was already dead. Maybe he had died long ago, on that horrible night beside Gregor's grave. Maybe this man here was nothing but a husk.

Theo bristled and snapped fiercely, "I always keep my word!"

Oh, thank God! I drew myself up.

"Prince Ferdinand Di Napoli has offended my honor."

I did not wait for him to answer, but turned and headed through the early evening gloom toward our rented car. As I crossed the snow-sprinkled yard, I could feel the heat of Theo's anger burning behind me like a flame.

CHAPTER
NINE

The Gate in the Crate

"Miranda, your suitcase is chirping," announced Mephisto.

"Quiet, pal, someone will hear you. Ma'am, haven't I told you before you should turn that dratted thing off when on a stakeout?" Mab muttered, exasperated.

"Relax, Mab, we're in a sealed car. No one is going to hear us. Only, I don't think I can reach the phone. Could you answer it, please?" I asked.

Mab grunted and reached into the backseat of yet another rental car. As he opened the carrying case and answered the phone, I kept a lookout on the warehouse door across the parking lot.

It was early evening of the following day. We were in Landover, Maryland, parked in front of the warehouse that was the last known location of Mephisto's staff. As soon as the warehouse employees cleared out, we were going in to have a look around.

After leaving Theo's, we had driven back to the airport without incident. Once at the plane, I had wanted to hurry on to Logistilla's, in hopes of reaching her before the Three Shadowed Ones did. Mephisto had refused to give us any additional directions, however, claiming we were not taking the hunt for his lost staff seriously. In return, Mab had offered to bash him with a lead pipe.

Since it was quite late in the evening, we had found a hotel for the night, where we could discuss the matter civilly. Eventually, we reached a compromise. Mephisto told us Logistilla lived in the Caribbean. In return, since Maryland was en route to the Caribbean from Vermont, we agreed to pause and check the warehouse where Osae had brought Mephisto's staff and see if it might generate any additional leads. Once this was done, Mephisto promised, he would give us the exact location of St. Dismas's Island, where our sister Logistilla lived.

So now we sat in the car, hunched down under a blanket, waiting in silence for the warehouse employees to depart. At least, we had sat in silence until my phone rang.

Mab spoke softly into the telephone. "Hello? Miranda Prospero's answering service. Chicago, eh? What can we do for you? Really, you don't say? Wait, I'll ask her." He covered the receiver with his hand, "Miss Miranda, it's that kid from the Chicago office, Simon? He says there's a gentleman at their office asking to see you, a Mr. Di Napoli. Mr. Ferdinand Di Napoli."

This was unexpected.

"Any suggestions?" I barely managed to keep my voice from coming out as one long squeak.

"I know!" Mephisto bounced up and down, his hand raised. "Set up a meeting with him, then don't show!"

"How the heck did he find us?" Mab growled. "Might not be a bad idea to hear what he has to say, Ma'am. I, for one, wouldn't mind asking him a few questions. Would you like me to go speak with him?"

Mab's tone of voice evoked images of single chairs positioned beneath unbearably bright spotlights. I laughed, despite my dismay. My palms were slick with sweat. I wiped them on my Irish Setter-ripped coat.

Meeting Ferdinand would cause a delay, and I was eager to carry out Father's request, warn my family, and return to the business of running Prospero, Inc. On the other hand, I did not feel the sense of impending doom that had oppressed me before our encounter with Osae the Red. My sister must be warned, but it could probably wait a day. Besides, the unlikeliness of Ferdinand reappearing in my life now was too great to be a coincidence. I wanted to discover the relationship between his reappearance and the Three Shadowed Ones.

"Let's meet him, then. I'll come too." The thought of sending Mab was appealing, but I could not run from my past forever. "Where?"

"Better make it some public place, Ma'am."

"I've never lived around here. I don't know any public places."

"Everybody knows public places in D.C., and that's only a few miles from here," Mephisto said. "What about the Capitol building, or the Lincoln Memorial?"

"Very well," I replied. "You may tell Simon we'll meet Mr. Di Napoli tomorrow at noon at the Lincoln Memorial. If he can't make it, so much the better."

"Tomorrow, at noon, at the Lincoln Memorial. Gotcha." Mab repeated the information into the cell phone. He hung up and looked at me. "You gonna tell your brother that this Ferdinand joker is going to be here?"

I sighed. "No. Theo would blast him before we got a word in edgewise. I think we should hear what Ferdinand has to say."

Besides, the whole point had been to get Theo to leave his farm and interact with the world. That would hardly happen if I did his legwork for him.

MAB hung up and poured himself a cup of hot coffee from a thermos which he, like all good detectives, kept with him in the car along with a wide-mouthed jar. He offered a cup to Mephisto and me, but we both shook our heads. It was growing dark, and we could barely make out the two figures who came out of the warehouse, waved to each other, and climbed wearily into their cars. The lights came on in one car and then the other. Both cars pulled out and drove away. We were left alone with two trucks, a Dumpster, and the warehouse.

"That's the truck I chased in the cab! I recognize the numbers." Mephisto popped out from under a blanket and pointed over my shoulder at one of the two green-and-blue sixteen-wheelers. He frowned. "Or maybe it was the one over there. Anyway, they're gone. Shall we go in?" Darting from the car, he started forward.

Mab leapt after him and grabbed him by the shoulder. "Hey, punk, where do you think you're going?"

"Get your hands off me. Into the warehouse, isn't that the plan?" Mephisto shrugged free of Mab's grip.

"If you want to set off the alarms and notify the police," Mab said.

"They didn't have any alarms when I was here before," Mephisto said.

"That was before the place got trashed, by you. If they're not bonkers or bankrupt, they've upped their security since then." Mab squinted, pointing through the gloom at the warehouse. "See that sticker by the door? That tells us they have a security system. Hand me the binoculars, Ma'am. I'll see if I can read it despite the dimness of the light."

I reached into the backseat and picked up the shoulder bag into which I had stowed equipment we might need. The gear Ariel had packed for us included a pair of binoculars, my laptop and portable scanner, a starlight scope, several LED headlamps with battery packs. Last night, we had added some bright-orange foam earplugs, the kind used at shooting ranges, for Mab's ears.

Climbing out of the car, I handed Mab the binoculars. "Check it out, Mab. Tell us what you can find out."

Mab peered through the field glasses. "Thomson Security Co.: I've run into them before. No motion detectors, usually, but the system is tied into a phone line which calls the security company and the police."

Smiling, I picked up the shoulder bag and handed the neon-orange earplugs to Mab. Then, I took up my flute. "You gentleman see to the locks. I'll take care of the alarms."

I WENT forward, whistling softly. Across the parking lot, three brick steps led to a heavy steel door. Climbing the stairs, I touched two fingers to my lips, then tapped them lightly against the door, just next to the doorknob.

"Spirits of lightning," I intoned, "deviate not one iota from the paths of your dance!"

Then, sitting down upon the steps, I raised my flute and played the tune I had been whistling. Upon my lips it had been a cheerful march. When voiced by the flute, it became something grander, rousing and yet solemn, bringing a tear to my eye even as it lifted my spirits.

As I played, Mab and Mephisto came hurrying across the parking lot, Mab glancing carefully backwards to make sure no one was in sight. Convinced we were alone, he pulled out locksmithing tools and set to work. Meanwhile Mephisto, who had not climbed the stairs, went over to the warehouse's windows and tried in vainly to peek between the closed slats of the Venetian blinds.

The lock clicked open. I kept playing. As Mab swung the door open, a tiny line of blue fire continuously leapt the path between the tongue of the doorknob and the metal plate on the lintel.

Mab ducked under the stream of living current and stood blinking in the darkness on the far side. I followed more slowly, maneuvering so as to enter without disturbing the lightning or my flute playing. Then, I was within the small hall beyond the door, my back pressed against a coatrack, and only Mephisto remained outside.

Mab called to my brother, who came meandering up the stairs. Upon seeing the open door, with its blue-white flickering arc, Mephisto let out a cry of delight.

"Oooo! Look at that, Miranda! How pretty! Can I touch it?" He raised his hand.

In horror, I watched my brother reach for the live electricity. The amount of current necessary to keep up this unnatural arc was far greater, by several magnitudes, than normally flowed through these wires. I wanted to shout at him, but if I stopped playing, the alarm would go off. Of course, my brother disrupting the current by electrocuting himself would also set off the alarms. Desperately, I kicked at Mab, who had turned away and was gazing into the inside of the warehouse.

Mab saw Mephisto. With the speed of a striking snake, he grabbed my brother's shirt and forced him down, away from the deadly blue-white arc.

"Are you crazy?" Mab's voice was unusually loud, as he still wore his earplugs. "You're gonna get yourself killed!"

Mephisto's eyes fixed on the electricity, and his face turned ashen. Swallowing fearfully, he squatted to the ground and duck-walked through the open door, far beneath the blue arc of the electricity.

Once Mephisto was inside, Mab slammed the door shut. I played another measure or two to insure the current returned to its natural path. Then I lowered the flute and waited, holding my breath.

No alarm sounded. We had made it safely inside.

THE narrow hall opened into the great cavern of the warehouse. To our right was a loading dock with openings to two truck bays. Before us stood six towering rows of shelves, each some twenty-five feet tall. Large wooden crates sat on the floor beneath the lowest shelf, which stood the height of a tall man. The upper shelves held electrical equipment, furniture, and boxes marked INVENTORY or "UCS". These shelving units stretched off into the darkness, toward the back of the warehouse, some tenth of a mile away. The middle four were accessible from both sides. The first and last units stood against the side walls.

A noise in the darkness startled us, and we ducked among the giant crates. The cause of our distress turned out to be the dripping of one of the great pipes running across the ceiling. Relieved, I reached into my shoulder bag and handed out the headlamps.

We split up according to our pre-agreed plan. Mab and Mephisto crept away to search the warehouse. They moved down the narrow corridor between two rows of shelves, the light from their headlamps falling upon the crates and causing shadows to leap and dance before them. Donning my own lamp, I set off as well. Since I was familiar with the running of Prospero, Inc.'s warehouses, my task was to find and check the records.

* * *

I FOUND offices on either side of the warehouse. The office tracking incoming goods was neat and orderly, while the one tracking outgoing shipments was a disorganized mess. It stank of burnt coffee grounds, and beverage stains discolored the piled papers. The computer directories and file cabinets in the outgoing office were in better order. Luckily, they did not require passwords to get past the screen savers, and only one cabinet was locked. Mab jimmied it open at my request, revealing personnel records and miscellaneous reports.

A quick search revealed the date of the break-in. Hooking up my laptop, I scanned copies of all files for that date and those of several days to either side. A few of the filthier pages I ran through the warehouse copy machine first, so as to avoid smearing some unknown substance on my scanner.

A perusal of their computer records confirmed that a shipment had gone to Chicago on the eve of the break-in. The street number of the destination point differed by two digits from the one Mephisto recalled. I scribbled the correct address on a piece of paper and stuck it in my pocket to pass along to Mab.

As I worked, my thoughts returned to the warehouse door. Opening locks was another of the Six Gifts of the Sibyl, and commanding lightning was a third. Had I been a Sibyl, the precious minutes of attention-drawing flute music could have been replaced by a word and a touch. We could also have avoided the game of electric limbo. I sighed. If only I could discern my Lady's mind and discover what held me back from achieving this final honor. But upon this matter my Lady remained mute.

BY the time I finished, Mab and Mephisto had nearly completed a circuit of the warehouse. Mephisto climbed over the boxes and stored couches, the shadows cast by his headlamp bobbing wildly. Mab moved slowly from box to box. Sometime, he dusted for fingerprints. Other times, he stopped and sniffed.

As he came to the end of one of the narrow passageways, he approached me. "There's something strange here, Ma'am," he said. "An odd scent. I've smelled it before, but I can't recall where. It's nothing natural, I can assure you that. Nothing good."

I sniffed. I detected a faint, dank odor mingled with the scent of cardboard, but nothing that struck me as clearly supernatural.

From the back of the warehouse, Mephisto called. "Do you think they're storing magic in these boxes? Like in *Raiders of the Lost Ark*?"

Mab snorted. "Your harebrained brother has seen too many movies. Whatever it is, it's strongest in the middle row. Over where Mephisto is now."

As he spoke, I heard an odd noise from over in Mephisto's direction. My brother called, "Hey, you guys, come look at this box. I think there's something alive in it."

"Alive? What makes you think so?" Mab began striding quickly in Mephisto's direction. I followed rapidly.

"It's making knocking noises. Wait a second, I'll open it up," Mephisto responded.

"Mephisto! No!" Mab and I shouted together.

"It's okay. I've almost got it . . . Oh-oh!" said Mephisto.

Mab and I ran. Our headlamps lit a semicircle of concrete floor before us, sending shadows scurrying to either side. Two rows over, Mephisto's noise of dismay turned into a scream. We ran faster. The screaming continued, mingled with growls. Then, there was a loud angry bellow, and Mephisto fell silent. The light of his headlamp rose high into the air and then clattered to the ground.

Mab and I sprinted through the darkened warehouse. I would have pulled ahead of him, but he grabbed my arm, holding me back. The corridor we ran down was separated from Mephisto's by a single unit of shelving. Ahead, a break in the shelving allowed access to the next passage. As we approached it, Mab stopped behind some large cardboard boxes and pulled out his lead pipe.

Slowly, we peeked around the boxes and down the passage beyond. The shadows cast by our overlapping headlamps swayed and leapt toward us . . . and kept on coming.

Slavering hounds of shadow and smoke, dark fangs bared, rushed silently towards us. Behind them, further down the corridor, rested a large wooden crate, the top of which had been pried open. More shadow dogs were swarming out of the open crate.

There was no sign of Mephisto.

"Barghests out of Limbo," Mab spat. "Jiminy Cricket! But I hate those shadow puppies."

From the pocket of his trench coat, Mab brought out the handful of leftover rock salt, which he tossed into the midst of the loping hounds. The lead dogs yowled and drew back, dropping to the floor to paw at their noses and eyes. Those behind leapt over their prone leaders and kept coming. They began to howl, an eerie sound that froze the marrow in one's bones.

Mab raised his pipe and backed away slowly, keeping his body between me and the barghests. He said softly, "You know what I'm thinking? I'm thinking this is the perfect environment for our shadowy teleporter. There's not much we can do against barghests. Our lights aren't strong enough to keep them away. By Setebos, I wish I hadn't thrown that stuff! We could have made a protective circle and stood in it until the sun rose. Let's get out of here. Where's your good-for-nothing brother?"

"Mephisto?" I called. There was no answer. "His headlamp is behind the crate there. Perhaps he's fallen."

"Perhaps he's dead," Mab growled. "We'll be dead too, if we stick around to find out. Isn't there anything you can do with that accursed flute? I got my earplugs."

"I could call down the electricity that runs the warehouse, but it would disrupt the alarm circuit and warn the police." I backed up uncertainly. The thousand-folded fan of Amatsumaru might be able to damage these semi-substantial foes. Then again, it might not.

"Do it! Better to be arrested than dog meat!" Mab stuck in his earplugs.

The hounds leapt, mobbing Mab. He struck them with his pipe, but no thud came. Mab's arm sank slowly through their substance, doing them little damage. Where their sable fangs closed about his wrist and shoulder, however, Mab's trench coat tore with a loud rip. Red blood welled up where they bit him.

The hounds nearest the wounds lapped at Mab's blood. The ruby liquid seeped into their smoky bodies. Their eyes grew as scarlet as blood. Their fangs paled. Their coats became a silky coal black. Their claws began making ghostly scampering noises against the concrete floor.

As the dogs leapt upon Mab, I drew back and hid among the boxes. Touching two fingers to my tongue, I pointed first at a light socket high overhead and then at the barghests. Raising my flute, I played the capture of the wolf from *Peter and the Wolf*. The melody surged from my instrument, rising and crashing and drawing my spirits along with it. Above, in the ceiling, the sockets began to hiss and buzz with curling blue fire. Almost immediately, a loud alarm blared.

The tongues of blue-white fire drew together to form a javelin of lightning, which leapt from the ceiling and fell among the barghests. The battle became too bright to behold, as a deafening crash ripped the air, and the smell of ozone filled my nostrils.

In the glare, it looked as if an electric white horse with a spiral upon her brow reared above the dogs and pierced them through with her hooves and horn. Then the sparks flickered and fled away. In the returning dimness, I could see Mab, rising slowly from where he lay upon his back. His blood seeped through the rents in his trench coat.

I approached him, glancing down the corridor toward the crate. The light of my lamp fell on scorched concrete beyond which cowered shadowy shapes. Of the more substantial blood-fed beasts, only one had survived. It slunk back among the boxes now, whimpering plaintively. Farther down the corridor, however, fresh barghests poured from the opened crate. My heart grew cold. I could not pull that trick again. Every fuse in the building would be blown. There was no electricity to call—unless I went outside and summoned a storm, a process that could take half an hour.

Oh, if only I were a Sibyl and could call lightning!

Mab wiped the blood from his eyes and looked toward the crate.

Taking out his earplugs, he said. "We better split, Ma'am! Some of the dogs are gone, but more are coming out of the box. Oh-oh, we have company!"

Standing in the darkness between the two rows of shelves, illuminated by the light of Mephisto's fallen headlamp, was a vast bat-winged shape. The creature was nearly ten feet tall, with a smooth and well-fashioned body, as if a black marble statue had sprung to life. Huge wings spread from its back, and many curling horns crowned its head. Tattered rags fluttered from its arms and legs. A surcoat clothed its body. In the darkness, I could not make out its device.

The demon stepped forward.

Mab rose haltingly to his feet and took a limping step back. "Run, Ma'am! Save yourself. I've got to try to close that crate. I'll follow you if I can."

I fled.

Halfway to the door, I looked over my shoulder. Over the incessant shriek of the alarm, I could hear the slavering growls of hounds, and Mab's curses and groans. There were no barghests following me, and the demon had not followed, thank goodness! I was nearly to safety.

Mocking words my brother Erasmus spoke years ago returned to me: "How easily our haughty sister extinguishes the lives of men, like so many flaming moths." Following close on its heels rang Theo's more recent statement, "*Sometimes I think Erasmus is right about you.*"

My relief turned to shame. I was leaving my best man back there. Worse, one of my brothers lay fallen. What if he were still alive? It took a lot to kill one of us. Had not I set out upon this odyssey specifically to avoid losing any more siblings?

I ran back toward Mab, gripping my war fan tightly. When I was nearly there, I turned off my lamp, crept back to the boxes we had originally hidden behind, and peered around the corner.

Mab had made it about a third of the distance to the crate. He was again being mobbed by the smoky hounds. They slavered on his arms and legs, licking at thin fountains of blood. Mab's face, suddenly dear to me, was slick with sweat, or was that blood, too? Beyond him, I could see the demon looming above the box.

Whispering a silent prayer to my Lady, I ran into the fray.

A skinny, lanky hound scented me. It growled and leapt. I slashed at it with my moon-colored fan. As the glimmering crescent of pale silver struck its dark body, the creature yowled. Thin streaks of gold appeared in its smoky fur where the silver blades wounded it, but it kept coming nonetheless.

Its pale gray fangs could not penetrate my enchanted gown. But the teeth of its mate found the flesh of my hand. I screamed.

"Damn it, Ma'am! I thought I told you to beat it," Mab growled, but the hope in his eyes told a different story. Pushing through the shadowy bodies of the hounds, I reached Mab and put my back to his.

"It's 'all for one, and one for all,' now," I replied bravely, recalling only belatedly Theo and Titus's rather unpleasant experience with the real French Musketeers. "We'll make it together, or we'll fall together."

"Idiotic strategy," Mab growled, but he kept fighting.

SLOWLY, we gained ground, drawing closer to the crate and the demon. The barghests snarled and leapt at us, their snapping fangs dripping with our blood. Mephisto's headlamp illuminated the scene from below, making shadows larger, and the hounds harder to see. Mab's curses grew audible above the blaring alarm. He cursed himself for being caught without chalk and holy water. He cursed Osae for making him leave it behind. Then, he cursed Mephisto for holding up the cloak and attracting Osae's attention in the first place.

The lead dog leapt forward, seizing Mab's arm in its jaws. Mab struck it repeatedly with his pipe, accomplishing nothing. But by the fifth blow, the dog had imbibed so much of Mab's blood that its body offered resistance, and the heavy length of lead bounced off its head with a resounding thud. Mab struck the beast on its sensitive nose, and it released him and went crying off toward the crate.

Its fellows drew back, circling Mab with raised hackles and stiffened legs. Then, all together, they rushed forward and fastened their jaws upon his limbs. Their fangs found his face and legs. Blood ran into his eyes. Mab fell to one knee

I was having troubles of my own. I chased off the first three barghests that came my way with a quick slash across the face with my fan. While I swung at a fourth, two others slipped in and found my unprotected ankles. Sharp needle-like pains shot through me, causing me to stumble. As I did so, a more substantial shadow dog, perhaps one that had fed on Mab, leapt upon my back, knocking me over. I went sprawling across the floor, my fan flying from my hand and rattling across the cement.

One of the dogs at my feet yowled and started to writhe. Handmaiden blood had some of my Lady's virtue. I had slain a vampire once, just by letting it drink some. The barghests seemed able to lap up my blood in small amounts, but this one had drank too much. It twisted and jerked in pain, getting in the way of its fellows and giving me a chance to pull my legs under me. I reached back and grabbed the heavy beast on my back, throwing it from me, though not before it savaged my wrist and hands. This sent a frisson of fear through me. If my hands were damaged too badly, I would not be able to play my flute!

Scrambling to my feet, I ran for my fan, knocking aside three dogs with my enchanted-gown-covered shoulder as I went. Picking up the fan again, I slashed from right to left. Golden ichor hung in the air like a ribbon before the barghests broke, howling. From the corner of my eye, I saw the glowing sapphires of the demon's eyes grow closer. I turned to face it. Perhaps the demon's flesh would be vulnerable to the bite of my fan.

Raising a powerful arm clothed in black tatters and tipped with claws of ruby, the demon slashed. The blow caught two barghests, rending their shadowy substance. The smoky hounds screeched and yowled. Steaming golden ichor spilled from their wounds. It had a hot, sweet, metallic smell.

"Geesh! Look at that!" Mab gasped weakly. "The demon is attacking the barghests!"

The pack of inky barghests slunk down and began growling at the dark intruder. The demon smiled a terrible smile and slashed again. More dogs flew. Lowering its head, the demonic fiend impaled two dogs on its many curling horns, tossing them screaming over the shelving unit to its left. More dogs turned away from us and began circling it.

"Quick, it's distracted the dogs. Let's shut that crate," Mab hissed. We ran rapidly forward, circling about the demon toward the open crate.

The demon lifted its many-horned head. From within its chiseled face, deep-set eyes the color of sapphires fixed upon us, ignoring the hounds. The creature spoke in a deep and melodious voice.

"Quickly now. Our retreat must be fleet of foot. Cowardly barghests have run crying through the gate in this crate to warn their hellish masters. Whatever will next emerge may not be so easily dispersed." Spying our confusion, the fiend frowned. "What troubles you, sister? Do not you recognize me?"

The demon, tall and majestic, came closer, kicking aside the smoky barghests that yapped at its knees. It stepped into the light of Mab's headlamp, which illuminated the device on the surcoat: a fleur-de-lis upon a field of sapphire.

"Mephisto?" I asked.

"Merciful heaven!" exclaimed Mab.

"Shall I aid your flight? The steps your short legs take are puny compared to my great stride," the demon said, stepping toward us and extending his hand.

"The crate! Shut the crate!" Mab shouted above the blaring alarm.

The great dark shape of my brother leapt toward the box, a single beat of the wide black wings carrying him over the snarling barghests. He lifted the lid and slammed it into place.

The smoky hounds growled and yapped. Mephistopheles lifted his ruby-clawed hand and reached toward them menacingly. They slunk back slowly, blending into the shadows until all that could be seen of them was the gleaming red eyes of those who had supped on blood.

Launching into the air, the demon Mephistopheles came sweeping along the corridor between the towering shelves. He swooped down and seized us both about the waist. A second beat of his powerful wings, and we were aloft, tossed under his arms like so many naughty children. Peering around the bulk of his back, wings, and sleek barbed tail, Mab and I met each other's gaze. As we were rushed through the air away from the yapping barghests, Mab shrugged.

The heavy steel door of the warehouse was before us. Our rescuer landed lightly, curling his wings like a paraglider. Stepping up to the door, he kicked, striking the door at chest height. The heavy steel door popped free of its hinges and slammed outward, falling over the three-step brick staircase beyond like a steel ramp. Maneuvering us through the doorway, Mephistopheles beat his enormous black wings again and sailed through the darkness, crossing the parking lot to land beside our car.

As soon as we were back on our own feet, Mab and I backed away from the imposing hulk of my-brother-the-demon. The sky was overcast, and the only light was coming from Mephistopheles's glowing jewel-like claws and eyes. I wanted to question him, to ask him why he looked so uncomfortably like a fiend of Hell, but there was no time. Above the blare of the alarm came the wail of rapidly approaching police sirens.

I prayed to my Lady to protect us and dove into the car.

Mephistopheles stiffened and sniffed the night air. He turned his head very slowly until glow of his eyes came to rest on my face. An eerie glint kindled in their sapphire depths. Something in the gaze unnerved me. Instinctively, I shut the car door between us, though I opened the window. He spoke.

"Do I disturb you, sister? Perhaps I have remained thus long enough. I return now to my puny and lackwitted form. Adieu."

Mephistopheles bowed his many-horned head and crossed his arms, grasping black muscular biceps with ruby-tipped fingers. He seemed to collapse inward, growing shorter and paler. Then, Mephisto stood before us dressed in his surcoat, the pink of his flesh showing between the black tatters of his ripped shirtsleeves and trousers. He stared about him, his eyes vague and wide with dazed confusion.

"Wha-what happened?" He rubbed his bare arms, chafing them against the cold autumn wind.

"Get in the car!" Mab pushed him bodily toward the backseat and dove in after him. "We've got to get out of here. Not only are the police coming, but also the barghests will soon be after us. Once they have tasted our blood, they can track us anywhere. Our only hope is to outrun them until we can get the components we need to banish them, or at the very least establish a ward. What are you waiting for?" This last was directed at me. I sat motionless in the front seat, waiting for guidance.

The parking lot had two exits. The one we had entered by led to the main road, down which I could see the police cars approaching. Their sharp blue lights, painful to the eyes, cut though the darkness. Our car would not be visible to them yet. As soon as their headlamps fell on the parking lot, however, they would see us. My only hope was to reach the other exit and get my car behind a copse of trees growing along the country lane there.

The night was black as pitch, and I recalled a Dumpster sat somewhere between us and the far exit. If I turned my headlights on now, the police would surely see us. If I drove in the dark, I might hit the Dumpster.

Of course, that was what starlight scopes were for.

CHAPTER
TEN

An Unexpected Encounter

With the starlight scope to my eyes, I drove slowly forward across the parking lot, avoiding the Dumpster. The parking lot rose slightly and met the country lane beyond. I had just rounded the bend and slid behind the trees when the piercing blue lights of the patrol cars entered the parking lot. I kept driving, slowly at first. Then, once there was the rise of a hill between us and the warehouse, I put my foot on the accelerator and shot forward as quickly as the range of the starlight scope would allow.

When we passed the third stop sign, I slowed down and turned on my lights. Mab, who was peering out the back window, swore softly. Mephisto leaned forward between the two front seats, nearly jarring my elbow as he did so.

"Yippie! We escaped the police! Why were they chasing us? Did we get my staff?"

"No, Mephisto, and they were chasing us because we broke into a warehouse. I can't believe I let you talk me into this. Can you imagine what would have happened if I got arrested? The C.E.O. of Prospero, Inc., a multinational corporation, nabbed breaking into a warehouse like a common crook? I think I'm getting too old for this sort of thing. Mab, what is going on back there?"

"I can see 'em, Ma'am, the barghests. They're after us, and they're running pretty darn fast."

"Oh, no!" I cried, adding more rapidly, "Holy Lady, be my shepherd. Guide me to a safe fold."

Like a bright beacon in the darkness, a warm certainty urged me forward, directing me where and when to turn. Obediently, I drove and turned as I was bid. We passed down narrow country roads. To either side, tree trunks gleamed, half-illuminated by our headlights. Mab watched the road behind me, cursing and swearing as the barghests gained.

"If they reach the car, they'll probably be able to get in, and we'll have to fight them. I doubt this vehicle has been properly warded," Mab said. "That's not my biggest worry, though. It's what happens if they reach the motor that really frightens me. Natural laws and the supernatural don't mix well. The engine will probably cut out."

"Well, do something! I don't want those ugly dogs slobbering all over me! Hey, Miranda, where'd all that blood on your face come from?" Mephisto said.

"Those slobbering dogs." I spoke the words automatically, my thoughts on our path and the road.

"Why don't you do something?" Mab snapped from the backseat. "You scared them away quickly enough in your fiend form. How'd you do that anyway?"

"Do what? What's he talking about, Miranda?" Mephisto called.

I glanced in the rearview mirror. Mephisto sat hunched in the backseat, his face contorted by confusion, as if he struggled to remember something unpleasant.

"I don't think he remembers, Mab," I said softly.

As we continued barreling through the night, I fought a growing sense of dread. Mephisto's strange transformation disturbed me. I had been certain, considering the terrible things my family had witnessed, that none of us would ever traffic with demons. It was quite a blow to learn that one of us might *be* a demon! Still, I held onto the lingering hope that Mephisto might have some reasonable explanation. Perhaps, if we questioned him later, under less stressful circumstances, he would be more forthcoming.

On the other hand, maybe there was no more palatable explanation. I remembered my moment of sympathy with Mephisto in Vermont, when I wondered how sane Mephisto might feel about the crazy one. If I lost my reason or, worse, my rank of Handmaiden, I would be desperate to regain it, though not desperate enough, I hoped, to give in to the lure of forging a deal with Hell. What of my brother? Might he have given in to such a temptation and made a pact with dire powers in hopes of regaining his sanity, even if only temporarily?

We were driving through the outskirts of town. Once, then twice, the car pulled suddenly as, according to Mab, the barghests seized the bumper in their teeth. Soon, we found ourselves on a busy street, passing diners and neon signs. Mab cried out, pointing at a passing pool hall.

"Stop there! Pool halls always have chalk for their cues. We could step on the stuff to grind it down. I bet it would work. Stop! Do you hear?"

"No."

"No? Has your brain left your noggin? Stop!" Mab cried.

The car jerked again as another barghest gained our bumper. Mephisto shrieked. His voice shrill, he cried, "Miranda! Listen to him. These barghests are about to eat us. I don't wanna be puppy chow!"

I glanced at the neon sign hanging sideways along the pool hall. Mab was right, such a place would have chalk. Chalk alone, especially of the poor quality we'd find here, would not allow us to banish the hounds. However, the pool hall sign indicated they sold food, so they probably had salt too. A circle of salt and chalk would keep the barghests out. If we could stay put until morning, the sunlight would force them away until the next evening. By then, we certainly could find what we needed.

I considered stopping. There was not only myself, but Mab and Mephisto to consider. Yet, the beacon of my Lady's light led onward. I pushed aside the gnawing fear in my stomach and shook my head again.

"No. That is not where Eurynome wants us to go."

"Has anyone told Her about the barghests?" Mab asked.

I kept driving. Mab stared morosely out the back window at the receding pool hall. Mephisto sat shivering, with his arms around his knees.

"Ah, Miranda, something happened to these clothes you gave me. Do you have any more?" he asked plaintively.

The car gave a thump. Blood-red wolf-like eyes peered in the back window. Pale fangs gnawed at the glass, slobbering at it with a faint black tongue. Mab swore, and Mephisto screamed. As I rounded the corner, following where my path was leading me, Mephisto perked up.

"Oh, goody, a mall!"

Sure enough, we were in the middle of a massive parking lot. A bright sign of blue and pink read "Landover Mall." Led by my Lady, I parked under a street lamp. When the barghests drew back, confused by the light, we made a break for it, leaping from the car and running for the mall's entrance.

"A mall? Oh, this is great, Ma'am! Just excellent," Mab yelled sarcastically as he sprinted for the door. "What does that horse-brained Lady of yours expect us to find here?"

"Her brain is made of lightning, Mab. Same as yours, or at least mine." I reached the double doors and plowed through both the outer and inner set. Then I slowed. Panting, I said, "Perhaps, she knows something about malls we don't. Perhaps they're warded. They are the churches of the modern capitalistic creed, are they not?"

As I spoke, the first barghest passed through the glass and lunged at me. We turned and ran again.

"Warded church of the capitalistic creed, my foot!" Mab panted as he ran. "Hasn't anyone ever told you that the first creed of blessed capitalism is: sell to all comers? That means me and the barghests too."

We raced pell-mell along the lower floor of the mall, passing staircases and kiosks, startling shoppers. The hallway led into a large open area. Above could be seen the stores of the upper level. There were three ways we could go. I glanced rapidly in all three directions. As I turned toward the leftmost corridor, a warmth touched my face, like the sweet breath of spring air. Instantly, I ran in that direction, calling for Mab and Mephisto to follow me.

The mall was decorated for Christmas. Bells and wreaths hung in store windows and along the railing of the upper level. Far ahead of us, a Christmas display had been set up, complete with fir trees, stuffed elves, and a Santa Claus to listen to the wishes of children. Many of the shoppers wore their winter coats. Some carried parcels wrapped in red and green paper.

Children screamed. Some pointed down the hallway, back the way we had come. Others cowered behind their parents' legs. The adults stared blindly toward where they were pointing, seeing nothing amiss, other than three adults running. Several mothers lectured their frightened children, ordering them to be silent, apparently embarrassed by the attention their children's wailing drew.

As we ran on, Mab called, "Where are we headed, Ma'am? Maybe we could find a mountaineering store. That chalk rockclimbers use works pretty well. Or maybe the food court? Or a place that sells drawing materials? Isn't that an art store over there?"

I glanced in the direction Mab was pointing. My face felt instantly colder. I continued onward, following my Lady's beacon.

"No. This way!" I replied with certainty.

Mab scowled. He gave the art store a last longing glance. Suddenly, an unarticulated cry of horror escaped his lips. "Ma'am! The barghests! They're feeding on the crowd!"

The smoky hounds, unseen by the crowd, were leaping upon and rending the shoppers. I saw a barghest bite the leg of a thin woman in a burgundy coat. The woman sagged suddenly, her face becoming tired and pained. She grabbed her leg, massaging her calf, where—to my eyes—the barghest lapped up her blood. Another man had a barghest gnawing at his throat. Eyes dazed, he looked for a place to sit. A small child had fallen to the ground. Two smoky hounds licked blood from his bleeding cheek. His angry overweight mother, oblivious to the barghest, dragged him back to his feet and slapped him for crying.

The sight was terrible; I felt sick to my stomach.

"You should have stopped at the pool hall, Ma'am," Mab said between gritted teeth. "At least, there wouldn't have been any kids there."

"Oh, Mab!" I cried out, shaken.

The lead barghests were nearly upon us. As we ran again, I prayed aloud. "Holy Lady, take not from others the safety and sanctuary that I have asked be granted unto us." The warmth of Her beacon did not waver. I ran, following it. Behind us, the barghests bayed.

Then they were among us, barking and yapping and howling. Fear gripped me. Whatever sanctuary my Lady envisioned for us, we would not reach it before the barghests devoured the lot of us. Just a few days ago, I might not have cared about the welfare of the shoppers, but I thought again of my aging brother with his wrinkled and careworn face. He did not look so different from the old man by the stairs, or the man near the ice cream store who was trying to comfort his frightened wife. All of these people wanted to live at least as much as I did. How terrible if we were to perish now and leave the innocent shoppers prey to the denizens of Hell.

Maybe Mab had been right. Perhaps I should have stopped at the pool hall and not trusted my Lady to take human needs into account. That thought took me aback. Did my Lady usually take the needs of those around me into account? I could not remember. I realized with growing chagrin that I had never noticed.

A sharp stinging pain shot through my ankle. A great shadowy beast clung to my leg. I cried out, kicking it and slashing at the beast with the polished shaft of my flute. My leg came free. Desperately, I threw all I had into one last sprint, running directly toward the warmth that guided me.

Suddenly, there was a small, white picket fence directly in my way. It was only a foot and a half tall, but I did not have time to react. My leg struck it. I fell sprawling, arms flailing before me.

I tumbled onto something soft and white. A green-and-white object tumbled over with me. Rapidly, I threw my arm up before my face, waiting for the attack.

None came.

Slowly, I sat up, clutching my flute. I was sitting just beneath a large Douglas fir, among the soft cotton snow of the central Christmas display. A jolly stuffed elf lay toppled beside me. Just beyond the tilted picket fence stood the barghest. Its red eyes glowed hot with anger. It growled and snapped, showing teeth as white as bone. So substantial had it become from drinking blood that the shoppers stopped and pointed at the angry dog. However, it did not cross the tiny picket fence.

I lay cushioned by cotton, gazing up at fake pine needles. Before me, the shadow dog leapt and slobbered, but each time he approached the fence, he cringed, drawing back. I was aware of him, and yet it was as if we were worlds away from each other. The fear I had felt when the dogs were chasing me fell away, and now I felt enveloped in an aura of safety and cheer, as if nestled against my Lady.

Mab and Mephisto had run toward me when I fell. The barghests assailed them. Mab, blood-streaked and gasping, backed toward me, warding off the dogs as best he could with his lead pipe. Mephisto had collapsed to a crouch. Cowering, his hands before his face, he shouted for the barghests to leave him alone. Leaping to my feet, I called to them.

"Mab! Mephisto! Over here!"

A large hand came down my shoulder, bringing with it a sense of peace. Behind me, a deep voice spoke.

"Madam, are you harmed?"

I turned and gazed up into a familiar face that was wise with age. The man who regarded me had bushy white eyebrows, keen blue eyes, a proud and kingly nose, and a long bushy beard. His red velvet hat and robes were trimmed with white fur and clasped about his middle by a shiny black belt. In one hand, he held a tall staff of yew wood hung with bells that rang softly. He smelled of peppermint.

"Father Christmas!" I breathed in amazement. As Mab and Mephisto came vaulting over the picket fence, I glanced toward the empty chair where the mall Santa had sat. "Is it really you?"

"Indeed, Miranda," he spoke in his deep booming voice. "Many years have passed since last we met, have they not? But you must excuse me."

Father Christmas strode past me. Just inside the picket fence, he stopped and raised his left forearm, laying his staff perpendicularly atop it, forming a horizontal cross between arm and staff. Throughout the mall, the barghests froze. They looked up from their victims and turned their blood-red eyes toward Father Christmas. The majority of them began to back up slowly, their heads lowered, their tails between their legs. A few braver hounds growled and began to creep forward, hackles raised.

Father Christmas pointed the iron tip of his belled staff straight between the eyes of the largest beast. In a tremendous booming voice, he said. "Begone! I revoke your invitation."

The entire pack of barghests howled. Turning, they fled. Some ran down the corridors toward the doors and the night beyond. Others vanished into the shadows, under staircases or behind store displays. In a blink of an eye, not a single barghest was left.

About the upper and lower levels, the crowds of shoppers, startled by the loud noise, turned weary faces toward Father Christmas. Among them were the barghests' victims, still bleeding from yet unnoticed wounds. The hostile gaze of the crowd took in Father Christmas and the three of us who stood beside him. Mephisto slowly backed away and hid behind a pine tree. Mab's hand reached into his pocket and closed about his trusty lead pipe.

Father Christmas raised his staff and shook it. The bells about the top jingled and rang.

"Merry Christmas," he boomed, "Merry Christmas!"

The shoppers straightened. Fear and tension drained from their faces. The plaintive cries of children changed to laughter and shouts of joy.

I watched my hands and ankle heal until nothing was left of the bloody bites and scratches but tiny, almost imperceptible scars. A sense of awe filled me. The barghests were spiritual creatures. The wounds they made must have been spiritual, too. When our fear changed to joy, they were undone. Elsewhere, the wounds of those who had been injured in the crowds also healed, though where the more substantial shadow hounds had damaged clothing, the rents remained. Apparently, the cloth was not affected by Father Christmas's holiday cheer.

Father Christmas strode around to the other three sides of his small enclosure, shaking the bells on his staff and spreading holiday cheer. On both the upper and lower levels, the shoppers smiled. Children hopped up and down, waving. Many pulled at their parents' coats and pointed. Even at a distance, I could make out that their happy mouths were forming the word "Santa!"

Mab took off his battered hat and stared after the dignified figure in scarlet and white who stood waving to the children crowded around the railing of the upper level, an expression of awe on his craggy blood-caked features.

He turned to me and said, in a subdued voice, "I beg your pardon, Miss Miranda. I guess that Lady of yours really knows her stuff."

"She does indeed!" I laughed.

"What are the chances that Santa would be right around the corner?" Mab marveled. "Seems almost eerie."

"Had we asked Her to lead us to Father Christmas and he turned out to be right around the corner, that would have been eerie. We just asked for a safe place, and this happened to be the closest one," I replied. When Mab continued to look dubious, I added, "Surely, you know there are supernatural beings scattered throughout our world. My Lady led us to the nearest friendly one."

"That's right!" Mephisto stuck his arm around my shoulders. "That's what having a Handmaiden for a sister is like! Everything goes better when she's around! Kind of like Coke."

"Ya know," Mab scratched his stubble, "Come to think of it, magic does attract magic. There may be a reason why the real Father Christmas showed up near where the demons have a warehouse. Their presence may have made it so that it was okay for him to come here in whatever cosmic Big Book of Score the Powers of Good use to decide these things." He made a note in his notebook. Then, his eyes drifted back toward Father Christmas. I touched his shoulder lightly. He started and blinked. "Huh?"

"Come on," I said, smiling. "Help me lift this elf."

We righted the jolly elf, removing some of the white cotton snow from its sharp pointed chin. Mab bent and peered into the figure's narrow impish face. "What did you say this was supposed to be?"

"An elf."

"Humph!" As he put his hat back on, he added under his breath, "Just goes to show how little humans know."

FATHER Christmas finished his rounds and shut the gate leading to the enclosure, stopping to speak a brief quiet word to a little boy and girl who stood by the entrance. The boy laughed and the little girl stared up at him with adoring eyes. He handed them each a red-and-green peppermint stick, then returned. Taking his place in the throne-like chair set upon a dais amidst reindeer and three-foot-tall candy canes, he beckoned for us to join him.

We approached Santa's Chair. A semicircle of Douglas firs surrounded the dais, forming a partial screen. In this small oasis of seclusion, away from the bustle of the mall, Father Christmas sat surveying the Christmas display, with its jolly elves' workshop and its moving toy train, as a kindly father might survey his children's playroom. His large hands, unadorned except for a single gold wedding band, rested regally on the arms of his chair. His eyes crinkled kindly as we approached.

Mab and I sat on the steps of the dais, basking in the sense of warmth and security this place radiated. Mephisto, however, rushed forward and plopped himself down at Father Christmas's feet, singing as he did so, " 'He knows when you've been bad or good, so be good for goodness sake.' What about me? Have I been good?" he asked.

Father Christmas stroked his long white beard and nodded his head slowly. There was a sadness in his keen blue eyes. "Yes, Mephistopheles. You have been good."

"Goody, I hate that icky coal stuff!" Mephisto started to rise. I feared he would attempt to sit in Father Christmas's lap. He asked, "Can I tell you what I want?"

"I know what you want, Mephistopheles," Father Christmas replied solemnly.

"You do?" Mephisto sat back down. "Oh." Then, perking up, he asked, "When do I get it?"

"When all my presents are delivered, child," Father Christmas laughed. "On Christmas, of course!"

I smiled indulgently, pleased to see the kindness with which Father Christmas treated my daffy brother. And yet, hearing his calm promise, I could not help but feel a lingering sense of envious regret. When I first met Father Christmas, so long ago, I asked him for the one gift I most desired: the *Book of the Sibyl.* Written by Deiphobe, the Sibyl of Rome, it purportedly explained the secrets of the Sibylline Order. Shaking his head sadly, Father Christmas had told me that was beyond even his ability to give.

"What of my people?" Mab cocked his head. His tone was challenging "Do you give my people gifts?"

Father Christmas met Mab's gaze squarely. "Do they give each other gifts?" Mab frowned, thinking. Father Christmas turned his keen and penetrating gaze toward me.

"Let us speak of things immediate. I have driven off the demons who pursued you. However, those beggarly dogs may not yet have lost your scent. You are safe within the circle of my hospitality. This place is as a temple bedecked in my honor. My power is strong here." He gestured toward the red and green banners hanging from the rafters and the Yuletide displays decorating the window of every store.

"Then we can stay here a while?" I asked.

Father Christmas smiled down at me kindly. "Of course! All who serve the Light are welcome."

I smiled and, reaching out, squeezed his hand in thanks.

"It has been a long time, Miranda," Father Christmas declared. "When was it we met last?"

"On the streets of London, near Mayfair, during the reign of Victoria," I recalled. "You wore robes of dark green, and two shaggy ponies festooned with bells pulled your sleigh. If I recall, there were burning candles in the holly wreath about your head."

I remembered the encounter clearly. It was just after vespers, and the evening bells were ringing. The air smelled of pies and spices, for the muffin man had just pushed by with his cart. Carolers were singing at the park, and snow was falling. I had met him once before, too, long ago, in Italy, though back then he wore yet another guise.

Father Christmas's keen blue eyes twinkled. "The mall security will not let me have lighted candles."

"Imagine, meeting the real Father Christmas at a shopping mall, and after a wait of well over hundred years!" I laughed in wonder.

It was unbelievable. Yet, nothing was impossible when divine guidance was involved. To think I had nearly doubted Her. Silently, I begged my Lady's pardon.

Father Christmas nodded solemnly. He frowned ever so slightly and stroked his long white beard.

"Hey, aren't you called St. Nicholas in Russia?" Mab asked.

"I am."

"Is it true what the legends say? That you're God's apprentice, preparing to take His place when He dies?" Mab asked.

"Ho! Ho! Ho!" Father Christmas's laugh was a deep and jovial sound. "How could anyone replace the Infinite?"

"Hmm, you have a point. . . . Sir, why don't my people give each other gifts?" Mab asked.

"Gift giving requires a free will. Mankind did not always give gifts. Do you know the tale of how they came to have the freedom to do so? Perhaps with its telling, we can while away the time you must remain here for my blessing to protect you. I know Miranda is familiar with this story, but perhaps she will not mind hearing it told yet again," said Father Christmas.

I knew the story quite well. The servants of Eurynome passed it down from generation to generation. It was an analogy only, not necessarily more or less true than other accounts, though it resembled rather closely the version told by the early Christian Gnostics, before the Church hunted them into extinction. We kept it alive because it glorified our Lady and served as a reminder of the infamy of Her great enemy, Lilith.

"Don't worry," I said. "I could hear that tale told over a thousand times, and it would not be too often for me."

"Then listen, my children, and I shall tell you the tale of how mankind came to be free." Father Christmas leaned forward and began. "Once upon a time, the fallen angels who dwell in the darkness were bitterly envious of the bright things they had left behind. Filled with overweening pride and wishing to prove their superiority to the Infinite, they fashioned a world out of the stuff of darkness and set in it a garden, which they filled with all manner of pretty things: flowers, fruit trees, animals, birds, and fish. In the midst of this garden, they created creatures formed in their own images."

"He means people," Mephisto looked back and forth from Mab to me. "Doesn't he mean people?"

I reached over and touched Mephisto's shoulder lightly, putting my finger to my lips. Mephisto covered his mouth with his hand and sat quietly, gazing eagerly up at Father Christmas, awaiting the tale.

"Their new creatures were homunculi, containing no spirit." Father Christmas's voice was deep and restful. "When the fallen ones exerted their will upon them, their hideous homunculi would stand and shamble about the garden, dancing and cavorting much like a marionette beneath the puppeteer's strings. When the fallen angels turned their will to other matters, their charges collapsed and lay inanimate upon the grass.

"Beholding this little pocket of color in the bleakness, the Divine Infinite felt pity for the fallen angels and their dolls. He moved across the face of their garden and breathed the breath of Life into their homunculi. The flopping homunculi stood and thought and named themselves mankind.

"The fallen angels were both horrified and delighted with this new turn of events—horrified because now their charges had the ability to escape them, but delighted because they now had prisoners to torment. Fearing that mankind might escape the garden, they laid great enchantments to blind mankind and bind their will. Thus bound and blinded, mankind could not perceive the nature of their fallen masters, nor could they perceive the walls that enclosed the garden. They lived much as they had before, bound and meek, obeying the fallen ones' every whim.

"Far above, among the shining spires of High Heaven, a daughter of the Divine Infinite beheld the creatures within the walls of the garden prison. Moved by mankind's plight, she left the Void, where she had danced, weaving worlds out of chaos, to travel down into the murk and darkness wherein the fallen ones' world was hid.

"Eurynome came across the oceans of the Void, a bolt of brilliance through the eternal night. The hosts of the fallen streamed forth to bar her way, but none could stand before her brightness. Searing the air as she plummeted, she pierced the wall surrounding the garden. Where she struck the ground, a tree grew.

"The fallen angels took council among themselves. Mankind must be stopped from eating the fruit of this new tree, else the darkness might be lifted from their eyes and the bindings from their will. The fallen ones chose one from among their number, the dark and cunning Lilith, called the Queen of Air and Darkness, to misguide mankind. Lilith crept among them, whispering to them that if they should eat of this tree, they would surely die. Mankind dutifully abstained."

As Father Christmas wove his tale, his voice grew more powerful and the gleam in his eye more keen, until I was amazed any shopper could mistake him for a costumed mortal. An aura of majesty surrounded him like a cloak, and the lights gleaming off his thistle-white hair shone like a halo. Folklore named him a saint, but I suspected he was something far older and more primordial. After all, saints were human. When Father Christmas spoke about High Heaven, I got the distinct impression he knew of it firsthand. When he spoke of Lilith and the demons, he seemed no more afraid than an adult might be of a child's nightmare.

"Then, one day," he continued, "as a woman sat beneath the blessed tree, a fruit fell into her hand, and she bit into it. Some say that it fell by its own volition, but others claim that Ophion, the Serpent of the Wind, Eurynome's dance partner from the Void, moved through its branches, disturbing them. If so, this might explain why some other versions of this tale recall a snake within the branches.

"As she ate, Eurynome's virtue went into the woman, and the mist cleared from her eyes. She became aware of her divine nature and beheld the imprisoning walls. Running to her mate, she shared the fruit with him, and he too beheld the truth. Hand in hand, they scaled the walls and escaped from the garden, to make a new life upon the face of the Earth. They were free now to love, to give gifts, and to do all those things, both good and bad, that free will allows."

While we sat spellbound, listening, the halls of the mall around us had slowly grown quiet and empty. Now a security guard approached, stepping over the low fence as he came toward us.

"I'm sorry folks, but the mall is closed; you'll have to leave."

Father Christmas stood, saying, "Come. I will escort you to your vehicle and ensure no dark powers approach you out of the night."

OUTSIDE, we found our rental car alone in the parking lot, bathed in a pool of garish lamplight. The magic of the story still encompassed us as we walked in silence, Father Christmas striding before us. When we reached our vehicle, Father Christmas raised his staff and uttered his benediction.

"Merry Christmas! And to all, a good night!" he boomed.

"Good night, Santa," Mephisto said.

"Good evening, Sir," said Mab.

"Good night, Father Christmas," I said. "I hope to see you before another hundred and forty years have passed."

"May your wish be granted!" Father Christmas bowed solemnly and strode off into the darkness.

CHAPTER
ELEVEN

Of Tall Dark Men

"So, do you think this Ferdinand chap will show?" Mab looked at his watch.

"With any luck, no," I replied.

We stood on the steps of the Lincoln Memorial, gazing back toward Capitol Hill along the green avenue known as the Mall. The serpentine length of the Vietnam Memorial, the World War II Memorial, the rectangular reflecting pool, the towering white obelisk of the Washington Monument, and the handsome buildings of the Smithsonian museums lay between us and the dome of the Capitol. It was an impressive sight, as grand as the cathedrals of Europe.

The wind was bitingly cold. Few tourists were about. A young couple in matching plum parkas sat within the memorial eating their lunch, and a small tour group of elderly citizens stood together in a tight cluster, reading the inscriptions on the inside walls of the memorial itself. These made up the entirety of those present, except for the three Italian stonemasons who were doing some repair work on the farthest of the enormous columns that lined the front of the monument.

I would have preferred to spend the morning flying down to the Caribbean, but since we could not depart from Washington, D.C., until after our meeting with Ferdinand, we had spent it shopping instead, with periodic interruptions as I fielded calls from Prospero, Inc. It was a novelty to me, who normally divided all my time between Prospero's Mansion and various branch offices, to spend a day as a tourist, visiting shopping malls and seeing sights. I found it surprisingly pleasant.

All three of us bought new outfits. Instead of my tattered white trench coat, I wore a heavy cape of creamy cashmere lined with scarlet satin, a knitted hat and matching muff trimmed with faux ermine. Mephisto had a new navy parka, black trousers, black boots, and, after some searching, a new lute. The bottom ten inches of his royal blue surcoat stuck out from underneath his new coat.

Mab had at first refused to replace his old gray trench coat, despite the terrible rents it now bore. But when the clerk showed him how the new coat would have twice the pocket room of the old one, Mab was sold. Those new pockets were now bulging with all manner of arcane items: chalk, salt, rosemary, garlic, and dried rose petals, as well as his notebook and a selection of stubby pencils, all blue.

Thus attired, we set out for the Mall to search for the offices of *Smithsonian* magazine, wishing to inquire about their most recent address for my brother Erasmus, who occasionally wrote articles for them. Upon arriving, we learned that *Smithsonian* magazine was not published at the museum. Mab made a note of the proper address, and we spent the rest of our time wandering though the museums, gazing at all manner of wonders.

The Air and Space Museum was the most delightful, for everything there was new and amazing to us. The history of man's desire to fly was laid out in loving detail. Just seeing the kites, balloons, and early planes brought a sense of exhilaration. Walking its halls, I could almost imagine there were other mortals who loved flight as much as I.

Among the photos on display near the Apollo moon-shot equipment, we found a picture of NASA administrative officers that included, toward the back, a man who was the spitting image of my brother Ulysses. The photograph was over twenty-five years old—not much of a trail there.

AS the sun approached its zenith, Mab and I had walked slowly up the steps of the Lincoln Memorial. It was just before noon, but neither of us felt inclined to hurry. Mephisto had abandoned us to sit on the first tier of the monument's steps and tune his new lute. As he tuned the instrument, he spoke to it, telling it how, in the past, he had played for Bess of England, for King James I, for Louis XIV, and how once—on an occasion I myself well remembered—for the Queen of Elfland.

Mab halted partway up the steps. "Look, Miss Miranda, there's something strange going on. I've done my share of supernatural investigations, and I can tell you something all the manifestations I have tracked down in the past had in common: They didn't happen in plain view. And they most certainly did not happen at shopping malls, or in front of gas station attendants, or turn up in hotel lobbies!"

"What are you getting at, Mab?"

"That's just it, Ma'am, I don't know. The powers of Hell always prefer subtlety. No sane man makes a pact with the Devil with his eyes open. Demons have to hide their true nature if they wish to woo mankind into their fiery pits. So much overt action on their part is damned peculiar."

"It's not so different from past situations. What about the demon manifestations of the seventeenth century, the ones that resulted in so many innocent women being burned as witches? Or the incubi plague in Milan, about the time of Gregor's and Logistilla's birth, that Theo put an end to? Remember, no one but us saw the barghests last night. No adults, anyway, though a few customers will remember seeing a big dog. The shapechanger, I grant you, was unusual. But from what Theo says, he sounds like a special case."

"The point is, Ma'am, you've got to be prepared to find this beau of yours caught thick in the middle of this."

"He's not my beau," I objected.

Mab ignored my protestations. "His turning up now after a five-hundred-year absence is mighty peculiar."

"Which is why I agreed to meet with him," I agreed.

"Heck, he might even be the cause of our troubles," said Mab. "How did he get along with Mr. Prospero?"

I thought back through the haze of years, but it was difficult to recall my youth. Or, rather, it was difficult to distinguish between Shakespeare's version of events and the real events. I could recall the face of the young boy who played me the first time *The Tempest* was performed, and that of the buxom redhead who, many years later, had been the first woman to perform the role. I could even recall, in crisp detail, down to the smell of the greasepaint, a performance in Paris where I myself performed the role of Miranda. Not surprisingly, however, my memories of the real events, upon which the play had been based, were sketchy. The real events had happened only once.

Of us, only Cornelius had made a serious study of the Ancient Art of Memory—possibly because if he forgets the location of an object, he barks his shins. Erasmus originally learned this art from Giordano Bruno, back in the late sixteenth century, about the same time Father was winning the good graces of Queen Elizabeth by summoning a tempest to destroy the Spanish Armada. It was not until Cornelius lost his sight, however, that any of us took this art seriously.

Cornelius always believed Mephisto's madness had its roots in faulty memory. Cornelius theorized Mephisto's mind had become so overburdened by memories that it affected his sanity—though why this would be true of him and not the rest of us, Cornelius had no idea. At Father's urging, he spent the better part of the 1740s trying to teach Mephisto the Ancient Art of Memory. At first, Mephisto improved under his tutelage, but as with all attempts to cure Mephisto, the progress proved temporary. Cornelius eventually became irate and refused to waste more time on the project. To this day, he insists that Mephisto deliberately resisted his assistance.

To Mab, I said slowly, "Father was uncharacteristically cruel to Ferdinand when they first met on the island and then later claimed this behavior had been part of his plan." I frowned and rubbed my temples. "At least, that's what I think happened. Certainly, that's the way Shakespeare tells it, and he heard it from Father. Ferdinand might feel he had cause to dislike Father, I suppose. But why now? Unless, he had to wait all this time to catch Father at a moment of weakness."

"But Ferdinand doesn't want Father." Mephisto had come up behind us, lute in hand. "He wants Miranda!"

"You know, the harebrain may be right." Mab squinted thoughtfully. "Maybe he showed up now because he knows Prospero's not around to protect you." Mab glanced around, eyeing the columns and the expanse of lawn and monuments beyond. "Perhaps we'd better fortify our position."

I held up my flute. Its polished wood gleamed in the subdued light of the overcast sky. "On a windy day like this? Outside, in the open? This is all the fortification we'll need."

We reached the top step and stood before the temple to the youngest of the four American Gods of Liberty. Their goddess, a giantess, guards the New York City harbor. Passing between the enormous columns, the massive statue of the god himself gazed at us with sunken, piercing eyes. He sat enthroned, surrounded by marble walls bearing his immortal words and murals portraying his freeing of the slaves. Mab took off his hat and reverently recited the Gettysburg Address. The elderly tourists stared at him. Then, a few of the men took off their own hats.

As I waited for him, I wondered why I had agreed to subject myself to the humiliation of this impending meeting. Why was I not doing something productive, such as warning my sister or researching the question of whether my brother Mephisto was possessed by a demon.

Last night, once we had settled at the hotel, Mab and I questioned Mephisto at length about his disturbing transformation, but he claimed to remember nothing. When we pressured him, insisting he tell us something, he became frantic and frightened and began crying. Either he was a better liar than I remembered, or he did not know why he had turned into a demon.

Returning to my side, Mab scowled at my flute. "You should have left that thing in the car. You'll desecrate the temple." He glanced back up at the statue. "Wish I'd known about him back when he was alive. Could have asked him to free us Aerie Spirits while he was at it. Those blue Yanks of his would have put a quick end to that accursed instrument."

BACK outside, we waited at the top of the marble staircase. After gazing out along the mall for a time, Mab glanced sidelong at the Italian masonry workers near the far column and whispered under his breath, "Psst, Ma'am. Those guys look a bit like you and Mr. Mephisto."

I examined them more thoroughly. "They're probably Milanese, Mab. That one in the black T-shirt looks cold, poor fellow." I paused. "Must be a Jewish Italian."

The man in question, a dark-haired and wiry fellow with a black mustache and wearing a black T-shirt despite the cold, had a tattoo of the Star of David on his left arm. The other two, a youth and an older man, also wore the Star of David as a pin or on a chain.

"Odder than that! Notice his ring, and the patch on the jacket of the guy next to him. If I'm not mistaken, that is the compass and 'G' of the Freemasons." Mab noted.

"Well, they are masons," I said. "Or, at least, they are repairing the masonry, and this is D.C. Do you know that the Freemasons have a huge temple near here, in Alexandria? Dramatic-looking building too!" I laughed, "And to think that the Freemasons used to be a secret society. How times changed."

"All the same, it's mighty odd," Mab said.

"How so?" I asked.

Mab shrugged. "From all I've heard, the Freemasons are a Christian organization. Whoever heard of an Italian, Jewish Freemason?"

"Only in America!" I replied gaily.

HOW much the world had changed in a few short years, since America had risen to prominence. The young woman in the plum coat wore blue denim jeans instead of a skirt. The appearance of these modern women struck me as boyish and unnatural. But, oh, the things they did achieve!

As I looked at the young woman, her pretty face framed by her plum parka as she smiled up at her balding beau, I felt a moment of such sympathy that, for an instant, I felt as if I were her, a young wife gazing admiringly at my protective husband. I drew back, alarmed.

What was happening to me? First the elderly lady on the overpass, then Mephisto in Vermont, and now this. I could not recall ever before having seen myself as someone else. Could I be under some kind of attack?

I glanced rapidly about, but saw no sign of an enemy. Beside me, Mab snapped open his notebook. "What's this guy going to be like?"

"Arrogant and proud," I replied. "Didn't you see how cocky he looked leaning against the hotel counter? I'm sure he will breeze off his minuscule five-hundred-year absence with a few smooth words. After that? Who knows? Probably hit us up for money or something."

Mab closed his notebook and returned it to his pocket. I saw his arm tighten as his fingers curled about his lead pipe.

"I'd like to put a few obstacles in the path of his smooth words!"

"We should go." I glanced at my watch. "Father is in trouble and we have siblings to find! We've lost enough time as it is, trying to chase down Mephisto's staff."

Below us, footsteps rang out on the steps. The young woman in the plum coat turned to see who was approaching. Immediately, her expression became soft and dreamy, and her hand came up to smooth her hair.

"Ah," I said, "he's here."

I TURNED, and the shock of recognition hit me. Any doubt as to his identity dropped away, along with the pit of my stomach. My mouth opened, but my voice would not speak.

A tall youth came running up the steps. He wore a London Fog overcoat and a pair of fashionable black gloves. His head was bare, save for his thick wavy black hair. As he topped the steps and came before us, Mab held on to his pipe. Mephisto hefted his lute experimentally. Ferdinand did not even notice them. Falling to his knees, he took my hands in his and began kissing my fingers.

A strange dizzying sensation buzzed where the pit of my stomach had once been. I wanted to pull my hands away and slap him.

I did nothing.

"Miranda! *La mia 'nnamorata bella!*" He spoke with a charming Italian accent. "You did not have to wait!"

Mab looked at his watch. "No trouble, you're only ten minutes late."

"No, no!" Ferdinand's smile was brilliantly white. "Not wait today. Wait for me." He gazed up at me with liquid brown eyes. "*Cara*, no one would have thought less of you had you broken your vow."

I tried to answer, but still no voice came.

"Vow?" Mab asked. "What vow was that?"

Ferdinand stood. My hands were still in his. He met Mab's gaze.

"The vow she made when first we met." He squeezed my fingers and gazed into my eyes again. "That we would wed, or she would die a maid."

Had I actually made such a vow? I could have sworn that had been Shakespeare's invention. Yet, as my cheeks grew warm under his lingering gaze, I had to admit I could well imagine my naïve and youthful self uttering some such foolishness.

"Miranda, *bella*. Every day, while I dwelt in Limbo, I dreamed of your fair form. Yet, never did I dream that you, at liberty in the world of men, dreamed of me as well. How lonely you must have been throughout the ages! Had you forgotten me and wed another, I would have thought no less of you."

Nothing was happening as I had expected. This youth who gazed at me so adoringly was nothing like the cad I had painted him to be after he jilted me. Instead, he acted like the very same princely young man I first fallen in love with back on Prospero's Isle. Did he really believe I had never married because I had been waiting for him?

"Ferdinand," I said, forcing words through my numbed lips. "Where have you been?"

"As I just said, *bella mia*, I have been in Limbo." When I did not respond, he offered, "Limbo, by the gates of Hell?"

"You mean you were dead?" My heart ached, as if an old wound, long scarred over, had suddenly ripped open.

"No, my darling. As Odysseus, Aeneas, and Dante before me, I walked as a living man in the land of the dead. Only, it took me a little longer than they to return."

"How did you get out?" Mab asked.

"Who is this man?" Ferdinand looked from Mab to me.

"This is Mab. He works for me," I said. "And this is my brother Mephisto."

Ferdinand acknowledged each man politely, then answered Mab's question.

"About three months ago, the Gates of Hell were suddenly wrenched from their hinges," he said. "While the demons rushed to repair the damage, I escaped. It was . . . as if all my dreams had suddenly come true. I had never thought to see the sun again. . . ."

Mab and I exchanged glances. Three months ago would have been mid-September, the very time when Father disappeared.

I have unwittingly unleashed powers best kept bound, Father had written, before warning me of the Three Shadowed Ones. And then he had vanished, a prisoner in Hell, if the dark angel were to be believed. Could this wrenching of the Gates of Hell that freed Ferdinand be the same event to which Father referred? How could one *unwittingly* wrench open the Gates of Hell?

"The world is much changed." Ferdinand glanced down the steps toward where a car rumbled along the nearby road. "But it is still beautiful. Though not as lovely as you, my darling." Then, he frowned. Letting go of me with one hand, he reached up to touch my hair. "What happened to your tresses, Miranda? I had recalled them black as obsidian."

Ignoring his question, I said, "Ferdinand, how did you come to be a living man in Hell?"

"You did not know?" Ferdinand asked, shaken. "Oh, darling, how you must have railed at me for deserting you! I thought . . . I was certain he would tell you once time had passed."

"Who would tell me? Tell me what?"

Ferdinand frowned, looking down. "I am not certain now, after all this time, that I should speak of it. It will only bring you pain."

"Ferdinand. I am not the naïve girl you once knew. I've seen many painful things. Please tell me!"

Despite my calm words, my heart was pounding in my ears. I felt stifled and frightened.

"You bet he's going to tell us," Mab growled fiercely, slapping his lead pipe against his palm, "or we'll send him back where he came from, in the usual fashion."

"Do you recall the day before we were to marry, I changed our plans? Instead of spending the night in your father's *castello*, we would go directly to Naples?"

I nodded, vaguely recalling something about how Father had wanted to delay the wedding a few weeks, and Ferdinand had refused.

Ferdinand continued, "He came to me to tell me we must spend our wedding night in Milan. When I would not agree, he told me you were the priestess of an ancient goddess, who, like chaste Diana, would desert you if you wed."

"Eurynome is not a goddess," I interjected. "She is a divine emanation, similar to angels, but of a higher order."

Ferdinand nodded politely. "He said he needed her continued blessing. As we spoke, I realized he had meant for us to wed, so you would be confirmed as heir apparent to the throne of Naples, and then to slay me before we consummated our love. That was why he made such a fuss about our waiting for our marriage bed, back on the isle. I tried to escape, but he called upon unseen powers. The earth gaped below me, and I fell living into Hell."

"He?" I asked in a small voice.

"Your father, *dolce mia*. The dread and dire magician, Prospero."

"You lie!" I slapped him across the face.

The noise resounded down the staircase. The workmen and the couple in plum turned toward us. I pulled the hood of my cape up over my knitted hat and turned my back toward them, heat burning in my cheeks. Ferdinand came around in front of me.

"I wish my words were false, *bella mia*," he said sorrowfully. "For I recall how well you loved your father. But, alas, I cannot change what is."

"Let me get this straight," Mab interrupted. "You are claiming Prospero sent you living into Hell and left you there, never breathing a word to Miss Miranda? That doesn't sound like the Mr. Prospero I know."

"I do not believe you! Why would Father play such a cruel trick on me? It makes no sense. If he did not want me to wed you, why did he not just forbid me? Or, if he knew what you say he knew, why not tell me you had died? Why continue to let me believe you had wronged me?"

"He wished to rule Naples though our marriage, but not to let you lose your maidenhead. By allowing you to believe I had wronged you, did he not close your heart against other men?" Ferdinand asked.

Now, I felt as if I had been slapped. I drew back but said nothing.

Ferdinand frowned sorrowfully. "Miranda, my darling, had I known my words would bring you such pain, I would have torn out my own tongue before I allowed it to speak them."

"Yeah, yeah, all very melodramatic," Mab grunted. "Ma'am, there's a lot about this jilted-at-the-altar stuff I still don't get. How come you didn't just think he was dead?"

"I did at first and wept for days," I spoke flatly, recalling. "Then, a few months later, I met a Milanese sailor—one from that original ship that had foundered on Father's isle. He told a tale of having seen Ferdinand in a port in Spain. That was when I knew he had followed the longing for adventure he so often spoke of . . . or thought I knew."

"That man lied. Never would I have willingly deserted you so. Surely you know that in your heart."

I said nothing.

"*Dolce mia*, you are shaken," said Ferdinand. "Do not lose heart. Maybe there is an explanation. A demon in your father's form, perhaps? I have beheld demons in fiery Hell who know the subtle art of stealing another's shape. When I broke free, dread Prospero had not appeared among the souls in Hell. Does he still live? Let us confront him and ask him."

"Mr. Prospero is conveniently missing," Mab said sourly. "We were hoping you could tell us something about it."

Ferdinand shook his head. "I regret that I know nothing that could help you."

The wind whistled sharply. Its gusts were icy cold. The Italian workers had ceased their labor. Their eyes focused on us.

"Perhaps, we should go somewhere else," I said.

"Let us find a café and dine while we speak," Ferdinand suggested.

As the four of us walked down the steps, I murmured to Mab that Ferdinand had found a nice excuse to hit us up for a free meal.

"YOU say you escaped from Hell three months ago, Mr. Di Napoli." Mab pulled out his notebook and stubby pencil. "What have you been doing since?"

We were sitting in a pretty Italian café a few blocks from the Mall. I sat next to Mab, across the table from Ferdinand, who was next to Mephisto. I had thought this choice of seating wise but was beginning to regret it. It allowed Ferdinand to gaze directly into my eyes, which I found disconcerting. I could not tear my gaze away.

"When first I regained Earth's face, I found the sunlit world so bright I could not see," Ferdinand replied. "I stumbled blindly, my hands before my eyes. Kind women came—social workers—and led me to food and shelter. They insisted I speak to doctors dressed in robes of purest white, who told me my wits had fled. In my youth, I would have slain a man for such slander. But years of taunts from demons and the damned had caused calluses to grow against such abuse. The utterances of these doctors disturbed me not.

"Instead, I treated them with greatest politeness. They announced my madness—which they called amnesia—was not harmful to my fellow men and let me be. The kind women found a place for me at a hall of learning, where I could study the things the doctors claimed I had forgotten. So, now, I attend the University of Chicago, and, to repay the kindnesses shown me, I make use of my meager skills to impart to my fellow students knowledge of swordplay, history, and the languages of the classics."

"How did you learn English?" Mab asked. "You speak it awfully well for one who has been in America only three months."

"In Hell, there is naught for a living man to do but talk with the dead. And so, I have talked. At first, my Latin sufficed to allow me to converse with many learned men. To speak with men of slanted eye or dark skin, however, I needed to learn new tongues. After a time, the tongue of scholars turned to Spanish, then French. Later again, English became the language the learned spoke. Of late, even the learned among the Orientals and the Africans have spoken at least a smattering of this tongue."

"And how did you just happen to come by Miss Miranda's hotel in Chicago?" Mab glared at him accusingly.

Ferdinand threw up his hands as if to demonstrate his innocence. "I inquired at the dread wizard's office. I explained I was an old friend of the owner. The young person with whom I spoke had overheard the name of the hotel where Miranda planned to stay, and she passed it on to me."

My gaze remained fixed upon Ferdinand as he spoke. His face reminded me of the statues of the gods of old and left me with the same dreaded longing to possess such beauty. I could well imagine my well-trained receptionist forgetting her security protocol and blurting out secrets to this man. He answered Mab's question with calm assurance and measured words. Yet, all the while he spoke, his gaze drank in my face as a man newly emerged from the desert might sip from a cool mountain stream. I could not recall, within my long memory, anyone ever having looked at me that way, not even back when he and I were to be wed.

"What's Hell like?" Mephisto rested his elbows on the table and laid his cheek upon his hand, smiling at Ferdinand.

Ferdinand frowned. "I am not certain *cara mia* would care to hear the horrors. . . ."

"Just leave out the torture and dismemberment parts and tell us about how the place is set up," Mab suggested.

Ferdinand frowned, then shrugged. "Much is as Dante described it. Only the virtuous pagans of whom he spoke were nowhere to be found. Apparently, Christ took them with him when he broke out, much to my sorrow. I would have given all that was mine for a chance to converse with them."

"So there are nine circles, each with a guardian, and all that?" Mab asked, taking notes as he spoke. "And you lived in the First Circle, the one called Limbo?"

As Ferdinand nodded, the waitress came with our food. Ferdinand smiled at her and thanked her kindly. The young woman blushed, flustered. She remained, hovering at Ferdinand's elbow until Mab gave her a sharp look. Mephisto pouted. Waitresses usually fussed over him.

"Limbo is not properly part of the Devil's kingdom," Ferdinand said, wrapping his spaghetti skillfully about his fork. "It is instead the realm of the god of the dead. The shades there are not tortured. They are merely forlorn.

"Of the rest of Hell . . . myself, I have traveled only as far as the Sixth Circle. Having read Dante in my youth, I knew that if I could make my way to the bottom of the Ninth Circle, I could pass through the gate there and reach Purgatory, beyond. So, I tried to descend, but the Hellwind always caught me and returned me to Limbo before I could venture half so far.

"Twice in my journeys, I reached the red-hot iron walls of the City of Dis, on the Sixth Circle, only to be turned to stone by the Gorgon that the Furies have set to guard that wall. Once, I remained stone for over sixty years—counting by the dates uttered by the shades of the newly dead—before some fiend conducting an inventory of souls dragged me back to my proper place and restored me. Only once did I actually pass Dis's gates, and even then, I hardly got beyond the first row of flaming sepulchers before one of the fallen angels who patrol that foul city threw me out again."

"How did you get past the Furies?" Mab asked. To me he said, "You never know what might turn out to be important one day."

"I accompanied the angels of High Heaven during one of their raids. Every century or so, they swoop down from on high, burning with Heavenfire, their pinions too bright for any of us—of those below—to see. They draw up with them the souls of those who have truly repented of their former sins. I begged them to take me as well, but they said that I, being flesh, could not dwell where they were going."

"Why didn't you just kill yourself and go along?" Mab asked.

"The angels explained to me that were I to deliberately shed my mortal clay, I would find myself a tree in the Wood of the Suicides."

"Isn't the Wood of the Suicides in the Seventh Circle?" Mab wiped tomato sauce from his chin with the back of his hand. "Wouldn't you have been closer to the bottom, where you wanted to go?"

"True, but I would have been stationary." Ferdinand smiled into my eyes. I dropped my gaze, studying my calzone.

"So?" Mephisto broke in. "When are you two lovebirds going to get married?"

I glared indignantly at Mephisto, trying to douse the fire that had ignited my cheeks by an effort of will. Meanwhile, Ferdinand's gaze rested earnestly on my face, as if life and death itself depended upon my answer.

When I said nothing, he spoke. "*Bella mia*, if you wish time before you answer the question your brother has so artlessly yet aptly asked, I will not begrudge it to you. Yet, I would still take you, if you will have me."

"I have no interest in marrying." I spoke coldly in my effort to force my voice to remain calm. "You or anyone."

Ferdinand put his fork down slowly. "I understand, my darling," he said softly. "You are still the servant of the Diana goddess, are you not?" When I nodded, he asked. "Might you ever change your mind?"

"It is unlikely."

"I would it does not come to this." Ferdinand held himself proudly, but it was clear it took an effort to force the words from his lips. "But if it does. I would agree to wed you for a day, in name alone, in the courts of these American peoples, so the vow you swore to me would be satisfied. So long as we never came together as man and wife, you could send an emissary to the Pope in Rome and request the union be annulled. Then, you would be free to wed elsewhere, should you ever desire to do so."

"I will remember that." I dropped my eyes, for the look in his was too revealing. I decided this was not the time to explain that ending a marriage no longer required intervention from the Pope.

The waitress brought us our check. I began to pull out my wallet, but Ferdinand refused to allow me to pay.

"I will not take money from the woman who will someday be my wife," he said fiercely.

The waitress gave me a cold look. Recalling my quip about Ferdinand and the free meal, I felt ashamed. I suddenly wanted to do something to help him, but knew just as strongly that anything I offered would be turned down.

The four of us left the restaurant and stood together on the street.

"We must go," I said to Ferdinand. "We are about some business for my father. If you tell me where you are staying, I will contact you when we return. You already know how to contact me through Prospero, Inc."

Ferdinand nodded and gave us his address. Mab wrote it down. Ferdinand turned up the collar of his overcoat and stood gazing at me uncertainly. He glanced meaningfully at Mab and Mephisto. To my surprise, they both stepped away.

"Miranda." He drew closer until he stood too close. His hand came up and touched my cheek. Then, tilting my chin up until I could no longer avoid looking him in the eye, he said, "I cherish a hope that, given time, you will recall your love for me. For it would be a sin, indeed, if torn from each other by such unkind fates, we did not make use of this, our second chance."

He leaned toward me, and I knew he meant to kiss me. I stiffened and drew back. He hesitated, and then drew away slowly. Lowering his head, so his lips were near my ear, he whispered, "No. I see the time is not yet right."

He touched my lips lightly with one finger. Then, bowing, he turned and walked off into the windswept afternoon.

CHAPTER
TWELVE

Dances With Elves

The afternoon sun hung low over the aquamarine waters. The winds blew steadily upon our sails, as sparkles of golden sunlight danced over the curling waves. To the starboard, a flying fish broke free of its watery home before splashing back into the depths; overhead, seagulls wheeled and sounded their cries.

Mephisto, Mab, and I were sailing out of Charlotte Amalie, the busiest cruise port in the Virgin Islands. We had spent the night in Maryland, feeling it was too late for a long flight after our meeting with Ferdinand. Then, rising early this morning, we flew to St. Thomas, as there was no landing strip on St. Dismas's Island. Once there, we chartered the *Happy Gambit*, a spinnaker-rigged thirty-foot sloop, and set sail for Logistilla's.

The prevailing wind speed averaged eighteen knots. We bounded along at a goodly clip, with Aerie Ones shielding us from excess wind and spray. While I could not deny the appeal of sailing with the sheet in one hand and the helm in the other, the appeal of lounging on the deck enjoying the sun and wind was even stronger today. It had been months, perhaps years, since I had taken a day off.

I charted a course to St. Dismas's Island and sailed out of the harbor. When we reached open waters, I whistled up the winds and turned control of the helm over to the local Aerie Spirits.

The *Happy Gambit* was a beautiful cedar-strip sloop. I sat on the bowsprit, floating above the waves, a cool breeze blowing in my face. I had changed my attire and now wore a yellow-and-white sundress with a wide straw hat tied under my chin with a ribbon of bright yellow silk that fluttered about my face as I gazed at the sea. It had been a long time since I had been sailing. My own sailboat, the *Witchcraft*, sat neglected in some dry dock in Portland. Sitting there, watching the water reflect the sky as our boat leapt from swell to swell, I resolved to find time to take her out again.

Sailing brought back such happy memories. It was hard to feel troubled when caught between the sky and the sea. One could almost believe one was flying. The warm Caribbean sun beat down on my face, as our hull moved melodically through the waves. What a splendid afternoon! What lovely weather! I loved weather, all weather, not just the good kind. I loved balmy days, fearsome storms, blizzards, and spring showers. And the colors! Every day brought something to be admired: the soft feathery patterns of cirrus clouds, the deep, dark grays of thunderheads, the lacy gold and peach of the early morning sunrise. The sky and its moods called to me.

My childhood had been spent upon an island that was barely more than rock and heavens. The Aerie Spirits continually orchestrated storms at Father's behest. Hardly a day went by without the howling of winds and the crash of thunder, and I had reveled in every moment of it! That my brother Erasmus, who had known me nearly all my life, could believe I had asked for the flute because I desired to seize control of Father's servants was mind-boggling.

What a shock returning to Milan had been for me. Perhaps my long life might have taken a different direction if my father had married a woman who showed any kindness to my young self. When we returned from the island, Father had expected me to wed Ferdinand and leave for Naples, so he had not considered my welfare when he chose his next bride. Hoping to consolidate his power in Milan and keep his brothers at bay, he chose a daughter from a powerful family. Isabella Medici was a gorgeous young woman with dark glancing eyes and clever calculating ways. She had no time for a lovely stepdaughter who knew nothing about society or womanly arts. Since I was content to mope about the castle, mourning silently, she ignored me.

Father's counselor, the wise Gonzalo, who in prior years had warned my father against his brother's treachery and who had helped him and my infant self escape, took a keen interest in me and sought to cheer me; however, he passed on a year or so after our return, leaving me friendless.

With time, I recovered my spirits and took my first trek to draw Water of Life from the Well at the World's End. The well stands beside the place where the River of Stars plunges off the brink of the world, falling into the abyss of the Void in a cascade of silvery light, surrounded by a spray of stardust. The journey there and back takes a year and a day, during which I was gone from Father's court. By the time I returned, my grief banished and my spirits buoyed up by the wonders I had beheld, I had been forgotten. I was a living ghost, haunting the great stone edifice of my new home.

The night I had met Theo at the top of the Filarete tower, Isabella Medici had given a party in honor of my uncle Antonio. Everyone at the *castello* had been invited. Everyone, that was, except the duke's awkward, savage daughter, who did not know how to eat or speak properly or how to behave like a civilized person. It was not that I would have been turned away—oddities were always diverting—but, rather, that no one bothered to rouse me from my private retreat, or to provide me with a suitable dress, or for that matter, to take any thought about me whatsoever.

My father treated me kindly, of course, but he was a busy man. In addition to his ducal responsibilities, which he left mainly in the hands of his wife and his brother Ludovico, he waged a war within the *Orbis Suleimani*. The details of this struggle were never made clear to me, but he was constantly drafting letters and sending Aerie Ones off with missives. Also, he was still drunk with the wonder of having fathered sons.

Nor did it seem to occur to my father that I might need attention. I had seen to my own entertainment on the island and had been perfectly content. He seemed to assume the same would be true in Milan. Only, on the island, I had Aerie Ones as companions, and, in my younger days, Caliban as my playmate. In Milan, the Aerie Ones were still with us, but Father, fearing that I might be slandered with charges of witchcraft, had forbidden me to speak with them when anyone else might see. And so, I did not.

I did go once and ask him what he thought I should be doing with my time. He asked why I did not help my stepmother, attend her parties, and whatnot.

"She does not seem to want me underfoot," I had answered simply.

"Well, perhaps you should make yourself scarce, then," Father had replied absently, as he turned the page of a highly illuminated tome. And so, I had done so.

Thus it was that I climbed so often to the top of Filarete Tower, even on cold nights, to talk with my airborne friends and play the old silver practice flute Father had given me.

Even today, the Aerie Ones remained my closest companions; they were the only ones with whom I could share my thoughts, my joys. I had never met another mortal who felt as I did, particularly about the sky. Everyone else in my family favored one type of weather over another. Even my dear Aerie Ones did not entirely understand. They were too much a part of the natural world to savor its delight. When I played my flute, summoning up a storm or a perfect blue sky, I could feel my soul stirring as if I could escape the bonds of earthbound life and lose myself in eternity.

"MA'AM, we're being followed!" Mab's voice called from the stern.

"Motor or sail?"

"Sail."

I laughed. "You have got to be kidding!"

I roused myself and headed down into the cabin to get my flute, nodding to Mephisto, who was belowdecks making up his bunk. My brother often suffered from seasickness, so he wanted to have his bed ready, in case he felt the desire to slink below.

As I climbed back up the ladder, I called, "Earplugs, Mab!"

Planting my feet on the undulating deck, I played a brisk tune. The music leapt and danced, lightening my spirits even as it mocked our adversary. Within moments, the offending sailboat was blown far off course. Every time the harried sailor tried to change his tack, the wind switched directions. Soon, his sailboat was but a tiny spot on the horizon.

Mab took out his earplugs. He carried a cola, drinking it through a straw. "Did you see the guy sailing that boat, the one with the moustache? He's the same fella who's been following us since the hotel last night. I'm sure of it."

"Last night! You mean the hotel in D.C.?"

Mab nodded. "I think he's one of those masons from the Monument. The one with the tattoo on his arm."

"Maybe the masons overheard us talking about escaping from Hell, and it piqued their interest." A disturbing thought occurred to me. "Do you think one of them is trailing Ferdinand? Maybe we should warn him."

I climbed down into the hold and pulled out my cell phone. It read "out of range." Seeing the phone reminded me I had forgotten to check in with Mustardseed to confirm that everything was on schedule. The Priority Accounts were too vital to risk; too many lives were at stake. We would have to head back to St. Thomas.

I climbed back up through the hatch, flute in hand. The sun beat down upon my face, but a cool sea breeze soothed my skin and ruffled my hair. I inhaled the salty air and beheld the cerulean sky reflected in the azure water. Sitting down on the polished bench beneath the railing of the cockpit, I said, "Oh, what the heck! Let's just go. Surely, they can get along without me for a day."

Mab sat down beside me and pulled out his notebook. Despite the warmth of the day, he still wore his trench coat and fedora.

"A lot of weird stuff been happening of late, Ma'am. Maybe we should review and make sure we're not missing a clue. According to my notes," he flipped open the notebook, found the page he wanted, and surveyed it, "some of these we've already answered, but the unexplained mysteries I've got listed include: what happened to your father, the incubus showing up while we were in the Great Hall, finding Mephisto by chance on the street, Di Napoli showing up while we were in Chicago, finding the Chameleon Cloak right outside your brother's place, stumbling upon the crate with the gate to the nether realms. And now . . ." He paused to scribble something. ". . . this guy from D.C."

"Let's see." I leaned back and considered his list. "We think we know where Father is, but not how he got there or what he was doing when he got into trouble. The incubus you explained: we let the wards down when we opened the door—and it was able to get through the outer wards because the demons have Father and thus Father's blood. Finding Mephisto was my Lady's doing. I prayed to Her, and She showed me the way. The crate?"

Mab said, "It was in the warehouse visited by the demon who stole your brother's staff. I bet you, as we keep going, we'll find out that crate is involved in this in some way."

"You're probably right. That leaves Ferdinand, the Chameleon Cloak, and the guy who was just chasing us as still suspicious."

Mab crossed a few things out and made another note. "Right. So, tell me about this sister of yours, the sorceress with the *Staff of* . . ." Mab flipped through the pages. "Says here: '*Transmogrification.*' Does she turn men into toads?"

"And pigs, and bears, and fish, and dogs, and ravens, and horses!" Mephisto emerged from below, carrying his pocketknife and a chunk of pale wood for whittling. He had put aside his winter garments and now sported shorts and a bright blue Hawaiian shirt.

"Logistilla has a selection of seven shapes my father built into the staff," I continued. "But if she can catch a reflection in the green globe at the staff's top, she can reproduce it."

"Sort of a latter day Circe, eh? Sounds like an utter sweetheart."

"Oh, she's not so bad. She gave me my first pet unicorn."

"What was it before she got ahold of it?" Mab murmured.

I could not help smiling. Mephisto chuckled too.

"Probably an old lover. She loves turning old lovers into things." Mephisto pushed a coil of anchor rope aside and plopped himself down on the bench beside me. "I like her staff, but I liked mine better." He pouted sadly, recalling his missing staff.

"Forgot to ask Di Napoli where he came out of Hell." Mab paged through his notes some more. "Was it in Chicago? Or did he come out of a wooden packing crate? We've got to do something about that crate as soon as possible, Ma'am. I dispatched two Aerie Ones and a mundane to watch the warehouse and steal the crate; so we can ward it, like you suggested, but . . ."

I cut him off. "When we get back, Mab. Let's warn my family first. There'll be time enough to seal up a gate to Hell later . . . besides, if Father's really down there, we might need it."

Mab frowned thoughtfully. "What do you make of what Mr. Ferdinand said, Ma'am? About Mr. Prospero, I mean."

I took my time answering, gazing into the dark waters of our wake. The blue-green sea stretched out around us like a thousand-faceted living jewel, undulating and shimmering.

"I don't know what to think, Mab," I said finally. "I've known Father much longer than I've known Ferdinand. It's hard to believe . . ."

"So, do you miss him yet, Miranda?" Mephisto interrupted. "What a nice guy, that Ferdinand. I hope you marry him soon. Only, I still think you should marry the elf lord."

"Elf lord? I'm dead against it, Ma'am," Mab jumped in immediately. "Humans marrying elves is a bad business. I wouldn't get involved with a misalliance like that, if I were you. What elf lord is this, anyway?"

"One of the Lords of the High Council!" chimed Mephisto.

Mab whistled, awed. "How did you meet one of them?"

Sighing, I took off my hat and leaned back against the railing, letting the cool breeze blow through my hair. The *Happy Gambit* skipped across the waves like a rock tossed by a child. Bits of spray escaped our airy shield, wetting my face and neck.

"It was in the mid-1600s," I said, "during the reign of Charles I of England. We were on our way home from a party when we saw an entrance in the side of an old barrow where only earth and stone should have been. We came upon them by starlight, where they danced beneath the arching boughs, all lit by tiny floating sparks. They were tall and stately folk, and their music sounded of night noises, dew, and softly ringing harps."

"Ma'am, that sounds suspiciously like Elfland. A dangerous place. I trust you turned tail and ran home," Mab growled hopefully.

"Don't worry. We neither ate, drank, nor accepted gifts. But we did dance, and dance, and dance, and dance." How graceful those elves had been. No human partner had ever compared to that night. "When they left, Mephisto thought we should all of us, Father too, marry elves. He had one picked out for me, one of the high lords. I believe he had chosen the Queen of Elfland for himself." I laughed at the memory.

"You didn't accept any assignations, did you?" Mab asked accusingly.

"I never saw him again," I replied primly.

I neglected to mention to Mab that the elf lord and I had agreed to a rendezvous. We were to meet seven years later by the banks of the Avon. I went on the appointed day, garbed in a gown I had convinced Logistilla to make for me. It was of the finest gossamer silk from Cathay, a forest green concoction with a bodice of gold, the split skirts revealing a silver petticoat embroidered with golden lilies.

The fickle elf lord never came.

Meanwhile, Mab was snorting at Mephisto, "Queen Maeve is hardly your type!"

The motion of the sea had already gotten to Mephisto, for he looked a pale sickly green. Clutching the rail and staring morosely into the sea, he did not rise to Mab's jibe, but answered in a flat distracted tone: "I know."

THE sun sank beneath the waves. Above, the deep, shadowy, purple clouds were shot through with fiery rose. Below, the sea mirrored the glorious sky, differing from the original only where a stray island broke though the reflected clouds. I sat for a long time at my favorite perch atop the bowsprit, watching the beauty of color, light, and water until the first stars appeared in the twilight fields of the sky.

The sight of the stars a-twinkle brought back memories of the night in 1627 when we had come upon the elves dancing outside their howe. I recalled the smell of apple wood upon their bonfire, and the brightness of the sparks that shot up from it. How tall and fey the elves had been, and how disdainfully aloof the elf lords' regard. All except one, who had mocked his fellows for their poor taste and led me into the dance.

He had clasped me about the waist and spun me hither and thither, midst music and enchantment. Many a dancer wishes he could make his partner feel as if she were flying, but this time, we did fly! He whistled, and the winds picked us up, swirling us amidst star and cloud and sky. His eyes, filled with laughter, changed their color with his mood. In them, I saw myself reflected as a constellation among the stars. It was the single most marvelous night of my life. Even the joy of skimming along upon the sea, amidst an illusion of endless sky, does not compare to the exhilaration of actually being among the heavens. Only my childhood flight and the music of my flute in the midst of a tempest could even began to compare.

The sea was without question my next most favorite place. Amazed, I wondered how I had spent so much time away from it. Sailing was the first skill I learned after we left Prospero's Island. Ferdinand taught me on the trip back to Italy, when everything was brave and new. He had stood behind me, the length of his body pressing against mine, his hands guiding me, showing me what to pull or tie. We had laughed and laughed, once falling to the deck together to avoid the swinging boom. We had not been able to remain there long; the ship was crowded, and privacy rare. Yet, before he gallantly helped me to my feet, Ferdinand had stolen a kiss. I had blushed and called him "my most true love."

Pain squeezed my heart, the ache of a wound I had thought long healed. I recalled the agony of those first few weeks after what should have been our wedding day, when I was certain Ferdinand lay grievously wounded somewhere and I had been unwilling to admit he might be dead. My father treated me kindly, but I could tell he did not believe Ferdinand would return. At the time, I thought he believed Ferdinand dead, but would not dash my hopes. Later, I thought Father had suspected the truth—that Ferdinand had run off pursuing a life of adventure. Now?

Now, I did not know what to believe.

As the sunlight dimmed, so did my mood. Like a leaf in the autumn winds, my well-ordered life was suddenly tumbling every which way. I no longer knew whom to trust, save my Lady. My abiding faith in my father, whom I relied on and loved above all men, had been shaken from two sides.

And what of those sides?

Theo's speculation that Father held me enthralled in an enchantment was just that—speculation. I dismissed it. Ferdinand's claims were harder to deny and harder to accept. I could forgive Father's binding me up, should it turn out to be true, because I trusted him. If he had done it, he must have had a good reason.

If Father had condemned my love to Hell, I feared my heart would burst. What kind of good reason could a man offer for sending an innocent teenage boy to Hell?

Then, there were my brothers to worry about. Theo was dying. There was no way to be certain my calling upon his oath would successfully rouse him from his stupor. And, if it did work . . .

Alarmed, I sat straight up and wrapped my arms about my knees. I had sent Theo after Ferdinand! But, Ferdinand was innocent. I did not want Theo to kill him! Yet, if I called Theo off, there might not be time to find another way to engage his interest. This might be my last hope of saving my favorite brother. If it came down to my brother or Ferdinand—well, I had lived without Ferdinand this long. . . .

Finally, there was Mephisto! All these years, the family had assumed his madness was harmless. Yet, two nights ago in the warehouse, he had transformed into something bearing a sickening resemblance to a fiend of Hell. A frisson of terror tickled my spine when I remembered the disconcerting way he regarded me when we landed beside the car, right after I called upon my Lady! If Father sent Ferdinand to Hell, was he responsible for Mephisto's state, too? And what, if anything, was the relationship between this larger, seemingly more alert form and Mephisto's madness?

A LOUD bellow broke my reverie, followed quickly by a high-pitched screech. The disturbance came from the cockpit. Grabbing a stay, I swung myself back onto the deck and began clambering along the port side of the vessel, squinting in the dim light. After shimmying past the anchor and hurling myself along the sloping deck beside the cabin roof, I found Mab crouched over Mephisto. His gray trench coat spread behind him in the wind. His hands encircled my brother's throat, throttling him.

A lantern swayed upon the mast. In its light, Mephisto's face was blue. His eyes bulged, and his arms were flailing. The pocketknife he had been carving with had flown from his hand. His piece of carving wood clattered off the cabin wall near my foot.

"You scurvy, good-for-nothing lout!" Mab shouted. "I'll wring your scrawny neck!"

"Mab! Mab! Stop! What are you doing?" I cried, but Mab did not hear me. Mephisto made a gargling noise but could get no words past his strangled throat.

Putting my flute to my lips, I blew a harsh command. Mab jerked into the air and was thrown against the mast.

"What is going on here?" I demanded.

Mab slid down across the helm, his trench coat catching on the spokes of the wheel. Reaching the cockpit floor, he rose to his feet and yanked his coat free, growling. Mephisto rubbed his throat. He slunk up to sit upon the bench again and stared with sullen, hurt eyes at his attacker.

"Your lousy, no-good brother tried to cast a spell on me." Mab jabbed a finger at Mephisto.

"Mephisto?" I turned to regard my brother.

Mephisto recoiled, blocking his face with his hands. "Did not! I was just carving. I was sitting here, minding my own business—as quiet as you please—when your stupid bodyguard went wacko and jumped me!"

"I'm not her bodyguard." Mab stalked forward.

"Calm down, Mab. Nothing will be achieved by fighting." I stooped and picked up the wooden figure by my foot, holding it up near one of the lanterns. The bottom was still an unworked rectangular block. The upper portion vaguely resembled a human face and shoulders. The very top, however, clearly and skillfully resembled a fedora and its brim.

"He was just carving you, Mab. You have to be less paranoid. Not every image of you is meant for voodoo, you know. Please be more careful! You could have hurt my brother. I think you should apologize to him."

"Yeah!" Mephisto stuck out his tongue at Mab.

Mab ran his hand through his grizzled hair. "Begging your pardon, Miss Miranda, but I am the expert on thaumaturgy here. And when I say I felt a spell trying to bind what little is left of my freedom of will, I know of what I speak. Your brother was trying to cast a spell on me."

"Oh, for heaven's sake, Mab. This is harmless! It's just a piece of wood. Look. It's . . ."

I halted midsentence. Something about Mephisto's carving seemed strangely familiar. During our conversation on the way to Theo's, Mephisto had hesitated when I asked him how he had lengthened his staff. What had he said? Something about himself being able to make more compacts without Father's help?

A cold shiver traveled down my spine. Other than Father's magic, there was only one method I knew of to make compacts of that sort. Merciful Heavens, no wonder he hesitated! With what Hellish powers had Mephisto trafficked, and what price had he paid for it? His wits, perhaps? I thought of the great black demon with his shining sapphire eyes. His soul?

I turned on my brother. "Mephisto! Mab's right, isn't he? This was going to be a figurine, wasn't it, like the ones on your staff?"

Mephisto squirmed beneath my gaze.

"I . . . I thought he'd be useful," he blurted out. "Ever since Chalandra took my staff, I've been so lonely without my friends. You have so many windy friends. I thought you wouldn't mind if I borrowed one sometimes. Would you? Please?"

"No way," Mab hissed. "No bloody way. Not even if Hell freezes over."

I struggled to maintain my composure, fury seething through my veins. I was furious with Mephisto for daring to take something that was mine, and with Mab, for daring to attack a member of my family. My first concern, however, was to see that the incident not be repeated. Yelling at Mephisto would not make any impression.

When I could speak calmly, I said in measured tones, "Mephisto, your figurines only summon. They do not compel. What happens if the creature you summon doesn't want to cooperate with you when it arrives?"

Mephisto gazed at me in horror. His face went slack and drained of all its color. His eyes opened wide in terror. His lips worked, but emitted no sound. His breathing became labored and rough. I had meant my comment as a prelude to a tirade; however, Mephisto's reaction was so extreme that I reconsidered. Had he once summoned up something he could not control? If so, the mere memory of the incident was enough to petrify him.

"I'm sorry," Mephisto squeaked.

I nodded and turned away.

"That's it?" Mab fumed. "Aren't you going to throw him overboard? Or cut off his hand?"

"He's my brother, Mab. Besides, I don't think he'll do it again."

"'Don't think' isn't good enough, Ma'am. If you want any more help from me, you're going to have to do a bit better than that!"

The sails snapped loudly, jangling, as the boom swung across the ship. We ducked. When I rose, my voice was as soft as thistledown and as sharp as steel.

"Are you threatening me, Mab?"

Mab crossed his arms and stared back at me, eye to eye. "You can't intimidate me, Miss Miranda. I know I don't have much free will. But I cherish what I have above all other things. Now, you do more than slap that slaver's hand, or I won't do another stitch of work for you."

My voice remained deceptively calm. "Mab, I give you my word. It won't happen again. Now, I suggest we let this drop."

Mab jutted his chin out and stubbornly shook his head.

"Look, Mab. I'm not going to drown Mephisto. He's my brother. So we're stuck on this boat together, at least until we reach Logistilla's. Let's put this behind us and make the best of it."

"If this is the kind of treatment I get after all I've done for you, I'm sorry I even tried. And, I, for one, am not stuck anywhere. At any time, I can leave this body and wing away from here. Now, I suggest you tie up your brother, or I'm leaving." Mab straightened, eyes glaring.

Staring back at him, I raised the flute. "Not away from me, Mab! Never away from me!"

Mab scowled. He took off his hat and threw it down. It bounced against the deck.

"You win, Ma'am," he said bitterly. "But, if you want me to do something, you're going to have to make me do it. I'm not going to do anything your accursed flute can't force me to do."

Mab snatched up his hat and put it back on his head, pulling it low over his eyes. He continued sarcastically. "Go ahead, Ma'am, play your exalted piccolo. Do you want me to spend my time blowing your sails or scrubbing the decks? Your wish is my command, milady. Should you want me to speculate about who is following us, or to make some guesses as to where your father is? Sorry, lady, you're out of luck. I don't think you'll be able to find a song for that."

Turning his back on me, he climbed out of the cockpit and stomped off to glower by the stern.

CHAPTER
THIRTEEN

Never Traffic With Spirits, Ma'am

The last of the light died away as the colors of the sunset bled across the ocean. As the first star rose, I went to where Mephisto sat huddled under a sail tarp, staring out into the darkness.

"It's Wednesday," I said. "Let's take a look at the Ouija board."

As Mephisto rose groggily to his feet, I called good-naturedly, hoping that if I did not make an issue of our earlier argument, Mab would forget it. "Are you coming, Mab?"

He did not stir. Nor had he moved, not one quarter of an inch, not one hair, since our argument more than an hour before. He stood beside the binnacle, facing out toward the sea, shrouded in the night's gloom. Seeing him so motionless, I was struck by the flimsiness of his human disguise. No man could stand as motionless as he on a rocking sailboat. He looked like a man, but in times of turmoil, the inhumanity of his true nature revealed itself.

I ordered the Aerie Spirits to keep the ship on a steady course, and Mephisto and I climbed down the hatch. The cabin was of teak and brightly polished brass and smelled of linseed oil and disinfectant. Large wooden leaves, attached to a rectangular board that was sunk through the floor and secured to the keel, had been unfolded to form the chart table. Lanterns were fastened to the port and starboard bulkheads.

We set up the chart table and laid out the Ouija board. I used a compass to align the axis of the board with north, while Mephisto lit four tall bayberry candles and used melted wax to stick them to the rounded corners of the chart table. Then, we sat down on the bunks, facing each other, shook out our wrists, and each placed two fingers on the planchette.

Our attempt failed miserably. We could not agree on what questions to ask, and Mephisto kept pushing the planchette about the board instead of waiting for the spirits to guide it. Frustrated, I doused the candles and folded up the board. After saying goodnight to Mephisto, I climbed into my bunk and prayed; however, my Lady had no wisdom for me tonight. Closing my eyes, I drifted off into sleep.

I STOOD *by the ocean on a stormy night. Hurricane winds beat the shore, as strong as those Ariel stirred up to force Ferdinand and his father onto our island so long ago. Only this time, the winds blew Ferdinand away from me. At least he looked like Ferdinand, though as is the way with dreams, I felt certain it was actually someone else. He called to me with outstretched arms; however, the wind ripped his words away before they reached my ears.*

The seeming Ferdinand refused to be daunted. He struggled toward me, and I toward him. My hair whipped about in the roaring winds. We drew close, almost touching. He bent his head, his lips near mine.

A lightning bolt struck the ground between our feet. A tremendous crash rent the sky and the air smelled of ozone. He was tossed back, sprawling across the sand. The lightning bolt arched its neck and brought its spiral horn down to hover just above his heart. The figure with Ferdinand's face scrambled backwards.

An enormous wave crashed between us, drowning the beach. The land where he stood receded from me. He ran to the forward tip of his landmass, screaming through the roar of the wind. Secure behind my wall of lightning, I could not hear him.

As the windblown figure of Ferdinand dwindled, there came a momentary lull in the storm. His words carried across the distance. "She's not a guard, she's a jailer!" he called. "Look, it is you who are imprisoned, not I!"

Now, I stood upon an island besieged by angry waters on every side. The island was no more than ten feet across. Upon it, I was alone but for a windswept oak. Girded about the island was a low railing of lightning, similar to the fence that girded the unicorn's enclosure in medieval tapestries. Here and there, among the posts and cross rails of electricity, I could make out the proud head and horn of unicorns facing the storm.

I WOKE, my heart pounding as I lay shivering in my bunk. Pale starlight came through the porthole above me. The dream seemed hauntingly real, and that sensation awoke my suspicion. I stirred to go find Mab, then stopped, as I recalled our recent argument. Softly, I swore. I needed Mab, and dream interpretation was not the sort of skill I could force with the flute.

Yet, the mere idea of allowing any spirit to roam free, even a spirit as well-mannered as Mab, left me feeling sick to my stomach. I had walked through the aftermath of too many supernatural battles, seen too many shattered towns, and too many broken, bleeding children, their lives destroyed by brawling sylphs or warring oreads or unrestrained djinn, to believe mankind could live in peace with unbound spirits.

In my youth, before Father started Prospero, Inc., earthquakes, tidal waves, tornadoes, and vast forest fires—the outward manifestations of spirit violence—were far more common and destructive than they are today. Those disasters, however, were nothing when compared to the magnitude of the catastrophes that took place before King Solomon bound the Four Lords of the Elements. Modern treatises do not correctly portray the magnitude of past natural disasters. Few chroniclers survived to describe the incidents. Where they did, their works have since been edited by the *Orbis Suleimani*. Scientists cannot agree on what destroyed the dinosaurs, but Mab could tell you.

Now, here was Mab, carrying to the extreme his affectation of having the feelings and rights of mankind. His pretensions infuriated me. I wanted to pick up the flute and dance him around the deck like a puppet to remind him of his true nature. Yet, I knew if I did, he would never forgive me.

As I wondered again why Father had given Mab that body of clay, an answer occurred to me. It was so astounding I cried out, oblivious of the sleeping Mephisto in the bunk across from mine.

Father had promised, when he first freed Ariel from the pine, that he would let the Aerie Ones go at the end of a millennium—half of which had already passed. Yet, Father did not want them free to strafe mankind again. Only recently, a tussle between Aerie Spirits and watery ones resulted in the flattening of houses in Florida and the destruction of levees in Louisiana, and that was while they were bound!

If Father wanted to keep his power in the world of spirits, he could not break his word. He needed to find a way to free the Aerie Ones, and yet keep them from harming mankind. His two options were: bind them anew, or teach them self-discipline! Creatures with self-discipline need not be bound by magicians. They could rule themselves by following the guidance of their conscience.

Only two ranks of beings acted with discipline: angels and men. Angels looked directly to God to set their course, and so could not be truly said to have self-discipline. That left men. Could Father have given earthly bodies to a few Aerie Ones as part of an experiment to determine whether they could learn self-control? If Mab could learn to rule himself, he could safely go free.

I could not free Mab, now, without destroying the flute and freeing all the Aerie Ones. Nor would I maim Mephisto to placate him. Yet I needed him. Not only did his notebook contain all the clues to our current adventure, but he was also the demonologist and the thaumaturge. He had recognized both the figurine and the Irish Setter as supernatural far before Mephisto or I would have. Nor would I have wanted to try my hand at disenchanting the Unicorn Hunter's chameleon cloak. Theurgy is my specialty, not thaumaturgy.

Then there were Mab's mundane detective skills. He knew how to check with credit bureaus and find people's bank account numbers. I still did not know the whereabouts of Erasmus, Titus, or Ulysses. I doubted I could find them without Mab's help.

And finally, there was the fact that I liked him. He made a pleasant companion. I prayed to my Lady again, this time asking specifically for guidance in dealing with Mab. For a long time, I received no response. Undaunted, I maintained my vigil. When an answer finally came, I picked up the wooden figurine Mephisto had carved and climbed the ladder to the deck.

THE dark form in trench coat and fedora stood motionless beside the helm, silhouetted by the moonlight. I padded forward quietly and pressed the wooden figurine into his hands. As his fingers curled about it, I spoke the words that had come to me—though they stuck in my throat.

"I am sorry, Mab. I apologize."

Mab turned toward me slowly, his face obscured under the shadow of his hat.

"Words aren't enough, Miss Miranda. What are you planning to *do* about it?"

How dare he speak back to me in such a fashion! Mab had worked with me long enough to know how rarely I apologized. That should have been enough for him. I wished I had brought the flute with me. A few well-chosen toots, and he would be curbing his manners!

I listened for my Lady again, but Her words made me balk. I had never hesitated to obey my Lady before—but surely there must be some mistake. Perhaps I had misunderstood. I dared to ask a second time, but the answer remained the same.

Obediently, I spoke them. "Whatever punishment you feel is just, Mab. What would you have me do to Mephisto?"

Whatever Mab had expected, this was not it. He cocked his head, taken aback. The moonlight now fell upon part of his face. A flash of bitterness crossed his craggy features, and his mouth opened as if he meant to make a quick retort. Apparently, he wisely thought better of it, for he shut his mouth and, screwing up his face, scratched his stubble.

"I guess we can't really kill the nut," he said at last. The coldness had drained out of his voice. "But he is a danger, Ma'am! And not just to me. He probably alerted Osae the Red to our position by pulling out that cloak, and he definitely caused the barghest attack when he tore open the crate.

"Okay. Just see that he doesn't do any more carving while I'm around, and when we get back to the mainland, he goes! You don't have to kick him out the second we touch down. I mean it's all right with me if you get him an apartment or leave him with a brother or something. But he goes. No more staff stuff."

"Very well," I said, although my heart was heavy.

Still, I was relieved he had not asked me to cut off Mephisto's hand.

ONLY the faintest moonlight shone through the portholes. Outside, we could hear the creak of the rigging, and the pounding of the waves against the hull. I sat on my bunk, a white lace dressing gown secured tightly about me. Beside me, Mab sat hunched, gazing intently at the curling calligraphy of the antique Ouija board. Across from us, a yawning Mephisto blinked owlishly in Hello Kitty pajamas.

Mab pulled out a silver cigar lighter and held it up to the first candle. Then, he lowered it again, turning it between his fingers.

"Ma'am, I'd like to go on record as objecting to this procedure. I realize you humans think of this Ouija board as a toy, but magic is never a game, Ma'am. It's a deadly serious business, as in: if you don't take it seriously, someone will soon be dead. Mortals should never traffic with spirits, Ma'am."

"I appreciate your candor, Mab. Now, let's get started."

"But what about all the salt you spilled on the floor, Mr. Bodyguard? Won't that protect us?" asked Mephisto.

"Bah! Table salt is good against your run-of-the-mill spirit—if you don't invite them to cross! But this board acts like an automatic invitation. As soon as I light the candles, it will invite every ambient spirit within leagues to pop over and offer us their opinion. Compels 'em to tell the truth, within certain limits, but that's about all the protection it offers. Stinking way to do business, if you ask me."

"Then, why did you waste the salt? Or did you just pour it for fun?" my brother asked. He peered under the table and presumably poked his toe at the salt circle Mab had drawn upon the deck. Mab slapped his arm.

"Cut that out! What little good it might do will be undone if you break the circle! As to what protection it offers?" Mab shrugged. "Well, it's about as effective as locking the barn door while blasting a hole in the back wall of the horse's stall. If, on the off chance, it should turn out the horse can't squeeze through the hole, at least he won't get out by the front door."

"It was Theo who suggested . . ." I began.

"Mr. Theo also suggested that using magic damned the soul, Ma'am. He would not be participating were he here tonight. Good man, your brother."

"Thank you, Mab. Your concerns are noted," I replied crisply. "Do either of you have any questions you want asked?"

"Let's ask what God eats for lunch," suggested Mephisto.

Mab glowered at Mephisto. "This is a serious matter, chump! And if I catch you pushing the planchette, I'm taking off some part of your anatomy. Besides, everyone knows what gods eat—nectar and ambrosia."

"Gentlemen, please! We only have a few minutes of Wednesday left. If neither of you have any pressing questions, I will begin by asking whether my dream tonight was normal or a visit from an incubus."

"What dream?" Mab asked sharply.

"I had a dream. There was something odd about it."

Mephisto giggled. "Oh, Miranda, you're such a dopey-head! Just because you dream about sex doesn't mean there's an incubus haunting you."

"Not that it's any of your business, Mephisto, but I did not dream about . . . intimate relations." I was glad the darkness hid my face.

Mephisto cocked his head to one side. "Then what made you think it was an inkie?"

"The Unicorn came to defend me."

My brother's mouth formed a soundless "O."

Mab swore. "Geesh! Okay, let's get cracking. Remember—ordinary humans may play with this board, but they don't have enchanted garbage hanging off their persons by the bucket load. So, as soon as I light these candles, everyone shuts up. Miss Miranda will ask the questions, and even then, only when her hand is touching the planchette. She will start with "Yes" and "No" questions, and only move on to more elaborate answers once communication has been established. If anyone else has to say something, put out the candles first. Or better yet, write it down. Here's a paper and pencil."

Mab ripped a page from his notebook, pulled an extra stubby pencil from his trench coat pocket, and handed them both to Mephisto. "Ready?"

When Mephisto and I nodded, Mab lit the candles. The three of us shook out our wrists and each rested two fingers on the planchette.

I closed my eyes, preparing. The bunk rolled beneath me as the sailboat skipped from wave to wave. The pleasant aroma of bayberry and burning wick drifted through the cabin. In the distance, a bell buoy clanged.

Opening my eyes, I asked, "Was I visited by the incubus Seir of the Shadows in my dream tonight?"

Immediately, the planchette wiggled and shot across the board to cover the "YES."

Mab pounced on the candles, extinguishing their fires, and plunging the cabin into darkness.

"You pushed it!" came Mab's accusing growl.

"I did not," Mephisto objected hotly. To my eyes, he was but a faint shape in the murk. "Why would I want Miranda to believe a dopey thing like that?"

"Gentlemen!" I commanded. "Time grows short. Let's try again."

"You might want to make your questions simpler, Ma'am," Mab said to me as he prepared to light the candles again. "If you had gotten a 'No,' you would not know if that meant 'There was no incubus,' or 'The incubus was not Seir of the Shadows.' "

"True. However, we are short on time. A 'Yes' answers both questions at once. I can always ask the simpler version if we get a 'No.' Shall we continue?"

Mab shrugged and relit the candles. We put our fingers on the planchette again. I asked the same question. The planchette moved under my fingers, traveling rapidly to cover the "YES."

A chill traveled down my spine. So, it had been a demon! How disturbing. And how nasty of Seir to appear as Ferdinand!

It was one thing to suspect a dream of being more than it seemed, but it was quite another to discover it was true. I felt uncomfortable, as if my most private sanctum had been invaded. I wondered what precautions could be taken to protect against future incursions. I wished I could ask Theo, but perhaps, Mab would know.

Still shaken, I moved on to the next question.

"Can Seir appear out of any shadow, anywhere?"

The planchette trembled, then began sliding across the board.

"NO."

Mab scribbled furiously with his left hand, having put his right hand on the planchette. It took me a moment to decipher his loopy scrawl.

"Only where he is invited?"

"YES."

Mab scribbled down two more questions. I read them in order.

"Is a vocal invitation sufficient?"

"YES."

"Is just saying his name, without intending it to be an invocation, sufficient?"

"NO."

Mab breathed an audible sigh of relief. I gave him a reassuring smile before I realized he probably could not see me in the near darkness. Meanwhile, Mephisto leaned over and began scribbling on the paper. Unlike Mab and me, he had put his left hand on the planchette, so he wrote with ease.

His note read: "Does line of sight act as an invitation?"

The board answered "YES."

So, if he could see us in the distance, he could step out of a shadow beside us. Eerie and disturbing, but point to Mephisto for thinking of it.

Taking a deep breath, I asked, "Is the man who introduced himself to us as Ferdinand Di Napoli a shapechanger?"

The planchette hesitated. In the silence, my heart seemed to be thumping loudly. Was this pause a suspicious sign? Or, was it just that the name of Ferdinand Di Napoli was not as familiar to these spirits as the Three Shadowed Ones?

Eventually, it moved again. "NO."

That was a relief! I decided to leave YES/NO questions and move on to more chancy territory.

"Where has he been the last several hundred years?" I asked.

The pause was shorter this time. Then, the planchette began moving, pausing here and there atop the handsome letters on the quaint antique board. Mab scribbled quickly, noting the pauses. The letters it hovered over spelled out:

"I-N—H-E-L-L."

Having moved beyond YES/NO queries, I asked another question that set my heart hammering.

"Where is my father?"

The answer was the same: "I-N—H-E-L-L."

This only confirmed what I already suspected, yet it was all I could do to keep from exclaiming out loud. Mab's fingers went rigid on the planchette, and Mephisto gasped. The candles flickered. The hairs on the back of my neck stood on end. I pushed on quickly.

"Is he alive?"

"YES."

My mouth had gone dry. I let out the breath I had not even realized I had been holding.

"How did my father come to be in Hell?"

"T-H-E—T-H-R-E-E—S-H-A-D-O-W-E-D—O-N-E-S—C-A-P-T-U-R-E-D—H-I-M—B-A-E-L-O-R—O-S-A-E—S-E-I-R."

"Who holds him now?"

"T-O-R-T-U-R-E-R-S—F-R-O-M—T-H-E—T-O-W-E-R—O-F—P-A-I-N."

"What was Prospero doing when he was captured?"

A pause then.

"T-H-E—S-E-C-R-E-T-S—O-F—D-R-E-A-D—P-R-O-S-P-E-R-O—A-R-E—U-N-K-N-O-W-N—T-O—U-S."

I shifted nervously on the bunk. I had forgotten how disturbing séances were. The air hummed with tension and the feeling of unseen presences. While I found the company of Aerie Ones soothing, these lesser spirits made me distinctly uncomfortable. I began to recall why it was that I had chosen to run the business side of things and leave the actual practice of magic to Father and Erasmus.

"What is one plus one?" I asked suspiciously.

"Two."

"Hmm." I burned to ask: "What happened to the mind of my brother Mephisto?" and "Why does he turn into a giant black being that looks disturbingly like a demon?" However, I did not know how Mephisto would react. If he objected or cried out, the results could be deadly. Reluctantly, I postponed the investigation of those questions.

I already knew the board could not answer my most burning question: "What is needed to become a Sibyl?" In past séances, years ago, I had asked the question numerous times in a myriad of formats. The spirits moving the planchette were not privy to Eurynome's secrets.

I returned to the subject of the Three Shadowed Ones.

"What can you tell us about Baelor of the Baleful Eye?"

"H-E—R-E-A-D-S—M-I-N-D-S."

What are the limits on his power?"

"E-Y-E—C-O-N-T-A-C-T—O-R—T-O-U-C-H."

As Mab scribbled down a question, I felt another chill travel down my spine. Suddenly, I wanted to put out the candles and climb back into my bunk. Mab was right. Humans were not meant to meddle with magic. I reached toward the candles.

Mab handed me his question. It was one he had asked earlier. After our recent spat, I was hesitant to disappoint him. I glanced up at the brass clock. It read five minutes to midnight. What could another five minutes hurt? I read the question aloud.

"Where did Ferdinand Di Napoli emerge from Hell into the daylit world?"

The planchette hesitated for a long time. Finally, it began moving slowly across the board, spelling out:

"E-L-G-I-N—I-L."

I stifled a gasp, but Mephisto was not so reserved. He blurted out: "Isn't that where Gregor is buried?"

The planchette began moving, jerking and pausing about the Ouija board. Like children listening to a ghost story, we awaited its answer; our breath held, the hair on the nape of our necks rising as the planchette spelled out:

"N-O—L-O-N-G-E-R."

CHAPTER
FOURTEEN

Logistilla

A candle flickered out; smoke rose from its dead wick like a ghostly rope. Mab leapt to his feet, gripping his trusty lead pipe, a finger pressed against his lips. He stood alert and motionless, slowly slipping his free hand in the pocket of his trench coat. Spinning, he threw a handful of table salt toward the port stern.

There was a screech, and a high-pitched voice issued from the back of the cabin, crying out: "*Fools! A curse upon the Family Prospero! By Twelfth Night, your doom shall be sealed. I go now to fetch my masters, the Three Shadowed Ones!*"

"Wait! I compel . . . Darn, it's gone!" Mab struck the table with his fist.

The flame atop the candle in the far corner, by Mephisto, leapt from its taper. It ignited the curtain beside Mephisto's bunk. Mephisto screamed and scrambled backwards. I grabbed for my flute, but could not think of any use I could put it to in this enclosed space.

"Where's the fire extinguisher?" cried Mab.

COUGHING and panting, we spilled out onto the deck. The smell of smoke clung to our clothes. Foam whitened Mab's hair and clung to his eyebrows.

"Next time, I use the extinguisher, not Rabbit-for-Brains, here," he growled, mopping his face.

"Sorry!" Mephisto still held the red fire extinguisher in his hand. He did not look the least bit repentant. "But I did stop the fire. That was good, right?"

"Darn that spirit!" Mab pounded his fist into his palm. "I would have liked an opportunity to get an explanation of that last Ouija board comment. What did that mean: 'No longer'?"

I would have replied, but the purr of a motorboat behind us distracted me.

"That spirit! It fetched the Three Shadowed Ones!" I peered into the darkness. "Mab, get the binoculars and the starlight scope!"

Still disgruntled, Mab disappeared down the hatch, returning with the scope. Making his way to the stern, he put it to his eyes and peered at the approaching boat.

"Is it Mr. Moustache?" yelped Mephisto. "Shall I let him have it?"

"With what? Your lute?" Mab muttered under his breath. "Yep. It's the same guy. That dratted spirit must have alerted him to our whereabouts! I see he got smart and came back with a motor this time."

"If he's working for our enemies, we don't want him to catch up with us, and we certainly don't want to lead him to my sister's!" I started down the ladder to take a look at the charts and fetch my flute.

"What can we do to help, Ma'am?" asked Mab.

"Reef the sails, batten down the hatches, and put in your earplugs," I replied. "We may be in for a ride!"

A LONE motorboat sped across the black twinkling ocean. As Mab and Mephisto secured the sails, I stood by the helm, my long slim instrument poised at my lips. Softly at first, the lilting strains of the "Hall of the Mountain King" could be heard across the darkened sea. The warm night breeze stirred and tugged gently at our shortened sail. As the beat quickened, and the music grew louder, the sailcloth tightened, growing taunt. So wild and raucous grew my flute's refrain that I had to resist throwing back my head and laughing with joy, forgetting to play.

Our sailboat surged forward. The motorboat increased its speed, attempting to intercept us. Faster and faster, my fingers flew across the flute. The winds howled, and the mast creaked. The waves grew, lifting pale-crested heads above the sable water. The motorboat leaped from one to the next, becoming airborne, then smacking down against the water. Before our path, however, where the green and red beams of our starboard and port lights fell, the sea was as smooth as glass.

Three times we pulled ahead of him, only to have him catch up again. By this time, we were quite close to our destination. If we wanted to lose him before we reached my sister's island, we were running out of time. Sparing a second to close my eyes, I consulted my Lady as to how to escape this menace, but no reply came.

Ahead, silhouetted against the night, were several small isles barely larger than boulders. A narrow passage ran between them. We sped toward it.

Again, louder than the swelling music, came the creak of the mast. I spared it an appraising glance. Our craft was rented, and I was uncertain of its condition. I regretted not having asked Mab to reef the sails more tightly.

The isles loomed before us. I could make out three great rocks rising from the waters between them. Measuring carefully, I found a single course between two boulders where a sailboat of our size could pass. It was a narrow passage, a very narrow passage. It would be madness to navigate it in the darkness, much less at this speed.

The motorboat was drawing closer. I could make out the face the man who manned it. He was gesturing elaborately and shouting, though I could not make out his words. Was he casting a spell? We had to lose him before we approached St. Dismas, or we would lead the Three Shadowed Ones directly to my sister's house!

A solution occurred to me, but it was risky. I closed my eyes again, praying for guidance through the obstacles ahead. This time, I felt Her presence immediately. With Her, there was no risk—"neither shadow of turning."

Returning to the deck, I doused the port and starboard lights. Pausing, I took a deep breath of the salty air, and listened to the clang of the red and green bell buoys, as they warned sailors off the rocks. The pale moon hung in the west amidst a field of stars stretching both overhead and underfoot.

I went to the helm and released the spirits who were piloting the ship.

"What are you doing?" Mab asked sharply.

"Giving over navigation of the ship to a higher power." I rested my hand on the wheel and closed my eyes.

Mab suddenly saw the rocks ahead. "Oh, Geesh! No. Please tell me we're not going in there? Jiminy Christmas! We're all gonna die!"

Mephisto just squeaked.

We raced toward the rocks. I felt the ship leap and lurch beneath me. The mast creaked ominously. Mab had taken off his trench coat and was preparing to leave the boat—and his body, if necessary. Mephisto sat on the bowsprit, shouting with exhilaration.

As we approached the deadly boulders, I suddenly felt fear. What if Mab was right? What if I lost my Lady's direction for even a moment when the crucial time came? We would all die, and my hubris would be at fault. I clutched at the helm and started to change our course.

The warm breath on my face remained steady, a soft, loving presence, comforting even as it led. Reassured, I banished my fear and closed my eyes,. She had never let me down. Why should I doubt?

Without opening my eyes, I followed my Lady's warmth, shining upon me like a searchlight, and sailed my ship through the narrow passage in the rocks. The craft lurched, and the mast creaked again. Mab muttered, and Mephisto screamed. My eyes nearly flew open at the last, but I remained calm and trusted my Lady's direction. The bell buoys clanged again, and I felt the presence of the boulders to either side, sliding silently by like great ghosts.

From behind came a resounding crash. Then, there was open water beside us. We had made it. Our pursuer failed to navigate the narrow passage. We were free of him. As I cheered, the warm beam of my Lady's regard vanished. I shivered, suddenly cold.

Before us lay the open sea and then St. Dismas's isle. Keeping my hand on the wheel, I sailed us around to the south side of my sister's island, where the natural harbor lay. As our craft slid up to the dock, I let go of the helm and breathed normally again. Mab dug the earplugs out of his ears, and Mephisto clapped weakly.

"What a ride!" He smiled wanly and sank to sit cross-legged on the deck. "At least we're safe now."

From the beach, an eerie green light flared, blinding us. Mephisto threw up his hands before his face. Behind the light, a woman's voice cried out.

"Invaders, you will not triumph. My power exceeds yours. Your companions have all been subdued. I grow tired of these attacks. This is your last warning. Surrender now, or face my ire!"

AS my eyes adjusted to the glare, I saw the greenish light emanated from a round ball on the top of a long staff. The sphere was held in place by seven prongs, each carved to look like a different animal. Holding the staff aloft, illuminated in its pale glow, stood my sister Logistilla. The high pointed shoulders of her enchanted robes gleamed in the eerie light. Its long split skirts blew about her, showing glimpses of a pale leg.

All around her, snarling beasts roamed the pale strip of sand. Wolves, panthers, hyenas, and wolverines slunk about her. They growled toward the ship, or rubbed against her legs. Their eyes glinted green in the light of her staff. From the waters came the gleam of other eyes: crocodiles, maybe, or perhaps, hippopotami. To the rear, near the forest, there lurked a hulking shape that could only be a bear.

"Hi, Logistilla! You can call off your bully boys, it's me!" Mephisto leapt up. He ran to the front of the boat and leapt up on the prow, spreading his arms. "Don't you recognize me?"

Logistilla lowered her staff and spoke in her husky voice. Her jet-black hair—as black as mine had once been—came to a widow's peak above her forehead. Her face was oval-shaped, and her nose Roman.

"For God's sakes! Mephisto! How dare you scare me like that! Getting me out of bed in the middle of the night, as if I had nothing better to do than dance attendance on my lunatic brother!" Turning to the beasts milling about the beach, she said, "Back off, boys. You'll get no dinner here."

The beasts slunk away into the forest. Logistilla examined the ship. Peering through the darkness, her eyes touched on me briefly.

"No! No guests, Mephisto! I can barely tolerate you as it is. The bonds of family affection do not stretch far enough to cover your trollops. If you bring her in, I . . . I won't be accountable for what happens to her." Logistilla toyed with her staff, glancing back and forth between me and the seven animal figurines carved into the staff's length.

"Sorry to disappoint you." I stepped over the rail and onto the dock. "But it's your big sister, Miranda."

"Miranda?" Logistilla raised both eyebrows. "What a surprise! Who would have thought you'd dig yourself out of your den long enough to look in on the rest of us? But, oh, I forget myself. How presumptuous of me to assume you came by to look in on your sweet younger sister. I had forgotten. The ice queen Miranda never does anything if it is not for the profit of Prospero, Inc. Not in the gown I made for you, I see. Too good to wear your sister's offerings?"

"This is my night dress," I replied, annoyed. "It's the middle of the night."

"Sure, sure, always full of excuses . . . who is this?" Logistilla eyed Mab as he climbed out of the sailboat onto the short dock. Mab raised a hand between himself and Logistilla's staff.

"Get that thing out of my face, Lady. I'm not afraid of you. You can't hurt anything but my bod—" Mab stopped and walked up to Logistilla, peering closely into her face. "Now I recognize you. I thought there was something familiar about that witch statue back at Prospero's Mansion."

"You've met?" My voice rose in surprise.

"Yeah." Mab stuck his thumb toward Logistilla's face. "This fleshly body I'm wearing? She made it."

Mab's news amazed me, yet I felt foolish for not having guessed. My only consolation was that Logistilla, who should have recognized her own handiwork, seemed as amazed as I.

"You're one of Papa's Aerie Ones?" She stepped closer and lowered her staff, shining the pale greenish light in Mab's face. She peered at his hand as he moved his fingers and thumb. "How amazing! You do that very well. I almost took you for a human."

"Funny, I almost took you for a human too," Mab growled back, glaring at her. He was irked, though whether at being mistaken for a human or at not being mistaken for a human, I could not tell.

Logistilla gave Mab a last look over. "Father wanted you to be a detective, did he ever tell you that? I patterned the body after a detective from the movies, only I used a trick I know with mirrors to make a few changes." She examined Mab's face. "Nice work, if I do say so myself." Turning back to Mephisto and me, she continued, "You two might have written before you came. But, no, how silly of me! That would require forethought and consideration. I?" She gestured dramatically at herself. "Expect forethought and consideration from my own family? Better to wish the sun would delay its rising by an hour on my behalf. I'd be less likely to meet with disappointment. Well, as long as you're here, you might as well come in. I would never want to be accused of being inhospitable. Have you eaten? No?" She clapped her hands and cried out. "Prepare a feast!"

"Are you going to serve us old lovers transformed into pies?" Mephisto had his arms spread wide and was turning in circles on the pale sand. "I hate meat pies!"

Logistilla stooped gracefully and stroked the back of an ocelot that had come down from the forest to rub its spotted head against her leg.

"Of course not!" she said indignantly. "I never eat my pets."

"WE can't stay long. We've got to warn the others. The Three Shadowed Ones are hunting our staffs," I told my sister.

"They want to destroy us all!" Mephisto added enthusiastically.

"Yes, of course, I could have predicted that. No time for Logistilla. Dear sister Miranda must hurry off to warn the boys," Logistilla purred. "What is it this time? Three Shadowy Huns? Whatever it is, it can wait until we're seated for dinner."

We had had changed out of our night clothes and joined Logistilla on the dock. Now, she led us across the pale beach toward the house beyond. Animals circled us or watched from the underbrush. Two large Irish wolfhounds walked beside us along the slate pathway leading to the house. In the forest beyond, the green light of the staff glinted off the tiny eyes of a boar. Behind the boar, I could just make out the towering hulk of the bear. Logistilla waved her staff toward it, frowning. The bear turned slowly and lumbered into the black depths of the forest.

Ahead, a Gothic mansion rose out of the forest, its many gables silhouetted against the starry night. To either side of the tall staircase that led to the porch, the blocky, geometric patterns of a formal flower garden could be discerned in the moonlight. Farther back, to the left of the house, the rails of a fence, enclosing pigs or perhaps sheep, could be faintly seen through the black trunks of the trees.

My sister, the split skirts of her deep blue robes flowing about her legs, led us up the stairs, over the sleeping lion before the front door, and into the foyer. Within, the hall and sitting room were surprisingly orderly for a house inhabited by so many animals, though the pungent musk of what might be boar and lion lingered in the air. I recognized some of the furniture from the French house we had lived in back in the 1860s, during Napoleon III's reign. Two Serengeti dogs prowled under a heavy-legged Victorian table, growling softly, and a dingo slept curled up on the flowered upholstery of an overstuffed Venetian chair.

We followed my sister down a darkened hall toward a door bright with candlelight. As she walked, Logistilla glanced at me over her shoulder several times, regarding me from beneath heavy lids. Logistilla was at best acerbic. More often, she was downright spiteful. I resolved to say what we had come to say and depart.

Mab, who had been peering into one of the darkened rooms we passed, scowled, "This place stinks of enchantments and worse!" His eyes narrowed suspiciously. "Who are all these guys? Old lovers?"

"Oh, don't be gauche. What kind of woman do you take me for! I could never tire of my lovers half quickly enough to populate this island," she objected. "The beasts here are clients . . . for the most part."

In spite of my resolve to stick to our mission and leave, curiosity prompted me to ask, "Clients? Of what kind?"

"Oh, so the wondrous Miranda speaks! Not to ask me about myself or after my health. No, only concerned with business. Very well, far be it from me not to satisfy another's curiosity. My clients are criminals and cripples, mainly. They serve me for three years. In return, I give them what they want."

"You mean all these animals are shapechanged men?" I asked.

"Every single one," Logistilla replied primly. "Well, except the crocodile. He's real." When we glanced with alarm back toward the boat, she snickered, "Just kidding."

"Surely, you don't mean to say that you are using magic directly on mortals?" Mab exclaimed. "By Setebos and Titania! Is there no end to this family's madness?"

I added, "It is bad form, dear sister. Remember what happened to Circe."

"How kind of you to concern yourself, my dear sister. Yes, there's such a danger that Odysseus might stop by and hang around long enough to father two children upon me. What a dreadful fate! Besides, Circe didn't offer contracts; I do. Sometimes, I even let them try it for a few days before they decide. All the same, it was easier back when that snake Cornelius was cooperating with me!"

"And just what is it these clients of yours want?" Mab asked.

"What do you think? Ah, but I forget, you're not even a human being. How ungracious of me to expect you to make use of a brain. Criminals want new faces, of course, and cripples want new limbs."

I listened, morbidly fascinated and mildly appalled, while Mab scowled. Little sister Logistilla was using transformation magic on the client himself, rather than just reproducing a product. The potential for such a venture was staggering. I considered what such a project could do for Prospero, Inc.'s revenues. Though, come to think of it, making such a service available to our mortal customers would likely cause more trouble than it was worth. As far as that went, Logistilla was welcome to keep her little operation here.

Making such a service available to our supernatural customers, however, had enormous potential. With such a service at my disposal, I almost certainly could have settled the quarrel between the Aerie Spirits and the watery ones a few years back, in time to avoid that terrible hurricane.

I was dreaming, of course. Logistilla had the *Staff of Transmogrification* and, with it, all the metamorphosis magic our family possessed. Except in the unlikely event that Logistilla could be convinced to join the company again, the resources for such a venture would never be ours. I sighed.

LOGISTILLA led us into a dining room. A long table had been laid out with a place for one at the nearer end. Silver dishes overflowed with fresh fruit. Pastries and steaming delicacies filled platters and crystal bowls. The sweet aroma of papaya and fresh bread mingled with the smell of wet fur. Above, two spider monkeys chattered as they lit the candles of the chandeliers.

Logistilla gestured with her staff, spreading her arms wide. The spider monkeys rushed from the room, returning presently with enough china and silver for three more settings. My sister swept aside the skirts of her deep blue robe to take the chair at the head of the table. She gestured for us to choose seats. Mab and I sat to her right. Mephisto sat to her left. Koala bears sidled up to our chairs and fanned us with large painted fans, which was pleasant, for the air was humid and hot. A fourth fan-bearing koala sat amidst the dishes, defending the feast from flies.

The pale green light emanating from the top of Logistilla's staff died away. The globe now appeared to be an iridescent ball the color of mother-of-pearl atop a slender willow staff. Seven prongs, carved into the semblances of a bear, dog, raven, rat, horse, toad, and pig, held the ball to the staff. Logistilla placed the staff in a special holder beside her chair. It stood upright beside her.

"Mangos anyone? Oranges? Breadfruit?" She began to serve.

"Three years is an awfully long time for a man to be a beast." Mab was carefully sniffing each dish before he took anything. Cautiously, he spooned some strawberries onto his plate.

"Oh? So, you disapprove? Just for the record, Mr. Snoop-into-Other-People's-Business, I give them a chance to buy their way out at the end of the first year. This does tend to favor the rich, I admit. But then, life just never is fair, is it?" She bent and scratched an enormous pit bull behind its ear. "Is it? Yes, my sweet."

"Can't you just reproduce money? Wave your stick around and 'zingo' you've got bags of lucre?" Mephisto helped himself to three slices of blueberry pie. "You used to do that all the time."

"That was coins," she pouted. "My staff was particularly good at reproducing coins, but American money has some sort of spell on it that interferes with my work. Such an inconvenience. Probably put there just to stop me."

"It was," Mephisto replied, his mouth full. "By Cornelius." He swallowed. "At least, Erasmus says Cornelius is the one who put that spooky eye in the pyramid on the money. That's probably what's stopping you from reproducing it."

"An *Orbis Suleimani* spell," I murmured.

"Cornelius! He lives to make my life miserable! Though he does have a very fine staff! Of course, I like mine better." She reached behind her and petted the globe of her staff fondly.

"He does work for the Federal Reserve Board," commented Mephisto. "Maybe he feels he owes it to the people of America to keep their currency magic-free. Besides, with neat digs like this, what do you need money for?"

"Taxes, mainly. You would think if a person owned their own island, taxes would not be a problem, wouldn't you? But, no. Some foreign power is always sweeping in and declaring itself sovereign. I just pay them and hope that's the end of them. I find it easier to pay than to protest.

"Then, there's my estate in Russia," Logistilla continued. "The bribes I've had to pay to keep the title to that place are exorbitant. And they refuse to accept anything but American currency. Or that's how it had been for years, anyway. Such a nuisance! Shepherd's pie, anyone?"

"Any shepherd in it?" Mab eyed it suspiciously.

"Not a one," Logistilla replied.

Mab and I both accepted a serving. Mephisto made a face and shook his head. "Russia's become boring this last century or so. All that violence and yuck. Why bother to keep a house there?"

Logistilla lifted her head regally and stared down her elegant nose at Mephisto. "That estate was granted to me by Peter the Great!" she said. "I'll be damned before I let some insolent pack of transient mortals take it away."

Mab glanced around nervously. "Wouldn't say things like that, Madam Logistilla. Bad luck to call willingly on the powers of Hell."

He poured salt from the shaker into his hand and sprinkled it about his seat in a circle. Turning to me, Mab whispered.

"Who was this great Peter fellow?"

"A king in Russia," I replied. "He spent a year traveling incognito around Europe during the 1690s. Our family traveled with him for a time. Logistilla and he . . . got along well."

"I would have made him a far better wife than that Catherine creature!" Logistilla said. "But perhaps it was for the best. I would have tired of him eventually. He was sometimes called the Bear, but the Russian people might have been a bit put out had he actually become one."

"Apparently, Catherine thought you had turned him into a stallion." Mephisto snickered, his face smeared with blueberries and marshmallow. "I heard it was her fatal flaw."

Logistilla gave him a veiled look. "Wrong Catherine, you buffoon. You're thinking of Catherine the Great. That's a myth, anyway! And thank you so much for mentioning such an unpleasant subject in my presence, yet again."

Mab looked up. "The death of Catherine the Great?"

"No, you fool," Logistilla replied. "Horses. I should have known the two of you were just waiting for a chance to humiliate me. And after I attempted to be such a generous hostess!"

"Wait, I'd heard you liked horses," Mab asked, confused. "I thought you were some kind of great horsewoman."

"I do love horses," Logistilla replied theatrically. "It is only when they are upon the lips of my relatives that they offend me."

CHAPTER
FIFTEEN

Raiding the Treasures of the Popes of Rome

Logistilla stood. "We have lingered over our repast long enough. Let us withdraw to the drawing room."

We followed my sister to a drawing room decorated with overstuffed Victorian furniture upholstered in deep blue velvet. The place smelled of pungent musk. Logistilla chased off several large beasts to make room for us all to sit. She gestured imperiously. A marmoset scurried over and poured a deep red port into our tall fluted glasses.

She took out a long cigarette, placed it in a long black holder, and murmured. "Look at that. Now we can smoke and drink port after dinner just like the men used to." She glanced at the rest of us and gave a throaty chuckle, "Even if there isn't a real man here."

"I didn't hear that!" Mephisto said cheerfully. He walked up to Logistilla and snapped her cigarette in half. "Besides, don't you know that nobody smokes anymore. Smoking is evil, nowadays. Right up there with murder and loitering. Or did loitering go out of style?"

"Oh, pooh!" murmured Logistilla, but she did not take out another one.

Mab pulled out his notebook, "All this talk about horses reminded me of something. You guys never told me the whole scoop about that Vatican caper. This is as good a time as any, considering that we really shouldn't try to sail out of here until the tide comes in. So, tell me about it. Who stole what?"

We all began talking at once, but Mephisto shouted over Logistilla and me.

"Oh, it was great!" he cried. "We broke in just before dawn, there was a huge commotion. First, Gregor walked out with the ring. Then, I stole the sphere. Miranda carried off St. George's lance. You may have seen it, Daddy keeps it by the fireplace. It's all black and twirly with gold edges? No? Anyway, Titus was supposed get something, I don't remember what, but after he dropped the fake dead body of Pope Gregory, he got too busy killing the guards. Ulysses . . . no, he wasn't born yet. Erasmus took the Shroud of Turin. Cornelius stole the Ark of the Covenant—only he opened it, the dope. Too bad about that. Daddy got the scepter made from a piece of the true cross. Theo rescued the spear of Joseph of Arimathea. With Theo, it's always a rescue. He never steals. And, who's left?" Our hostess glared at him. "Oh, yeah. Logistilla held the horses."

"What a night it was!" I cried, recalling our wild escape ride across the sky.

"Held Xanthus, Pyrois, Aethon, and Phlegon I will thank you to remember," huffed Logistilla. To Mab, she said, "They left me holding the horses, while they got all the glory and the goodies. Then, they never let me live it down. After that, any time we planned to do anything, it was always 'Oh, we can't rely on Logistilla, she's only good for holding horses.' Or, 'Here's some horses to hold, Sister Dear, you excel at that.' The ingrates!"

"You made your getaway on the Horses of the Sun?" Mab cried aghast. "Where was the sun that day? On vacation? Do you know those horses are relatives of mine? Nephews, I guess you'd call 'em."

"It was dark, silly." Mephisto spoke despite his mouth being full of banana bread.

"But what about the other side of the earth? Ah, never mind . . . why did you need horses at all?" Mab asked. "Why didn't you just take . . ." He flipped through his notebook. ". . . the *Staff of Transportation*?"

"The travel staff was new." I chose a candy from a box of bonbons offered by the marmoset. "Father made it while we were in Italy. It had never touched the earth of the British Isles, so it could not bring us there. Instead, Father sent Mephisto to capture and harness the Horses of the Sun."

"It was a royal pain," Logistilla complained, gesturing with her wine glass. "We could only take with us what we could carry by horseback. I had to winnow my childhood, my whole youthful life, down to two saddlebags."

"Back up a step." Mab held up a hand. "You were living in Italy? Last I heard, your family fled Milan and ended up in England."

"You mean the famous ignominious retreat after they were betrayed by Uncle Antonio?" With a wave of her hand, Logistilla dismissed events that happened well before her birth as ancient history. "That was in 1499; this was 1623."

I jumped in. "After that, we moved to Scotland, though we spent much of our time in London. In 1589, we moved back to Italy, this time as private citizens. The Spanish were ruling Milan then." I recalled how strange it had been to see their unfamiliar faces living in our old *castello*.

"What was that all about?" Mab scribbled as he talked. "I mean, why did you go?"

"I'm not sure of the details, but it had something to do with the internal squabbles of the *Orbis Suleimani.* Father was constantly sending Titus and Cornelius to and fro on errands related to these matters. They had been born during our stay in Scotland; this was their first time in Italy."

"And their first time carrying staffs!" Mephisto piped in.

"Titus and Cornelius." Mab made a note and then looked up. "Where was everyone else?"

"Theo stayed behind in England for much of this period, fighting under the Earl of Essex. Erasmus married an Italian girl, a merchant's daughter. When she died in childbirth a few years later, he and his surviving children returned to England, where he participated in the king's translation project, helping to create what later became known as the King James Bible. I was with Father, of course," I finished.

Mab scribbled down what I had said and counted my brothers quickly, tapping each name with his pencil as he muttered it. "Where were you, Harebrain?"

"Here and there," Mephisto gestured airily. "I was in Germany, learning a new trade."

"But you went to Italy . . ." Mab glanced down again ". . . by 1623?"

Mephisto tilted his head thoughtfully. "Well, I went back to England and hung out with the School of the Night for a while . . . or were those the guys who hunted Miranda? Mainly, I practiced gathering . . . stuff. Then, the Spanish Ambassador stole something from me and sent it to Rome. I wanted it back, so I went to Italy."

"What was it?" asked Mab.

Mephisto squinted. He frowned. He rubbed his temples, concentrating. Finally, he shrugged. "Don't remember."

I sighed. Sometimes, Mephisto's memory losses seemed far too convenient.

"Okay, so Mr. Prospero sets up house in Milan and remarries?" Mab asked.

"That's right," Logistilla nodded. "Gregor and I were born in 1593."

Mab did some quick addition. "Hold on! This makes no sense! Gregor was born in 1593 and pope by 1623? The College of Cardinals confirmed a thirty-year-old man as pope?"

Logistilla put down her wine glass. "The whole adventure began in 1618, when Gregor and I were about twenty-five. We were visiting our mother's family in Rome, and we happened to be the only ones present when a cardinal collapsed and died. Alexander Ludovisi, I believe it was. As a lark, Gregor asked me to use my staff—Papa had only recently lent us use of our staffs for the first time—to make him look like the cardinal. Only, once he was the cardinal, he turned out to be a natural. Within two or three years, they made him pope.

"Gregor made a pretty good pope, actually," she continued. "Most of the popes back then were as corrupt as the devil, carousing and wenching and taking bribes as fast as the money poured in. Gregor was devout. He refused to take bribes and cleared the cardinals' mistresses out of the Vatican. He'd been pope about two years when Papa discovered there was still a great deal of true magic in the hands of the Catholics.

"Father was outraged to learn the Church was doing so well against his darling Protestants because they had magic on their side," Logistilla continued. "By then, the whole family had turned Protestant, with the exception of Gregor and myself. And I've never been a great believer. So, when Papa asked us to break the power of the Catholic Church once and for all, by stealing their enchanted talismans, we agreed."

"Even Pope Gregor agreed?" Mab asked.

"He was called Pope Gregory XV. Well, he was young then—despite wearing an elderly man's body—and tired of the effort of being pope. Also, he was disillusioned by the lack of piety among the church officials. Gregor thought he was doing the faithful a favor by removing power from the hands of the criminals who were milking them in the name of Our Lord."

"He thought the magic was harming the Catholics," I explained. "He's a little like Theo that way. In fact, Theo probably got his ideas from Gregor. He was a strange fellow, Gregor. For all his love of the Catholic Church, he had the soul of a Puritan."

Logistilla drew herself up, frowning severely. "Do not malign my dearly departed twin!" She turned to Mab, pouting again. "Gregie-Poo was a pussycat and don't you let my icicle of a sister convince you otherwise."

"Er, as you say, Ma'am." Mab lowered the brim of his fedora. Remembering that he should not be wearing a hat while sitting at a lady's table, he quickly took it off and laid it on a chair beside him.

Sipping my wine, I recalled our daring escape that long-ago night in 1623, the wind whipping by as we clung to each other in our chariot pulled by the sons of Zephyrus. Stars sparkled overhead. As the Horses of the Sun mounted higher, the constellations swayed and danced, as if we had entered some higher realm, where Orion and Cassiopeia were living entities. That night was the end of an era for us. It was the night we left Italy for the final time.

Arriving home in Scotland after the raid, we freed our godly steeds, sending them back to their bright master, then stumbled laughing, windburnt, and exhilarated, into the Hound and Eagle Pub. Cornelius went upstairs to lie down and rest his eyes—back then we still expected his sight to return presently—while the rest of us gathered in the common room. Excitement still crackled in the air. Easygoing Theo got into a fistfight. Mephisto left with two barmaids, and normally rowdy Titus relaxed by the fire, spent from his battle with the guards. Only Father remained silent. He sat by the bar watching his children, the furrow in his brow deepening.

The next day, Father took back our staffs and commissioned Mephisto to carve statues for Logistilla and Gregor, who did not yet have them. It was some time before we saw our staffs again.

MAB finished scribbling down Mephisto's accounts of who stole what and looked up. "Okay, there's the scepter with the piece of the True Cross, the ark, the lance of St. George, the spear of Joseph of Arimathea . . . that's the same weapon as the Spear of Longinus, right? The ring? That would be Solomon's Ring, the original Seal of Solomon. I'd heard somewhere it used to belong to the Pope."

"That's where the tradition of kissing the Pope's ring came from," said Logistilla. "Only a human being could bear to kiss that ring. It was the Pope's way of testing whether or not he was being beguiled by a demon."

"And the sphere?" asked Mab. "Would that be Merlin's globe or John Dee's?"

"They are one and the same," I replied.

"Worse and worse! Dangerous object, that. Said to be one of the few seeing glasses capable of looking into truly vile places."

"Mr. Dee once told Father that the angels he communed with warned him never to look anywhere infernal," said Logistilla.

"Good advice," Mab growled. "Where's all this magical garbage now?"

"The lance, the scepter, and the shroud are at the mansion," I said. "Cornelius still has the ark—we thought it only fitting considering the high price he paid to get it. The spear was later built into Theo's staff. Father used to have the Seal of Solomon, too, but I'm under the impression something happened to it."

Mab nodded. "It was one of the two pieces Ulysses kept the time he stole the Warden. What happened to the sphere?"

"I broke it during the original raid," Mephisto said sadly. "I had to throw it at some guys who wanted to kill me. But it was great!" His face lit up. "It exploded in a huge mushroom of fire!"

Mab looked at Mephisto with an odd expression on his face. "I heard a rumor about that sphere once," he began, but Mephisto interrupted him, speaking rapidly.

"There were lots of rumors about the sphere, and most were wrong. But, it's gone now. So, it doesn't matter. Oh, well. Too bad."

Mab eyed Mephisto thoughtfully, but he did not voice his original thought. "I gather Cornelius did something similar when he opened the Ark. Foiling his attackers, I mean."

"The guards who attacked him were transformed into dust," I replied. "Only, he himself looked too soon, as he was covering it. That's how he lost his sight."

"Bad business, the Ark," said Mab.

Logistilla arched her perfectly formed eyebrows and looked at Mab with new interest. As Logistilla raised her glass to her lips, our eyes met. Her lip curled up slightly. To Mab, she said, "You seem surprisingly sensible for one of your kind. There's a question I've always wanted to ask a spirit who talked sensibly. Who was Christ Jesus really? I know what we Prosperos believe, but then, we're all Protestants now. What do the spirits believe?"

Mab sat back and scratched at his stubble. "Opinions differ, Madam Logistilla. No one seems to know for sure. Or, if they do, they aren't telling. Some say he was the son of a wrathful sky god named Jehovah. Some say he was Lucifer's son. Some say Adonai's. Some think he was a stranger, from Outside, or a renegade from the universe of Muspell. But, I think that's pure conjecture. Personally, though, I doubt all of the above."

"Oh? Why?" Logistilla asked. I listened, curious. It was not a topic Mab and I had ever discussed.

"Simple. Devils don't give you something for nothing, and this Christ guy did. Angels don't break the law, creating miracles and all that. As for the tribal sky god theory, the old deities are no longer powerful enough to keep mentions of their works from being edited by—well, the guys you called the

Orbis Suleimani. Mithra and Jove have been relegated to fairytales. Christ Jesus has not. As for who Christ actually was? I have my own opinion."

"Ah, the *Orbis Suleimani*, or the Boys' Club, as it should be called." Logistilla sniffed. "I've never understood why Father would not let us women join. Even their splinter group, the Freemasons, don't allow women. Or didn't last time I checked. Things are changing so quickly, these days."

Mephisto said. "Father did not create the organization, Dopeyhead! He was just a member. Solomon started the organization. Hence the name: 'the Circle of Solomon.' "

Mab frowned suspiciously, "You know, that's probably where Mr. Prospero stole his magical tomes from."

"Father would never steal books!" Logistilla said, appalled.

"Why not?" Mephisto shrugged. "He stole stuff from the Vatican, didn't he?"

I frowned, recalling Antonio's taunt the day we lost Milan. " . . . *in the old records you left behind in your haste to rob us of our sacred library*." By *us*, had Uncle Antonio meant the *Orbis Suleimani*?

If so, why did Father claim—well, imply—the books were rightfully his? Could this ownership dispute have had something to do with the division in the *Orbis Suleimani*? For the first time, I found myself curious about the split in their organization. Mephisto had probably once known what had caused it, but it was unlikely he remembered today. The *Orbis Suleimani* had tossed him out long ago, for not being able to keep track of their business or their secrets.

"There may be a good deal about Father you don't know," I murmured. Theo and Ferdinand's claims regarding Father's trustworthiness clamored for my attention. Dutifully, I ignored them.

Logistilla gestured, and tiny furry hands served us bowls of sherbet.

"Miranda, why are you here?" she asked. "Mephisto, I can understand, he's probably short of funds. Stupid thing to do, big brother, lose your staff. You, however, my sister; what would pull you out of your cocoon?"

"Something has happened to Father."

Logistilla laughed out loud. "Oh, dear, you are going to have to do better than that!"

"You don't believe her?" Mab asked, outraged.

"No, certainly not. Nothing rattles Papa. Besides, if something had, why would she come to me? Unless he'd been transformed into a newt. Has Papa been transformed into a newt, Miranda? Perhaps, if you stopped dawdling on this Sibyl business, you would be able to turn him back yourself, without my help. Or is transmogrification not one of the precious Gifts of the Sibyl?"

"Transmogrification is not a Gift of the Sibyl, as you well know, Sister," I replied through clenched teeth.

Mephisto, who had been frowning angrily down at his hands, now raised his head and shouted at Logistilla. "He is too in trouble. He's in Hell!"

Logistilla sat motionless, shocked. What little color she possessed slowly drained away from her pale face. Her bottom lip trembled.

"Father unleashed an enemy he could not control," I said. "He left a note asking the rest of the family be informed of the danger."

Logistilla recovered quickly. "Left the note to you, Miranda, did he?" she asked scathingly. "Well, you always were his favorite. There was little enough the rest of us could do to get his attention."

"He just left a note, Logistilla." I was growing bored with her constant accusations of favoritism. "I happened to be the one who found it."

"So . . . how did it happen? Where did our faultless paterfamilias go wrong?"

"We don't know," Mab replied. "We're trying to track that down now."

"Papa didn't tell his perfect Miranda what he was up to?" Her eyebrows arched, and her lips formed a moue of amusement. "Who would have thought? I assume Cornelius and Erasmus must know. They're thick as thieves with the Boys' Club, and all Father's dastardly doings."

"Which dastardly doings would those be?" Mab reached for his pencil.

"It's just a turn of phrase," Logistilla responded primly.

Pencil in hand now, Mab asked, "How about you? When's the last time you talked to Mr. Prospero?"

"Me? Oh, Papa comes by now and again. I'm helping him with certain . . . work." Logistilla eyes sparkled maliciously. "But, I'd prefer not to talk about that. If Papa hasn't told his precious Miranda all about it, there must be some reason he doesn't want her to know."

Mephisto had been pouring wine back and forth between three sizes of tall fluted crystal glasses, his face intent. Now, he lowered the glass in his hand. "Do you really think Daddy does it on purpose? The secrecy thing, I mean? I thought it was second nature to him, sort of like protective camouflaging in moths. You know, over the generations, moths change to blend in with new backgrounds, but it's not like they do it on purpose. I think Daddy's like that, don't you?"

"I blame that Antonio person," Logistilla replied, sniffing.

"Uncle Antonio? The Great Betrayer? Or was he the cool uncle who used to take me whoring?" He tipped his head back thoughtfully, as if he were trying to recall the misty past.

"Probably one and the same, from what I've heard. I never met Uncle Antonio, or Uncle Galeazzo and Uncle Ludovico, for that matter—they all died before I was born." Logistilla gave Mephisto and me an arch glance. "But none of Papa's brothers sound like real winners to me. Face it, this Antonio person betrayed Papa when he was young and vulnerable, and Papa's never gotten over it. Papa's spent his whole life worrying some family member might up and betray him at any moment. That's why he's so closemouthed with us. He doesn't trust us! His own children, and after all we do for him!"

I frowned, not liking what Logistilla was implying. "Father is far older and wiser than we, Logistilla. We should not question his purposes."

"Older and wiser, my foot! Papa is much closer in age to you, Miranda, than you and Mephisto are to me," Logistilla replied. "After all, how old could Papa have been when you were born? Thirty? Fifty? He didn't become immortal until after you brought him the Water of Life, right?"

"Didn't Mr. Prospero have the magic of the . . ." Mab flipped through his notes, "*Staff of Decay* at his disposal? Can't that be used to keep a person young, as well as to age them? Or did I get that wrong?"

"It can make you young," Logistilla replied slowly, "but it can't heal illnesses and wounds, the way the Water of Life can. Erasmus experimented at one point with trying to keep people young using his staff alone. After a few uses, they became fragile and weak. It could extend life ten years, twenty years, maybe thirty, but not longer.

"Even so, Papa's brothers and sister were still alive when Mephisto was young, and we know Papa wasn't using his magic to preserve them! You know how niggardly he is when it comes to sharing immortality. So, we have a pretty good idea of how old he was.

"But, back to my point, Miranda, you were born one hundred and thirty-five years before Gregor and me, and Mephisto, here . . ." She fluttered her long narrow hand in his direction. "Mephisto's a hundred and seventeen years older than we. I certainly don't venerate the two of you based on your greater age," she concluded.

"Maybe you should," Mephisto replied. "I could do with some venerating. It's a bit stuffy in here."

Logistilla chuckled, and Mab snorted, shaking his head in disgust. I chewed my candy in silence. My sister's math was correct. Father was closer to me in age than I was to her, and yet, somehow he had seemed ancient with wisdom, even when I was a child, in a manner my brothers and I had never achieved. I wondered why. Was Father different from us in some fundamental way? Or was my great admiration for him proof of Theo's perfidious theory?

"So, tell me about our new enemies," said Logistilla.

"Three demons called the Three Shadowed Ones. They are after our staffs. So far, they have gotten Mephisto's and Gregor's," I said.

"The Three Shadowed Ones? Not the very same who hounded us after . . ." She frowned. "The incident involving equines of which I refuse to speak?"

"Yes. Do you remember them?"

"Quite well." Something about the way she spoke disturbed me. Before I could respond, Logistilla turned to address Mephisto. "You mean it was this enemy of Papa's who stole your staff?"

Mephisto turned his head away and sniffed pointedly.

"They can't be far away." Mab looked around suspiciously. "They sicced a human servant on us on our way here, and some two-bit spirit big mouth claims they've cast some kind of doom over your family so that you'll all be dead by Twelfth Night, or something."

"Really?" Logistilla stiffened. "That's disturbing!"

"I wouldn't worry about it too much, Madam Logistilla. Low level spirits like that are notorious liars; but, on the other hand, it never hurts to be careful. Here's a list of precautions you might want to take." Mab began scribbling rapidly.

I asked carefully, "I know spirits exaggerate, Mab, but do they predict doom upon a particular date if there is nothing to it?"

"Well . . ." Mab scratched his head; his gray-black hair stuck out all awry. "That's a good question. The general answer is: sure, they are always predicting the end of the world on such and such a day. Problem is, 'such and such a day' is usually well in the future at the time of the prediction. Twelfth Night, on the other hand, is less than three weeks away. That kind of prediction usually has some teeth behind it. It suggests that these Three Shadowy Creeps are up to something no good."

"That's . . . disturbing," Logistilla mused. My sister suddenly whipped her head around to face me. "Gregor's? Did you say they have Gregor's staff?"

"Yeah." Mephisto put his hands on his hips.

"But it was buried with his body!" Her voice rose.

"Well, they have it now," I replied. "They used it to attack the mansion."

I sipped my wine. How had the Three Shadowed Ones come to have access to Gregor's coffin? The more I thought about it, the more the Ouija board's last message troubled me. If Gregor's body was "No Longer" in Elgin, Illinois, what had become of it? Had Father moved the grave? If so, for what reason? And why had Ferdinand climbed out of Hell to find himself in the same town where Gregor was, or had been, buried? A number of possibilities came to mind, none of them pleasing.

Logistilla lifted her glass to her dark red lips and sipped. Her expression became calm again. "My island's been invaded three times in the last month. Twice by a dark shape who fled when my pets went out to meet him. Once by men who are now part of my retinue. I have no way of telling whether the incidents are related. Oh, and one other thing: Both times the dark shape came, my staff gave off a flash of green light of its own accord. It's never done that before. It was the oddest thing."

"Did the dark shape have red eyes, red like fresh blood?" Mab asked. Logistilla nodded. "That was the incubus Seir of the Shadows. He's one of the Three. He's after your staff. You better watch out, Ma'am; one of their number is a shapechanger." Mab gestured toward the sleeping beasts littered about the room.

Logistilla threw back her head and laughed again. "Do you hear that, my pet?" she asked, addressing the pit bull. "They're worried about a shapechanger! Here! On St. Dismas!" She let out a long, throaty chuckle. Shaking her head, she added, "No worry there! My pets would notice a stranger in their midst immediately. They're much smarter than ordinary beasts, you know. A shapechanger, you say? Not Theo's old shapechanger, is it? What was his name?"

"José the Red?" Mephisto offered.

"Osae," Mab corrected him. "Yeah, the very same."

"Really! How very peculiar." She turned toward me. "I assume you've reached all the others. I can't imagine you'd bother getting around to me until the end."

"Hardly. I've seen you, Theo, and Mephisto here."

"Yes, of course, your dear Theo." She laughed harshly. "Not quite the dashing figure he once was, is he? What a pitiful waste of flesh."

"I sent Cornelius a letter," I replied, refusing to rise to her bait. I had never made a secret of the fact that Theo was my favorite. "Have you seen any of the others?"

"Oh, Cornelius," she snorted. "I wouldn't trust him as far as . . . but no matter. The others? Erasmus throws a New Year's Eve party every year. Care to go? I'll give you my invitation. And Mephisto came by a few months ago with the sob story about losing his staff. Taken by demons of Hell, was it? Really, Mephisto, you should be more careful whom you take to bed. Why don't you tie them up or turn them into goats while you are sleeping? It would be safer that way. Other than Mephisto, Erasmus, and Cornelius? I haven't seen anyone in years."

Logistilla lifted her wine glass again, holding it up between herself and the chandelier. As she stared into the swirling red liquid, she asked, "Have you heard anything from Ulysses or Titus?"

"I thought Titus was living in the Okefenokee Swamp with his children," Mephisto spouted. "At least, until recently."

That was news to me. I had not known Titus had children. Until two years ago, he had sent me a birthday card every year. They always arrived the day before my birthday, like clockwork. However, he had never mentioned children, or even a new wife.

"Titus is such a fuddy-duddy these days," Logistilla scoffed. "He probably sat down somewhere a year or so back and hasn't bothered to get up. Pah! And he was such a dashing figure in his youth!"

"It's 'cause he's so big," Mephisto offered cheerily. "Makes it hard to move!"

"So, you haven't seen Ulysses?" Logistilla asked again.

"What is the trouble with Cornelius?" I returned to her earlier topic. Last I had heard, Logistilla and Cornelius had been on the best of terms. She could never have held the title to her Russian estates through the Communist regimes without help from the *Staff of Persuasion.* What had caused their recent falling out?

Logistilla lowered her glass and pursed her lips. "Perhaps I shouldn't say."

I did not intend to give her the satisfaction of seeing me beg. I waited. She obliged me.

"Doesn't it strike you as peculiar," she said, glancing nervously over her shoulder before leaning forward in a conspiratorial manner, "that Theo has kept this latest resolution of his, right up through growing into an old man? I mean, how many such resolutions has Theo ever kept before?"

She had me. I bit. “What does this have to do with Cornelius?”

“It’s just that the day we met to try and summon up Gregor’s spirit, the day Theo made his rash vow?” Her eyes gleamed spitefully as she reveled in my discomfort.

“Yes?” I tried to keep impatience from my voice.

“I thought I saw . . . I could be wrong, I realize. I could be misinterpreting . . .” She glanced over her shoulder again and leaned closer, dropping her voice. “And to tell you the truth, I had forgotten about it until speaking with you today.”

“What did you see, Logistilla?”

“Just after the ritual ended, just before Theo made his speech?” Logistilla whispered. “I saw Cornelius holding the *Staff of Persuasion* in front of Theo’s eyes—you know, his staff that hypnotizes and makes people obey?—I could not hear his words, but I could see the movement of his lips. He was saying something about ‘abandoning magic.’ ”

CHAPTER
SIXTEEN

The Three Shadowed Ones

I left the house and walked out onto the beach, a pale strip before the black of the ocean. It was almost dawn. As soon as it grew light, we would depart. Meanwhile, our sloop rested peacefully beside the dock, the tall mast with its reefed sail silhouetted against the faint light along the horizon, its rigging clinking softly in the low breeze.

To either side of the tall Victorian house stretched woods, black and murky save for the gleam of a single pair of eyes. As I walked along the edge of the forest toward the shore, swinging my flute, the door of the house creaked behind me. Turning, I saw Mab approaching.

"You okay, Ma'am?"

"I guess so." I stopped swinging the flute and hugged my arms, suddenly cold. "It's just . . . difficult to hear such things about my family. I know I haven't always liked them, but I didn't . . . I didn't think we would betray each other."

"Are you sure your sister's accusations are legit?"

I nodded sadly. "Several times over the years, I've seen Theo get very enthusiastic about something only to have a sudden dullness come over his eyes. That's the effect of the *Staff of Persuasion*. I've seen it before. I'm dismayed I did not recognize it, but who would have imagined one of us would do such a thing? To think Theo might die, because of Cornelius! It's . . ." I trailed off and stood a time, watching the pale light slowly spread across the sky.

My mind was not on Theo or Cornelius, but on Father. Cornelius's betrayal hurt, but it did not shock me. I had liked Cornelius quite a bit when he was a boy. Over the last century or so, however, he had become devious and subtle, so much so that I almost expected something like this from him—though why he would strike out at Theo baffled me. I had thought everyone loved Theo.

Father, on the other hand, I loved and respected—or thought I did. But Father had wielded the *Staff of Persuasion* throughout my entire youth. Did I admire Father? Or had he enchanted me so I could not believe otherwise?

I stared off into the starry horizon. My family was crumbling away, falling to death, madness, and betrayal. For the first time, in as long as I could remember, I felt lonely.

"Mab," I said, "do you recall the day I told you about the Three Shadowed Ones? You thought Father was probably dead already and said, 'Sorry to hear it, Ma'am.' What if our positions had been reversed? What if it had been Father telling you the Three Shadowed Ones were after *me*? Would that have been your only reaction, 'Sorry to hear it, Sir'?"

Mab had been staring out to sea with his hands thrust into the pockets of his trench coat. As he turned toward me, an object fell to the ground. He stooped, picking up the partially carved wooden figurine of him Mephisto had made, the one I had slipped into his hand the previous evening on the ship. Mab stood a moment, gazing at it, before answering.

"Yesterday, Ma'am." He slipped it back into his pocket. "But not today."

"THERE'S something you should see, Ma'am," Mab said presently, after we had stood silently a bit longer. "I don't know what it means, but I think you oughta see."

He led me around the back of Logistilla's house. Amidst the slender trees, decomposing leaves had been kicked aside, revealing a set of storm cellar doors.

"Found this place because the bear was scratching around over here. Figured it was a food store, but it had a funny smell about it . . . enchantment funny, I mean. So I thought I should take a look—just in case."

Mab opened the doors and started down the stairs, descending into utter blackness. He gestured for me to follow and, once I was below ground level, he scurried back up again and shut the doors behind us, leaving me floundering on a rickety wooden stairway in pitch darkness. The air was cold and smelled of damp earth. Somewhere in the distance, water trickled over rock.

A light flicked on, revealing Mab's hands and legs. He had lit the headlamp I had given him back at the warehouse. Apparently, he had stuffed it into one of the many pockets of his new trench coat. Strapping it to his head, he turned and shined the light down the stairs.

Below lay a vast underground cavern, a natural cave complete with an irregular stone roof and stalactites. Covering the floor, stacked one upon another as far as the eye could see, lay naked bodies.

"Are they . . . dead?"

"Don't think so, Ma'am. No stench of death."

"Then . . . wha . . ."

"Empty bodies, Ma'am. Far as I can tell with my instruments, these have never seen life. My guess is Madam Logistilla made them."

"But . . . why?" I cried. "Why make a stadium full of bodies? What does she plan to do with them?"

"Don't know, Ma'am."

"Could they be for her clients? Could there possibly be this many animals on this island?"

"Don't think so, Ma'am, not unless she's turned some of 'em into birds and bugs." Mab shook his head disapprovingly. "Seems like a rather macabre hobby. If you ask me, your sister should give up this shady business of hers and turn her attention to some wholesome pursuit that does not stink of the arcane. If she must be a collector, let her collect lacy picture frames or those little porcelain Hummel dolls. Something decent!" Mab's voice held more than his customary touch of bitterness. I did not fault him. He had been through a difficult day.

Gesturing for Mab to bring the light closer, I descended the staircase into the chilly cavern and examined the expanse of naked bodies stretching out before me. Some lay neatly with arms crossed across chests and eyes closed, like corpses. Others had been casually tossed, one upon the other, vacant eyes staring outward. Nearly all the bodies had olive skin, Roman noses, and dark, shiny hair. Italians. My sister was living above a cavern filled to the brim with the naked bodies of Italians.

I stepped around a stack of them, and my stomach lurched. The bodies I could see from the stairs had all been adults in the prime of life. These were children. Little dark-haired boys and girls lying lifeless on the ground. One of them reminded me so much of young Theo that tears came to my eyes.

I backed up slowly.

Mab came up beside me and swore softly. "Maybe she's bonkers, Ma'am . . . went the way of Mephisto. All this living alone with animals can't be good for her. Not to mention . . ." His voice died off.

"Not to mention what?"

"Well, Ma'am, I don't like to spread rumors. I'd rather not speculate just because of a hunch."

As I walked back to the staircase, I tried to recall an instance of one of Mab's hunches being wrong. "Go ahead, Mab, speculate away."

"All right, Ma'am, if you insist, but I want you to remember that this is just speculation." When I nodded, he spoke hesitantly. "There's a . . . *smell* upstairs, a smell I didn't like."

I chuckled. "Which one? Bear? Dingo? Or wild boar?"

Mab was not amused. "I wish, Ma'am . . . unfortunately, I'm not talking about anything so wholesome as animal musk. I'm talking about a real stink, as in 'stink of corruption.' In one of the side rooms, one of the rooms we passed by, I could have sworn . . . now mind you Ma'am, I didn't go in to investigate . . ."

"Yes, Mab, get to the point. You could have sworn . . ."

"Smelled like demon, Ma'am." Mab spoke in a quick rush.

"You think the Three Shadowed Ones have been here?" I asked, dismayed.

Mab rubbed the back of his neck, "With all due respect, Ma'am, the Three Shadowed Ones are posers. I don't mean they haven't caused trouble for you and your family, or that they're not dangerous, or that we should not be wary. But in the grand scheme of things, they're just posers, lesser minions in service to the Powers of Hell. This . . . this smelled like a Power of Hell . . . one of the big Seven.

"Those big guys . . . they leave a stench you never forget! Had some dealings with the Lord of the Flies long ago when I was—well, I think you know I wasn't so nice a guy back then." He hunched his shoulders. "Let's just say there are reasons those Greeks used to call me the 'Bad One.'

"Anyway, the big guys, they have this . . . call it a smell. The stink of corruption hangs about them like a cloud of ill omen. It reeks like nothing else on Earth or below. Your sister's room? Whatever was in there, it reminded me of that.

"And did you notice how nervous she was acting when she told you about Mr. Cornelius using his staff on Mr. Theophrastus?" Mab's eyes narrowed. "Almost like she expected someone to be looking over her shoulder."

I whistled softly to cover my shock and fright. "When you said demon, you meant devil? As in The Devil? As in the Prince of Darkness and his cohorts, the Rulers of Hell?"

"Yeah. A devil."

"That's bad," I whispered, shaken.

I grabbed for the rail, but the staircase did not have one. My hand closed on empty air. I wobbled perilously but managed to retain my balance. Beside me, Mab opened his mouth, shut it again, then shook his head.

"Gotta say it, Ma'am. This project your sister was working on with Mr. Prospero? Well, I just wish we knew more about it, is all."

"Me too, Mab," I said. "Me too."

We retreated rapidly up the stairs, leaving the cavern of naked bodies behind us.

MAB and I returned to the docks, where we gazed out across the ocean at the rosy fingers of dawn. The vista was lovely, but it was hard to shake the memory of stacks of naked bodies and pale children, as still as death. My imagination, overly vivid from lack of sleep, pictured armies of Italian zombies rising to serve some nefarious cause.

If my supposition the night before was correct, perhaps Father intended these bodies for Aerie Ones. I found this theory difficult to accept. Where could Father intend to put such a large group of people? Back in the 1920s, they could have arrived at New York Harbor on a boat and no questions would have been asked. But today? To mingle with modern society, they would need birth certificates, driver's licenses, or, at the very least, passports.

True, documents could be forged. Mephisto, Erasmus, and Ulysses were each a fair hand at forgeries. Nowadays, however, identification documents required secret watermarks, special materials, and electronic histories. Updating my ID, which our trip to Joliet had shown would soon be necessary, was going to prove difficult enough. False IDs for thousands of people? Including a credible history for credit checks and other computer-related identity searches? Such a project would require a tremendous amount of effort.

Perhaps, Father intended them to blend in among one of the dwindling indigenous populations, somewhere in the Southern Hemisphere. If so, why were they all Italians? Surely, Father realized that Italy had moved into the modern age and was no longer the idyllic land of pastures and country villages of his youth!

Could Father intend the Aerie Ones to live as their own community, either here or on Prospero's Island? Playing the roles of adults and children alike? A clever idea on the surface, but the more I thought about it, the more I doubted it would work. The incarnated Aerie Ones who showed signs of developing self-control, like Mab and my dear departed friend Gooseberry, were the ones who interacted with human beings. Those that did not—such as our enforcer Boreas, another of the incarnated Northerlies—remained as fierce and uncivilized as they had been before they put on a fleshly form. It was not his body that had transformed Mab into a being with judgment and perspicacity, I realized, but his interaction with mankind.

And then there were the little bodies. I did not think Aerie Ones would make good children, as their whimsical nature would be encouraged rather than curbed. But maybe I was wrong. Perhaps they would make excellent youngsters.

"Ma'am! Watch out!"

Startled by Mab's shout, I swung about to find Logistilla's bear looming over me. The enormous creature, even larger than Osae the Bear, stood on the dock, blocking any view of the island or the house. Its huge paws, with long curved claws, reached toward my face. I shouted and leapt back. Mab's shoulder knocked into me as he thrust his body between me and the bear. Despite the difference of their size, he courageously brandished his lead pipe before the bear's nose.

The enormous towering bear hesitated. Then, slowly, it continued to stretch out its arm. It reached past Mab and, very gently, brushed my face. The soft pads of its paw rested against my cheek. Mab stood there a moment longer, then stepped back, frowning.

"Poor sucker was a man once." He put away his pipe.

I reached up and touched the thick matted fur of the bear's paw. The musky smell was nearly overpowering, yet had a pleasant quality. The creature plaintively gazed back at me, its huge eyes looking sadly into mine. In the dim dawn light, I could just make out their rich brown color.

The door to my sister's house swung open. Logistilla's voice cut through the darkness.

"Miranda? Where did you . . . No! *You*! Get away! Get back in the forest now! Shoo!" When the bear did not move immediately, she brandished her staff, pale beams of green light emanating from the ball at the top illuminated the darkness. "Quickly now, before I turn you into something more vile!" The bear drew back and lumbered off into the forest. "And stay there! What impertinence!" She turned toward Mab and me, smiling. "I'm sorry. He's harmless, really. But, just to be on the safe side, why don't you two come inside?"

As we followed my sister back into her house, I watched the bear disappear among the dark trunks. Whispering to Mab, I said, "The poor man. I wish there was some way I could stop Logistilla. Men should not have to live this way."

"No one should have to live this way, Ma'am."

* * *

I QUESTIONED Logistilla about the bodies when we returned to her house, but she merely became enraged that we had been prying into her business, called me a snoop and a sneak thief, and accused Mab of trying to make off with her silver. Finally, she sniffed haughtily and declared that if Father chose not to make me privy to his secrets, who was she to go against his wishes? We could get nothing else out of her.

The three of us departed my sister's house at dawn and slept on the sloop, leaving the Aerie Ones to sail the craft. Five hours later, we sailed into the harbor at St. Thomas, returned the chartered boat and then set off for the airport.

The afternoon was beautiful. We strolled through the Royal Dane Mall on our way back to the airport, peering into the quaint little shops tucked in among alleys and walkways off Dronnigens Gade. Warm palm fronds tickled our faces, and brightly-colored banners rustled in the light wind. In these pleasant surroundings, it seemed almost surreal to recall that my family was in danger, our staffs hunted by demons who wished to destroy us. And yet, it was so.

The warm breeze brought back memories of our family's great journey, the one that transformed the *Staff of the Winds* into the weather-mastering instrument it was today. Ever since Father whittled my flute from that cloven pine back on Prospero's Island, it had been his dream—and mine, of course—to capture all Eight Winds and thus control the weather in all directions of the compass. Ariel and Caurus Father captured in my youth, and in the early 1500s we tracked Zephyrus to his lair in the Outer Hebrides islands (which was how we came to take up residence in Scotland). Some two hundred years later, we still controlled only the Southeast, Northwest, and West Winds.

Our travels in the company of Peter the Great took us deep into the heart of Russia. When the tsar returned to his court, we continued north, passing over the Rhipaean Mountains into Hyperborea. There, we finally cornered the elusive North Wind. With Boreas at our command, we were able to capture the fiercest wind of all, the Northeast.

After the bone-chilling cold of Russia and Hyperborea, Father promised our next journey would be through gentler climes. Some fifty years later—after that terrible earthquake in 1755 brought us to Lisbon—he kept that promise. All of us, except for Logistilla who was pregnant and remained with her husband, departed Europe for places farther east, setting out on what we later called the Great Wind Hunt.

During this extended journey, we supped on exotic food and subdued menacing spirits while tracking the remaining winds. We cornered Afer, the Southwest Wind, in Egypt, and captured Notus, the South Wind, below the Cape of Good Hope. We then chased Eurus, the East Wind, through India and China, before it escaped us by hiding in Japan. We did not follow because, at the time, the Shogunate had declared the country closed to foreigners. Outsiders found on Japanese soil were slain.

We dwelt in China for a few years. Then, in 1792, we received a request for help from En the Ascetic, the immortal Japanese sorcerer, whom we knew from the Centennial Masquerades. Mount Unzen had erupted, and the ensuing tsunami had killed over 14,000 people. En wished us to come and subdue the *oni* responsible.

With the help of the *Staff of Persuasion* and the *Staff of Transmogrification*, we crossed the Japanese countryside in disguise, hunting down numerous *tengu, oni,* and violent *kami.* The dragons, who dwell beneath the islands and shake the earth, eluded us, but no Japanese volcano since has slain so many. To show his gratitude, En brought us to his secret temple. There, by playing upon his enchanted shakuhachi, he lured the East Wind into the open. Finally, three hundred years after Father first captured Ariel, all eight winds were ours!

Throughout these journeys, Father would pause and touch the *Staff of Transportation* to the earth, so the staff could return to that spot. The Great Winds Hunt took us thirty-six years, all told. The return trip was accomplished in under one minute.

Where was Ulysses now? I wondered, sighing. That staff was wasted on him!

"Ma'am," Mab called. He had gone ahead to find a shop that carried newspapers from the mainland and now stood before a newsstand, scratching his jaw. "That Priority Account you decided not to sail back and check on yesterday. What was it for?"

An icy jab of fear traveled through my stomach.

"Why?"

"Better take a look at this." He jabbed a finger at a paper. The headline read: RUMBLING AT MOUNT ST. HELENS: ASH FALLS ON NEARBY TOWNS.

Frowning, I handed him some change. He bought the paper, and I read the article on the spot.

"This doesn't bode well, Mab." I folded the paper and tossed it into a nearby trash can. My cell phone still read "out of range." "This is definitely a breach of contract. I'd better call headquarters as soon as we reach the airport!"

We picked up our pace. The sights were still lovely and the air balmy, but the afternoon had lost its charm for me. What would I do if our Priority Accounts stopped honoring their word, now that Gregor and Theo were not around to oathbind them and terrify them into submission? Currently, as a stop gap, I was requiring new contracts be sworn upon the River Styx. Our meager supply of Styx water grew smaller each year, however, and some of what remained was needed for other purposes. More than once, I brought this up with Father, but he had never given me a satisfactory answer. Now he was missing, and the problem was on my shoulders.

Mephisto tripped along in front of us, kicking stones and shouting instructions to them. I could feel Mab glaring at me. He was waiting for me to tell Mephisto that we were deserting him. I figured there would be plenty of time for that on the plane. After all, I was not going to abandon him on St. Thomas.

As we reached Vimmelskaft Gade, Mephisto turned into a narrow alley that the map showed to be a shortcut, then suddenly backed out again, bumping into Mab and exclaiming excitedly, "Uh-oh!"

"Hey, Harebrain, what's your prob . . . oh . . ." Mab trailed off, staring down the alley. He threw out a hand to indicate that I should stay back. I ignored him and rounded the corner. A shiver of dread passed through my body from the roots of my hair to the soles of my feet.

We were gazing down an alley paved with dusty yellow brick. A few palms grew on one side. There was an opening into a café, and the air smelled of fragrant spices, though I also caught a whiff of decaying flesh. In the middle of the alley, blocking the way, three demons stood shoulder to shoulder.

The first was an inky figure with sharp horns, wrapped in a billowing opera cape. His scarlet eyes matched the runes carved into the staff in his hand. Next to him, a stocky man in a robe of thick gray fur leered menacingly. His red hair stood in caked peaks that resembled a punk hairdo, though he followed a far older custom. The third, clad in moldering mummy's wraps, towered over the other two. A gold pharaoh's death mask hid his face, and the red-and-white double crown of the Egyptian kings adorned his head. The eyes of the mask were dark slits, so the direction of the gaze beneath could not be discerned. It was from this last figure that the stench of death wafted.

Quick as the wind, Mab pulled a container from his pocket and, deftly pouring it, formed a protective circle about us. Mab's face was slick with sweat. Putting his finger to his lips and then drawing it across his throat, he indicated that we should keep silent if we valued our lives. Then he passed his hand in front of his eyes, while pointing toward the demons with his elbow, which I took to mean that we should avoid glancing in the direction of the splendid golden pharaoh mask, lest we accidentally make eye contact with the mind-reading Baelor.

So, the three of us stood bunched together, trying not to look at the demons while still not daring to look away, lest they catch us off guard. Mab's precautions are often excessive, but this time I applauded his quick thinking and vigilance. The palpable malice that issued from the demons—sweeping over us and causing me to feel sullied, unclean—diminished after Mab completed his salt ward. Even so, the sensation was as frightening as it was unpleasant, for the demon's infernal presence conjured up memories I loathed to recall.

The alley fell away, and, suddenly, I was back several centuries, following Theo and Titus into an abbey that had been visited by an incubus. The demon's unholy get had eaten their way out of their mothers' wombs, leaving the dead nuns lying with their entrails spread about them in pools of blood. It was the smell of Baelor of the Baleful Eye that brought back this particular memory. The sight had been terrible, but the odor had been worse, as the stench of the nuns' rotting corpses mingled with that of the decayed matter spilled from their exposed innards.

I pulled my attention back to the present, only to again breathe in the demon's stink and find myself transported yet again into my past: the time we found a corpse in an abandoned boneyard, its limbs spread out about the graves, the head bloated and hollowed, as if some creature had been wearing it like a mask. That one gave Logistilla nightmares for years.

This memory was followed by another equally ghastly: a visit to an asylum with Erasmus and Cornelius to question inmates driven mad because some sorcerer had trafficked with a demon. The poor souls screamed horrifically, flinching from invisible foes. They gnawed on their own lips until their mouths were raw and torn. They would have done worse had they not been restrained. The first few had been found eyeless, with gnawed stumps where their fingers should have been. The would-be sorcerer was dead, his blood splattered across the walls of his house. The patients in the asylum were his unsuspecting neighbors. Their only crime: they lived too close to the wrong man.

As bile rose dangerously in my throat, I felt I could not bear much more of this. I closed my eyes and prayed.

Like a soft breath of cool freshness, my Lady's blessing embraced me. The glaring images of mangled bodies and lives gone wrong faded from my thoughts. I felt cleansed, pure. Mab and Mephisto also raised their heads and stood straighter. Apparently, my Lady's blessing extended to them. I thanked Her.

Ahead of us, the third demon moved. From behind his back, he brought out a tall staff topped with a winged lion. It consisted of small figurines similar to the one Mephisto had begun of Mab, strung together like a long totem pole. Birds and angels carved from pale woods made up the first two feet of the staff. Mundane creatures made of apple, cherry, and oak followed, and dangerous mythical beasts of dark mahogany or ebony made up the bottom. The jeweled eyes, set into the carven faces, winked in the bright sunlight like so many points of colored fire.

"My staff!" Mephisto darted forward.

Mab and I both lunged, grabbing him by the hair and shoulders. My brother struggled, twisting and writhing, but there were two of us and only one of him. Furthermore, his recent injuries and vagabond life had taxed his strength. After a brief struggle, he went limp and confined himself to muttering darkly, never taking his eyes off the staff.

Mab wildly glanced about us. One-handedly, he drew out his salt and fixed the circle where Mephisto had scuffed it. From his scowl, I gathered that he would have liked to redraw the ward entirely, but to do so he would have had to release Mephisto.

The stench of death was growing. I fought off the desire to gag and wished I had an extra hand to cover my mouth. I noticed my arms, were trembling from the effort of restraining Mephisto. This was not good.

We could remain here, but for how long? The sun would set soon, and the demons' power would only get stronger as night approached. True, we had a ward, but salt was used to hold off ghosts, ghouls, and vampires. More powerful beings, such as these, could cross such a barrier if they exerted a little effort, especially now that Mephisto had scuffed it.

What other options remained? Run? If so, where would we be safe? Where could one run when fleeing demons? A properly consecrated church would offer sanctuary, but nowadays one could not rely on churches having been properly consecrated.

If we could not stay and we could not run, that left fighting. Fight with what? My flute? Lightning hurt demons, but the sky was blue, and there was not a power line in sight. On a clear day like this, raising enough of a storm to draw a lightning bolt might take as long as twenty minutes, and that was assuming I let go of my brother to play. By then, we could all be dead.

A tornado? Calling up a twister did not require a storm, and I could do it one-handed. In an enclosed alley like this, however, it would be as likely to suck up us as them, not to mention the effect upon the town.

That left us facing demons of Hell with a fighting fan, a lead pipe, and Mephisto's new lute—and that was assuming Mephisto would fight beside us, rather than commit suicide by lunging for his staff. Of course, it might throw the fight in our favor, if Mephisto suddenly reverted to his giant black bat-winged form. If he was not transforming now, to gain his beloved staff, then I doubted we would get help from that quarter. Besides, I did not necessarily want help from a demon, even if it thought it was my brother.

What we needed was Theo's *Staff of Devastation*, or the Ring of Solomon, or one of Mephisto's mythical beast friends. Alas, the mythical beasts were on their side now.

Seir of the Shadows spoke in soft dulcet tones. "Children of Prospero, our quarrel is not with you. Return that which has been stolen, and no harm will come to you."

His voice flowed like music, as pleasing to the ear as his handsome sable features were to the eye. Yet, it was a repulsive pleasantness, evoking passions I did not care to experience. My Lady's breath encircled me again, shielding me from his influence.

Mab, too, stood grimly, refusing to speak. Mephisto, however, showed no such restraint.

"Stolen? You stupid Inkie! We're not the thieves, you are! Or at least that Irish Setter guy with the Celtic hairstyle is! He stole my staff. And look. It's right there! King Tut is holding it in his hand! Do something, Miranda! Make them give it back!" Mephisto stamped his foot.

He had begun to squirm again, and I feared Mab would deck him, or worse, let him go and abandon him to the demons.

Seir replied courteously. "Long ago, Dread Prospero stole nine books that were in his trust. We, the Three Shadowed Ones, are the guardians charged with their return."

"Daddy didn't steal anything!" Mephisto cried. "Unless you count grumpykins Mab here, who wasn't stolen, just compelled; so he still didn't. Besides, we don't even know where those books are!"

Seir gestured with the *Staff of Darkness*, then pointed it at the *Staff of Summoning*. "Two we have already retrieved. A third, the lady Miranda holds in her slender hands: the eldritch flute known as the *Staff of Winds*."

His words made no sense, even to Mephisto, who cried out impatiently, "Those aren't books!"

"Great Prospero altered their form, but we are not deceived."

Was this true? Could that be what Father meant by *they have been put to a greater purpose from which they cannot now be retrieved*? I dared not let the question distract me now.

Osae the Red cocked his head and leered at me; his gaze traveled over my pale peach sundress in a fashion that turned my stomach and caused a frisson of fear as I realized I was not wearing my enchanted tea dress. He rasped, "Just give us the flute, and there won't be any trouble."

"Are you crazy! No!" Mephisto put his hands on his hips, even though we were still holding his arms, and stuck out his tongue. "What's with you guys, anyway? Are you culturally challenged? Shouldn't the guy with the Irish name do his hair like a Celt, and the goofy shapechanger wear the mask? With a name like Baelor, if you want to hide your face, you should paint it with woad!"

The tall Egyptian figure touched two fingers to the golden lips of the pharaoh mask and pointed them at Seir. The incubus's face went slack, and his body became rigid. A deep, jarringly inhuman voice issued from his mouth. The voice made my hackles rise.

"*Puny mortals, vile flesh worms. I know the secrets of your innermost thoughts. I know your insatiable desires, your pathetic hopes, your private fears. I know why the once proud Prospero Family has grown twisted and warped; why Theophrastus's wrath leads him to embrace death, and Titus grows too slothful to maintain his vigil; why Logistilla is consumed by envy, while despair gnaws upon the innards of the once-proud sorcerer. I know your petty secrets, too, Prince Mephistopheles, and yours, O Maiden of Ice, and I spit upon you both in my contempt.*"

Mab stiffened, and I felt my heart beating in my throat. What did Baelor—I assumed this was Baelor somehow speaking through the incubus—mean? Was there a reason for all this madness that had been afflicting us, an explanation?

I longed to cry out, to beg him to tell me, but, of course, he was a demon. Anything he said would most likely be a lie. This did not mean his boasts were empty. Demons were notorious for telling just enough truth to lead men astray.

Seir continued in his inhuman voice, "*I know you as well, Caekias Boreal, who currently plays at a guise called Mab. Why do you allow yourself to be enslaved by these mortals, born but what must die? I know your inner nature. It is akin to mine, filled with wrath and boiling desire. Why do you aid their efforts to oppress you?*"

Mab had remained granite-faced since completing the ward, but I saw him wince when Baelor called him by his ancient name. Was it a name of power, by which Mab could be compelled? Or was he merely reluctant to be reminded of his past?

Before the demon could continue, Mephisto begin to shout. His voice rose in panic, but I noticed a subtle gleam in his eye.

"Come on, Miranda! Detective! Do something, or they'll use it! If they use my staff, we're doomed! All kinds of horrible things can come out of my staff. We'll never get away!"

I shook my head, embarrassed for him. Even demons could not be that stupid. Mab must have felt similarly, for he muttered very softly, "Oh, great one, Harebrain. What you going to do next? Ask them to throw Br'er Rabbit in the briar patch?"

"*I give you one last chance, vile vessel of clay,*" the deep voice of the mind reader spoke through the incubus's sable mouth.

The incubus relaxed, glanced about alertly, and spoke in his own sweet voice. "Lady Miranda, will you surrender the *Staff of Winds*?" When none of us replied, he continued. "Then, as Prince Mephistopheles suggests, his own handiwork shall bring about your demise." Seir tilted his head, his scarlet eyes regarding Baelor, who raised the *Staff of Summoning*.

They had fallen for it. I could not believe it.

The masked mind reader placed his long gold-clad fingers upon the jeweled eyes of one of the figurines, and tapped the *Staff of Summoning* upon the ground. A trick of the light made the pattern of shadows on the hot bricks look remarkably like some great beast.

Then, a real great beast crouched in the alley. The creature had three heads: an enormous lion with a thick tawny mane, a goat with huge curving horns, and a dragon with a mouthful of cruel teeth. Behind these came the agile body of a goat. Its tail, which was curled up over its shoulder, ended in a great orange stinger, shiny with poison. As the creature stalked toward us, it opened its sharp-toothed serpent mouth and breathed curling bursts of hot, fetid fire.

Mab let go of Mephisto and gave him a push toward the thing. Then, he stepped back and put his hands in the pockets of his trench coat, frowning. Reluctantly, I released my brother.

From beyond the beast came Osae's breathy laughter. Seir's soft voice followed. "Surrender the *Staff of Winds*, and we will call off the chimera."

"Death first!" Mephisto called back, grinning widely.

Seir's voice floated over the back of the monster. "As you wish."

The chimera growled and charged, its steel hooves throwing up sparks as they thundered against the yellow bricks. Fire curled about the green scales of its serpent snout, smelling of brimstone. Mephisto rushed forward. Stopping abruptly in front of the thing, he spread his arms and yelled at the top of his lungs,

"Hello, Chimie! Don't you recognize me?"

The great beast piled forward, ignoring the greeting. Too late, I remembered Mephisto's words when his lute broke: *My friends don't recognize me.* Horrified, I watched as the creature set upon my brother, knocking him to the ground and opening its giant lion maw to swallow his head. My mad brother was about to meet a very unfortunate, yet sadly fitting, end, eaten by his own chimera. I leapt forward to help him, but the dragon head breathed fire at me. Jumping back, I patted out the flames on my skirt.

"Damn," whispered Mab. "We'd better run for it. Maybe, if we run out into the traffic, the mythical beast'll get hit by a car."

"If we're not hit first." I drew back slowly, my hand gripping my flute tightly in one hand and my fan in the other.

"Hey . . . wait a second." Mab paused. "Well, would ya look at that!"

The chimera had halted. Slowly, the lion released Mephisto's head and sniffed him with its huge wet nose. Mephisto lay absolutely still, his dark locks singed. From where I stood, I could see his eyes were squeezed tightly closed. Perhaps, he was praying.

The chimera's three heads sniffed Mephisto. The lion's great pink tongue slipped out and licked Mephisto's cheek, its goat head butted his stomach, and the serpent head began to rub against his leg. My brother opened one eye and then the other, an expression of unadulterated joy spreading across his face. Reaching up, he scratched the lion head behind the ears. From its body came a rumbling noise. Could the chimera be purring?

"Hi, there, Chimie," Mephisto cried. "It's me. You know me! Your boss? The guy who loves you and feeds you? The one who is supposed to own that staff?"

Peering under the scaly serpentine tail, Mephisto called to the Three Shadowed Ones. “Pity that staff doesn’t let you command the things you summon, isn’t it, guys? Oh, well. Your loss!” To the chimera, he said gaily, “Get ’em, boy!”

The chimera leapt toward the Three Shadowed Ones, flame spurting from its serpent mouth. Immediately Seir of the Shadows winked out like a snuffed candle.

I caught a whiff of freshly-struck matches. Then, a silky masculine voice whispered in my ear, laughing. “Give me the *Staff of Winds*, my dearest love, and I shall not trouble you again.”

With a single motion, I whipped the mirrored fan of Amatsumaru behind me and slashed his throat. Turning, I saw my blow had fallen short, merely drawing a razor-thin line across his windpipe. A tiny ribbon of crimson blood appeared across the black satiny skin of the incubus’s neck. It matched his eyes.

“Ah, my mistake,” he said politely and vanished. Reappearing between his two companions, he threw an arm about them both.

“*Think not that you have escaped us.*” This time, Baelor’s jarring voice issued from the shapechanger’s mouth. “*If you keep the staves, you are thieves. If you return them, you aid the cause of Hell. Either way, your place among the damned is assured. By Twelfth Night, it shall be sealed!*”

Darkness welled up from Gregor’s staff, and the three demons vanished like a shadow before the sun. The chimera reached the place where they had stood and pawed the ground, sniffing.

“Stupid dopes,” snorted Mephisto. “They could have just used the staff again to send Chimie away.” Turning to us with a hand on his hip, he announced, “Always pays to know your tools!”

WE could not take the chimera on the Lear, so we opted to have lunch while we discussed our options. We found an empty café overlooking the beach. Mab and I sat on the rounded white plastic chairs beneath a blue awning that kept some of the day’s heat off our faces. Mephisto rested on top of the chimera, his hands knotted about the mane. The waiter who approached us gazed at the chimera with an expression of puzzlement and growing terror.

“Stage prop,” Mab said tiredly, waving a hand at the monster. “We’re from Hollywood.”

The terror died from the young man’s eyes. He stared, intrigued.

"Is there a role for me in your movie?" he asked, in his lyrical island accent.

"No," Mab replied flatly.

Cowed, the waiter took our orders and retreated.

"Are we really doomed and damned?" Mephisto asked from the back of the chimera. "These pesky spirits have been flinging about an awful lot of prophecies of gloom lately."

"Most likely," Mab replied tiredly. "You play with fire, you get burned. You play with the Powers of Hell, you get damned."

"We are not damned yet!" I declared. "Nor shall we be, if I can do anything about it!"

"That's the spirit, Miranda," my brother cheered. "Knock 'em dead! Or alive. Or something."

As we waited for our food, I noted that Mephisto was playing with a black dirk with a ruby set in the pommel. I asked to see it.

"I found it at Logistilla's." Mephisto handed me the knife.

"It looks familiar," I said.

"Titus and I made it," Mephisto explained, "for one of Gregor's Centennial Masquerade costumes."

"Centennial Masquerade?" asked Mab. "That's when all the world's immortals gather once a century to chat, right? In costume, as if that's going to help hide their identities. Let me see if I remember . . . on the night of the first full moon after midsummer on the last year before the new century." Mephisto and I nodded. Mab continued, "I attended once. I was part of a costume with a few other guys. I got to control the left knee. Had a grand time blowing humans' tunics around and carrying off their hats." Seeing our frowns, Mab added quickly, "This was a while ago, of course, before we worked for Prospero."

"You went!" I said, amazed. "I've heard gods and spirits come among us sometimes. I never believed it though."

"Elves come, too," said Mephisto.

"Yeah, King Alastor usually goes," said Mab.

"Really?" I asked. "How does he dress?"

"Like himself," said Mab. "Huge antlers, mirrored purple cloak."

"Oh, him! I thought he was a Fomori. No wonder he didn't have an Irish accent." I had danced with the King of the Elves in a London ballroom and had not known it!

"Miranda's elf went once, but she didn't recognize him," said Mephisto.

"I don't own my own elf, Mephisto," I said wearily, though Mephisto's words prompted me to wonder. Had the elf lord come after all? I remembered the wry humor in his stormy eyes and felt mildly sad that he had not chosen to reveal himself. Of course, I reminded myself, Mephisto might be inventing the whole thing.

Mephisto was speaking happily into the chimera's lion ear. "Chimie, you and me! We're going to show this old world. We'll get my staff back, won't we! They'll see!"

"What in creation are we going to do with this thing, Ma'am?" Mab gestured toward the chimera.

"Easy," Mephisto replied. "I just hold on to Chimie until they tap the staff to call him back. They will. They're demons of Hell, after all. They're not allowed to leave magical beasts hanging around on the sunlit plane. Then, when Chimie goes back, I go too and grab my staff. Easy as pie!"

"Begging your pardon for asking, but how do you get away after that?" Mab asked.

"Hmm," said Mephisto. "I know!" He halted and looked at me hesitantly, a speculative gleam in his eye. "What happened to that cloak, the one Mab found at the thrift shop?"

"It's gone," I said.

"Gone! Gone how?" Mephisto sat straight up.

"We destroyed it," said Mab. "It's gone, finished, kaput."

"When? I don't remember!" Mephisto cried plaintively.

"At Theo's, while you were asleep," I said.

"You let Theo see it? Oh, you dopey-heads! Now, how am I going to be able to sneak around? I only left it at the thrift shop because I needed money. You had no right to destroy it!"

The hair at the nape of my neck stood on end. I asked softly, "Only left what, Mephisto?"

Mephisto's face went suddenly pale, as if he only just realized to whom he was speaking. He smiled a nervous smile and babbled, "Anyway, I'll find a way to escape without it. You see, they won't be expecting me. And once I can grab my staff, I'll have all my friends. They can't make my friends their friends just by tapping the staff, can they, Chimie? I'll call Behemoth and Leviathan and Nessie. Or maybe the monstrosity from the Black Abyss. See how well the Three Shadowed Ones deal with him, eh?" Mephisto continued rapidly. He swung his legs out so that he was stretched across the chimera as if it were a Roman couch, one hand entangled in its mane, the other outstretched. "Teach them to trifle with Mephistopheles, Prince of H . . ."

Before he could finish, he and the chimera vanished; fading away as if their presence at the table had been nothing but a trick of the light.

CHAPTER SEVENTEEN

Prospero, Inc.

"Tell me he was not about to say Hell," begged Mab. He leapt to his feet, darted around the slate patio of the café, and peered down the hill toward Charlotte Amalie port, as if to make absolutely certain Mephisto and the chimera had not departed in that direction.

Despite its being December, the weather on St. Thomas was sunny and beautiful, with a salty breeze blowing off the sea. As our waiter approached, the aroma of fried fish, garlic sauce, and coconut supplanted the other scents, even as the clink of dishes drowned out the distant ships' horns and cries of seagulls from the harbor.

I started to rise, to tell the waiter that there was a change of plans and we had to go, but the food smelled so good. I sat down again. I had eaten nothing since last night at Logistilla's, and there would be no opportunity to eat on our plane. Whatever was wrong at Prospero, Inc. could hold another fifteen minutes, while I had my lunch.

"Wish I could," I said to Mab as soon as the waiter had departed. I took a bite of my conch in garlic. It was delicious. "What could he have been thinking? He hasn't seemed all that crazy, except for the thing with the lute. How could he suddenly have forgotten he was not Mephistopheles the demon?"

"Maybe he wasn't going to say Hell," Mab drawled. "Maybe he planned to say 'Harlem' or 'Hollywood,' but I kinda doubt it. None of those places have princes nowadays. Prince Mephistopheles sounds suspiciously like Hell to me. . . . Maybe he didn't forget. Maybe he is the demon Mephistopheles."

"What?" I spit conch across the table.

"It's just I don't remember a demon named Mephistopheles back when I was wreaking havoc as the Northeast Wind. When was that Faust play written, anyway?"

As he spoke, Mab approached the place where Mephisto and the chimera had stood. Slowly, he inched his way around the chimera's tracks, leaning over and sniffing the air. When he had circled the place, he scowled. "No otherworldly scent. That's good for him—means he's still on Earth—but, it makes things harder for me. Earthly scents are harder to pin down."

Mab pulled a sextant, a slide rule, and a handful of brown rice from his pocket. Kneeling, he took a reading off the sun with the sextant, tossed a handful of rice in the air, and took a reading again as the grains pattered to the dusty earth. He stood silently for a time, calculating his results with the slide rule. Then, scratching his stubble, he repeated the whole process again.

I watched him work and sipped my tannia soup, savoring the creamy texture and mild, nutty, potato-like flavor. After five hundred years, it often amazed me there were still foods I had never tasted.

"It's no good," Mab growled finally. "The doorway dissolved too quickly. There's no spatial drift."

"What does that mean?"

"It means he hasn't been taken from this world. Even a short dimensional hop would have allowed some unearthly air to escape through the cracks between worlds. And if there's one thing I can detect, it's unearthly air. The brief whiff I got smells more like Rome or Chicago."

"That's good enough, I guess. I'd ask you to do more, but by the time we found him, either it would be too late, or he'd have his staff again—in which case, he'll be fine. Since I agreed to send him off on his own anyway, I'll leave it like this."

"Ma'am . . . what did he mean about the chameleon cloak? Was it his? How could it have been?"

I recalled our visit to The Elephant's Trunk thrift shop. The clerk had smiled and headed for Mephisto immediately. I had dismissed her interest as romantic. Could she have been smiling because she was already acquainted with Mephisto?

A cold chill ran down the back of my spine. As soon as Mephisto departed, she brought his companion, me, to the chameleon cloak!

"Do you remember how he thought that gas station and The Elephant's Trunk looked familiar?" I asked Mab. "They were familiar! He'd been there before!"

"Your brother was acting weird at the thrift shop. The only excuse I can offer for not having noticed is that he always acts weird."

"But why?" My voice rose. "How could Mephisto own a chameleon cloak? He knows their vicious nature! He helped destroy the originals."

"Maybe he didn't," Mab offered. "Maybe he squirreled one away and had it all this time."

I shook my head. "No, I was there when Mephisto, Theo, and Erasmus destroyed the originals. I watched as each one was unmade. Mephisto must have gotten this one more recently. But where? And why?"

And how long ago? All this time, I had been assuming Mephisto's interest in ponchos over the last century or so was based on nostalgia for his old royal tabards, but might it not have the sinister purpose of hiding his chameleon cloak? I tried to remember when Mephisto first started wearing a poncho. It had been many, many decades, at the very least.

Mab shrugged. "Who knows why Harebrain does anything? Maybe he's actually a demon-haunted horror, or perhaps he wanted it for the reason he gave us, camouflage. Where'd he get that big demon body, anyway? That's what I'd like to know!"

"Me too, Mab. There are a lot of things I'd like to know including . . ." I ticked my questions off on my fingers, starting back at my thumb again when I reached my pinky. "What is up with Mephisto? What's up with Logistilla and her cavern of naked Italians? Is my sister trafficking with the Devil? Is my brother? Is my father? Why did Cornelius use his staff on a brother, and what can be done to disenchant Theo? What was my father doing when he released the Three Shadowed Ones? How do we rescue Father from Hell? What is going to happen on Twelfth Night?"

I took a breath and continued, "Where did Father get his books? Could the virtue of his tomes—their magic—have been in the paper, rather than in the words written upon the pages? Is that why Father could not cast the spells again, once he made our staffs? What really happened to Ferdinand? Where's Gregor's body?" And silently, I added: what is this secret Baelor spoke of that is destroying my family?

Mab flipped through his notebook, looking for additional loose ends. "Dang lucky Mr. Theo showed up when he did at the gas station. I wonder what Harebrain meant about him being prompted by an angel. And . . . Oh!" He tapped his finger on the page before him. "You left out whether Prospero has you under a spell, Ma'am."

"I'm not concerned about that. But, I'll tell you another thing I'd like to know! How did that knife end up at Logistilla's?"

"Knife? What knife? The one Harebrain was playing with?"

"I just remembered why that knife was important. It was on Gregor's body when he died!"

"So, maybe his sister kept it as a keepsake . . . to remember her brother by. Weren't they twins?"

I rubbed my temples, which were beginning to ache. "You don't understand, Mab. It was on his body when he was shot. By the time my family got there, the knife was gone. According to the police report, the killer took it. Now, if the last known person to own this knife was the man who killed Gregor . . . how did Logistilla get it?"

"Maybe she hunted down his murderer and turned him into a newt?" suggested Mab. "Dang! I had meant to ask your sister if we could interrogate the men she mentioned recently adding to her retinue. What an idiot I am! Guess I was distracted by the scent of devils and empty Italians."

Pulling out his notebook, he added our questions to the list he was keeping.

AT the airport, I phoned headquarters and learned that the shipment of phoenix ash promised to the salamanders of Mount St. Helens had never reached its destination. Our truck had crashed somewhere in Arizona, spilling barrels of the precious deadly substance across the road.

Returning to the Lear, we flew directly to Prospero, Inc.'s corporate headquarters in Seattle. I immediately dispatched Mab with a team of experts to clean up the crash. Afterwards, he was to continue on to Elgin, Illinois, to see if Gregor's grave held any clues. Meanwhile, I dealt with the problem of locating another six drums of phoenix ash before the Mount St. Helens salamanders blew their top, literally.

According to modern lingo, Prospero, Inc. was a multinational corporation; however, as it was originally founded in the same era as the East India Company—with a similar royal charter—I still referred to it by the older nomenclature of "company." Early in the twentieth century, we incorporated under the laws of the State of Delaware, leading to our current appellation of Prospero, Incorporated—or as most of us called it, Prospero, Inc. As our supernatural clientele have become familiar with this name, I have kept it, even though the folks at marketing press me, from time to time, to modernize. Mr. Charles Chapman, the vice president of marketing, jokes that our name is so out-of-date, some of the younger employees believe they are working for a printing firm known as Prospero Ink.

Upon arriving, I passed Charles Chapman in the bustling hallway. Father had hired him when he was just out of college, and he had now been with the company thirty-five years. He believed me to be Father's granddaughter, the daughter of the Miranda he had known in his youth. He often paused to tell me how I was the spitting image of my mother, which was more pleasant than Philip Burke, the oldest of our salesmen, who liked to tell risqué stories of his exploits with "my mother" back in the fifties and sixties, none of which even remotely reflected the truth.

After commenting that he remembered my mother wearing that very green dress, Mr. Chapman asked after my father. I smiled and nodded and murmured something unintelligible. As I walked on, I wondered how he would have responded if I had told him Father was in Hell. "Befuddle the mortals" was not a game I cared to play, but it had once been a favorite pastime of Mephisto's and Erasmus's. They had taught it to Ulysses, who took to it like a seal to the sea. For a time, he got a kick out of blurting irrelevant bits of supernatural lore to unsuspecting mortals and then tapping on his staff and disappearing in a burst of light. My father eventually made him stop, ordering him not to make things difficult for the *Orbis Suleimani* after pictures of him using his staff appeared in a British tabloid.

I took an elevator to the tenth floor, nodded kindly to the ladies manning the phones in the upstairs foyer, and pressed my hand against the white rectangle to the left of the locked doors marked "Priority Wing." What looked like a security device was actually a magical talisman that did exactly what a security device would have done—but we had been using ours for nearly four hundred years. The doors swung open and then, with an audible click, locked again behind me. I breathed a sigh of relief.

The company was divided into two major divisions: the Mundane Branch, run by normal humans, and the Priority Branch, staffed by incarnated Aerie Ones. The first handled mundane business concerns: factories, chains of retail stores, and other business ventures of the ordinary sort. The second supported our supernatural customers.

Long ago, King Solomon charged the *Orbis Suleimani* with the task of conquering the supernatural entities whose struggles and strife caused what humans called natural disasters. The great innovation of our company, which was fundamentally a branch, or perhaps an offshoot, of the Circle of Solomon, was the discovery that if we provided wares that spirit creatures wanted—usually some commodity owned or produced by a different kind of supernatural being—they would cooperate willingly, with a minimum of oathbinding and fuss, saving both tremendous effort and countless lives.

Prospero Incorporated carries out this charge by facilitating the exchanges between these entities. We provide phoenix dust to salamanders who otherwise caused volcanoes; cinnamon sticks from the nests of Cinnamologus to the phoenixes; pearls from the nereids to the oreads of the earth, who could make every gem but these; and the black blood of the oreads to hungry djinn. It had taken years, centuries, to negotiate the agreements we currently maintained, and their success was based on a delicate balance between our various clienteles. This balance helps to stabilize the supernatural community. Were even a single link in the chain lost, it would herald untold disaster!

AS I swept into my office, I called to my assistant. "*Presto*, Windflower! I need everything you can get me on phoenix ash depositories!"

Windflower rose from her desk, glanced at the filing cabinet, looked down the hallway toward the library—most of which had been scanned into our database—and sat down at her desk again, where she began typing furiously. She had been a swift westerly breeze before her incarnation, and still retained her innate quickness.

I sat down at my own desk and pulled up the notes that Mustardseed, our vice president of Priority Contracts and the de facto head of the company when I was unavailable, had written thus far. Of all the Aerie Ones, Mustardseed was the most competent at interacting with the human world, and his sharp tongue could keep our supernatural employees in line. He was invaluable; Prospero, Inc. would be lost without him.

Mustardseed reported, among other things, that our current inventory included only a few ounces of phoenix ash. I was not surprised. The stuff was volatile, liable to burst into flame, not the sort of substance we kept stocked in our warehouses.

Without warning, Windflower was standing at my elbow, a disconcerting habit of hers. She was clad in a poppy red Grecian dress with a high golden waist and gold trim along the V-shaped neckline. Her pale blond hair was piled up in the same Grecian style I often wore. Windflower had been my assistant in company matters well before she took on a fleshly body. Apparently, she had picked up her fashion sense from me.

Windflower handed me a steaming mug from which issued the heavenly rich aroma of my favorite Peruvian coffee. I accepted it gratefully and held it in both hands, inhaling.

Her voice rang out cheerfully, "This is what I have so far, Miss Prospero: upon rising from the ashes, the young phoenix embalms the ashes of its parent/former self in myrrh and brings them to one of three sacred depositories: the ancient city of Heliopolis, a hidden valley in the Kunlun Mountains, or a cavern deep beneath the city hall in Tempe, Arizona. For obvious reasons, we usually retrieved our phoenix ash from Arizona. However, that supply now lies scattered across Interstate 10."

"Is there any left at the depository?" I asked, taking a sip of my coffee. It was hot, but not too hot, with the perfect amount of sugar and cream. "Can we gather more from the Tempe location?"

Windflower shook her head vigorously, causing the violet pasqueflower-shaped bells on her hair comb to jiggle and ring. "Not enough to fill one drum, much less six"

"Six drums! That's quite a bit of ash!"

"That was the renegotiated amount after the disaster of 1980. Most of the other volcanoes only receive a few ounces."

"So, what's our next best choice, Heliopolis?" I leaned back in my chair. "The new one or the old one?"

"The old. It is now the Tell-Hisn district, just outside of Cairo."

Glancing at my screen, I paged up until I found the reference to Tell-Hisn I had just scanned. "According to Mustardseed's report, it's the largest depository of phoenix ash in the world, and we have operatives in the area. He says that we provide ash from the Heliopolis depository to Mount Vesuvius, Mount Etna, Mount Fuji, Mount Paricutin, and Krakatoa. I wonder why we haven't used it for St. Helens before?"

"I can answer that, Miss Prospero," Windflower said quickly. She was a veritable encyclopedia when it came to Prospero, Inc. matters, which was, of course, why I had chosen her for my assistant. She had worked for the goddess Rumour before Father captured her people. "The Tell-Hisn cache is frequented mainly by Bennu. The Egyptian Bennu produces a higher quality ash than the American Phoenix."

"Ah! I remember. Father feared that if we ever provided the salamanders of Mount St. Helens with Bennu ash, they would come to expect a similar quality of ash in the future."

"Do you wish to discontinue that policy, Miss Prospero?"

I considered. The Egyptian ash was much more expensive to retrieve than its American variety, and, considering the amount of ash the St. Helens salamanders had demanded after the last fiasco, the cost would be exorbitant.

On top of that, there were the dangers of trying to transport six barrels of volatile ash across the Atlantic on a regular basis.

"Not unless it turns out to be absolutely necessary," I concluded. "Where was the last site? The Kunlun Mountains. In Northern China?"

"South of the Gobi Desert. Phoenixes live in deserts, of course. Their ash caches are near the world's great deserts."

"Is there one in the Australian Outback?" I asked hopefully. Australia was much easier to do business with than Mainland China.

Windflower shook her head, jingling. "Phoenixes are not native to Australia, though there are reports that Xi Wang-Mu has tried to introduce them."

"Xi Wang-Mu? Was that the Chinese fellow who slew the flood dragon?"

"No, that was Lu Yan. Xi Wang-Mu is a woman."

"Oh! Of course, the woman with the phoenix! One of the Chinese Immortals. I had tea with her during the Centennial Masquerade that was held in Cathay. The beginning of the eighteenth century, I think it was." I thought for a moment. "Doesn't she live in a cave in the mountains, somewhere in China?"

"In the Kunluns," Windflower replied with a smile.

"Well that's helpful," I mused. "Now, we just have to figure out how to get the ash out of China."

"And to discover what she wants," Windflower added.

I shook my head. "No. She is a compassionate soul. If she asks for anything at all, it will be for someone else."

"Shall I dispatch one of my people to speak with her?"

"Yes. Wait, no. It will take three days for an Aerie One to get there. Have a pilot fly the messenger to Siberia or South Korea. It will be quicker from there."

Windflower toyed with the anemone-shaped brooch fastened at her right shoulder, her eyes lowered. "That's embarrassing."

"It's an emergency. The ash arrived merely hours over the deadline back in 1980, and the salamanders blew up nearly half the mountain. We can't take any chances."

"If you insist," she sighed. She whisked to her desk to give the order. I took advantage of her departure to drink my coffee, but she was back, comb bells chiming, before I finished swallowing my first sip.

"Done, Miss Prospero," she declared. "Now, once we contact Xi Wang-Mu, assuming she's willing to help us, how are we going to get the ash out?

No lone Aerie One is going to be strong enough to fly six barrels across mainland China. Even a group of us could not do it. You would need a major storm for that."

"Ah, now there's the rub," I pressed my fingertips together.

There were a number of methods of extracting the ash. We could ship it, but to get it through customs, we would need the help of Cornelius, who would have to travel to China in person. The *Staff of Persuasion* only worked within the sound of his natural voice. Under the circumstances, he would go if I asked him to, but China was a tricky place to visit, even for us. I was worried that by the time I reached him and he arranged for a flight, it might be too late.

Ulysses could get there and back in nearly no time, assuming he had Cornelius's help to make it from the city of Datong, where the *Staff of Transportation* had previously touched the earth, to the Kunlun Mountains. But I had no idea how to reach Ulysses.

All other methods at my disposal were too slow, which meant there was only one option left. I was going to have to deal with the Black Market.

"LADY Miranda, what a pleasure," purred Alberich of the Nibelungs from the other side of the phone line. "We are always eager to do favors for Handmaidens of Eurynome."

Silently, I cursed myself for not requesting that Mustardseed make this call. Mustardseed was a wizard at negotiations, but even more important, he could have offered a variety of enticements. As soon as the King of the Nibelungs heard the word "Handmaiden," the options collapsed to a single currency, one I was extremely loath to spend.

"Alberich, a pleasure as always," I replied crisply. "How is your kingdom under the earth?"

"Not as rich as it once was when I had my ring, my lovely ring. Have you seen it?"

"No. Is it lost again? I am sorry to hear that."

"A thief crept into the heart of my palace and made off with it," grumbled the sovereign of the dwarves. "I blame Mime. I've had him clapped in irons for the last half-dozen decades, but he will not confess. But, enough of me. What may I do for you, Lady Miranda?"

"Nothing large, a trifle really." I kept my voice light. Though I needed the ash as soon as possible, the last thing I wanted was for the Nibelung king to discern that this was an urgent matter. He would instantly quadruple the price. Better to offer an incentive to have the matter expedited once an initial price had been settled upon. "I need some goods moved and I was wondering what you would charge to have your boys do it."

"Prospero Transport Company wishes us to move goods for them?" Alberich chuckled. "What is the world coming to? You run one of the best transportation systems on the planet. Why not move it yourself?"

The question stumped me, but I recovered quickly.

"We had a little . . . mishap with one of our trucks. I wish to replace the lost goods without my brothers learning about it."

"Of course," Alberich replied smoothly. "You know we live to serve in such delicate situations."

"Wonderful," I replied airily. "I need six drums of phoenix ash moved from the Kunlun Mountains in Cathay to our headquarters, here in the New World."

"Six drums of . . ." he sputtered. "Six *drums*?" Regaining his composure, he continued. "You do know that stuff is liable to burst into flames if shaken or dropped?"

"I do."

"Moving hazardous materials will increase the price, of course," the dwarf king said glibly. "And then there are the added handling fees for engaging the services of the Cheng-huang, our representatives in that area. They are efficient and thorough, mind you, but too many years of service to the Jade Emperor have made them sticklers for paperwork. Many forms to fill out, a nuisance, you understand."

"Of course," I replied blithely. "What will the charge be?"

Alberich muttered, as if engaged in some massive calculation. Eventually, he cleared his throat.

"Three ounces of Water of Life seems like a fair price, doesn't it?"

"Three *ounces*!" I cried, outraged. I had expected him to open by asking for Water, but this was ridiculous! I could save a hundred and twenty lives or summon as many deities for such a price. "A fair price if I were asking you to deliver me the moon!"

And so the dickering began. I offered all sorts of treasures, from rubies from the river nymphs of the Ganges to a box of stardust I once brought back from the World's End, but while he lowered the amount he was asking for, Alberich held fast to his request for Water of Life.

Eventually, he lowered his demand to six drops, one for each barrel. I pursed my lips and considered. I could afford to part with six drops. It would mean that I had to return to the Well at the World's End one year sooner, but more than six people might be killed if we did not receive the phoenix dust on time. So, on the surface, the bargain seemed worthwhile.

What troubled me was the precedent. Were it to get out that Prospero, Inc. was willing to pay for services in Water of Life, even once, our careful network, through which supernatural entities helped supply each other's needs, would evaporate. No longer willing to settle for dryad bark, fairy dust, and black blood of the earth, every deva, sylph, and djinn would demand Water of Life. Instead of facilitating trade and good relations between magical creatures, we would find ourselves in the business of bribing them from our own pocket.

Even this might not be the worst thing, were I a Sibyl and able to create Water of Life at will. But I was still a Handmaiden, and now that I was running Prospero, Inc., it was getting harder and harder for me to take off the year and a day necessary to make the journey to the World's End. It would be harder still, I realized with a pang, if Father were not around to keep an eye on the company while I was away.

It sat ill upon my shoulders to trust the fate of the company to the discretion of the King of the Nibelungs. No, I needed to find another way.

CHAPTER
EIGHTEEN

The Secret Known Only to Cats

Nestling the phone on my shoulder, I scribbled a note to Windflower, asking her to run down to records and bring back the folder on the Nibelungs. I could not find it in my computer, which meant it was among the thousands of files that had not yet been scanned into the system. Then, I stalled for time, asking Alberich about his family.

I need not have bothered. Windflower had returned with the folder before Alberich had even begun complaining about his ungrateful children.

As the dwarf king launched into his list of the offences that Hagen had committed of late, I nodded my thanks to Windflower and examined the file. My eyes narrowed. No. It could not be that simple . . . could it?

"So, you will provide the phoenix ash in return for six drops," I clarified, when he had paused to breathe. "You have something to store the Water in, of course. It can't just be stacked underground. Nor can you keep it in an ordinary bottle. You have a carafe of cut-crystal Urim to put it in?"

"I figured you would provide . . ." he began.

I laughed. "There is not enough phoenix ash upon all the earth to entice me to part with one of my vials."

"Ah . . ."

"But, I'm sure you can work that out," I continued off-handedly. "And, of course, you are prepared to guard such a treasure. You have a method to keep it from being stolen, a way to see that it isn't carried off, as your ring was? The ring may be recovered some day. A thief has merely to drink the Water and, gulp, the drinker is stronger, faster, and wiser, and your wealth is gone."

"Yes, well . . ." he muttered, flustered.

"Water it is then . . . unless there is something you would prefer."

There was a long silence on the other end. Then, Alberich said hesitantly, "There is something else we crave. Something you might be able to provide."

"And that is?"

"Gold!" his voice was hot with greed.

"You mean ordinary gold?" I deliberately raised my voice in surprise.

"Ordinary?" he raged. "Gold is never ordinary. It is frozen sunlight, the solid manifestation of that which we cannot see, for we cannot view the daystar lest we turn to stone. It sings to us. So precious. So beautiful . . ."

"You drive a hard bargain, King of the Dwarves," I concluded when we had agreed upon the amount. "But I believe we have a deal. A pleasure doing business with you, as always. And . . . oh," I finished casually, "tell your boys, I will throw in a bonus of thirty-five percent if they expedite shipment."

Hanging up, I hit an intercom button on my phone. "Mustardseed. Contact our Arimaspian team and send them to raid the caves of the Hyperborean gryphons until they gather enough gold to pay our bill to the Nibelungs. I'm e-mailing you the details. Have the gold minted into bullion and delivered to Alberich in Iceland, *presto*. Then, have a company Lear standing by to receive the ash and fly it to straight to Mount St. Helens."

I paused and took a breath "While I have you on the line, have there been any major archeological discoveries since I last checked?" I did not say more, but Mustardseed knew well what I wanted: discoveries that might include the scroll inscribed with the last of the Sibylline Books, the one that contained the secrets of the Order of the Sibyl. "No? A shame. Very well. This matter is settled."

By that evening, the Chinese phoenix ash was on its way to Mount St. Helens. The spilt ash had been removed safely from the highway. Mab was in Elgin, Illinois, and I had dashed off a letter to the address Logistilla gave me for Erasmus. In it, I explained about the Three Shadowed Ones and the possibility of some tragedy before Twelfth Night, which loomed ever closer. I urged him to spread the word to any other family members with whom he might be in touch. There was nothing else I could do for my siblings until Mab returned tomorrow. I turned my attention to the matter of Father's disappearance.

Every day that passed was another day my father spent as a prisoner, tortured in Hell, another day for the doom predicted by the fell spirit on the *Happy Gambit* and, again by Baelor, to grow closer. I did not know what the doom was, and I had not the slightest notion of how to rescue Father. It was like being told that one's father was frozen on Pluto or spirited away to the Andromeda galaxy. There was no precedent for retrieving someone from such places.

My only hope was to discover more about the project Father had been working on when he disappeared. If I could figure how he came to be in Hell in the first place, maybe I could find some clue as to how to retrieve him.

While I was away, the weather had grown bitter. When I came home, I found that Ariel had lit the ancient diesel heater. The hum of it could be felt throughout the house, and the smell of petroleum hung in the air. Retreating to the lesser hall, where the pleasant cinnamon of the phoenix lamp overpowered the odor of fuel oil, I curled up in an armchair with Father's latest journals, the ones Peaseblossom had brought back from Father's island for me.

Flames burned merrily in the great hearth. The old heater sent hot air through the radiator vents, but the lesser hall was still drafty. A fire did much to increase the room's cheer. After a time, the heat made me thirsty, but I hesitated to call the butler, as I dreaded yet another conversation about whether or not I would free the Aerie Ones. Theoretically, I could have fetched my own cup of tea, but though I had lived in this mansion for well over fifty years, I had only a vague notion of the whereabouts of the kitchen.

Nearby, my familiar, Tybalt, Prince of Cats, lay curled on a great rosy silk pillow with gold tassels, twitching as he dreamed. He had stalked into the hall earlier in the evening, announcing he had come to keep me company. Apparently, napping was his idea of companionship.

Tybalt had been able to confirm that Father was in Hell. When I returned from Seattle, he told me one of the feline guardians of Kadath had overheard a dark peri discussing the matter with a cacodemon.

As I was scanning a treatise Father had composed on the subject of the Lethe, the river of forgetfulness, Tybalt opened a single golden eye and stretched. At least, if I spoke to him now, he could not accuse me of sending the Dream Gods scurrying.

"Ask Ariel to send a servant with a cup of tea, would you?"

Tybalt lifted his proud black head and looked to the left, down the length of the tapestry-hung hall. Then, turning his head slowly, he gazed to the right, examining the hearth and the phoenix lamp. Finally, he fixed his golden gaze upon my face and asked: "Were you addressing me?"

"You are the only one here."

Lithely, he jumped to the floor and sat before me as proud and dignified as a statue of the Egyptian goddess Bast.

"Do you take me for an errand-kitten? I am a familiar. It is a calling with a long and respected tradition. I do not perform errands. Perhaps you have momentarily confused me with your flunky, Mab."

"No danger of that. Mab does what he's asked to do," I answered. "So, just what *are* you supposed to do, O Familiar?"

"Advise you on arcane matters and guide you through the supernatural so that your soul does not wander astray." The cat stretched.

"Ah, but isn't fetching messages to and from the spirit realm also a duty of familiars?"

"Indeed."

"While Ariel is not technically in the spirit realm, he is a spirit. Thus, bringing a message to Ariel, even one so simple as to prepare tea, is within the duties of a familiar."

"With cats, technicalities make all the difference," replied Tybalt.

I could have made an issue of it, but I decided it was not worth the effort. Tybalt had been with me for centuries. His manners had always been atrocious. Under any other circumstance, I would have dismissed him for his impertinence, but he had been a gift from Father.

In the old days, before we had our staffs, calling upon Father's magic had required the casting of intricate spells. One Christmas, after we had suffered a few magical mishaps, Father presented us with kitten-shaped familiars. (This was back in Milan, so there were only the four of us: Mephisto, Erasmus, Theo, and myself. Later, he gave familiars to Cornelius and Logistilla as well. The other three, Titus, Gregor, and Ulysses, never took enough of an interest in magic to need one.)

Last I had heard, Erasmus, Cornelius, and Mephisto still had their familiars—Tybalt particularly hated Erasmus's familiar, Redesmere, whom he considered his dreaded rival—but what had become of Theo's cat, I had no idea. As for Logistilla's, she had taken to changing its shape every few years. For all I know, it might have been one of the spider monkeys or the marmoset.

Since I no longer practiced ritualistic magic, I no longer needed a familiar. Yet, somehow, I had never gotten around to banishing Tybalt.

Aloud, I said, "The Three Shadowed Ones have predicted a doom will fall upon my family by Twelfth Night. The date is getting closer and closer, but we don't yet have any inkling of what the threat might be. Have you heard anything?"

Tybalt's tail twitched with annoyance. Apparently, he did not think much of fell spirits who threatened his humans. It gave me a warm feeling. For all his arrogance, Tybalt was fiercely loyal to my family.

"Not as yet," he said, "but I can inquire."

"Perhaps you can help me with another matter. I'm trying to unravel the mystery of my father. . . ."

"I am very good at unraveling things," interrupted Tybalt, absently batting at the pillow's golden tassels.

I smiled at that. "I'm trying to puzzle out what my father was up to. What do you make of this poem?"

I read from Father's journal.

"I invoke the consort of Divine Zeus,
Mother of the nine sweet-speaking Muses;
Free from the oblivion of the fallen mind,
By whom the soul is joined and reason increased.
All thought belongs to thee,
All-powerful, pleasant, vigilant goddess,
'Tis thine to waken from lethargic rest
All thoughts residing within us, neglecting none.
From the dark oblivion of night, you enlighten the inner eye.
Come, Blessed Power, wake thy mystic's memory of the holy rites
And break the chains of the River Lethe."

Tybalt tilted his triangular head, " 'Ode to Mnemosyne' by the poet Orpheus?"

I jerked my head up in surprise. "Orpheus wrote this? You mean a real ancient Greek man named Orpheus, the man who spawned the myths? Wasn't he the founder of the Eleusinian Mysteries?"

"Indeed," replied the cat.

I quickly flipped through the journal pages, glancing at several earlier essays. Father had copious notes on the Eleusinians and their rituals, stuck in amidst the many drafts of his metaphysical treatise on Death and Rebirth, and the various renditions of what I had taken to be his poetry. But if these poems were actually Eleusinian prayers . . . perhaps I had discovered a theme.

"Do you know anything about the ancient Eleusinians?"

"Certainly. They were a cult of ancient Greeks who tried to imitate the secret of cats."

Despairing at receiving any help from this quarter, I sighed. "Tybalt, not everything in the world relates to cats."

Tybalt rose gracefully to his feet and began to stalk away. "If my wisdom is not appreciated, I will withhold it. No need to waste water trying to fill a sieve."

I sighed again. "Please. Continue."

Tybalt stepped onto one of the large silk pillows and walked three times in a circle. Taking his time, he settled down comfortably, pausing to lick a back paw and scratch an ear. Finally he raised his proud head and spoke.

"The Eleusinians wished to discover our great secret—how to pass through the gates of death and be reborn without forgetting one's former self. By ancient covenant, cats are allowed to pass over the River Lethe nine times without drinking of its waters. The Powers That Be hold that if a cat is not wise enough to learn to stay out of trouble after nine tries, he might as well be sent back *tabula rasa*."

I had to hand it to him. When one looked at it that way, the Eleusinians were trying to learn the "secret of cats."

"That matches what Father has written here. His treatises and the Eleusinian rituals both deal with death and rebirth. So, these poems are actually invocations—possibly all written by Orpheus—to Mnemosyne, Persephone, and Demeter. They were the goddesses worshipped by the Eleusinians, weren't they?"

"The Maiden, whose proper name I will not utter lest her attention be drawn nigh, was the key to the Eleusinian mysteries," Tybalt replied loftily. "As the wife of the God of the Dead, she had jurisdiction over Rebirth. If you should happen to be family, she would be inclined to grant you a favorable pleasant next life. The Eleusinian mysteries involved a ritual to make one the adopted child of the Grain Goddess, the Maiden's mother . . . and, thus, a member of her family."

"You mean, the Eleusinians convinced Demeter to adopt them, and then hoped to be judged favorably and given good lives the next time they were born, due to nepotism?"

"That's the basic idea," replied Tybalt. "Except they hoped for more than just a good life. They hoped Persephone would make a special exception for them and allow them to be reborn without having to drink from the Lethe—so they could keep their memories."

"Did it work?" I asked.

"For a time," replied Tybalt.

"What finally went wrong?"

Tybalt tilted his head, his gold eyes bright and fixed. "These days, most of those who wish for a better life appeal to a higher power."

"Hmm . . ." I ruminated over what Tybalt had revealed. "It seems everything in Father's latest journal revolves around one project. In fact . . ." I flipped through some more pages. The crisp paper turned easily beneath my fingers, "the only thing he mentions that is not related to rebirth is his horticulture project."

Tybalt eyed me evenly. "Would that be the horticulture project in the Wintergarden?"

"Here?" I cried. "In our Wintergarden?"

"I accompanied him when he went to check on it, last time he was here. He was kind enough to put down some shavings for me to capture."

"Interesting! I'll have to go down there and take a look," I mused.

The Wintergarden was technically in Prospero Mansion; however, it was not on Earth. A journey there could take as long as four days. I made a note to make time for such a venture.

Tybalt stared into the fire. His body tensed, as if he were preparing to spring forward and bat at the dancing flames. Then he turned his head and regarded me again, saying, "The Eleusinians vanished long ago. I had thought the Eleusinians' lore vanished with them, for they were good at keeping secrets. How is great Prospero gaining his wisdom concerning their rituals?"

"According to this journal, he has been summoning up the ghosts of the dead and invoking the lesser messengers of the Greek gods in order to question them."

Tybalt froze mid-yawn and fixed me with a bright golden stare. "Summon the gods? I am no Mab to chasten the curious, but even by my standards, Master Prospero skirts dangerously near the line between daring and foolhardy. No cat would be so foolish as to trouble the gods! That might attract the interest of their father, horned Alastor—a fate I would only wish upon a dog, or Redesmere."

"Alastor is the king of the elves," I said. "You are thinking of Jupiter."

"Mortals!" Tybalt eyed me disdainfully. "Your cumulative knowledge amounts to almost nothing. A bit here, a tiny glimpse there. You weave it together and declare that you have figured out the universe. All your myths and gathered lore are but hints of the truth; a truth that can only be glimpsed by eyes that dare not blink." He lowered himself regally, so that he sat in the posture of the Sphinx. "As for Alastor and Jupiter, the two are the same. Alastor is his name when he rules over the Seelie Court. The Lord of Heaven is what he is called by his children, the Greek and Roman gods. His Scandinavian children call him Odin. None of these names, however, is what he is called among my people."

"And by what name do you call him?"

Tybalt turned his head and began washing his shoulder. "That can be of no interest to you, as you are not a feline."

Sometimes, there is no point in talking to cats.

THE fire crackled. A log floated by, carried by an Aerie One. I read on, picking my way through passages written in Homeric Greek, a language I had not used in decades. On the pages beyond were sketches in my father's steady hand; pictures of the "Gate of False Dreams" and the "Gate of True Dreams," a sketch of Charon, the ferryman of the river Styx, and renditions of Eleusinians at their rituals. A rough sketch on a following page showed Father's horticulture project. It seemed to involve sprouting a cutting of some kind.

As I was studying the sketch, Tybalt leapt up onto my chair again. Settling upon the arm and beginning to wash, he asked casually, "Has Mab gone to hunt down the saboteurs?"

"What saboteurs?"

"The ones who destroyed our truck."

"The truck with the phoenix ashes? What makes you think it was sabotage?"

"We familiars hear things."

"Interesting . . ."

Ariel's voice interrupted, fluting softly. "Mistress, there is a visitor at the front portal. He refuses to surrender his name."

"Maybe he's one of the saboteurs," suggested Tybalt.

"Or a policeman with grim news," I said, standing. "Or a Jehovah's Witness. They have been here three times in the last two months. Was he wearing a uniform, Ariel?"

"He was not a Beefeater, if that was the direction of your inquiry," Ariel replied.

I sighed. There were disadvantages to having servants who did not get out much. "Bring the magic mirror, Ariel, the one that shows the house and grounds."

* * *

WITH a whoosh, a large oval mirror in a highly-polished peachwood frame flew into the lesser hall and came to rest on a marble stand made especially to hold it. I knelt before it.

Gazing into its misty gray depths, I chanted, "Mirror, mirror, on the floor, show me who is at the door."

The mirror's misty surface cleared to reveal the imposing facade of the front of the mansion. Snow swirled over the granite stoop. A lone man stood with his back to the mirror. The collar of his elegant charcoal cashmere overcoat was raised against the cold. His coat was so well-tailored that it emphasized rather than hid his lithe and athletic build. His expensive black kid gloves matched his coal black hair. He wore no uniform and carried no Bible.

"He shows remarkable understanding of the First Law," Tybalt observed, referring, of course, to the First Law of Cats: *Always look good.* In cat etiquette, this extraordinarily important law was followed by two others: *Always have at least three escape exits,* and *When in doubt, wash.*

"I had not realized saboteurs could be so . . . catlike," he finished, washing.

Almost as if he had heard Tybalt's voice, my mystery visitor turned to glance down the gravel driveway stretching from the house, through the tall pines, to the road a quarter of a mile away. He now faced the mirror, his vivid brown eyes focused somewhere beyond us. I stared at his face, saying nothing.

"But then, he looks more like a statue than a saboteur," Tybalt batted at the image in the mirror.

I continued to say nothing. The hall seemed to be shaking, though I suspected it was caused by the beating of my heart.

"Show him in, Ariel." My voice sounded somewhat breathless to my ear. Tybalt tilted his head and fixed me with an inquiring golden eye. "It's all right," I said. "I know him."

CHAPTER
NINETEEN

The Prince of Naples

Ferdinand strode into the hall and tossed his coat over the back of a chair. He stopped when he saw me, his eyes drinking in my face. He stood thus for a moment, before pulling off his gloves, one finger at a time, and tossing them atop his overcoat. Then he came toward me, both arms outstretched.

"Miranda, *bella mia*!" Kneeling before me and seizing my hands, he drew them against his lips. His eyes gazed eagerly into mine, and he smiled happily. "How I have missed you!"

"Hello, Ferdinand," I replied cordially. "What are you doing here?"

There came a low *grrrrr*. Tybalt sat crouched upon the large pillow. His claws needled the weave of the silk, as if preparing to attack. His golden eyes watched me, waiting for a sign. Seeing him, Ferdinand drew back and asked: "Are you a demon spirit? Or a harmless mortal creature?"

The black cat looked at me, for he never spoke in front of mundanes. I nodded.

"Why are you asking me? Cats don't talk," Tybalt replied. The firelight flickered in his eyes.

Turning his back on us, he circled three times and curled up on the pink silk pillow to sleep. As I sat down, there came the rustle of Aerie Ones passing among the draperies and tapestries as they gathered along the length of the hall. I was about to reassure them, figuring they were as alarmed by our visitor's behavior as Tybalt had been, when Ariel spoke. His words startled me, for I had forgotten their acquaintance.

"Now I recognize you, Prince Ferdinand, whom once I drowned, then brought again to life's shore. There young Mistress Miranda happened upon you, stretched upon the sands of her father's island, waterlogged and stinking of brine. You were the first man her naïve eyes beheld, save for her father and wretched Caliban. Half my long captivity at the hands of the magician

Prospero has passed since last I beheld your face. You have changed much!" came Ariel's voice. "Be as welcome here as you were unwelcome in Prospero's more humble abode upon that long-forsaken island."

"Ariel, my old friend! Is it truly you?" Ferdinand laughed. His voice rose with excitement. He bounded to his feet and gazed upward, here and there about the hall, as if by an effort of will he might see the invisible spirits of the air. The intensity of his reaction startled me, as I had not recalled he knew Ariel and the others more than briefly. His stay in Hell must have been unspeakably awful, if a reunion with even the vaguest of associates engendered such enthusiasm. "Oh, glorious! I accept your hospitality, kind spirit, and thank you for remembering me."

"Of course, we recall you," came the fluted answer. "For only in those few fair days when you dwelt with her was Mistress Miranda truly happy."

"That is enough, Ariel. You are all excused!" I rose and smoothed my skirt. There was a rustling, then silence. The fire crackled. The room smelled pleasantly of burning wood.

As the Aerie Ones retreated, Ferdinand came toward me. I moved stiffly to stand beside the hearth. He hesitated, then threw himself into an overstuffed Victorian chair, stretching out his long legs, and smiled at me.

"Only happy when you are with me, *bella mia*? No, do not say anything. Ariel has revealed all!"

"That was long ago." My voice was cold and distant. "What brought you here?"

"I am to spend Christmas vacation at the home of one of my professors in San Francisco. I took an early flight so I could spend this evening with you. I called yesterday, but there was only a machine," Ferdinand said.

"I was in Seattle on business."

"Ah! I suspected you were still away. Please, Miranda *bella*." He gestured toward another Victorian armchair across the Persian rug from him. "Sit down, and let us speak of what we have seen in the long years since last we met. I have told you of my adventures. But what of you? When did you leave Milan? Where did you go?"

I gazed into the fire and considered. If the Ouija board could be trusted, he was who he said he was, and his story was true—at least the part about having been trapped in Hell. Nor did he exude the unpleasant aura of menace I had come to associate with demons. There was a still a mystery here, surely, but it could do no harm to talk with him. It might even be pleasant. I took the chair he had indicated.

"Very well, let us talk."

We spoke long into the night. He told me tales he had heard from those he met in Hell; witty tales, pathetic tales, tales that wrenched the heart. I told him of our life since Prospero's Island. Of our triumphant return to Milan, Ferdinand already knew, so I described what had come after; how Father had ruled Milan kindly and well for thirty-five years and how Uncle Antonio betrayed us to Louis XII of France and his French sorcerers. I described our flight to Switzerland, and how we settled in England, our life in the courts of Henry VIII and Queen Bess, and Theophrastus's friendship with the impetuous Earl of Essex.

I told him the tale of how I had lost my raven hair; how Erasmus and I had quarreled; how he had used his staff upon me, leaving me with the thin and colorless hair of an old hag. I spoke of how I humbled my pride, bent my knee, and begged him to restore it—for the *Staff of Withering* could bring youth as well as the ravages of time—and of how he had laughed, claiming that my plight amused him. I told of the year-and-a-day journey I had taken to the World's End, and of how washing my hair in that fountain had restored its life, but not its color, leaving me with the silver-white locks I still bore today.

I spoke of how Mephisto and Cornelius used their magic to create the tulip craze in Holland and of the disastrous crash that followed; of life with Logistilla in Denmark, while my brothers marched against the Spanish with Marlborough; and of Gregor's second term as pope. I described Erasmus's and Cornelius's part in the East India Company; the high life in France under Napoleon III; and the steamer that took Theo and me to America in 1910. Finally, I summed up the tragedy that had befallen us since we arrived in this new land: how Gregor's death had led to the breakup of my family.

It was well past midnight when I came to the end. Ferdinand laughed happily and leaned back. Between his hands, he held a mug of steaming mulled cider. A silver tray holding fruit and scones rested upon the coffee table, which had once belonged to Louis XIV.

"Ah, Napoleon III, a charming man, yet sad. I know him well. He dwells in the Second Circle and is still much as you described him to be in life. We often played chess, he and I, to while away the long hours," said Ferdinand. He ran his finger along the coffee table. "Louis XIV, I have known too, though not as intimately, and I have met several of those French sorcerers who drove you from your homeland: Malagigi, his brother Eliaures, and their sister Melusine—the one with the serpent's tail. How many other prominent, and not-so-prominent men must I have met below who knew you during their life!

"Pity, I never knew to question them about you," he finished, smiling into my eyes. "The dark and dreary hours would have seemed so very much lighter if I could have spent them being regaled with tales of your wit and beauty. I could have spoken of you as a girl, and of your sweet and innocent charm. They could have told me of you as you grew, perhaps describing the serenity and stately grace you have gained with the passage of time."

I sat silently, regarding my hands, which were folded in my lap, and listened to the crackle of the burning wood. I was uncertain how to respond to his constant stream of compliments. None of my usual defenses against such behavior seemed to operate. Cool haughtiness availed me nothing, for Ferdinand just laughed and said, "*Mia*, Miranda, come! You cannot fool me with these arctic blasts. I know you better than that." Nor did it help to remind myself that I was Miranda Prospero, Handmaiden of the Unicorn, and he but a mortal. For Ferdinand was not a mortal, clearly—as he walked upon the Earth, and yet was older than I.

So long had it been since I had sat comfortably, speaking with an equal, that I could not recall when such an event had last occurred. With the exception of Theo, I had seldom been comfortable with my siblings, and no mortal I had met since we left Milan was truly my peer. Even Theo, whom I dearly loved, was a younger brother to be protected and coddled. With the exception of one fair summer night in 1627, I could not remember a time I had talked with a man I considered an equal, since I last sat with Ferdinand, speaking earnestly of our life and hopes, the night before we were to wed, over five hundred years ago.

As I mused, my gaze must have strayed to the figurine sitting on the mantelpiece, the only memento I owned of that fair summer night. Ferdinand's gaze followed mine. In the rapid way in which he did everything, he rose and bent close to examine it. He uttered a short exclamation, but his back was to me, and I could not make out what he said.

"What beautiful craftsmanship! Who is it?" He held up the tiny statue of polished beech wood. It was a wonderful likeness of a handsome man with upswept features and tiny sapphires for eyes.

"Oh, that?" I said, smiling. "That's my elf."

Ferdinand stood a moment longer with his back to me, but I could see the lines of tension in the muscles of his shoulders. When he turned toward me, his face, normally so vivid and vital, was as blank as a mask. The expression in his eyes, however, appeared almost tortured.

"And what did he mean to you? This elf man?"

I gazed at the little elf figurine. What had he meant? He had meant freedom and exhilaration, and a promise of something wondrous beyond the life I knew. A false promise, I acknowledged with the tiniest tinge of bittersweet regret, but oh, how enchanted I had been by what he had pretended to offer!

I did not say this to Ferdinand, of course. Instead, I laughed gaily.

"Ferdinand! Are you jealous of an elf I met once, three hundred years ago? Oh, that is delightfully amusing."

Ferdinand would not be distracted. He placed the tiny elf on the coffee table and, putting his foot on the irreplaceable Persian carpet, leaned over to gaze ardently into my eyes.

"You did not answer my question, *bella mia*—what did he mean to you that you would keep his likeness here on your mantel all these many years?"

"He did not mean anything to me, Ferdinand. I keep it because Mephisto made it for me," I insisted, gesturing at the little elf. "Mephisto wanted me to marry the elf."

"He told you that?" Ferdinand asked, shocked.

"Mephisto is always coming up with schemes like that. It is a pretty piece of craftsmanship, though, and I kept it because it reminds me of happier days. Carving this piece was one of the last things Mephisto did before his mind began to go."

"And the elf? He meant nothing to you?" There was a plaintive quality to his voice, as if my answer to his question mattered enormously.

"Nothing, Ferdinand. Now, please sit down. Surely, you don't expect me to defend every gift, object, or likeness I might have acquired in five hundred years? Besides, it is no concern of yours."

Ferdinand sat back in his chair, oddly deflated. It was a moment before he answered.

"You are still my fiancée." He met my surprised gaze. "Neither you nor I have yet renounced our betrothal. No mortal man you may have met while I was locked in Hell could be a threat to me. Unless you had met him in the past score or so of years, he is now far more trapped in the drab afterworld than ever I was. To learn you were wooed by an immortal, however, and an elf lord at that . . . had you lost your heart to such a one . . ." Ferdinand fell silent. He lifted his steaming mug to his lips and sipped of the warm cider.

After a few moments, he spoke again. His voice seemed altered, almost as if his previous lightheartedness had been an act, and only now did he speak from the heart.

"You must excuse me, Miranda. When you have lived above, and now must dwell below, and your only crime was the chaste love of a virtuous woman, the affections of that woman take on enormous significance. Eventually, when the truth is known about the Quee . . ."

Ferdinand doubled over, coughing. His mug tumbled free, causing him to cry out as the hot cider scorched his thigh. He slipped to the floor, choking. He hands flew to his throat, almost as if he struggled to fend off some invisible attacker.

Startled and frightened, I leapt up and went to him. A glass of water stood upon the tray. I knelt down and offered it to him. He took a sip and smiled at me as best he could. After a couple of swallows, he managed to catch his breath, and began mopping at his soaked thigh with a linen napkin from the tray.

"Thank you, *bella mia.*"

We knelt close together upon the Persian carpet. The fire hissed and cracked behind us. Ferdinand stared gratefully into my eyes and lifted his hand to touch my cheek. I rose quickly but took his outstretched hand, helping him up. We faced each other, our features lit by the flickering firelight. A foot or two of space separated our bodies, but I was aware his presence. Even with my eyes closed, I felt I would have known exactly where he was; in the same manner that I knew, without needing to look, the location of my own arm.

Ferdinand watched me intently, but his gaze was no longer directed at my eyes. I found myself unaccustomedly aware of the pleasing cut of my tea gown and the narrowness of my waist. The sensation was disturbing.

"You should drink more carefully, unless you are overeager to return to the afterworld," I said with a twitch of a smile. "You had been saying?"

"Ah, yes. As I had been saying . . . Ah, when the truth is known . . . about your father, I hope it will not be too hard for you to take."

Ferdinand's glance disconcerted me, and his words touched upon a subject I had striven to forget these last few days. I turned away to gaze toward the hearth. Even with my back turned, I remained aware of him.

"My family is coming apart at the seams, Ferdinand," I said, admitting aloud what had been tormenting me. "They desert each other and betray each other. I don't understand them. I cannot understand how they can ignore their familial duties!"

"Perhaps, they do not know what is expected of them," Ferdinand offered softly.

"How could they not?" I countered fervently. "How could anything be more clear than what Father expects of us? Father tells us what needs to be done. All we need to do is follow his orders! What could be less obscure?"

"Not everyone is like you, *bella mia*. What you are saying is . . . unusual." Out of the corner of my eye, I could see he was watching my face and frowning.

Haltingly, I said, "Theo believes . . . that . . . that Father has cast a spell on me so that I cannot help but obey him."

Ferdinand nodded slowly. "It may be true. Most immortals do not remain steadfast as you have, remaining loyal for five hundred years to your Lady and your father. Even your father—has he not wandered from his main pursuits at times?"

"But, it is so clear to me!"

"Is it clear, *bella mia*? Or is it that all other choices have been obscured?"

I turned toward him, tipping my chin up to look into his face. "Do you think I am under a spell?"

Ferdinand stared down into my eyes. "Darling, I cannot say. It may be that you are. However, it may also be that you are more like an angel than other mortals. Angels do not swerve from their duties, for they see no path but the most virtuous one open to them." His fingers caressed my neck, brushing aside a lock of hair. I jerked, startled by his touch.

"I saw an angel once," I blurted.

Ferdinand tilted his head and gazed at me, his brows drawing together. "But I thought you would have seen many angels, being the daughter of Prospero, who summons them to do his bidding?"

"Yes, of course I've seen many angels. I suppose it was an odd thing for me to say." I laughed. Then, gazing up at Ferdinand, I added more softly, "But once, I saw an angel that was not summoned by magic. She came for me, entirely on her own. It happened a long time ago, and I have never spoken of her visit to anyone, not even Father."

"Tell me of it." His voice was hushed.

"It was during the awful months after . . . our wedding." I faltered, embarrassed by the blush that rose to my cheeks. Ferdinand took my hand in his, patting it gently. "I was very distressed, then. I thought . . . I thought I might prefer to be dead."

"No! *Bella mia*!" Ferdinand squeezed my hand. "Oh, better we had never met than that I should have caused you such pain."

I continued, "One evening as I wandered aimlessly about *Castello Sforzesco*—you remember the long reddish-brown corridors—as I walked, a terrible sadness came upon me, and I dropped to my knees and prayed, not to my Lady, but to Heaven, asking for release.

"As I knelt on the cold stone, my head bowed with bitter despair, a warmth came over me. A soft golden light shone down on me, bathing my body and the flagstones.

"When I looked up, I saw an angel. Her garments were of purest green, her waist and sleeves inset with silver and pearls. In her hands, she held a partially-opened scroll, of which I could only make out the first few letters. Her delicate silver slippers did not reach down to the flagstones, but hovered above them. Five pairs of seagull wings sprang from her shoulders; some folded behind her, others spread wide behind her. Five halos floated above her head: a circle of white light above which hovered a ring of ocean spray, and then one of water lilies bejeweled with drops of water like little silver pearls, one of river foam, and the top was a circlet of shining gold. It was from this last that the light came.

"She hovered there above me, a beneficent smile touching her perfect lips. When she spoke, her voice was a sound of inhuman beauty, the sound that music strives to imitate. And she said," I spoke the words in the original Italian, as they had been spoken to me, long ago, " '*Rejoice, my child, do not despair! All joy in Heaven and on Earth awaits you.*'

"Awed, I asked her name, and she replied, '*Muriel Sophia.*' At that moment, I was startled by footsteps in the hall behind me. When I turned again, she was gone. However, the sorrow weighing on my heart began to lift. Over the next few weeks, it broke apart as ice on a mountain pond breaks apart with the thaw, and my life slowly began to take on meaning again."

Ferdinand said nothing; his eyes were filled with a quiet awe. He stood near to me, holding my hands. I could smell the pleasant musk of his body. Slowly, his gaze not leaving my eyes, he lowered his head toward mine.

Century-long habits are hard to break. Almost without my knowledge, my hand flew to slap his face.

I have, over the years, slapped the faces of a thousand impertinent men, from farmers and scalawags to the nobility and royalty of three continents. I am far older than they, and, with my Lady's blessing upon me, far swifter. None of them, not even the famed sword fighters of France, ever dodged my blow. Ferdinand, however, casually caught my arm mid-flight. He held it where he had seized it, and his fingers closed tightly about my wrist. Still staring into my eyes, a slight smile playing about his lips, he began to kiss my palm.

As his lips gently caressed my sensitive skin, tremors of bliss shot through my hand, spreading along my arm and through the entire length of my body. I felt transfixed, unable to resist as Ferdinand proceeded to kiss the tip of each of my fingers.

Still grasping my wrist, Ferdinand reached out with his other hand and lightly touched my cheek. His fingers caressed my cheekbone and the line of my nose and chin. He curled his hand behind my neck, drawing me toward him. Of their own volition, my head tilted back, and my eyes half-closed.

Bending, he brushed my mouth with his. My lips parted. I leaned into his kiss, and heard myself moan softly. Then, his arms came tight about me, embracing me, and he crushed me to his chest.

The sensation coursing through me, as he held me, was all the more amazing for its familiarity. It was the same warmth that touched me when I called upon my Lady. Only now, it was as if that warmth had woken up and taken on a life of its own. It coursed through my limbs like a living thing, spreading wildfire. The feeling was dizzying, and far headier than the finest wines. As Ferdinand raked his hand through my hair and bent to brush his lips against the soft skin of my neck, it occurred to me I had been wrong all these years; there was a pleasure greater than the knowledge of a task well done. My arms snaked about his neck, and I returned his kisses as best I could with my untutored lips.

We stood thus entwined, the fire crackling behind us. He kissed me more deeply, and the hall around me faded. I was aware only of Ferdinand and of myself. My heart raced uncontrollably. I shivered, alarmed by the wild, intoxicating sensations bedazzling me. My fingers trembled against the hard muscles of his back. I feared both that he might continue and that he might stop.

It occurred to me that we were appropriately engaged. We could marry, and I would never need to be farther from him again than this.

Like an icy wind on a pleasant spring day, memory cut through my dazed fantasy, and I recalled who I was and what I was about. Sibyls could marry but not mere Handmaidens. A Handmaiden must remain a virgin if she wished to maintain her position. I would have to choose between Ferdinand and my Lady. The choice was an easy one.

I pulled back my head and said, in as cool a voice as I could muster, "I would like you to leave now."

I would have sounded calm and dignified, except I was short of breath.

Ferdinand did not object as I half expected, half hoped he would. He stood a moment as if stunned, an indecipherable expression in the depth of his brown eyes. Then, he nodded with a sad smile.

"If that is what you wish, *bella mia,* then I will go. I know all this is new for you. Alas, it is far past the time I should have left. I am expected elsewhere tomorrow and must be on my way."

Crossing the room, he slipped into his cashmere overcoat and wrapped a white pilot's scarf I had not previously seen about his neck. Dressed thus, he looked very much like the cover of a glossy men's fashion magazine.

Coming back to me, he said, "It was a charming evening, was it not?"

"Yes . . . I had a lovely time," I said, to my surprise. I had intended to be cold to him, but, yet again, his manner cut through my haughtiness. "It has been a long time since I have spoken to anyone as we spoke tonight."

"And I may see you again?" He bent down to look into my averted eyes.

"Very well," I replied haltingly.

"When?" he asked. "You must tell me when, *bella mia*! I must have something to look forward to!"

The intensity of his gaze flustered me.

"Ah . . . New Year's Eve, my brother Erasmus is throwing a party. It's in . . . I forget where, Ariel will give you the address on your way out," I blurted out. Louder, I called, "Ariel, give Ferdinand the address Logistilla gave me."

Until the words left my mouth, I had given no thought to Erasmus's party. If Ferdinand accepted, I would be obliged to go. I found myself torn between an unrealistic hope that Ferdinand's New Year's Eve would already be unavoidably occupied, and an intense wish that he would attend.

"Your family will be there?" A keen spark of interest showed in his deep brown eyes.

"Some of them," I replied speculatively. Little help as my family might be in other ways, I could trust them to thoroughly interrogate anyone who might make extravagant claims about Father. I was curious to see what Cornelius, who claims he can hear truth in a person's voice, would conclude about Ferdinand's story.

"I would like that, *bella mia.*" He took my hands. "I would like to meet your family." He bent his head and kissed both of my hands. "And now I must trouble you to call a taxi, for I have no other vehicle."

Ariel gave Ferdinand Erasmus's address, while I called for a taxi. When it came, I accompanied Ferdinand to the driveway. The snow, which had tapered off during the night, had recently resumed. A blanket of white lay over the lawn and surrounding trees. All seemed hushed. I walked beside Ferdinand down the snowy slate path to where the taxi waited in the curving drive.

"New Year's Eve then, *bella mia*," he whispered to me, as he opened the rear door of the red-and-white cab. I nodded silently, shivering in the chilly night air.

Ferdinand bent to climb into the seat. Straightening suddenly, he swung around and seized me, crushing me to him. He kissed me harshly, his lips bruising mine with their roughness. I kissed him back and slipped my shivering arms beneath his coat to embrace him, the warmth of his body spreading slowly to me.

The snow swirled about us. The taxi driver waited patiently. When Ferdinand finally drew away, there was a furious and untamed gleam in his eyes that flickered like a raw flame. I feared he would seize me again, or carry me off with him, or refuse to leave. A moment later, however, his customary gentleness returned. He kissed me demurely upon the cheek.

"Till the New Year, *bella mia*," he whispered in my ear.

Then he was in the taxi, and the driver was pulling away. I watched the cab disappear down the long drive leading to the road. When I could no longer see the red taillights, I brushed the snow from my shoulders and went inside.

As I walked back, each step felt so light, I was tempted to look over my shoulder to make certain I was leaving footprints in the snow. I felt as if I were standing on the air, just like the angel I had described. A delightful tingling ran from the roots of my hairs down the length of my body, causing me to laugh out loud. Reaching the lesser hall, I seized the statuette of my elf and danced about the hall with it, my gown swirling as I went. Even the steady curious gaze of Tybalt, where he lay curled upon his silk pillow, did not dampen my lightheartedness.

CHAPTER
TWENTY

The Chapel of the Unicorn

I awoke the next morning to sunlight streaming through the curtains of my enormous canopy bed. The bed had been built during the reign of Elizabeth I, when such beds were first in style. As I luxuriated upon the massive mattress, it amused me to recall that, back then, our whole family had slept crammed into this single bed.

What pleasant dreams the night had brought. I dreamt Ferdinand kissed me, and no fence of lightning appeared to drive us apart. Only . . . I sat upright. I ran a finger across my lips. They still felt tender. Then, it had not been a dream at all, had it?

The phone rang, and an Aerie Spirit wafted the receiver to my hand. I leaned back against the headboard and greeted Mab, whose gruff voice came wearily to my ear.

"Greetings, Miss Miranda, how are things back there?"

"Very well, Mab," I replied enthusiastically. "It's a lovely morning!"

"No additional disasters?"

"Not a one. No inkling of what may befall us by Twelfth Night, either, but I have the company on high alert, to be on the lookout for more attacks, just in case."

"Good thinking, Ma'am," Mab grunted. "I sent the truck parts we recovered to our forensics guys. I'm hoping they will be able to tell us the cause of the crash."

"Let's hope they find it was just an accident, though Tybalt doesn't seem to think so."

"Begging your pardon, Ma'am, but I wouldn't trust the talking fur ball. He has this quirky notion that facts should not stand in the way of an exciting theory. Hardly a reliable witness."

With nothing to gain from participating in the Mab-Tybalt feud, I changed the subject. "How is it going where you are?"

"Okay, Ma'am. This is what I found out." There was a short pause, during which I could hear him flipping the pages of his notebook. "Your father visited Prospero's Mansion in Oregon on September 17th—while you were in Japan. I'm not certain exactly where he went next—looks like he spent a few days in New York, perhaps visiting your brother Cornelius."

Cornelius again. I shuddered. *Please, Lady, do not let him have worked evil upon Father, too!*

"Anyway," Mab continued, "he showed up here in Elgin five days later, on September 22nd, which happens to have been the fall equinox this year. The old priest who takes care of the graveyard where Gregor was buried says Mr. Prospero arrived about two p.m. He had a judge's order allowing him to exhume your brother's body and brought in a backhoe to dig up the grave. Then the bulldozer departed and the old priest left Mr. Prospero alone with the coffin."

"Exhume Gregor!" My mind boggled. "Wha-what happened next?"

"Well, that's just it, Ma'am. No one seems to know. The priest says your father never showed up to sign the rest of the paperwork. Nor have any of my people been able to find hide nor hair of him since. The backhoe driver was the last person who reported seeing him. It's as if Mr. Prospero walked into the graveyard and vanished off the face of the Earth . . . which may be exactly what happened."

None of this made any sense, unless . . .

Could Cornelius be in league with the demons? Could he have sold out Father in order to free the Three Shadowed Ones and get his hands on Gregor's staff, perhaps hoping to earn some nefarious reward from his infernal allies? Perhaps, ensorcelling Theo and tricking Father were part of some greater, overarching plan.

No. The idea was ridiculous. Besides, Father claimed he freed the Three Shadowed Ones. Of course, he thought it was an accident. . . .

"This doesn't sound good, Mab." I spoke slowly, hoping to mask my confusion and dismay.

"I questioned the old priest as to whether there were any other unusual occurrences," he continued. "He mentioned two weird things. First, late that same night, a man was found wandering around that same graveyard in a state of amnesia. Or at least the priest called it amnesia; apparently nothing the guy said made sense. The old priest took him to the local hospital, which in turn shipped him off to Chicago. I spoke with the doctors, to ascertain whether it might have been Mr. Prospero. They described a young Italian man, who I am tentatively assuming was Mr. Di Napoli—at least, until I find evidence to the contrary."

"Well, that's a relief!" I sighed. Slipping from my bed, I began laying out my emerald tea dress and clean undergarments. "More corroborating evidence for Ferdinand's story!"

Knowing that Ferdinand might be on the level made me feel better about last night's visit; however, I refrained from mentioning it to Mab. The experience was too precious to share just now, and I did not wish to field the barrage of questions such an admission would surely bring.

Over the phone, I could hear a scratching sound, as if Mab were doodling on a notepad as he talked. "The other thing was: on September 23rd, a trucking company showed up and carried away a crate. According to the old priest, they were supposed to be taking away a broken headstone. However, the priest showed me the broken headstone—it was still there. Then, he showed me the paperwork. Guess what company owned that truck?"

A feeling of icy dread clawed at my stomach. "The same company that owns the warehouse we investigated in Landover, Maryland?"

"You betcha!"

I sat down in front of my vanity and rested my forehead against my palms. It had just dawned on me that the theory Tybalt proposed that first night might be correct. Perhaps Father had not told me what he was about because he feared I would disapprove—and with good reason.

Rallying, I picked up my brush and began untangling my long silvery locks. It took a certain knack to keep the phone nestled snugly on one's shoulder while dressing one's hair, but decades of practice helped. Of course, one of these days I would get a speakerphone, and yet another of my highly-honed skills would go the way of galloping while riding sidesaddle, placing the bedwarmer just so, and dancing in a bustle—victims of the relentless march of progress.

"I don't suppose the priest had any idea what Father wanted to do with Gregor's body?" I asked. Mab gave a negative snort. I continued, "Did he say what became of Gregor's body and coffin?"

"The priest never mentioned a body. He thought the trucking company took Gregor's coffin instead of the broken headstone, which may be the case. It can't be in the crate we found, because that crate was the wrong shape for a coffin, unless . . ." Mab's voice dropped. "Ma'am, I fear the coffin, and probably your brother's body too, may have fallen through the gate into Hell."

"It's a good thing I'm a Protestant now," I said faintly, putting down my brush. "Otherwise, I might find that information tremendously disturbing."

Ordinarily, the news that my brother's dead body was now in Hell would have inspired cold fury within my breast, directed at whomever had disturbed his eternal sleep. However, the culprit was apparently Father. I comforted myself with the assurance that Father had not intended to lose Gregor's body, and thus, that it has been the Three Shadowed Ones who were to blame . . . unless, of course, Cornelius were at fault. Given a choice, I would rather blame the demons.

"By the way, Ma'am, I've been meaning to ask, and seeing your brother's grave—or lack thereof—reminded me. What does Gregor's staff, the . . ." I heard pages flip as he consulted his notes, "*Staff of Darkness* . . . what does the *Staff of Darkness* do? Other than issue darkness . . . I mean, it does do something else, right?"

"Enforces oaths. If you swear an oath on it, you cannot break that oath without dying. Also, it drains life—not enough to injure a human without prolonged exposure, but enough so that the darkness can be used as a ward to keep out spirits, much as the rock salt did."

"Swear oaths, you say? Similar to swearing on water from the River Styx, then?"

"Exactly. We used it to guarantee our contracts would be upheld," I sighed, "and it's mighty hard running Prospero, Inc. without it! Also, the darkness that seeps from it absorbs life, keeping certain kinds of spirits at bay . . . the same kind that cannot cross the Styx. It's a wonderful staff, though I prefer mine."

"I see. Interesting . . ." There came a pause. "We swore on that thing, didn't we, Ma'am? That's how we Aerie Ones became enslaved to you Prosperos. . . ."

"Employees, Mab, not slaves. Slaves serve against their will."

"When the penalty for changing one's mind is death? Sounds pretty 'against my will' to me! Wish there were some court where I could go complain about being compelled to swear under duress."

"Back to the matter at hand, Mab," I insisted sternly. "Where do we stand now? What have we learned?"

"Basically, the priest's story seems to corroborate Di Napoli's story. Other than that . . . your father goes into a graveyard and digs up a dead relative. He never reappears, but a truck shows up and removes a crate. The truck belongs to a company that just happens to own a crate with a gate to Hell in it.

"My guess is this: the crate from the graveyard contained a gateway into Hell. The same gateway through which your father disappeared and Di Napoli emerged—probably herded out by the demons, so that his reappearance would cause havoc. Furthermore, I hypothesize this is the same crate Mephisto so kindly opened for us in Maryland—a crate which, by the way, is now securely packed in one of our warded warehouses. Thanks to the good work of some of my men."

I brushed my hair in silence, considering all that I had heard. Mab waited respectfully. I heard him take a gulp of something, probably—from the sound he made after he swallowed it—the cold dregs of a forgotten morning coffee. It was later in the day where he was.

"Begging your pardon, Ma'am," Mab asked finally, "but what was Mr. Prospero thinking? Digging up your dead brother on the fall equinox?"

"I don't know, Mab." I considered the matter. "My guess is he was trying to summon up my brother's ghost, and he got some kind of demon instead. The demon then dragged him bodily into Hell—leaving behind an open gate, which allowed both Ferdinand and the Three Shadowed Ones to escape."

"Yeah, but what did Mr. Prospero expect to gain from summoning your brother's shade? And why did he need the body? Why not just use his hairbrush or some old belonging? What kind of magic was he aiming to perform that he needed a corpse? Nothing white, I can tell you!"

"I don't know, but I can make a possible guess. Father has been studying the secrets of the ancient Eleusinian mystery cults. With those secrets, it is theoretically possible that Gregor could be reborn without losing his memories. Their rituals were usually held around harvest time. Perhaps the fall equinox was a propitious day for this, so he tried to summon up my brother in hopes of sharing with him the secrets he had gleaned. Though how he thought Gregor would find his way out of Hell to be reborn, I don't know. Nor do I have any idea why he needed my brother's body, unless he had tried before without it and was unable to locate Gregor's soul."

"Interesting," Mab muttered darkly.

I said, "I would not envy Gregor, finding himself stuck in the body of an infant with the memory of a grown man. Nor would I want to be the woman who gave birth to a baby who remembered his previous life." Visions of the cigar-smoking baby I had seen in some cartoon flashed through my head.

Mab growled, "Bet you Prospero planned to take Baby Gregor to your sister Logistilla. Then, voilà, a flick of her wrist, and she turns him into an adult. After all, she's had plenty of practice producing full-grown Italians. Only, Prospero doesn't know darling Logistilla was in on it with the guys who killed Gregor. Unless she had his knife because she hunted down his killers, took the dagger back, and turned them into turtle soup."

"A comforting hope, Mab," I replied, "but I doubt it. I'm sure if Logistilla had caught Gregor's murderer, we would all have heard about it, over and over again. No, I fear her having the knife has some more sinister cause. Exactly what, I don't know—perhaps having something to do with that devil you smelled."

"Speaking of that knife," Mab drawled, "I visited the archive at the town hall in Elgin. Apparently, they still have some police records regarding the shooting of your brother. They aren't immediately accessible though—have to be printed off a microfiche machine or something. I paid their fee and gave them the address of the mansion. The clerk promised to mail us a copy of whatever he finds."

"Good thinking! Tell them we'll pay more if they expedite it," I said absently, for my thoughts were consumed with suspicions regarding Logistilla and Cornelius.

They had been quite close until their recent falling out, always whispering together at stockholder meetings, back when Logistilla still owned stock. Could this plot against the family have reached as far back as the death of Gregor? Could Cornelius have wanted the *Staff of Darkness* even then, and been thwarted when it was laid to rest with Gregor's body?

I would have dismissed this theory as foolishness, were it not for one thing: I did not, for an instant, believe Logistilla's claim that she had forgotten about seeing Cornelius use his staff on Theo, only to have the memory conveniently pop up again while we were dining together, over half a century later. It was possible, but since we were speaking of something as important as Theo's life, her claim struck me as unlikely. Yet, if she had remembered all along, why had she waited so long to tell anyone?

Unless she had been Cornelius's accomplice. In which case, she was willing to tell me now because of their recent falling out. I wondered again what the cause had been. Could it be that she feared for Theo, or that she had balked at involving Father? If so, I applauded her attack of conscience. Of course, all of this was speculation.

"Ma'am?" Mab repeated.

"Er. Very good, Mab," I said. "Though I'll be surprised if they turn up anything. I recall Ulysses did some investigating at the time, but no one was very helpful."

"Won't know what they have until we see it, Ma'am."

"Very true, Mab. Hurry home! There is still much to do."

"Yes, Ma'am. Will do."

BUNDLED in my white cashmere cloak and a pair of fur-lined suede boots, I set out into the enchanted gardens behind Prospero's Mansion, and passed through the gate in the high stone wall that enclosed the forest beyond, seeking the chapel hidden in its midst. I walked between the straight black trunks, my boots crushing the mix of snow and soft needles carpeting the earth. The pungent scent of pine tickled my nostrils, and brought to mind other walks through other forests on other continents.

I always enjoyed walking through this forest, but today it seemed even more lovely than usual. For the first time since I had read Father's letter, my spirits felt light again. I was no longer afraid that some terrible doom was going to descend upon us; spirits called up by séances were notably untrustworthy, and demons were notable liars. There was still almost two weeks until Erasmus's New Year's Party. Most of the siblings were likely to gather there, though hopefully, by now, Erasmus had received my letter and warned those with whom he was in contact. That left only Titus, who seemed to be missing. There was little I could do about this until Mab returned, however, so I had decided to use the time to attend to other matters.

As I went, one of my pet unicorns, a descendent of the original mated pair Logistilla had given me one Christmas, came to greet me, nuzzling my pockets for sugar or carrots. I pulled out some oats and stroked the soft whiteness of his nose. He was merely a mortal creature, not a supernatural being, like my Lady. Still, I loved him.

The chapel was hidden amidst the tallest trees of the enclosed forest and could not be seen until one was almost upon it. It was a small white structure with stained-glass windows and a white spiral steeple stretching above its steep black roof. Two keys, a long, old-fashioned cast-iron one and a modern brass one for the deadbolt, were required to open the thick oak door, behind which lay a single chamber.

Inside, the chapel was simple and clean, whitewashed walls above oak wainscoting. A spiral candlestick, as tall as a lance, stood in each of the four corners. In the center of the chamber, a small altar held a book and some candles. Across the back wall, a tapestry woven by Logistilla portrayed the

Greek concept of Eurynome—a woman dancing with the Serpent of the Wind as She created the world out of Chaos.

Sunlight filtered through the pines to strike the stained glass in the eastern windows. Dust motes danced along sapphire, emerald, and ruby beams, which dyed the slate tiles with gem-like colors. The effect was striking. I could stand and admire the kaleidoscopic light shining through the colored glass for hours.

Each time we rebuilt the chapel in a new location, I replaced yet another window with a stained-glass portrait of one of the Sibyls of Eurynome. The women and the style of the art differed sharply, but each bore a spiral of ivory upon her brow, like a white flower with five curving petals: the Mark of the Sibyl.

The four women I had chosen to portray were Eve, Cassandra of Troy, Phemonoe of Delphi, and Deiphobe of Cumae, the Sibyl who helped Aeneas find his way to the underworld. It was she who wrote the nine famous scrolls known as the Sibylline Books, including the scroll containing the secrets of my Lady's order that I so desired. I once had another window portraying Herophile the Pilgrim sitting upon her prophesy stone, but it had been shattered by Cromwell's followers when we lost the English Civil War.

What had become of these women? I wondered for the millionth time. With their access to Water of Life, every Sibyl should be able to live as long as she pleased. And yet, in all our travels, both on Earth and otherwise, I had never met a single one. Everywhere, we encountered rumors of how a Sibyl had once lived there and, sometimes, tales of how one had been slain by the Unicorn Hunters, but neither I nor my family had ever located a living Sibyl.

Even Handmaidens were becoming rare. In my youth, I would meet another Handmaiden every so often, and we would swap secrets and discuss our duties. But it had been more than a century since I had met the last one. Where had they all gone?

I crossed the chamber to stand before the altar, my cashmere cloak dappled with bright splashes of color. The altar's lacquered front bore symbolic images for the six gifts of the Sibyl: a key to represent opening locks; a mortar and pestle for curing poison; an overflowing cup for the Water of Life; a lightning bolt for command of electricity; a mirror for the gift of visions; and a broken chain to represent absolving people of foolish oaths.

How strange to recall how this chapel, or another like it, had once been the center of my life. In my youth, I spent my waking hours praying before this altar, waiting for insight or instruction, perhaps pausing to watch the play of the light through the beautiful glazed portraits. Back then, inspiration came to me sporadically, seldom and far between. Receiving the answer to a question often took hours or days of patient prayer. Over time, it became easier, until the wall between my mind and my Lady's grew so transparent, I could hear Her—when She chose to speak—even in the midst of the tumult of daily life.

Once this occurred, I was sent back into the world to join my family and aid their work. Since I could hear Her voice so clearly, I was certain She would guide me to take the steps necessary to achieve Sibylhood. Yet centuries had passed, and still I waited.

So many memories had been lost to the mists of time, and yet, as I stepped within these walls and smelled the stone and candles, my vigils in this chapel returned so vividly. I also could bring to mind the exact colors and shapes of the portrait of Herophile the Pilgrim. I had been praying before her window when the guards arrived, the time I was arrested for witchcraft. We were living in Rome, during Gregor's first term as pope. When I heard the boots of the guards coming up the path, I knew Gregor must have betrayed me, for he hated Protestants and disapproved of my devotion to my Lady.

That night, he came to see me where I was chained. He slipped into my cell under the cloak of darkness, not as an old man but in his own youthful shape. I had been praying when he arrived, pointing out to my Lady that this might be a good opportunity for me to be raised in Her esteem, as Sibyls could open locks. I was certain Gregor intended to have me put to death.

He stepped upon the straw covering the cell floor and pulled back the hood that obscured his face. He was taller and stockier than my other Italian brothers, though not as large as the Scottish Titus. Gregor had thick wavy dark hair and penetrating black eyes. His arms and shoulders were large and muscular—he had been apprenticed to an armorer in his youth. I wondered if he had come to strangle me personally.

"Greetings, Sister."

Gregor spoke in Italian. His voice sounded hoarse, as if from disuse. Before he had been transformed into the Cardinal, he had spoken with a pleasant baritone. Logistilla must have made some error that night in returning him to his true form, however, for his voice sounded low and breathy. From that day forth, whenever Gregor was in his own shape, he retained the low, husky voice. The last time I heard him speak, at our Christmas celebration about three years before his death, his voice was still the gravelly bass I first heard that night in my cell.

"Have you come to ask me to repent?" I asked, twisting my arms in their stocks.

"Would you?" he asked.

"Never!" I composed myself to die.

"I thought not." He spoke without a trace of humor. "I came to tell you I have found a way to save you, but you must be patient. You must promise, if I do this, you will wait for your legal release, not to disappear or flee away by magic."

"Free me? Why are you doing this?" I hesitated to give my word, lest this be some trick. "I thought you hated my Lady. Are you even *fond* of me?"

"It does not matter if I approve of your heresy, or even if I am fond of you," my brother replied huskily. "What matters is that you are my sister."

True to his word, I was released a few weeks later. The guard who unlocked the chains explained I had been spared by the grace of Pope Gregory XV, who had passed a Papal Bull reducing the penalties for witchcraft. The new Bull decreed the death penalty appropriate only for witches who were proven to have made compacts with the Devil or to have committed homicide through magic. To this day, that decree remains the last Papal Bull ever issued on the subject of witchcraft.

CIRCLING the altar, I knelt and slid back a panel, revealing a little cabinet. The top shelf held matches, a candlesnuffer, and other simple tools. The bottom half contained a black metallic safe with a combination lock. I spun the dial through the combination and swung open the safe door.

Within, upon a bed of green velvet, lay a heavy black case. Its intricate silver fastenings had been designed by Titus. Only someone who knew the secret to solving their puzzle could open the case. To my dismay, I saw I had left the fastenings unlatched the last time I had been here, some decades ago. Chiding myself for absentmindedness, I opened the box.

As the lid came up, the light of day glinted against the crystal cut sides of vessels within, causing a prism-like flash of light. The black velvet lining was molded to hold the special decanters that held my precious supply of the Water of Life from the Well at the World's End: a large diamond carafe and four tiny matching pear-shaped vials. These vessels had been given to me by the Keeper of the Well and were fashioned of the only material that could store Water of Life. Erasmus had studied them in his alchemy days, and declared this material was not diamond but crystallized Urim. It was because I had so few of these vessels that I could bring back so little Water from each trip to the World's End.

Within the case, the carafe and two of the small vials glinted snugly in their proper places, but the two remaining pear-shaped indentations were empty. I had intentionally left one vial at Theo's.

Where was the last one?

Silently cursing that Mab should be away at such a time, I drew one of the two remaining smaller vials out of the case and put it in my pocket, disturbing the case and its contents as little as possible, so as not to tamper with the evidence. Then, after locking the safe and closing the cabinet, I yanked on the pull-rope hanging beside the tapestry, ringing the bell in the steeple. A moment later, the door blew open, and Ariel's fluting voice asked what I desired.

"Ariel, we have been robbed. One of the vials of the Water of Life is missing. It has been some years since I have opened the case. I have no notion when it vanished. Quickly, call one of Mab's assistants, or someone trained in his art. Have them dust for fingerprints and do what else they may to discover who has touched it."

"I go and return as my mistress commands." The door rattled again. Moment's later, Ariel returned. "I have done as you decreed. There is another matter I would broach, Great Mistress. There is that which has been promised me, but not delivered."

I sighed. "Ariel, your contract is with my father," I repeated for the umpteenth time. "It serves no purpose to debate this matter with me."

Ariel's fluting voice continued. "The winds bring rumors of Prospero's death. If Prospero is no more, then our fate doth rest in the hands of his eldest child. Will you not set us free now, eldest child of your father?"

"Who has repeated such slander? I will not hear such evil spoken of my father!"

"But if it should prove true that he has perished . . ." Ariel began.

I cut him off. "There will be no talk of Prospero's death. Go about the task I have assigned you." Ariel sighed and sped away, and I was left standing in the dappled light.

Gone was the lighthearted calm that had accompanied me into the Enclosed Forest. The fear of the demon's predicted doom closed in around me like a cloak. Ariel's question had shaken me. I had never considered how the Aerie Ones' obligations to our family might be affected by my father's disappearance. It was one thing to continue to tell Ariel and Mab I could not free them because my father did not wish it. It was quite another to have to take responsibility for their captivity upon myself.

My gaze fell upon the bronze seal of the Order of Sibyls, where it hung above the heavy oaken door. Around the image of a unicorn rampant circled the words: RELEASE CAPTIVES, ABSOLVE OATHS, BANISH DARKNESS. A shiver went through me.

Had I ever read these words properly before? Eurynome, my holy Lady, forsook Her place in High Heaven to free the children of man in the Garden. Could my involvement with the imprisonment of the Aerie Ones be the reason that the coveted Sibylhood has eluded me?

I so yearned to be a Sibyl, a true servant of my holy Lady. Sometimes this desire was but a faint longing. At other times, it burned me like a living coal. Sibyls could wield the Six Gifts, and, unlike Handmaidens, Sibyls were free to marry.

Remaining unwed through the long years had been no hard task, since losing my Handmaiden status would have denied me the Water of Life, and damned my family to mortality. Secretly, in the depth of my heart, however, I have always longed for the kind of love my father had spoken of when I was a child.

We would take our meal atop the bluff overlooking the northeast shore of the island, and Father would speak to me of my mother. As he described his love for her, his keen blue eyes would glow, as if some light, kindled within his heart, were shining through them. Father took four more wives over the ensuing years, but none of them sparked such adoration.

My father had been a callous youth, so he often told me, foolish and bent upon selfish goals. Meeting my mother had transformed him. All his efforts since then—his life's work to improve the Earth for mankind, which had culminated in the current activities of Prospero, Inc.—all were inspired by my mother. Her influence had lifted him out of his previous wickedness and made of him a better creature.

Sitting atop the bluff with the wind in my face and the cries of seagulls in my ears, I had vowed to myself I would not wed unless I, too, could have such happiness. Of course, at the time I had imagined it would be only a short while before I found a man who stirred such devotion in me. It never occurred to the child I had been that I might remain unwed forever.

Were I a Sibyl, I would be free to pursue such a love.

Yet, even if I wanted to free the Aerie Ones, sacrificing my beloved flute and denying myself its music forever after, duty forbade me from doing so. It was not just the damage they might do were they free. There was also the matter of Prospero, Inc. To lose the Aerie Ones would be to destroy the company, and all my family's work. Half the employees at Prospero, Inc., and all those who managed our supernatural accounts, were Aerie Ones. If I let them free to pursue their own amusements, the company would fail. Even if I were willing to reveal our secrets to mankind, some of the most important tasks would be impossible to accomplish without supernatural servants.

Were Prospero, Inc. to founder, its contracts would be violated. If that were to happen, the technology upon which mankind depends would begin to fail.

Earthquakes and hurricanes, mankind might endure; however, worse fates would befall us if Father's covenants failed. Blood of the earth, known today as petroleum, only burned evenly because my father bound the oreads from whose veins it flowed. Nor would machines run smoothly if lightning, the servant and herald of my Lady, were no longer bound to run along a wire. Nothing mankind achieved in earlier ages rivals the grandeur, the accomplishment, or the quality of life of the modern age—all of which would be lost if the spirits of the natural world could act without restraint. The pre-industrial age had been unpleasant for men and worse for women. I could not free the Aerie Ones if it meant reducing mankind to that again.

I stood in the chapel staring up at the seal, astounded by the enormity of Father's accomplishments. Had he done all this deliberately? Had he foreseen this modern world, in which men moved mountains and walked upon the moon, when he first began binding spirits? Or, had he merely trusted mankind to prosper, once they were free of the ravages of unruly supernatural forces?

And what of Mab and the other incarnated Aerie Ones? Was spending time as a human the answer to the problem of freeing them? I certainly hoped so, especially as Mab's talk about devils had filled me with foreboding. I much preferred to think that the stacked naked bodies at Logistilla's were meant for our airy folk: the Aerie Ones, and the sylphs, sprites, apsaras, gandharvas, and other spirits of the air who serve them.

Contemplating all this filled me with renewed admiration for my father. I felt ashamed for having doubted him. Next to his accomplishments, accusations of ensorcelling me and damning Ferdinand paled to naught.

CHAPTER TWENTY-ONE

A Cold and Bumpy Ride

"I heard about the theft, Ma'am," Mab drawled. "Sorry I wasn't here when you discovered it."

He plunked himself down in the chair Ferdinand had chosen the night before, resting his booted feet on an embroidered ottoman. Mab's return was a refreshing distraction. Having spent the rest of the morning immersed in Prospero, Inc. business—I wanted to ensure that no other Priority Accounts went awry—I had only just returned to the lesser hall to continue reading Father's journals. Having finished the recent ones, I had begun delving into some of his earlier volumes. When Mab arrived, I had been in the middle of a horrifying dissertation called *On the Detrimental Effects Upon the Soul of Prolonged Exposure to Demons.*

"Were your people able to detect anything?" I asked, gratefully closing the journal.

Mab shook his head, scowling. "The culprit, whoever he was, wore gloves."

"Do we have any leads?"

Mab grimaced and scratched his jaw. "That depends on what you mean by a lead, Ma'am. At first, I suspected Mr. Prospero, thinking maybe he knew trouble was coming and thought a little Water of Life might help his chances. Now that I've seen the site of the crime myself, however, I don't think so."

"Why not?"

"Two reasons, Ma'am. One, if Mr. Prospero wanted Water of Life, why wouldn't he have asked for it? It's not like you'd tell him no. At the very least, I would have expected him to leave a note. He certainly wouldn't have sneaked into the chapel with gloves on to hide his trail.

"And two, the fastenings on the case were bent. Mr. Prospero knows how to decipher Mr. Titus's locks. He would not have had to damage it to open the case."

"Any other suspects?"

"Well . . . I don't have any evidence, but I have a suspicion," grunted Mab. "I think it was the perp . . . er, I mean, Mr. Ulysses. I think he took it the time he was here stealing the guardian Warden and that other stuff. It has his M.O. all over it. He has the shady know-how to break into the chapel and open the safe, but lacks the brains to decipher the puzzle lock."

"Ulysses again, eh?" I frowned. Was no one loyal to the family any more? But then, Ulysses never really had been loyal. "What would he want with a vial of Water of Life? He knows I'll give him some if he needs it."

"Begging your pardon, Ma'am, but that's only if *he* needs it. What if he wanted it for someone else? A honey or a business partner?"

I frowned and shook my head. "Father forbade me to share the Water with anyone outside our immediate family."

"Maybe that's it, then? He wanted the Water for some selfish use, so he stole it."

"Maybe," I replied, unconvinced.

"Let's take a different tack. If we're going to locate the teleporter, it's not going to be by tracking his movements. We're gonna have to figure out how he thinks, and where he's likely to hole up. I don't know a whole lot about Mr. Ulysses. What can you tell me about him, down to what he likes to eat on Sunday evenings, and the color of his socks? Start with how his staff works." Mab whipped out his notebook.

"Okay, the *Staff of Transportation* can bring him any place it has been before. So, while he can teleport, he has to travel overland any time he wants to set up a new arrival point."

"How does he like to travel, when going overland?"

"Ulysses's mother was a Victorian lady. Trains were a new invention when he was young, and Ulysses loved them. He used to have the most awesome toy train set. As far as I know, he still travels by train when he goes by land."

"Ulysses: train nut," Mab noted. "What else?"

"He takes pride in always being well-dressed, to the point that he's usually more concerned with the cut of his coat than with any matter of substance. Had he been born thirty years earlier, he would have made a great Corinthian. Yet, despite his frivolity, he was closer to the grim and solemn

Gregor than to anyone else in the family—though they had a falling out a couple of years before Gregor's death."

"Let me guess: you have no idea what the argument was about?"

I nodded, smiling sheepishly. Mab snorted in disgust.

"Humans," he scoffed. "No curiosity."

"I've always held it was a virtue not to get involved in family quarrels."

"Maybe Harebrain would know. He claims he's kept track of your zany family."

"If we see him again, we can ask him." I frowned. Mephisto's exit still troubled me, but he had returned unscathed from stranger expeditions than this. So I remained hopeful. "I know you couldn't tell me where Mephisto went, but if he's on Earth, can't something be done to find him? I would at least like to confirm that he is safe."

"I'll have some of my men look into it. He's got some credit cards we used to track him to Chicago. They're maxed out, but there's a Swiss bank account that makes an automatic payment on them around the middle of the month, so he might try to use them again. What else?"

"I remember the three of us, Ulysses, Gregor, and I, decided to go vampire hunting one All Saint's Eve. Gregor was an old hand at such things—he and Theo had hunted them in Hungary during the vampire infestations of the seventeenth century—but Ulysses and I were untutored in this business and had no idea what we were about. Nearly staked an old man through the heart before we discovered he was an albino. You should have seen us skulking about the countryside with our stakes and torches." I laughed, recalling.

"Did you catch any vampires?"

"Only two."

"Good for you!"

"Other than that? Ulysses is a thief. He loves jewels. He once stole the Hope Diamond and wore it to a dinner with the family. He put it back again before anyone knew it was missing, or at least the media never mentioned it," I said. "That's about all I can think of."

"Your own brother, and that's all you know?" Mab asked skeptically.

"He's hasn't been around nearly as long as the rest of us—didn't come along until just before we all started going our own ways. He never knew Sane Mephisto, and I never had occasion to spend much time with him. Oh, excuse me. In answer to your first questions? He eats caviar on Sunday nights, and his socks are gray. Everything he wears is gray, even his domino mask."

"Yeah, I noticed that on his statue in the Great Hall. What's with the little mask around his eyes?"

I shrugged. "I don't know, but he almost always wears one. It's his signature garment, I guess, a gray tux and a domino mask, sort of like my tea gown and Mephisto's surcoat."

"So. Ulysses. Perp. Likes trains. Domino mask. Falling out with Gregor. Got it." Mab made a note. "Now, back to the Water of Life: perhaps he's selling the stuff. There are many eccentric humans who would pay a fortune for extended youth. Maybe that's how he gets the money to enjoy his fancy lifestyle, caviar and all."

"Maybe . . . I wish we knew when the theft took place." I frowned. "Did we ever follow up on that photo in the Smithsonian?"

"Yeah, I had one of my people check it out," Mab said. "He was able to confirm that a Ulysses Prospero worked for NASA in 1975."

"Maybe he was in need of money," I said. "Odd, though, it's unlike Ulysses to work rather than just steal something. Oh!" I pressed my hand to my mouth, as the possibilities occurred to me.

Mab pushed back the brim of his hat. "Could he do that? Mark the Voyager with his staff and journey to another planet?"

"He could, though not Voyager. He would have to pick a landing vehicle, like Sojourner—otherwise, he'd find himself drifting in outer space. But he could do it. He once sent a carpet he had touched with his staff to a man who had stolen something from us. As soon as the man placed the carpet in his house, Ulysses teleported to it and retrieved our belongings. In principle, that's no different from touching a NASA probe and then going to another planet. Wasn't the Viking Lander launched in the mid-'seventies?"

"Hmm. Clever bloke," muttered Mab. "Maybe he's selling the Water of Life to get the equipment he needs to live on Venus or the Moon or something."

"Could be. But, we won't know for sure unless we find him, and lately that's been seeming less and less likely. Let's put this aside for now, and return to the more important matter of warning my other siblings. With the Three Shadowed Ones out there, it's important that we reach them as soon as possible."

"So, who's left?"

"Other than Ulysses? We've spoken to Mephisto, Theo, and Logistilla." I sighed. None of those conversations had concluded satisfactorily. "We have an address for Erasmus, and we're going to his New Year's Eve party. I wrote a letter to Cornelius, but chances are he'll be at the party too. Most likely Ulysses will be there as well. That just leaves Titus, who seems to have vanished."

"Do we have any leads?" asked Mab.

"Only that, according to Mephisto, he has a house somewhere with children in it, but we have no idea where, though at least with Titus, we can still be pretty certain it's on planet Earth. I did check with the caretaker of his old place—the place from which he used to mail my birthday cards—but he hadn't seen my brother in over two years."

"Harebrain said something about the Okefenokee Swamp." Mab flipped open his notebook. "I had one of my people check on that, too. He could not find any piece of property in that vicinity listed to 'Titus Prospero.' Of course, your brother could be using an assumed name."

"It's a shame we don't know the names of his children," I said. "Even the best search engine in the world won't produce information without input. There's no list we can check to locate 'Titus's children.' "

"We don't keep such a list," Mab smirked, "but we know someone who does."

I started to laugh but one look at his craggy face told me he was serious.

"You think we should fly to the North Pole in the middle of December and ask Father Christmas if we can look at his list?" I cried.

"Have any better ideas?"

"Um . . ." I thought about my giant taciturn brother, and the birthday cards he had sent me so dutifully. I recalled the many companionable walks we had taken together through the windblown Highlands, my brother striding beside me in his funny tartan hat with the pom-pom on top. I thought of the prediction of doom upon the Family Prospero. Could the cards have stopped coming because he was in trouble? If so, with Twelfth Night getting closer, time might be running out to save him!

"Let's go."

WE left by Lear jet early on the morning of the twenty-first and crossed the Canadian border in good time. Snow blew through the air, and wind speeds were rising. Mab wore his earplugs, and I kept up a string of jolly Christmas carols on my flute. We had no trouble with turbulence.

Our trajectory took us over northern Canada and the icy flats of the Arctic Sea. I sat in the copilot seat, enjoying the endless fields of snow as they passed beneath us, or, when they were eclipsed, the flurries of dancing snowflakes. What a joy to fly in interesting weather!

As we came out of a particularly thick cloudbank, something crimson flashed amidst the swirling white. Unable to make it out, I played a quick trill. Obediently, a gust of wind blew away the flakes obscuring our view.

"By Setebos!" Mab cried. "It's Osae the Dragon."

A giant red dragon with steely gray eyes was bearing down on our little plane. Fire flickered beneath his curving fangs. The motions of his leathery wings created little flurries of snow to either side of him as he flew.

Mab pulled out an earplug and demanded, "How did they find us?"

I shook my head. "Seems awfully foolish of them to attack us in the air during a snowstorm, doesn't it? Considering air is our element." I twirled my flute. "I wonder what they hope to achieve."

Mab snorted. "Oh, it's stupid, all right. For one thing, how do they plan to catch us? Look at the wings on that sucker. We're in an airplane. Those kind of wings don't outfly airplanes. Do they expect us to wait for them like the proverbial sitting duck?"

"What course do you recommend?"

"I'd recommend an old-fashioned Red Baron-style dogfight," Mab said with glee. "Sadly, that's out of the question, since our side does not have any guns. My second choice is: outrun 'em."

"Sounds good," I replied. "You pilot. I'll play."

Mab put his earplug back in, and I cleared us a path through the falling snow. The sky before us opened, wide and white, and the sinuous crimson serpent soon fell astern. Mab and I smiled smugly and settled in to enjoy the long flight north.

ABOUT twenty minutes later, we caught another glimpse of scarlet among the clouds ahead of us.

"It can't be," muttered Mab.

The crimson dragon snaked out of a cloudbank ahead of us. Snow dusted his back and wide red leathery wings.

"There's no way he could catch up!" Mab sputtered. "Think there might be two of 'em?"

He turned the plane and sped away again, jetting off to the right before returning to our course. The winged serpent fell away behind us again.

THE third time the dragon appeared before us, Mab pulled out his earplugs, swearing.

"This time he's practically on top of us! How the heck is he doing that?" Mab demanded. "Guess those wimpy wings are better than I thought."

A shiver traveled up my spine. "If he's ahead of us without having passed us . . ." I began. Mab's cry cut me off.

"There! On the wing!"

Standing, I crossed to the cabin and peered through one of the small, round windows. A dark inky shape crouched upon our wing. His black opera cape billowed wildly. As I watched helplessly, he threw a large object into the air intake.

The left engine stalled.

"Darn!" muttered Mab. "We gotta land. Even with the help of the accursed flute, we're not going to make it to the North Pole on one engine. Oh-oh. Incoming!"

Billowing flames shot toward us, rolling against the glass. If the flame was that close, the dragon could not be far behind. I dived back into the copilot's seat and braced myself. Not a moment too soon, either, for the plane began to groan and shake.

"Sounds like it's wrapping itself around us," Mab said nervously. "Do you think it could be strong enough to damage the plane?"

"I don't know, but I don't like the sound of it. Do we have parachutes?"

"Yeah, but we're too low for them to work reliably, and I wouldn't want to risk it in this weather. Besides, if we're not safe in the plane, how are we going to protect ourselves from the dragon once we get outside?"

"Good point. "What else can we do?"

"Nothing, unless you want to get out there and fight him hand-to-hand. Can you hit him with lightning?"

I shook my head. "Not only is it difficult to get a good lightning bolt during a snowstorm, but also we could electrocute ourselves. We don't know what condition our . . ."

The plane lurched to the right, accompanied by a terrible grinding tearing noise. I managed to keep my seat, but Mab, who had been half standing, in an attempt to watch the dragon, was thrown to the floor. He slid against my legs, pinning them against the instrument panel. A sharp pain shot through my ankle, causing me to cry out. Meanwhile, Mab's head made an unpleasant crunching noise where it struck the base of my seat.

Ahead of us, through the front window, a long slender titanium wedge could be seen sailing off into the snowy nothingness below.

"Ah, Mab . . . was that our left wing?"

" 'Fraid so," Mab muttered, his voice edged with pain. "Ma'am . . . things aren't looking too good."

"At least the body of the plane hasn't been breached. Though, I'm not sure it could survive another one of those . . . oh no!"

Smoke began curling about several spots on the ceiling where the vinyl covering was melting. In two places, tiny flickers of flame were visible.

"He's doing that from the outside? With just the fire from his mouth?" whispered Mab. "That's impossible!"

"Tell that to the flames."

I made a dash for the fire extinguisher, nearly falling when my injured ankle did not support me. Grabbing the extinguisher, I aimed it at the hot spots and fired. Liquid splashed across the ceiling, covering it with a white puffy cream. Foolishly, I remained standing, stooping to examine my ankle. The plane lurched again. The fire extinguisher and I went flying.

WHEN I came to, I was lying in the back, under a suitcase, with something sticky running into my eyes. Mab appeared over me and moved the luggage. As he did so, a jarring pain shot through my temples.

Mab did not look so good. Rivulets of blood ran over his face and down his neck.

"Are you all right, Ma'am?" he asked hoarsely.

"Guess so," I whispered. "How about you?"

"As well as can be expected."

"Who's flying the plane?"

"The dragon . . . so to speak."

"Great." My throbbing head fell back to rest against the carpet. "Do we have any kind of plan?"

" 'Fraid not, Ma'am. We're pretty well cooked."

"Any suggestions?"

Mab sat back on his haunches, bracing himself against a seat in case the plane should lurch again. "That depends on whether or not you feel well enough to play your piccolo. Otherwise, the only thing I can think of is that I might be able to abandon this body and go for help."

The situation seemed surreal. I had become so accustomed to having a solution to every predicament.

"Sometimes I forget that I, too, am mortal." My voice rang oddly in my ears.

"Ma'am, you're scaring me!"

"We must protect the flute," I continued, ignoring him. "We can't let it fall into the hands of the servants of Hell." Darkness danced at the edge of my vision. My eyes slipped closed. "Holy Lady, please protect my people."

Abruptly, the plane rose up, shook, then began to drop. The gentle weightlessness of free-fall caressed us. Mab slapped my face to wake me and shoved the flute into my hands. He was floating above me, scowling horribly.

"By Setebos and Boreas, Ma'am . . . play! The dragon just dropped us."

SOMEHOW I found the breath, though I cannot recall what I played. Mab hurriedly stuck in his earplugs. The plane continued to fall, the air whistling around us. Then, the whistle became a roar as gale-strength winds lifted us up, missing wing and all.

Mab, his face pressed against a window, whistled softly himself. "Well, would ya look at that!"

Outside, flying away from us, was a giant brown-speckled bird, bigger than an eighteen-wheeler, with a head like a hawk's, each wing the span of a football field. In its immense claws, it carried Osae the Dragon. The crimson serpent squirmed and writhed, trying to free himself, but the roc had pierced the dragon's body with a talon, so the shapechanger could not alter himself without tearing his body in two. As the two supernatural creatures sped away, I gave a feeble cheer.

"Sake's alive! The magnificent roc! Did your Lady send it?"

I laughed weakly and pointed to the left. "No. That roc works for a much less spiritual master."

Through the swirling snow came a white stallion flying on feathered wings. He sped across the sky as easily as an ordinary horse might gallop across a meadow. The winds carrying our plane troubled him not at all. Atop his back, laughing and waving his staff, rode my brother Mephisto.

"I can't believe it," Mab muttered, chagrined. "We've been saved by the Harebrain! I wonder if he's been following us all this time?"

"Maybe he's been following the Three Shadowed Ones," I murmured.

Mephisto turned Pegasus about, and the stallion dipped his wings, giving the universal air signal for "follow me." Via the flute, I directed the winds to carry the plane, and we set off after the flying horse. Pegasus dived through the swirling whiteness to land lightly on a wide snowy bank. With the help of the flute and the winds, we came to a safe, if bumpy, stop beside him.

* * *

MEPHISTO leapt from the winged horse and ran pell-mell to greet us. He was clad in a fur-trimmed parka and fur boots, such as reindeer herders wear, which allowed him to move easily and quickly across the icy environment. In one hand, he held the *Staff of Summoning*. Wonder of wonders! He had actually recovered it from the demons!

Mephisto burst into the cabin of the plane, then stopped cold, gaping at our blood-covered faces. All three of us gazed at each other in silence.

Finally, Mab muttered morosely, "Head wounds. Look worse than they are."

At our direction, Mephisto located the first aid kit and bandaged our heads and my ankle. This was made more difficult because he had handcuffed his staff to his wrist and could not put it aside, so that when he let go of it to help us, it flew about as his arm moved and banged into things. Once I could sit up properly, I gave Mab and myself a drop each of the Water of Life, to stabilize our condition and speed our healing. Then we gathered together what equipment we could salvage, and all climbed onto the back of the flying horse.

"Are you sure he can carry us all?" Mab asked dubiously. Mephisto and I laughed.

"He's a magic horse," Mephisto explained.

When this did not seem to placate Mab, I added, "He's not limited by earthly constraints such as size or weight. We used to fit our whole family on his back."

"What about Seir?" demanded Mab. "He's still around. He could turn up any moment."

"He wouldn't dare come near me, now that I have my staff! He knows what kind of horrors I could sic on him," Mephisto replied gleefully.

That answer did not make Mab feel any better, but we set off nonetheless. It pained me to abandon the Lear, which had been my main mode of transportation for decades, but it was clearly damaged beyond repair. Prospero, Inc. had plenty of other private planes, of course, but only this one had been custom designed to be piloted by Aerie Ones. It could fly in nearly any weather. I sadly waved goodbye as it fell away behind us and was lost in an ocean of snow.

We headed for the North Pole, which Mephisto insisted was only a little ways away. When Mab complained we could never possibly find it flying blind, Mephisto just grinned and tapped his staff against his foot.

The snow flurries beside us looked remarkably like a flying reindeer.

Then, a real reindeer was flying beside us. Mephisto called to him, telling him to fly home, and then told Pegasus to follow Donner.

The Arctic sky moved swiftly past us. Even the pounding in my head could not dim the joy of flying by winged horseback again! I reveled in the cold winds as they caressed my face and tousled my hair. Much as I enjoyed the flight, however, my injuries proved too great for me. As I surrendered to the darkness, finally escaping the throbbing pain in my head and ankle, I could have sworn I saw, in the distance, a red-and-white barber pole.

CHAPTER
TWENTY-TWO

The Mansion of Father Christmas

I awakened to the smells of baking. For a time, I lay in unbelievable comfort amidst down pillows and flannel sheets. Everything was warm and cozy; even my dreams had been pleasant, with no incubus to haunt me. I felt I could stay here, exactly as I was, forever.

The sounds of someone munching near my ear stirred my curiosity. I opened my eyes.

I lay in a small chamber with cedar walls and a thick burgundy rug. Rose-colored towels sat on a pink-and-white dresser, piled neatly in front of its oval mirror. Next to my bed, Mab sat on a matching pink-and-white chair, munching a freshly baked sticky bun. The smell of the spices and warm dough made my mouth water.

"Morning, Mab," I said experimentally. "I dreamed an elf brought me soup."

"An elf did bring you soup, Ma'am. And a real, honest-to-goodness elf, too. Not one of those deformed pixies that were on display in that mall of yours."

"Oh, really?" I slowly levered myself up. I felt whole. "How long have I been asleep?

"Three days. You slept like a babe . . . while the rest of us worked like dogs trying to get ready for Christmas Eve. Ol' Santa even got Mephisto to do his fair share."

"That's a miracle in and of itself! So, it's Christmas morning?" I asked.

"If anything could be called morning in the land of no sun." Mab paused while he finished his next bite. "Clever of you to miss the work and wake in time for the feasting. I recommend we ask our host what we came here to ask him, and get out of here immediately, Ma'am. No point in dawdling."

"Certainly! We've wasted precious time already. Three days! Who knows what progress I could have made on rescuing my father, or averting the coming doom?" I was interrupted by my growling stomach. "Good lord, I'm starving! Apparently, I've only eaten soup for three days. Did you say something about a feast? A Christmas feast?"

Mab frowned stubbornly.

"What aren't you telling me, Mab?"

"The elven High Council is expected for the feast, Ma'am. The further we are from here by the time they arrive, the better."

"And miss the High Council?" The name alone kindled memories of fireflies and dancing.

"I was afraid you'd say that, Ma'am," Mab sighed, adding morosely, "Oh, why couldn't you just have stayed asleep one more day!"

Mab retreated while I rose and dressed. I unwrapped the bandages covering my head, but could find no sign of an injury. After brushing out my hair with a coral-handled brush I found on the dresser, I met up with Mab and began making my way through the winding corridors of Father Christmas's house.

It was a magical place! Wondrous smells filled the halls: cedar, pine, peppermint, sizzling meats. Bells and garlands hung everywhere. I padded across the polished wooden floors in thick red socks someone had thoughtfully left beside my bed. To either side of me, doors opened into workrooms. I glimpsed stately blond elves, garbed like Swiss yodelers, in embroidered lederhosen, standing in rows before long workbenches, each cleaning his tools and scrubbing his spot of bench. Farther along, other doors led to cozy bedroom suites, and one opened on a cedar-lined sauna surrounding a hot tub the size of a swimming pool. Sweetly scented steam filled the chamber.

Around a corner, I came upon a great jet-black door held shut with massive steel chains. Next to that door, a hip-high pedestal held a silver circlet inset with some kind of polished horn.

Nowhere, however, could I find any sign of the kitchen. Finally, I caved and asked Mab.

"I don't know, Ma'am," he said warily. "Might not want to go there. That Mrs. Claus is a mean one. If she catches you, she'll probably make you go feed that bear. Very dangerous business, the bear. Already ate two elves this week."

"If the bear eats the help, why do they keep it?"

Mab shrugged. "Don't rightly know, Ma'am. Maybe it's too vicious to get rid of. Maybe they use it to dispose of unwanted help. Either way, I can vouch that the beast is dangerous. Mrs. Claus insisted I feed it last night, and I nearly got my head bitten off. I recommend you find a nice safe place to sit, and we'll flag down some passing elf to get us something to eat."

"Why didn't you just refuse?"

"Refuse Mrs. Claus!" Mab paled. "You haven't seen her, Ma'am. She's formidable!"

"Santa!" A harsh voice bellowed from farther down the hall. "Santa! Where's that man gotten to?"

"What's that?" I whispered, shaken.

"That's her," Mab whispered. "Our hostess."

"Poor Father Christmas! How can the most generous man in the world have a harridan for a wife?"

"One of the great mysteries, Ma'am. Along with why mortals always do the opposite of whatever they're told," he commented, as I continued turning corners and peering into chambers.

"Are they here yet, Mab?" I asked.

"Who?"

"The High Council?"

"No."

"Then, why are you worried?"

"There may be worse things than elves lurking in this house, Ma'am," Mab replied dryly. "Besides, I'd like to avoid another encounter with the bear."

DESPITE Mab's entreaty, the next corner turned out to be the one I was looking for. I stepped around it and into the heat of an enormous kitchen, where we were pleasantly assailed by the scents of fresh dough, of simmering soup with basil and onions, and of soap made with lavender. A dozen elf maidens worked busily, clinking dishes in the huge sinks, striking their long wooden spoons against the sides of the boiling pots as they stirred, or banging rolling pins against new dough on the butcher-block counters. Above their heads hung rows of giant copper pots, as shiny as new pennies.

Bustling through the middle of this, clad in a candy-striped dress and an apron, was Lady Christmas, whom Mab called Mrs. Claus.

"Santa!" she bellowed again.

Now that she was before me, I saw I had been deceived. While her voice was loud and strident, Mrs. Claus's plump rosy face smiled widely as she called out for her husband, and her eyes danced with merry cheer. I began to warm to her immediately and ceased feeling so badly upon her husband's behalf. Lady Christmas was no harridan—merely a loving wife with a very loud voice.

Seeing us, she sailed forward and seized my hands in her large warm flour-covered ones.

"Oh, honey, you look famished. Quick now, girls, fix our guest a plate. You may call me Martha," she added, smiling kindly.

An elf maid arrived with cups of steaming cider, and a second one brought us a crystal platter of pastries. I accepted the cup and two pastries, as did Mab. A second elf maid rushed in to explain that Father Christmas had been detained but would arrive presently with the ham.

"Careful," Mab muttered to me under his breath, "or she'll ask you to feed the bear."

"Feed the bear! How nice of you to remind me, Mab," cried Martha Claus. She gestured toward a silver tray upon which lay three bloody slabs of meat. "All right, girls, who will feed the bear?"

Silence. No one answered. Mab's eyes shifted quickly over the gathered company, and he stepped surreptitiously behind a large pot, out of his hostess's line of sight.

"No volunteers? Very well, I shall choose. Who was it that dropped a tray on the Gnome King last month? Nimbrithel? I choose Nimbrithel."

The elf maid in question did not protest; however, all trace of color drained from her face. She was taller than most, and as graceful as a swan, with alabaster skin and ashen-colored locks. Gravely, she unclipped a lovely necklace of silver and dewdrops from around her white throat and pressed it into the hand of her nearest neighbor, whispering a few words only the other elf maiden could hear.

"What is she doing?" I asked Mab softly.

"Her last will and testament. She is choosing who she wants to inherit her stuff if she doesn't come back," Mab whispered.

The young elf maid walked solemnly to the tray and, lifting it, cast her sorrowful gaze upon an oak door at the far end of a small alcove. The other elf maidens lowered their heads and stood poised with eerie expressions of poetic sorrow, but no one moved to stop her. Only our hostess did not seem disturbed. Her indifference shocked me. Perhaps I had not been deceived after all. Perhaps, her harsh voice gave a truer glimpse into her soul than her beneficent smile.

"Too bad Mr. Theophrastus isn't here," muttered Mab sadly. "He'd put an end to this slaughter. Took out Osae the Bear with one shot . . . or was it two?"

"Lady Christmas . . . Martha," I said, speaking up. "You can't send this young woman to her death for no reason. Wouldn't it make more sense for one of the knights do it?"

" 'Twould, if we could spare any more knights. But the truth is, we can't. Knights are hard to come by," she replied cheerfully. "We used to have a trained bear feeder. Alas, he met an unfortunate bear-related fate. Don't worry, she'll most likely survive. Seven out of ten do."

"Why not just kill the creature?" I asked.

"What? Kill Santa's bear! I say!" Our hostess exclaimed in horror.

Nimbrithel, the doomed elf maiden, reached to open the door. As she gave the kitchen behind her one last look, our glances happened to meet. Gazing into her eyes, which were as reflective as mountain pools beneath a cloud-covered sky, I was struck by the grace with which she accepted her fate. For an instant, I felt as if it were I standing in the doorway, my hand on the knob, calmly prepared to risk my life rather than shirk my duty.

Then, I was myself again.

"Give me the tray. I'll take it!" I stuck my hand into my pocket and felt the reassuring cold of my war fan.

"Absolutely not!" snapped Mab.

From the doorway, Nimbrithel spoke, her voice devoid of emotion, "If it pleases you, Mademoiselle, that is too cruel a fate for our guest. I shall go."

"No . . . please, allow me. I shall take it amiss if you do not," I replied coolly. Crossing to where she stood, I pulled the tray from her hands.

"Very well, if you insist. Nimbrithel, give her the tray. You are reprieved," chimed my hostess.

"Ma'am, no!" cried Mab, alarmed. "Even I nearly got chomped on. Please, Ma'am, it's too dangerous."

"He is vicious," offered the reprieved elf maid, "You know not what you will be facing."

"I have faced demons," I replied grimly. "I do not fear bears."

"No, Miss Miranda!" cried Mab. "Let me go. I survived once."

"I'll be just fine, Mab. . . ."

"At least, let me come with you."

"And risk it eating both of us? No, I can handle this, Mab." I strode toward the door, "Besides, as you have so often reminded Mephisto, you are not my bodyguard."

He backed off slowly, glowering. "Well, okay, but don't say I didn't warn you . . . and be careful on the ice."

Nimbrithel took a thick red wool cloak with a lining of soft downy white from a peg by the door, draped it over my shoulders, then opened the stout oak door.

"Carry it out just beyond the edge of the building." She added in a sad, soft tone, "I shall not soon forget what you have done for me this day. Long after the bear has gnawed on the last of your bones, elves shall recall your name in song."

Holding the tray firmly with one hand and curling the fingers of my other hand around the silver fan, I waited while Nimbrithel unlatched the heavy oak door. Then I stepped out into the yard beyond.

The sky and the earth blended together into a pure pearly white, broken only by the brown blur of the tall palisade that surrounds Father Christmas's house. The assault of the arctic chill was immediate; however, the cloak the elf maid had draped over my shoulders proved to be surprisingly warm. I suspected it was woven from the beard-hairs of fire giants. Huddled beneath it, I went quickly along the side of the house to the open area where she had told me to leave the food, watching warily for any sign of motion.

Rounding the corner, I came upon a great black bowl. I slid the dripping meat into the bowl and propped the tray against the wall. Then, I began looking for the vicious creature that claimed so many lives. I was determined to kill it and protect Father Christmas's people from future mutilation.

I moved slowly forward, keeping a sharp eye out for a large furry shape. The snow beneath my boots was a maze of prints, both human and bear, so there were no clues there.

As I came around the corner of the building, I saw it: a huge white polar bear, nearly indistinguishable from its frosty background. The monstrous animal was twelve feet tall, even larger than Logistilla's bear. Stepping back around the corner, I hesitated only long enough to make sure it had not seen me. Then, with one hand gripping my weapon and the other clutching the cloak that protected me from the biting arctic cold, I ran forward, determined to slice the beast's head from its shoulders in a single try.

As I raced toward the gigantic polar bear, my quarry slowly raised its head and spoke.

"Oh ja. Looks like snow?" asked the bear. His voice was calm and peaceable, and he spoke with a Swedish accent.

Startled, I tried to slow down and slid helplessly instead along the slick icy surface. The bear regarded me curiously, making no move to rise. I saw now that it sat slumped, its enormous clawed paws crossed over its round lap, gazing at me with coal black eyes and what could only be described as a bear's version of a benign smile. He made no move to attack.

"Are you . . . Did . . . ?" I stammered, belatedly regaining my footing.

"Told you the 'vicious bear' story, did they? Tsk-tsk." The bear shook his head. "They should not do that. It is unkind."

"You're not vicious?" I asked carefully.

"I am gentle as a kitten," he replied.

Recalling Tybalt's kittenhood, I did not find that metaphor particularly reassuring. However, I folded the fan and slid it back in my pocket. "I see . . . Mab said you tried to kill him."

"The Aerie One with the fedora? They played the same trick on him. He hit me on the nose with a truncheon before he realized his mistake. But he was very polite about it afterwards."

"What! You mean Mab *knew*?" I cried, flabbergasted. Mab had tricked me on purpose? The very idea!

"Would you care to play cards?" asked the Swedish polar bear.

"No, thank you. It's a tad cold for me," I said, surprised the bear was not deafened by my chattering teeth. I pulled the cloak tighter, and retrieved the silver tray.

"Nice chap, that Mab. He played a hand," the bear commented philosophically. When I would not relent, he said kindly. "Thank you for bringing my breakfast."

"My pleasure."

Stepping back into the blessed warmth of the kitchen, I stood hugging my arms and waiting for the chill to subside. Martha Claus smiled cheerfully and took the tray from my chilled fingers. The kitchen elves kept to their tasks, though many were smiling and a few giggling outright. And Mab . . . Mab was leaning against the alcove wall, whooping like a loon.

"You set me up, Mab!"

"T-true, M-ma'am," he said, hardly able to speak due to laughter, "but, y-you gotta admit. I-it was funny."

"I admit nothing of the sort!"

Before I could continue my tirade, the elf maids presented me with a wonderful-smelling breakfast laid out on a silver tray, and Mother Christmas whisked me off to a charming little table by a window through which I could see the bear, who waved.

* * *

MAB and I eventually left the kitchen and went in search of Mephisto. We found him in a little chapel looking out on fields of ice, where he knelt in prayer. When Mab exclaimed this seemed out of character for the harebrain, Mephisto replied hotly that it was Christmas, and only heathens did not go to mass on Christmas. Mab pointed out no mass was being performed, to which Mephisto replied that this was not his fault.

For myself, I was relieved to see my brother could kneel in front of a cross without his feet smoking.

I knelt beside him, and the two of us gave thanks together for the bounty we had received during the previous year. While we prayed, Mab wandered about, examining the crucifix and sniffing the altar.

Father Christmas found us on our way back from the chapel. He no longer wore the Coca-Cola Santa outfit we had seen at the mall. Instead, he looked much as I recalled him from our meeting during Queen Victoria's reign: scarlet raiment under dark green robes trimmed with ermine, high black boots, and a crown of holly encircling his white hair. He carried his staff, a tall length of polished wood from which living holly leaves sprouted, and some mischievous elf had woven a sprig of mistletoe into his long snowy beard. When he smiled, warm crinkles appeared around his blue eyes, and I was suddenly reminded of my father. Saddened, I realized this would be the first Christmas I spent without Father in a hundred and twenty-three years.

"Ho-ho-ho!" he greeted us.

Mephisto did a somersault in mid-air, landing like a gymnast with his arms spread.

"Presents!"

Father Christmas laughed jovially. "Just so!"

"Even me?" Mab asked, surprised, when Father Christmas seemed to include him. "I thought you didn't give gifts to my kind."

"I have made an exception upon this occasion of your visit to my home," Father Christmas replied.

"Oh . . . that's nice." Mab was both pleased and dubious. Leaning toward me, he whispered rapidly, "Was I supposed to get something for him?"

I shook my head.

"You sure? This isn't one of those things like leprechauns, where they make you shoes, but if you don't pay them, they stick you with two lefts?"

"No," I laughed. "Father Christmas is no elf, despite what the poets might say. He is generosity itself. One of the very few we can accept gifts from without fear."

"Still," muttered Mab, "I'd feel better if I had something to give him."

FATHER Christmas led us to a huge feasting hall. Garlands of pine boughs decorated the walls, and the doors were hung with mistletoe. Long oak tables had been set with plates and silver. Three lovely elf maidens carrying large cornucopias walked about the hall, filling the long fluted cups. At each setting, they tipped the horn of plenty and commanded, "Cornucopia, make red wine," or "Cornucopia, make brandy." The requested liquid poured from the mouth, filling the glass.

"That's nifty!" Mephisto bounced over and peered up one of the long hornlike devices. "Does that thing make food, too?"

"Oh, yes," the elf girl replied sweetly. She spoke with a heavy Swedish accent. "Though I only know how to make sweets. Mrs. Claus, now, she can make roast beef and shepherd's pie and piping hot mashed potatoes come from the cornucopia."

"Cocoa all around!" called Father Christmas jovially.

The graceful elf girl ran lightly off, returning quickly with four huge red-and-green mugs. She then produced hot chocolate, complete with thick foam and whipped cream. At Mephisto's request, she even coaxed her cornucopia into making marshmallows. Father Christmas gestured for us each to take a sweet-smelling cup, and led us across the great chamber to an enormous hearth where a huge fire burned, as great as any Guy Fawkes Day bonfire.

To our left was a living spruce so large that a hole had been cut in the roof to allow the tree to tower over the house. Gold tinsel and frosted red-glass balls, each containing its own tiny light, hung from its branches. Beneath the tree, atop the red-and-white skirt that surrounded the trunk, lay presents wrapped in green paper and tied with pink ribbon.

Mephisto rushed forward and began tossing presents to and fro, looking for one bearing his name. Mab approached more slowly, scanning the pile more dubiously. I would have walked forward, too, but Father Christmas bent down beside me and spoke quietly in my ear.

"Your gift will come later, dear child."

Mephisto's box contained a black cavalier's hat with a tall indigo ostrich feather.

"Well . . . that's dumb!" he pouted. "When we were at the mall, you promised me the thing I most wanted!" Cheering up, he added, "But then I did get my staff back, and that was what I really wanted. So, maybe a stupid hat is not so bad."

"Mephisto!" I cried, shamed by his rudeness.

"Miranda . . . it's a hat! That's as bad as getting presents from Logistilla. She always gives clothes—icky presents."

This was too much. "Mephisto, Logistilla makes invulnerable clothing with magic woven into them. That's hardly something to complain about!"

Mephisto stuck out his tongue. "You can have your opinion. I have mine. But I wouldn't want to be a spoil sport, or rain on your Christmas parade, so," he gave Father Christmas his biggest smile showing all his teeth, "thanks anyway, Santa-Baby!"

"You're welcome, Mephisto," Father Christmas replied, not in the least dismayed.

Mab opened his package, revealing a waterproof notebook and a tiny silver space pen of the sort that provided its own pressure. "Hey, now I can write underwater. Bet that'll come in handy!"

I turned to reprimand him for his manners, as well. Then I saw the big grin splitting his face. His comment had not been intended as sarcasm. Mab was genuinely delighted with the pen.

As Mephisto put the pink bow back on the hat box and began waltzing it about the large hall, I turned to Father Christmas.

"Has Mab explained why we came?"

He nodded his snowy head. "Yes. You wish to look into the Scrying Pool of Naughty and Nice, which my elves watch to compile our famous list. It would be my . . ."

A bell rang in the distance. Father Christmas stood and swallowed the remainder of his hot chocolate, wiping the foam from his mustache. "You must excuse me. My guests are arriving. As soon as they are comfortably settled, I will come and find you."

CHAPTER
TWENTY-THREE

The Scrying Pool of Naughty and Nice

We lay hidden in a snow bank as the High Council came across the moonlit snow. Arrayed in their finery, they rode in single file, each upon a long-maned sable horse draped with bells. Their cloaks of state flowed over the rumps of their steeds, trailing along the snow behind them. The cloaks were mirrored, like pools of ice, reflecting the pale arctic moonlight, each with its own touch of subtle color tinting the silver: royal purple for the elf king, followed by gold, black, flame red, white, green, scarlet, and indigo. Each lord wore a crown: gems for Ivaldi Goldenarm, the craftsman, whom earth elementals served; jagged spears of ice for Valendur the Dark, lord of water spirits; flickering flames for Vandel Spitfire; white swan wings for Carbonel, lord of beasts; a hoop of living wood bursting with roses and ivy leaves for Delling, the Forest lord; a cruel crown fashioned from edged dagger blades and curving tines for the warlord Aundelair; and a diadem of iridescent pearls for the sorcerer-scholar Fincunir. The elf king alone went crownless. No circlet could pass over his towering antlers.

The snow insulated us a bit, but I still shivered. There was a knot in my stomach, which I tried to attribute to the cold. Drawing the hood of my borrowed fur coat closer about my face, I peered down the line of the procession again, searching for a cloak of deep blue and a crown of stars, but I could not find them.

Beside me, Mab stirred and muttered, "Hey! Where's our elf?"

"'Our elf?'" I asked, though I knew exactly whom he meant.

"Astreus, the Lord of the Winds. The elf who represents us Aerie Ones on the High Council."

"I was just wondering the same thing," I observed.

Mab's eyes narrowed. He shot me a suspicious look. "Wait a second . . .

that elf you danced with, the one Mephisto wanted you to marry . . . You don't mean it was . . ."

Mephisto interrupted him. "Hey, Miranda, where's your elf? I don't see him."

I sighed.

AFTER the stately procession passed, we crept back to the main house by a circuitous route, so as not to draw attention to ourselves. Mephisto wandered off to swim in the sauna-pool, while Mab and I gathered steaming mugs of hot cocoa laced with mint liqueur, and followed Father Christmas down the narrow cedar-paneled halls to the scriery.

The scriery opened off the hall, a dark room lit only by the silver light shining out from the large black marble basin. The light reflected off tiny crystal chips set into the ceiling. These "stars" formed unrecognizable patterns, until I leaned over and looked into the waters of the basin. There, the concave surface altered the shape of the patterns overhead so they formed the familiar constellations. Staring into the pool, I experienced the illusion that I was looking up at the dome of the night sky.

Father Christmas lifted his holly staff and tapped it three times lightly on the floor. In his deep booming voice, he said, "Ask what you will."

"Is there anything we should be wary of?" asked Mab.

Santa shook his head. "My pool can show you no evil things. This pool sees with my authority. The secrets of adults are not mine to reveal. Its waters will only show you children."

"So we don't have to worry about accidentally looking, say, into the depths of Hell or the Unendurable Citadel?" Mab said.

"No. No earthly scrying pool will show you the Underworld. For that, you would need Merlin's crystal sphere."

"Good thing Mephisto destroyed it!" I murmured emphatically.

"Ah . . . about that sphere, Ma'am . . ." Mab began.

Father Christmas's deep voice interrupted him. "Look where you will. I would stay and assist you, but I am needed elsewhere to prepare for the feast." Smiling, he drew the door closed, leaving us alone in the semi-darkness.

Stepping up to the side of the pool, I looked into its star-studded waters and said, "Show me the children of Titus Prospero."

Ripples of light spread from one star fleck, filling the pool and obscuring the rest of the night sky. In the center of the spreading ripples, an image appeared. It grew until it filled the entire surface. Two boys of about nine and eleven years sat in what appeared to be a large library, perhaps in a mansion. The older one read a book. Large round glasses gave his thin face an owlish appearance. The younger one looked more athletic, reminding me, with a pang, of a youthful Theo. His slumped shoulders betrayed his boredom. He bounced a ball against the wooden floor.

The older boy glanced at the younger. When he spoke, a sweet inhuman voice, issued from out of the empty air beside Mab and me, repeating the words he spoke. The crystal pristine voice spoke rapidly, though unhurriedly, in order to faithfully convey the boy's rambling, rushed chatter.

"Typhon, must you make so much noise with that ball? Because if you must, then that's okay, but I am trying to read here. I just got to the part where the hero is trying to save the pig from the man with the antlers, only you are making a such a racket I can't hear myself think, much less read. So I would be much happier if you were quiet. You could read a book, too, you know. Maybe one on sports? You seem to like sports. I read a good one once, *The History of Sportsmanship*. It's on the shelf behind you. Or, maybe you could dribble your ball downstairs?"

The younger boy ignored him and continued to dribble his ball on the library floor. He looked petulant and lonely.

"Or not," said the older boy, sighing and continuing to read.

"Interesting. They look very much like us," I said. "Wonder where they are?"

"Ask the pool to pull back the image," said Mab.

I threw Mab an uncertain glance, but gave it a try. "Pool, pull the image back and show us the outside of the house," I commanded.

It worked. Mab grinned smugly. The image now showed an old Southern plantation house flanked by sycamores dripping with Spanish moss.

"I know that place," I said, surprised. "That's Logistilla's house in Georgia! She didn't breathe a word about this when we questioned her about the family. I wonder if Titus is staying there as well. Pool, show us who else lives in the house." But either no one else did, or they were adults, for the image did not move.

"Guess it wouldn't work to try and trick it by claiming Titus never really grew up or something," Mab said thoughtfully.

"No. Maybe with Mephisto, but not with Titus. He's the most stolid of us. But at least we know where his children are. We can send an Aerie One to spy the place out, and see if Titus is there, too," I finished, though I doubted it. Why would he have stopped sending me cards if he were merely in Georgia?

Just for the heck of it, I commanded, "Show me Prospero." Again, the image remained fixed on the red mansion and the dripping moss. "Show me Titus Prospero's children again."

The image returned to the two boys. I bent over the water, examining the room. The library was multi-level, with more books visible on a balcony above. To one side, on a raised dais, stood the most intricate doll house I had ever seen. As tall as the older child, it stood open, displaying to the viewer the interior of a toy mansion with twin wings.

"How strange! Mab, do you see that toy house? What do you make of it?"

Mab leaned forward, peering into the scrying pool. "Huh! That's Prospero's Mansion, Ma'am. That's your house!" Mab bent even closer, his nose just above the water. "Looks just like it, Ma'am, down to the last detail . . . except a few of the toy doorways are made of ivory. I can see the little statues in the Great Hall! There's the lesser hall, the library, Mr. Prospero's study, and that underground corridor that runs to the Vault, and the Wintergarden. And, look! At the top! There's the eyrie! Hey, they've even got my cot in there!" He frowned and scribbled something in his notebook, muttering, "Better ward it again next time I'm at the mansion."

"Why would Titus's children have a doll house that looked exactly like Father's house, down to the furniture and furnishings?" I asked slowly. "That seems . . ."

"Occultish?" Mab drawled. "Yeah, I was thinkin' the same thing."

"So, if this is Logistilla's place . . ." My voice trailed off.

"You think that's Logistilla's voodoo house? I don't like it, Ma'am. Specially not after that devil stench I smelled at her place." He frowned, his gaze fixed on the doll house. "We still don't know how that incubus got into the mansion."

I shivered and began chafing my arms. "We haven't found Titus, but we've learned some interesting things nonetheless. I guess that's all we're going to see here, unless there are other children in our family I do not know about."

The image shifted again. This time, it showed a group of dark-haired children playing in the street. As I watched, a man dressed in jeans and a blue shirt called to one of the children to come home. Apparently, the pool showed adults if they happened to pass close to children. Mab and I leaned closer.

"Why is the pool showing us this scene? Who is this boy? . . . Hey! I recognize that man! Mab, where have we seen him before?"

"I think . . ." Mab peered closer. "I know! He was one of the workmen at the Lincoln Memorial. He was the young guy hanging around with the fellow Harebrain nicknamed Mr. Mustache."

I leaned closer, examining the brass ring on the workman's hand. Gasping, I grabbed Mab's shoulder. "Oh, Mab! We are such fools! Look at the symbol on his ring! That wasn't the Star of David those masons were wearing! It was—"

"The Seal of Solomon," Mab finished. His voice trembled slightly. "Ma'am, those guys aren't Freemasons. They're *Orbis Suleimani*!"

"No wonder they followed us down to the Caribbean!" I whispered, releasing Mab to pace about the room. "The *Orbis Suleimani* are devoted to removing all traces of magic from Mankind. If they heard us talking at the monument. . . . That man in the motorboat! Mr. Mustache!"

Mab's face was grim. "If he was one of them, he might not have been sent by the Three Shadowed Ones after all."

"Oh dear, and I had been congratulating myself for taking him out so cleverly." I shivered suddenly. "I hope he survived the crash . . . unless the *Orbis Suleimani* is in cahoots with the Three Shadowed Ones, which could be the case if Cornelius has gone bad." I froze. "Ferdinand! He was with us in D.C. He's probably in danger, too! Do you think the pool was trying to warn us?"

"I wouldn't burst your buttons, Ma'am. If they haven't gotten him by now, he's probably safe. Either way, there's no point in our running off half-cocked to look for him."

"Still, perhaps, we should leave immediately, as you suggested. Without waiting for dinner, I mean."

"Glad to hear you talking sense, Ma'am," Mab agreed, adding under his breath, "Even if I don't much care for the cause."

IN the end, we stayed for the feast. We did inquire about leaving, only to discover a terrible blizzard raged outside. Even the reindeer with the nose-light refused to guide us through this storm. I offered to dispel the blizzard with my flute, but our host asked that it be allowed to run its course as he had already requested it to hold off until after Christmas Eve. As this left us with no way to depart before the weather cleared, our choice was to sit in our rooms or attend the feast.

The feast was not until late in the evening, so Mab and I decided to join Mephisto in the sauna-pool. I do not approve of the modern swimming suits—they reveal more flesh than they cover, but an elf maid had provided me with a proper bathing outfit, one that covered the shoulders and thighs while leaving the limbs free to enjoy the water. They had even gone to the trouble of providing me with one in emerald green. Garbed in this, and toting the huge shaggy lime-colored towel that I found folded beside my new swimsuit, I hurried down to join the men.

I walked into the steam-filled chamber and breathed in the moist sandalwood-scented air. It was like nothing I had seen elsewhere. The room was like a sauna, with cedar walls and ceiling, but much larger than any public sauna I knew. Hot rocks, over which water poured occasionally, formed a ring around a medium-sized swimming pool, filling the chamber with steam. Its heated waters bubbled from the pressure of air jets. The setup looked simple enough, but whether or not it required magic to keep up the thick steamy atmosphere, I could not tell.

The water was very warm. I luxuriated in the hot bubbling water, floating pleasantly in its relaxing warmth. Nearby, Mab, dressed in a pair of black bathing shorts, hung just beneath the surface with only his eyes and nose above the water. Farther along, Mephisto played with a large colorful beach ball. He leapt and splashed about, trying to interest us in his games, but Mab and I were both content merely to soak up the warmth.

As he floated, Mab pulled out his new Space Pen and began scribbling happily upon the pages of his waterproof notebook, underneath the water. I closed my eyes and breathed in the cedar-scented air, thinking back upon previous Christmases spent in exotic places, or with my family, in happier days. Christmas, to me, brought to mind the ringing of bells, exchanging presents, scrumptious feasts, and, in the earlier days, attending Mass. In later years, my siblings became less religious, and we stopped going as a family, though Father never missed attending church on Christmas Day—not until this year, anyway.

Even after Father retired, we still spent Christmas together. I would fly out to Prospero's Island to collect him, and we would attend mass in Notre Dame, or the Sistine chapel, or at one of the great Protestant Churches. We had talked about spending this next Christmas at the Duomo in Milan. Neither of us had been home in ages. It was to have been a special outing, just the two of us.

How terribly sad to know that while I basked in warmth and luxury, my father suffered the torments of Hell.

I splashed my face with hot water, so as to conceal any tell-tale tears, and recalled another Christmas when I had feared I would not see Father, though that occasion came to a happy conclusion. It had been a cold December, about forty years after our raid on the Vatican. After barely escaping the Roundheads with our lives, we had fled England. Returning ten years later, we found Cromwell dead, and the nation ruled by tolerant King Charles II. Father and Erasmus quickly made themselves useful to the new regime, and we were again the darlings of a British court.

Christmas of 1666, however, promised to be a lonely one, as only Mephisto, Erasmus, Logistilla, and I were home. Father and the rest of our brothers had left months before, chasing yet another meager hope of curing Cornelius's blindness by visiting some hot bath or holy relic. They had been expected for weeks, but there had been no sign or word.

The four of us who remained were an incongruous lot; yet, as the holidays approached, our spirits rose. Carolers knocked at our door, singing "As It Fell on a Holie Eve" and "Angels, From the Realms of Glory." We filled their hands with coins and steaming mugs of a strong ale called "nog," for everyone believed it was bad luck to send carolers away empty-handed. We had no Christmas tree—that tradition had not yet been brought over from Germany—but we did have a nativity scene Mephisto had carved many years before. Mary and Joseph were a bit the worse for wear when we first took them out, but after Erasmus gave them a fresh coat of paint and a touch of gilt, they looked quite festive.

After the others returned from church, we gathered in our finery for Christmas supper. Ribbons were newly in fashion, and Logistilla dripped from crown to sole with brightly colored "ribands of the finest satin." Erasmus and Mephisto (who no longer showed any concern for what he wore and thus had been clothed by Erasmus) were dressed in the new "English style" made popular by the king, who hoped to rival the French as an instigator of fashion. I thought they looked quite handsome in their long black cassocks lined with pink-and-white silk, though Logistilla insisted they looked like giant magpies. Less concerned with the dictates of fashion myself, I wore a gown of severe dark green with a falling lace collar of the sort popular during the reign of the current king's grandfather.

Just as we sat down to our Christmas supper, the door burst opened and in came Father, along with Theo, Titus, Cornelius, and Gregor. Returning from the Continent, they were decked out in the latest French style, wearing long justaucorps and handsome dark periwigs of wavy curls, except for Gregor, who wore his cardinal's robes, despite the danger to Catholics in England. Entering the house, they swept off Cavalier hats festooned with jaunty ostrich feathers—much like the one Mephisto had just received, which might have been what recalled this scene to me—and came forward, smiling, to embrace us.

Titus burst into laughter when he saw Mephisto's and Erasmus's attire, and informed them that the French king had recently taken to dressing his footmen and servants in this "English" manner. That was the last time I saw either Erasmus or Mephisto wear their magpie coats. There was much anger against the French king for this slight, especially among the English noblemen, who muttered that such indignity would incite even a stone to seek revenge. Yet, soon the whole court, including King Charles himself, were again garbed as French fashion dictated.

We all sat down together around our Christmas dinner, though what was to have been a large feast for four looked somewhat meager when shared among nine. Still, despite Cornelius's most recent disappointment, there was an air of festivity and joy.

"You missed a horrendous fire," Erasmus explained as Father began carving the shoulder of mutton. "Near all the city was destroyed. I did hear it called the new Great Fire of London."

" 'Twas worse than the fire of 1212?" asked Father.

"Over thirteen thousand houses lost. True, some of these fell to the Duke of York's gunpowder. Buckingham claims York was overzealous in his efforts to stop the conflagration, but the number remains."

Theo whistled. "How many killed?"

"Six!" Erasmus grinned.

Father's white bushy eyebrows shot up. "All those houses lost and only six souls died? Surely, the Hand of God rested upon London."

"Or the hand of Prospero!" Erasmus chuckled. "Mephisto and I ensnared the Sovereign of the Salamanders early the first day. Lacking our staffs, we had not the strength to compel him to stop his inferno, but we offered what we could. We promised if his minions curbed their taste for the living, restricting their diet to inanimate materials and beasts, we would reward him with a droplet of Water of Life. He did as we requested, and we paid the toll." The laughter drained out of Erasmus's face. "Sir, if we had but had our staffs! Thousands of men are destitute, camped in tents at St. George's Fields, and Moorfields, or as far out as Highgate. All of which could have been avoided."

"In their despair, many have turned to dishonest means. Our prisons are frightfully overcrowded," huffed Logistilla, who often visited the prisons as part of her charity work.

"And this after the Black Death claimed nearly twenty thousand souls only last year." Gregor bowed his head in prayer. "O Accursed City! The men of England suffer for the sins of their libertine Protestant king!"

Father looked up from his mince pie, frowning. "From whence came the Water of Life you proffered this monster?"

"From my personal reserve. I mind not forgoing one year's drop in return for the lives saved," replied Erasmus.

"Would not Miranda help you?" Father voice rose sharply. I opened my mouth to explain that my brothers had never approached me, but Erasmus cut me off with a snort of derision.

"That miser? A lamentable proposition, sir! She would rather all Londoners cook than waste one drop of her pearly riches! She would not even come out and help us."

Again, I wanted to object—the day Father departed, he had asked me to mind the house, and so I had done so. As I opened my mouth to explain, however, Theo threw me a pleading glance, indicating he would be grateful if Christmas dinner did not turn into a quarrel. I was so happy to have him home! As a favor to him, I held my tongue.

We ate, accompanied by animated descriptions of the travelers' adventures. The fare was excellent, and every time one of us raised an empty glass, a wine bottle would float up and fill it, as Aerie Ones rushed to do our bidding. Logistilla was commended by all for her choice of dishes, Mephisto roused himself from his morose stupor—his malady was much worse in those days—to juggle jam tarts for our amusement, and even Gregor allowed himself a smile.

As the last dish was being cleared away, Cornelius spoke up in his soft voice.

"Father, I would speak."

Father held up his hand, and the rest of us fell silent. Cornelius stood. The dusty-blue silk covering his eyes matched the shade of his justaucorps. "All this rushing to and fro, pursuing will-o-the-wisps, achieves nothing but to raise and dash our expectations. By the Grace of God was I blinded, and only by the Grace of God will my sight be restored. Let us abandon our attempts to find a cure and turn our efforts to more useful ends."

He sat down. The rest of us gaped at him in astonishment. Curing

Cornelius's blindness had been our main effort for four decades, that and Mephisto's madness. We were not sure how to respond.

Father finally broke the silence. "This news brings me sorrow, and yet I think it wise. I would reward you for your noble sacrifice. What gift do you desire? Name it!"

"Nothing for myself." He bowed his head. "Grant this boon instead to Erasmus."

A furrow formed between Father's brow, but he said only, "As you wish."

Erasmus laughed. "You know already what I desire. Our staffs! Had they been with us, instead of moldering away at our mansion in Scotland, we could have forced the salamanders to retreat. We could have saved the London we have known and loved these many years!"

"So be it." Father inclined his head gravely. "I retain the right to collect them again when I deem fit, but they shall be yours for a time."

We children gave a resounding cheer, and finished our Christmas feast in high spirits. As it turned out, Father would only let us keep the staffs for a decade before he collected them again, but we did not know this at the time. So the rest of the evening rang with comradery and good cheer.

In retrospect, the memory of this joyful Christmas was accompanied by a sense of bittersweet sorrow. At all Christmases after this one, either one of us was not present or some members of the family were feuding. The year 1666 was the last happy Christmas we all spent together.

THE door at the far end of the sauna opened, dispelling the ghosts of Christmas past. Three tall dark-haired men strode into the chamber. As my gaze penetrated the obscuring steam, I sat up, startled. We were being joined by three of the lords of the High Council: the elf lords Vandel, Carbonel, and Delling.

The stately elves did not glance in our direction. They spoke to each other in their soft lilting tongue while they unbelted their long black robes and let them drop to the floor, revealing lithe golden bodies which were . . . entirely unclad.

I glanced away and kept my eyes averted until the elven lords were safely immersed in the water at the far side of the pool. Mab had inched closer to me, as had a subdued Mephisto. The three of us huddled on the drowned steps set into the pool wall and wondered whether the elven lords realized we were present.

I peered through the steam to get a better look at the wet elves. Lord Vandel's back was to me. Along his golden shoulder blades ran identical scars, the shape of upside down teardrops. As Lord Carbonel fell back to dunk his head beneath the water and rose again, shaking a spray of drops from his long hair with catlike grace, I saw a similar set of scars marred his otherwise perfect back.

"Mab," I whispered softly, "those scars. What are they?"

Mab looked, then turned away, grief stricken. "That's where their wings were cut off, Ma'am . . . when they fell."

CHAPTER
TWENTY-FOUR

The Feast of Christmas

We were to feast with elves!

The great hall was even more splendidly arrayed than it had been in the morning. Holly decked the doorways, and garlands of pine boughs, bound with red ribbons and hung with silver bells, decorated the walls and snaked their way about the back of each chair. Red-and-green-leaved poinsettias, as tall as small trees, stood here and there in giant pots covered in red foil. In the center of the hall, between the tables, stood a fifteen-foot blue spruce draped with tinsel and colored ornaments. Amidst its branches, a hundred shell-shaped oil lamps burned brightly, their lights twinkling against the glass of the ornaments.

The long oak tables were laden with delicacies. Tall green candles in gold candelabra burned brightly amidst overflowing dishes of roast beef, turkey, venison, wild boar, grilled salmon, and hunks of juicy baked ham. Mince pies and steaming bowls of candied sweet potato surrounded the meats, along with platters of breads, various cheeses, fresh fruit, and an array of unfamiliar elvish delicacies. Wooden troughs held large salads of fresh vegetables and herbs, and armies of porcelain pitchers offered a variety of dressings.

The merry company was decked out in their finest furs and satins, as was our little party of three. Mab, who had not brought any finery with him, was garbed in a handsome outfit of green and black velvet that had been loaned to him by some helpful elf. He wore it now, despite his complaints that he would feel more comfortable in his trench coat and fedora, and it suited him well. As for Mephisto, he was dressed in a splendid doublet and hose of blacks, greens, and rich earthy browns. Where he had gotten it, or what denizen of what supernatural abode had helped him to don it, I did not ask.

Garments had also been left for me: a Victorian gown with a dark green velvet bodice trimmed with silver satin, velvet panniers, and a skirt of jade green crêpe de Chine. A lovely concoction, and I longed to wear it. Were events to go awry, however, I would never have forgiven myself for having put aside the protections of my enchanted tea-dress while dining with elves. Reluctantly, I declined it. I did, however, put on the jewelry that had been provided: drooping emerald earrings, a matching necklace, and a set of jade hair combs.

A lovely elf maiden led us through the labyrinth of scents and noises to our seats at Father Christmas's table. I was amazed, considering the august company present, when she placed us just to the right of our host—until I recalled that in elven protocol the most important figures sat at the center of the table, across from each other, while individuals of lesser worth spread out to either side, according to their station. By elven standards, the three of us were relegated to the table edge, a position of obscurity. Still, by European standards, sitting just beside our host put us at the head of the table. Determined to have a pleasant evening, I interpreted our position in the more favorable light.

Father Christmas wore an even more ornate version of the red and green velvet robes we had seen him in earlier that afternoon. At the far end of the table sat his wife, her jolly red face beaming with smiles, and a gown of autumn colors garbing her plump body. She waved to Mab and me as we took our seats, welcoming us cheerfully.

At the center of our table sat Alastor, the elf king, his antlers towering above the crowns of his lords. To either side of him sat the lords of the High Council. Lesser elves of note filled in the rest of the seats, save for ours and six seats across from the king, which had been left empty for the queen and her attendants. I noted with uncomfortable dismay that no place had been saved for Astreus. Apparently, he was not expected.

It disturbed me to sup with elves, so firmly had I been schooled in the evils of accepting fairy food. I knew the fare came from our host and hostess, and even Mab did not fear accepting food from Father Christmas. Yet I found the company so unnerving, I almost requested we be allowed to sit at the next table with the ice sprites and gnomes, both creatures whose natures I comprehended better than that of the cruel, quixotic, whimsical elves. But that would place us below the salt, a position inappropriate for our rank and station. Besides, the elves had been such pleasant company during the one occasion we had encountered them previously. Perhaps I worried needlessly.

Mab inclined his head toward me to make some comment, but his words were lost beneath a fanfare of trumpets. The queen of the elves and her ladies had arrived.

The elven queen glided between the tables. Layers of chestnut, white, and cream gossamer draped her lithe body, forming a high-waisted gown with long flowing sleeves and skirts which rustled as she moved. Her bearing was elegant and regal, but her face was that of a sixteen-year-old girl-child, delicate and fresh. Strings of diamonds, glittering like dew, decorated her auburn hair—or perhaps they were strings of dew that sparkled like diamonds. A golden tiara framed her lovely childlike face and glittered in the candlelight.

Behind her came her ladies, each fairer than the last. Fragile layers of moss green and sea blue draped Undine's slender form, and lilies adorned her blue-green hair. Behind her came graceful Sylvie, living butterflies perched upon her silvery locks. Lengths of sky blue, ice blue, and the purple of a brewing storm fluttered around her svelte body as she flowed forward. Floramel followed her, in a gown the color of orange blossoms, rose petals, and lilacs. Her dark locks were woven with exotic orchids. Gloriana's gown imitated living fire, as tissue-thin layers of red, orange, and candle-flame yellow flickered around her fair form. Her crimson hair was arrayed with columbines, bird-of-paradise flowers, and wine-red roses. Last came the incomparable Iolantha, the gentlest and most compassionate of the elf queen's ladies, dressed in gossamer of white and gold, her chestnut hair adorned with dogwood flowers.

As the elf queen and her retinue came forth through the hall, all rose. Mab, Mephisto, and I rose as well, and stood politely as they seated themselves. The elf queen took her seat, and regarded the gathered company with gracious mirth, her dark eyes sparkling as she prepared to speak. Then her eyes fell upon us, and all amusement died.

"Must we dine with Aftercomers?" she demanded archly in her sweet voice, her childish face stern beyond its apparent years. "Alastor, have them sent forth!"

I sat down abruptly, wishing I had sat among the ice sprites after all. Once, long, long ago, I had been thrown out of a feast. The humiliation still rankled, especially when I recalled the grating laughter of the French courtiers, how they had made merry over our plight as Father and I were dragged out, and dumped into the dirty straw outside the feast hall. It was soothing to remember that time had outstripped them, and they were all dead now. That succor would never heal this wound, should we be shamed before the immortal elven court. The elf queen had been charming to us the one night we had met under hill. I had not anticipated this reaction.

The king of the elves laughed. "What report will be given of our hospitality if we turn guests away during a blizzard, dear queen? Our host's guests at that? We can hardly refuse them seats at our host's own table."

"The girl then, but not him!" Queen Maeve pointed at Mephisto.

"Whyever not? How is he different from any other mayfly?" King Alastor's tone seemed solicitous, yet his gray eyes danced with cruel merriment. Queen Maeve drew herself up, her dark eyes snapping.

Before she could speak, Father Christmas's deep voice boomed across the table. "He is my guest."

"Well and good, then, we shall move." The queen started to rise, halted, paused, then sat again. Her color high, she stated flatly, "I shall not impose upon my subjects by asking them to trouble themselves. We shall remain, and endure."

I focused my attention intently upon my plate, determined not to smirk. The events that had just transpired had not been lost upon me. The queen had begun to rise, but the king had not. Uncertain how many courtiers would follow her should she depart, she had decided that it was better to eat with Aftercomers than to risk losing a contest with the king over the loyalty of the court.

I was grateful for Father Christmas's support. Our host's open blessing and the tacit approval of the elven king, however, were not enough to buy us acceptance. None of the elven courtiers seated nearby spoke a word to us or even acknowledged our presence. Rather than make a fool of myself by attempting to discourse with them, I turned my attention to our host and listened with pleasure to his amusing retelling of the highlights of his escapades the previous night as he delivered this year's gifts.

Snatches of conversation floated down our way. The elf lords spoke of battles fought and cruel games played upon unwary adversaries. Ivaldi described a journey into the bowels of the earth, the gem-studded splendor he had encountered, and a game of hurling played against the Nibelungs. Valendur, Carbonel, and Aundelair described conquering the unconquerable peak of Koshtra Belorn, and of what glory they had beheld while standing upon the icebound top of the world. Vandel told of a furious battle between a thousand of his best knights and the Sun. One by one his knights had fallen, until he stood alone. Yet, he had dealt the Sun a grievous blow before surrendering the field. Delling spoke of a fabulous pleasure palace of flower petals and thistledown held together by cobwebs and morning dew, while Fincunir entertained the king by recounting a chess game he had played against a mortal who thought himself invincible because he took his instructions from a machine.

Across the table, Floramel and Sylvie delighted the queen with tales of a changeling boy they had stolen and taught the elven arts of raising mushroom rings and calling fireflies; while Undine and Gloriana entertained with stories of their star-crossed mortal lovers, and of tricks they played upon the Wayfarers. Iolanthe recounted a conversation she had overheard between an angel and a water nymph.

Yet, all the while, no matter what the elves said, their conversations conveyed the feeling that they were really speaking about something else entirely, that their poetic words and stunning revelations were but a façade, a veil drawn across their secret meaning, which they communicated to each other by hints and innuendos no Aftercomer, unfamiliar with the intimate dealings of their court, could ever hope to comprehend. I found it eerie and bewildering.

Mab ate quietly and kept his mouth shut, but Mephisto was not so discreet. When the elves sitting near us would not speak with him, he began shouting his questions down the table toward the elven lords.

"Yoo-hoo, elf lords? Anyone know where Lord Astreus is?" he called gaily.

The bottom of my stomach fell away so violently that I grabbed the table, as if to keep myself from falling. While I was terrified for my brother's safety, I also found myself listening attentively, as if something very important rested upon the answer. Chagrined, I tried to return my attention to my meal.

The elf lords regarded each other. Ivaldi Goldenarm, their craftsman, answered first. While as graceful and well-featured as any elf, he was the stockiest member of the council, his face rounder than his brethren, and his muscled shoulders wider. "A well-fashioned question, brothers. Can any here answer true? I know not where our absent brother tarries."

"Oft doth wanderlust afflict him and rob us of his presence." Delling looked to be no more than a youth, though he was as ancient as the rest. "Ever does he seek new vistas where nary a foot has trod."

"The wind goeth where it listeth." Carbonel Lightfoot offered a morsel of bread to the mink that lay curled across his shoulders. The little beast accepted it eagerly, its bright eyes darting about the hall. "So, too, our brother, be it to the secret home of the phoenix, or the gardens at the top of the world, where the wolves gather one night a century to watch the lunar snowdrops bloom, or to the far shores beyond the Walls of Night."

"Many seasons have come and fled since last my eyes beheld him, either in truth or in the dark waters of my far-seeing pools." Valendur the Dark's eyes were black as coals, and his face held unearthly beauty. "Yet, all places do my pools reveal, except the Void and the Infernal Abyss."

"Last time I saw him, we danced for joy. 'Twas during the great celebration we held in Forestholme, in Astreus's honor, the one seven-year that Hell forgave our debt." Delling lifted his fluted wine glass. "A toast to that wondrous day! And to our absent brother for arranging it. May we have many others like it!"

The elves raised their glasses and drank with the toast. I toasted as well, clinking my glass against Mab's. It never hurts to be polite.

Before the conversation could resume, however, Mephisto's voice cut across the table again. "King Alastor? What happens to elves who are tithed?"

Silence.

From the shocked expressions around the table, I gathered Mephisto had just committed some awful faux pas. Perhaps elves did not like to discuss the fact that they handed one of their number over to Hell every seven years. I could not blame them. Perhaps, the queen had been right to fear dining with Mephisto. The uncomfortable silence was broken by Lady Christmas, who called happily from the foot of our table for someone to pass the stuffed mushrooms.

Mephisto, fool that he was, would not let the matter drop.

"You didn't answer my question, your majesty," he shouted. "What does happen to elves who are tithed?"

"Shut up, harebrain!" Mab growled through his teeth. "You're going to get us all killed. Or worse . . . there are worse things than death that elves can do to people, you know."

"Yes. I know," Mephisto whispered back, his voice gravely serious. "Like tithe them."

From further down the table, Aundelair the Cruel spoke. He was called the cruel not because of his treatment of others, but because of the harsh standard to which he held himself. He was famed for never having broken his word, no matter how dire the cost of keeping it.

"We do not speak of such things," he said gravely, regarding Mephisto with his cutting blue gaze. Apparently, his brother Fincunir did not agree.

"What my brother hesitates to say is that, in truth, we know not." Fincunir's voice was light and mocking. "We know as little of the secret councils of Hell as we know of the will of long-abandoned Heaven. And if you believe talk of the tithe disturbs us elven lords, you should see how we scatter like frightened field mice at Heaven's mention."

Fincunir's words brought frowns to the faces of several of his brethren; however, their efforts to chastise him were interrupted by a loud hollow booming that echoed from beyond the great hall.

"What is that?" Mab asked warily.

"That is a knocking at the Uttermost door, the door that opens upon the Void," said Father Christmas.

"Do not heed it!" ordered the elf queen. Father Christmas frowned but said nothing.

More knocking came. Father Christmas nodded to the elven serving maidens in their pretty gowns of red and green. One rose and began walking toward the great archway that led toward the outer hallways.

"Open not the door!" commanded the elf queen. The elf maiden hurried back and resumed her seat.

Once more the knocking came. This time, Father Christmas himself rose to his feet. In a booming voice, he called out, "Enter, Man, and be welcome! Merry Christmas!"

"You fool!" hissed the queen. "You know not what you let . . ."

A dark cloud, as black as soot, billowed into the chamber, seeping between the tables at the far end of the hall. Amidst the blackness was a figure blacker still. My stomach tensed as I peered, seeking blood red eyes. Thank goodness I had worn my protective enchanted dress. But, my flute! I had left it in my room, assuming we were safe from Hell's servants here. Would it be in greater danger if I ran for it or if I remained?

As the black cloud reached the tables where the candles burned, it vanished like mist before the sun, leaving behind a faint odor of dry ice. This was not the black substance that issued from Gregor's staff, but a gust of unnatural black snow. As the snow evaporated, the figure standing in its midst became visible. I caught glimpses of gray fur and deep blue enameled leather.

So it was not Seir of the Shadows after all. Whom, then, did the elf queen fear?

The black cloud parted. Several people gasped, including the queen . . . and Mab . . . and me.

The figure who strode toward us was of a height and stature with the other elven lords. His handsome garments were of wolverine and silver fox inset with dark blue enameled leather, slashed with black satin. From his shoulders flowed a mirrored cloak with a tint of deep blue, the feasting guests and candlelight reflected in its surface.

Piercing gray eyes gazed out from beneath hair the color of storm clouds. His features were elven and aristocratic. Upon his head, where should have sat a crown of stars, was the silver and horn coronet I had seen resting beside the chain-bound door. Had Father Christmas opened all those chains with just his vocal invitation?

"It's him!" whispered Mab. Rising, he rushed forward and knelt before the newcomer. "Lord Astreus!"

"Mab!" Lord Astreus gave a laugh of delight. His voice was a rich baritone, pleasant to the ear. Laying his hand on Mab's shoulder, he said, "Rise, good spirit. I thank you for your homage. Return to your seat and enjoy this merry food and company."

Mab came walking back, smiling to himself. Meanwhile, Mephisto grabbed my arm and whispered loudly, "Look, Sis! It's your elf!"

My heart leapt at the sight of him. "So it is."

King Alastor slid back his chair and turned to face the newcomer. His back was to us, revealing broad shoulders, dark hair, and a massive rack of antlers.

"A clever entrance, Astreus Stormwind. Most impressive, and one certain to inspire curiosity in your audience."

Lord Astreus strode down the length of the hall and knelt before the elf king, his head bowed respectfully before his liege. Yet, there was a subtle gleam in his eye that ill matched his subservient pose. "Your majesty. It does my heart good to look upon your face again. I have dwelt too long in gruesome darkness and gazed upon much unfit for elven eyes."

The elf king gestured, and Lord Astreus rose to his feet. The elf king regarded him in silence. Finally, he asked, "And where have you tarried, these three centuries, since last you danced with us at Forestholme? Come share with us tales of the sights you have seen and the far places you have journeyed. We have missed your counsel and your company."

Astreus replied with knightly courtesy. "Sire, I have been about the business of the queen."

King Alastor turned to Queen Maeve and quirked his brow. "Indeed? What pursuit is it you send my courtier about which keeps him so long from my side?"

"Lord Astreus teases, Sweet Alastor. 'Tis no business of mine," she replied, the color high in her cheeks.

Lord Astreus regarded the queen. A smile born of something other than mirth curled at the corners of his lips, and something unrecognizable flickered in the depth of his eyes, which had shifted color from gray to storm black. "Indeed, your majesty is mistaken. For I would not tarry at such tasks were it not by your explicit will and order."

Queen Maeve laughed sweetly. " 'Tis a private matter, milord, of which I will speak to you anon."

King Alastor inclined his antlers in assent. To the servers he called, "Maidens, bring a chair for our Lord Astreus, for he has the look of one who has traveled far and is need of rest and succor. Gentle lords, make room, that Lord Astreus may sit at my right hand."

"Thank you, Sire," Lord Astreus replied. He glanced about the hall, breathing deeply of the aroma of the feast. As he looked over the assembled company, his glance fell upon me and passed on. I wondered if he recognized me, or if he even remembered the tryst he had made and broken. Probably not.

Unexpectedly, his gaze returned, fixing on me with dawning recognition. His dancing eyes were now as blue as sapphires.

"Miranda!"

"Trifle not with the Aftercomers," declared Lady Floramel. " 'Tis the queen's wish that they be shown no favors, beyond that of being allowed to sup in our august company."

Astreus halted. He cocked his head and gazed at the queen with eyes as silver as mirrored glass. Anticipating he would heed his queen's will, I sighed with unexpected disappointment, which was quite foolish. After all, he was an elf. It was amazing he remembered me at all.

"Surely, Lady Floramel, you mistake our queen's intent," Astreus replied. "For no elf, be she maid or queen, would fail to honor the Handmaiden of Divine Eurynome, who is adored by all *true* elves." Bowing toward King Alastor, Astreus continued, "Sire, I appreciate the favor you show me, but respectfully decline. Do not oust my brethren from their seats on my behalf. Let me sit, instead, beside this fair maid, and speak with my servant Mab regarding the fate of my people. For I have been long absent and would hear how they fare."

"My lord, an elf lord supping with a mortal maid? 'Tis not done!" said

Queen Maeve. Her voice remained girlish and sweet, but her young eyes were wintry. King Alastor regarded the queen, then Astreus, then me. His gaze was penetrating, as if he saw far more than mere appearances might reveal. As he examined me, a half smile on his lips, I noticed anew that the elf king was a comely man, well-favored, and much admired by maidens and matrons alike. He had a reputation for beguiling ladies who drew his regal attentions. As my Lady's Handmaiden, I was immune to his charms, but I lowered my lashes demurely nonetheless.

Now I was most glad I had not chosen to sit among the ice sprites. Astreus's defense of me more than made up for the elf queen's slight! Yet, as I waited for the elf king's decision, my initial delight faded. What motivated Astreus? Did he truly desire to dine in my company? A flattering thought, but rather unlikely, considering that he had not only failed to appear at the rendezvous he himself had solicited, a mere seven years after we had first met and danced, but also he had avoided my company at whatever Centennial Masquerade Mephisto claimed he had attended. More likely, this was some subtle stratagem meant to discomfort the elf queen, whom he seemed bent on needling. If so, I wished he would leave me out of his schemes. The elf queen was not an enemy I wanted to cultivate.

Finally, the elf king spoke. "I see no harm in letting our wayward lord sup beside Eurynome's lovely handmaiden. He has been away so long on your behalf, my queen. Be merciful, and do not stand between him and his chosen amusements. Sit, Lord Astreus, dine, and be merry. When this feast is through, come to me, and we shall speak at greater length."

Lord Astreus bowed. "It will be my pleasure, Sire."

The queen frowned, and her ladies pouted, but there was nothing to be done. The elf king had spoken.

Victorious, Astreus came to stand beside me, his chosen entertainment. As he went to place a chair brought by a serving maid between Mab and me, he halted with some surprise. "Mephisto!"

"Astreus," replied Mephisto. They gazed at each other solemnly, and a glint of something like hope leapt in Astreus's eyes, changing their color to leaf green. Then, Mephisto gave his usual goofy grin, and the glint died away. Oblivious, Mephisto chattered on. "Good to see you again, Mr. Elf."

"And you, my friend. I see the years have not changed you." Astreus's voice was tinged with sadness as he took his seat.

"Not at all," Mephisto agreed happily. "Grape?" And he tossed a grape, bouncing it off the elven lord's forehead.

Astreus caught the grape. "Ahh . . . so this is to be my welcome, is it? At least, I shall be able to say that my Christmas feast was not without its merriment."

AS the feast continued, the elf lord sampled the many delicacies and expressed great appreciation for the wholesomeness of the cuisine. His conduct increased my suspicion that he only chose to sit among us to displease the queen; for while he claimed he wished to sit beside me, he hardly spoke two words to me, directing most of his conversation to our host and to Mephisto. Yet, several times I caught his eyes, now a brilliant blue, resting upon me, and his golden hand casually brushed against mine as he reached for the candied rose petals and the glazed juniper shoots.

As we supped, it occurred to me that I might be safer here, among the elves, than in Ferdinand's presence. Elves were dangerous, true, yet they were dangerous in a manner I understood. If one obeyed the rules and did not ask for favors, or eat their food, or accept gifts, all would be well. With Ferdinand, every step was unexplored territory. There were no rules to protect me or to tell me how to proceed.

As I ate, I could not help comparing the two men. Ferdinand radiated warmth and sincerity. I felt comfortable in his company, and found I could speak easily about nearly any subject. Astreus, on the other hand, was capricious and untrustworthy. Yet, there was something fascinating about him, something fey and light that lifted my spirits and made all manner of impossible things seem suddenly within my grasp.

I dismissed this, for the most part, as some quaint elfish trick. Yet whenever I glanced in his direction, I found it difficult to draw my eyes away, and when he caught my glance and smiled, I could have sworn the Northern Lights danced around us both.

AS we waited for dessert, Astreus addressed Mab, who had been watching him in quiet adoration, and the two began to converse about old times. The elf lord was quick to laugh, his eyes crinkling with his mirth, yet Mab continued to treat him with the utmost awe and respect. As they discussed the Aerie Ones, Astreus asked how each one fared today. Mab answered as best he could. More often than not, however, it was I who provided the latest details.

Lord Astreus smiled into my eyes. "I see you know my people well,"

His gaze went to my head like sweet wine, but I did not care to be intoxicated. The sting of having waited for him for hours by the river, while the stars revolved and finally set, had never quite faded, and his smile now brought it into sharp relief.

"I like to think of them as *my* people," I replied warily.

The mirth in Astreus's eyes grew still, and they changed from sky blue to a colorless gray. His aspect changed as well, suddenly seeming more fey and unearthly. In a voice scarcely above a whisper, he asked, "Is that so? And yet, they served me freely. To you, they are but slaves."

"They are not slaves," I replied haughtily, taken aback. "They swore an oath."

"Ah . . . oaths." The corner of Astreus's mouth curled cruelly. "And do you condone the imprisonment of living spirits, who toil and suffer because of words they cannot unsay?"

"They agreed," I insisted.

Behind him, Mephisto had stopped eating mid-bite and had turned rather green. He began waving his hands about trying to get my attention. When I spared a glance his way, he shook his head desperately and mouthed, "Ix-nay on the O word."

Meanwhile, Astreus spoke, "Perhaps they did. But, are they free to depart should they so wish?"

"They have agreed they would not," I answered, annoyed by his tone.

"You elude my question: can they depart at any time of their own choosing?" Astreus's tone was calm, but there was something terrible in his pale eyes, something that froze my blood, as if he had seen some sight so appalling that the horror of it now spilled out of him and contaminated me.

I eyed Lord Astreus cautiously. Was this the same carefree elf I had danced with on that summer's night, centuries ago? Had this relentlessness burned in his eyes back then? Such intensity seemed out of place in an immortal creature. Last time, I recalled, he had been like the other elf lords: detached, lighthearted, unburdened by the cares of the world. Either something was very different, or the qualities I saw now were but a studied pose, or some trick of elven glamour. Either way, I decided to give him an honest answer.

"No. They cannot."

"Then they are slaves, and you their slaver."

"No!" I cried, refusing to back down. "They are voluntary servants who gave their word."

"Is that the way of it?" His voice was now as soft as the breath of the Angel of Death.

Astreus stood and spoke in a voice that carried across the hall. "I fear my queen had the right of it: mortals are indeed unfit companions for elves. I have learned the error of my ways, and beg your pardon, your majesty."

The elf queen smiled. "You are forgiven, Lord Astreus. Come, sit here beside me. Maidens, attend to him."

Astreus strode away, joining the queen, while I stared down at my food, my cheeks afire. I knew now, without any doubt, he had deliberately not kept our tryst. As his laughter drifted down the table, mingled with that of the queen's ladies, I wondered if he and his companions had sat in some nearby tree, laughing at the foolish mortal girl who had fallen prey to his charms. No longer hungry, I covered my dessert with my napkin and prayed the evening would soon end.

CHAPTER
TWENTY-FIVE

And Should You Grant My Heart's Desire . . .

Amidst swirling snow, the elven court danced upon ice. Ropes of Christmas lights were strung on poles above the pond. Points of red, blue, and green twinkled through the whiteness and illuminated the ball. Beneath these diminutive stars, the elven courtiers, cloaked by the flurrying snow, twirled and glided across the ice like waltzers in a dream, and not one slid or lost his footing.

From somewhere beyond the dancers, elven music drifted. The song had the grandeur of a symphony and the wildness of swing or jazz but was more like a waltz than anything else to which I could put a name. Hearing it evoked memories of the warm breath of summer and the scent of long-crushed grass, for the music had changed little since my family and I had heard it that fateful day in Scotland, so many years ago. Yet, it was always new, for, unlike their mortal counterparts, elven musicians had no repertoire and seldom played the same melody twice.

The whole elven court had turned out to hear the music and join the ball. King Alastor opened the dance with Queen Maeve, his purple cloak swirling around them as they twirled. The Lords of the High Council partnered the Queen's Ladies. Father Christmas waltzed with his plump and smiling wife. Mephisto was out there, twirling and whirling with the best of them, and even Mab could be seen circling solemnly in the company of an elf maid. Everyone danced . . . except me.

I stood alone, isolated by blowing snow, envious of the dancers, for I loved to dance, but was too ashamed to venture among them. Who would dance with me now? Mephisto? Mab? Father Christmas? Perhaps, and maybe I would glean some small enjoyment from it. However, the whole court would recognize that those three were taking pity on me, and that seemed worse than not dancing at all. So, cold and alone, I allowed myself a behavior I had not indulged in for many many years: I felt sorry for myself.

Perversely, it was not my humiliation before the elven court that left me so despondent, but the realization that I had been fooling myself for centuries. I was never going to become a Sibyl. I had been a Handmaiden for five hundred years, more than ten times the life span of most mortals. If I had the qualities my Lady sought for in Her most cherished servants, She would have elevated me long ago.

Not that I disliked being a Handmaiden. It gave me the blessing of my Lady's guidance, without which I would surely be lost. It was She who had brought Father's message to my attention, led me to where Mephisto sat playing his lute, directed me to the thrift shop where we found the chameleon cloak, and guided me to find sanctuary from the barghests at Father Christmas's feet.

If I had not known there was such a thing as a Sibyl, I would have been entirely content. But I did know, and that was what rankled—knowing that whatever quality She sought, I did not have it.

So, I remained alone amidst the whirling snowflakes, watching the dancing from afar and wallowing in self-pity, comforted only by the solitude provided by the blizzard.

Also, Father Christmas had forgotten to give me my present. Such a trivial thing should not have been of significant consequence, yet I felt as if it were the worst blow of all.

The dancing continued, and the cold grew more biting. Brushing snow from my arms, I wished my brother Theophrastus were with me. Not the grumpy old man, but the noble and brave Theophrastus of yesteryear. He would never have allowed any cocky elf to insult me and walk away unscathed. But Theo was dying on his farm . . . or out hunting Ferdinand! I winced. Now *that* was a situation that must be sorted out as soon as I returned home. Perhaps I could send Theo after Astreus instead. Hunting down an elf who spent his time in the Void should be enough of a challenge to keep him busy. And if Theo caught up with him—all the better!

How ironic that Ferdinand had been jealous of the elf figurine. Ferdinand was worth a thousand of Astreus!

As I thought this, Astreus himself stepped from the snowy whiteness. He towered above me, the wind streaming through his storm-gray hair. His mirrored cloak, with its brilliant blue tint, billowed from his shoulders, and snowflakes speckled the silver and black fur trimming his dark blue garments.

Yet, he seemed as at ease in this icy arctic clime as he might be in the eternal spring of Mommur, where the elven court resided.

Just watching him enthralled me. He moved with the sleekness of a snow leopard, all poetry and grace. Yet I was so consumed with fury at him for waltzing up as if nothing were wrong, after his despicable treatment of me during the feast, that I could hardly form my thoughts into words. Furious, I crossed my arms and turned my back on him.

"You have some nerve!" I blurted out finally.

Astreus spoke to my back most courteously. "I have come to beg your forgiveness for having missed our tryst by the river. I would have moved Heaven and Earth to greet you there. As luck would have it, neither Heaven nor Earth was available to me."

The meaning of this last comment was so shocking, assuming he was telling the truth, that, for a moment, I could not reply. Was he saying that he had not left me standing by the river as a prank after all?

Any pleasure this revelation brought was short-lived. Why was he bringing this up now? Had he recalled our ancient tryst, only to forget the insult he just dealt me before the entire court? I supposed it was possible. The nature of elves and their memories remained a mystery.

Astreus stepped in front of me, as if he were oblivious to the connotation of my having turned my back to him. (Or perhaps he was. For all I knew, elves might turn their backs upon one another as a sign of favor.)

"Did Mephistopheles give you my message in time?" he asked. "Or were you condemned to wander by the riverbank, waiting in vain?"

"Mephisto? . . . oh, that! No, he did not find me until the next day, and even then I could not understand what he was babbling about. He was dru-unk . . ."

Or was he?

That next morning, after I had waited all night, Mephisto had shown up and babbled drunkenly about a message sent by Astreus—a story I had believed, until this moment, to have been concocted by Mephisto. Only, looking back, I realized Mephisto had not been drunk . . . he had been crazy. I had not recognized it at the time, because I had never seen him without his sanity before; I had not recognized the symptoms. Mab had once asked me when Mephisto first showed signs of madness. That had been the day.

Meanwhile, Astreus was saying, "I am most sorrowful to hear this. I had hoped he would reach you to spare you any discomfort. Please grant me your forgiveness for whatever distress I may have caused."

"You are forgiven—for that." I crossed my arms. Astreus smiled. His eyes were as blue as a clear winter's sky, and they bored into mine with such intensity as to leave me lightheaded. He extended his hand.

"Will you dance with me, Lady?"

The sheer audacity of his request left me thunderstruck.

"My lord, you have not yet apologized for humiliating me before the entire feast hall!"

"That is true."

"Will you apologize?"

"No."

"Then I shall not dance with you!"

"Come," he took my hand. I snatched it away.

"If we dance, the others will see us together," he explained. "They will assume my performance in the hall was caused by my dismay at some rebuff of yours, and not by any shortcoming upon your part."

"Why should they think that?"

"Why else would I depart with such obvious dismay and then seek you out again, unless it was because I disliked the coldness with which you received my suit?" He spoke as if this conclusion were so obvious that even the smallest of children could not possibly miss it. "They need not know the truth. Come, I will spin you about, and when we part, the others shall come clamoring to partner you, eager to hear from your own lips the subject of our quarrel, and how we came to be reconciled."

"But we are not reconciled," I stated.

"It shall be our secret."

I wanted to refuse, but it was hard to speak while laughing. The sheer audacity of his position on the subject amused me. Astreus did not wait for my answer. He seized me about my waist and drew me, swirling, among the other dancers. I could not pull away now, not without making a scene before the entire company. Resigned, I let him take the lead and turned my concentration to the steps; for I had no elvish surefootedness to keep me from falling on the ice. All eyes were on us now, and a knowing mirth twinkled in the elf king's gaze. The queen, however, regarded us coldly.

The music and the twinkling lights sang to me, enchanting me with their beauty. Astreus spun me about, his arm tight around my waist, until I was dizzy with laughter and exhilaration. Then, he bowed and left to dance with other maidens, while, true to his prediction, the lords of the High Council swarmed about me, each seeking my hand to dance.

I danced with Aundelair and Valendur, with Vandel and with Fincunir. This last even spun me beneath the mistletoe, which had been hung above the pond, and brushed his cool lips across mine, his eyes mocking all the while. Then, Father Christmas himself asked me to dance, and Mephisto, and Mab, and six handsome blond elves of Father Christmas's staff, whose names I never caught. When I stopped to catch my breath, the elf king himself came to request a dance.

He bowed over my hand, his towering antlers inclining toward me. His eyes burned with strange compelling emotions that made the company seem to fall away, until there were only he and I. Before I could accept, Astreus appeared out of nowhere and caught my other hand, saying softly in my ear, "Come away with me."

I blushed, made uncomfortable both by the intensity of the king's gaze and by the caress of Astreus's breath upon my neck. Flustered, I blurted, "I do not wish to offend your king. He claimed my attention first."

King Alastor laughed, shaking his antlers. "If, of all the many charms here at Bromigos's, Lord Astreus has eyes only for you, it would be niggardly of me to stand in his way. Go with him, fair maiden, and bring him what cheer you may." And he strode off in search of some other partner.

As he departed, I whispered to Astreus, "What is Bromigos?"

"The name we call our host."

"Father Christmas? I thought his name was Nicholas."

"Such a generous man can afford to answer to many names," he replied, drawing me away from the dance.

Before we could leave, however, Lady Sylvie ran up, laughing, and plucked at Astreus's sleeve, her eyes of perfect blue gazing merrily into his. Butterflies fluttered about her, surrounding her in a cloud of winged color. As she came to a stop beside us, they settled to form a many-colored living cloak that graced her shoulders and swayed about her body, as if the cloak billowed in its own private wind.

She was so lovely, lively, and quick that I felt slow and cumbersome in comparison, an unfamiliar sensation, for I was used to comparing favorably with other mortal women. I frowned, recalling with dismay the taste of the straw outside a certain feast hall in Paris.

Unwilling to give Astreus an opportunity to humiliate me yet again, I stepped back politely; however, he kept hold of my hand.

"Lord Astreus," the elven maiden cried, "so long you have been absent from our company. Surely, you could not be so cruel as to creep away without dancing with me even once?"

"Another time." He inclined his head politely.

"But I have missed you so!" Sylvie glanced at him sidelong while tugging on his arm. "And we have so much of which to speak, our two domains being commingled, my sylphs and your many aerial servants." She lowered her long silvery lashes until they brushed her high-boned cheeks. "Surely you will not deny me this tiny request?"

Astreus remained unmoved. "Another time."

She pouted prettily. "What has this mortal maid, who will be here today and thrown upon the fire tomorrow, to offer you, compared to me, your immortal companion? Come away with me. I'm sure the Aftercomer will wait. Where else has she to go?"

Astreus paused, and, with sinking heart, I knew what would come next. Again, I tried to draw away demurely. Better to be seen yielding the field willingly, than to be humiliatingly thrust aside. Astreus gripped my hand firmly, however, and would not release it. He looked neither at Silvie nor me but stood gazing off across the dance floor toward where, amidst snow and twinkling lights, the elf queen twirled in the arms of her partner. For an instant, Lord Astreus and Queen Maeve regarded each other, both of them with eyes as blank as mirrors. Then, Astreus turned and bowed to Sylvie.

"Another time," he repeated a third time.

Without another word, she turned and drifted back into the dance.

HE led me a short distance, the swirling snowflakes closing in about us, until the dancers and their merry music seemed distant and muffled. It was as if we were alone in our own little world, insulated from everything else.

Astreus halted and leaned back, gazing straight up. Laughing, he squeezed my hand.

"Isn't it beautiful?"

I craned my neck. Above, the sky was a vast and endless field of dancing snow. Countless tiny specks of white whirled along spiral paths and swirling eddies in their progression toward the ground.

"Yes!"

Astreus closed his eyes. Snowflakes fell upon his lashes. He spread his arms, pulling my hand along, as if we were about to dive into the sky.

Then we did.

The earth fell away beneath my feet, and we ascended, ever faster, into the twirling snow. Soft snowflakes swept against my face like birds' wings, melting into cold wetness upon my skin. The wind tousled my hair, tugging at my hair combs until they came free and tumbled earthward. I caught one with my free hand, but the other comb fell away and was lost in the blizzard below. My silvery hair, now free, whipped about my face and shoulders.

Joy, for which I could not possibly find words, sang throughout me. We were flying!

Up, up we rose, until the clouds of the storm fell away beneath us, and I found myself in a clear night sky, beneath a field of stars. Below me, I could see a vast distance. Beyond the storm lay an ocean whose frozen waves sparkled violet. Above, a brilliant glow that was not quite Northern Lights and not quite a rainbow danced, shining purple, lavender, lilac, and magenta.

With a dawning sense of awe and alarm, I realized we were no longer on Earth!

The winds that had lifted us slackened, and we began to fall. Astreus whistled sharply. A trumpet-call answered. Above us, one of the starry constellations tore itself free from the unfamiliar sky and plummeted toward us. As it grew closer, I saw it was a giant black swan the size of a sloop, with stars for eyes. The graceful bird swooped beneath us and caught us, so that we spilled, laughing, onto the soft plumage of its back.

Righting myself, I stroked the silken feathers of the sinuous neck. The black swan spread her wide wings and soared upward. The dancing lights and the violet seas fell away, while all around us the constellations stirred to life. Many were new to me, yet a few were familiar. I recognized the River Eridanus—which flows through the Milky Way to eventually, cascade down beyond the World's End—and Orion with his great belt, arrow nocked in his bow. He turned his head, regarding us as we flew past. Other giants, whom I did not recognize, watched us as well: a sleek star-eyed cat, a pack of lean hounds, a woman carrying a jar of oil, a ship with sails of starlight. As we glided past a giant seven-tailed steed, it tossed its head, striking the black swan with its long nose and sending us careening, but the great bird righted itself before Astreus and I were thrown from its back.

We flew past the Big Dipper, splashing through the milky liquid that flowed from it. Giddy with wonder, I licked the moisture from my lips. A sweet freshness dazzled my mouth, tasting part of milk and part of cool stardust. As I swallowed, I found I could now hear laughter and the baying of hounds . . . and music.

Entranced upon the black plumage, I listened to the Music of the Spheres. I had never heard the symphony of the fixed stars before, and yet I recognized it instantly. Its crystal perfection, so vast and marvelous and fine, rang like harmonic living bells, filling the Void, until there was no emptiness left. My heart swelled with the music, until I feared it would burst. Then, I was swept away, no longer aware of heart or limbs or "me"—only music.

When I came to myself again, I lay stretched out on the black swan, my head pillowed upon her down. Astreus leaned over me. His eyes were as violet as the sparkling seas below. There was a bitter taste in my mouth, and I saw he held in his other hand a black vial, which he returned to the folds of his cloak.

Gazing up at his slanted features which were illuminated by starlight, I was aware of several things at once. The first was that I had just done something extraordinarily foolhardy. Not only had I allowed myself to be drawn away and beguiled by an elf, but I had also ingested an unknown supernatural substance without thought for the consequences. If, assuming I ever returned home, I could still draw sustenance from earthly food, I should consider myself extraordinarily lucky, and offer thanks and blessings to my Lady immediately.

The second was that I lay on my back nestled in cushioning feathers, gazing up into the startling eyes of an elf. There was something dangerous about even being near elves; just breathing the air near them was enough to fill one's head with strange dreams, as if they walked awake in a place we only visited in sleep—a place not meant for mortals. He was so near that I could not help but breathe this air, as crisp and sweet as a fresh wind. It was as if a secret wind blew wherever he went; a wind that threatened to sweep me away again, into a world of sky, stars, and madness.

The third was a sense of unshakable peace, a calm serenity left behind by the Music of the Spheres, as if I had—for a time—found my way to a lost home I had not known I was missing.

I sat up, dazed and blinking, still agog with wonder and awe, and scooted backwards, until I leaned against the graceful curve of the giant black swan's neck. The bitter taste in my mouth caused me to grimace. Astreus leaned back on his haunches, laughing at me.

"What did you give me?"

"Just as mortal philosophers distill the essence of poppy in hopes that such droughts will give their thoughts wings, so we elves have draughts that do the reverse. Your soul had flown far from your body, joining the celestial choir. I summoned it back."

"I thank you."

"Do you?" He cocked his head, his eyes dark and starry. " 'Tis unusual for a mortal to be transported so. I had thought merely to show you a glimpse of the glories of my realm. The magic you guard for your dread father must have seeped into your soul, transforming it and making you more like us." His eyes narrowed, and he caught a stray lock of my hair. "Last time we met, your hair was as black as obsidian. Is it the mortal disease that has caused it to turn into spun silver?"

I shook my head and drew my hair out of his fingers.

"Family quarrel."

Astreus smiled subtly. "Perhaps mortals are not so different from elves."

The living constellations were gone, as was the velvety midnight sky. Instead, the air glowed with a rosy hue.

"Where are we now?" I asked.

"At the back of the North Wind. Below lies my stronghold."

Hyperborea! A cold country, but so very beautiful, haunted by gryphons and one-eyed Arimaspians, where the sun lay always beyond the horizon. I wondered what Astreus's home would be like, and what he might intend the two of us to do there, alone together. The thought both pleased and terrified me.

"I will not dally with you, Astreus," I said, my heart beating quickly.

"Would a hawk woo a she-dove?" He laughed, mocking. As he tilted his head to regard me, his eyes were as yellow as any falcon's. The analogy did nothing to soothe my mounting wariness. "No more an elf pursue a mortal maid."

"Then what do you want?"

He stood, as surefooted atop the black swan as he had been upon the dance floor of ice. "Anon, there will be time enough for you to learn what I require of you when our feet are again planted upon the ground." He peered downward. "Nor need you fear that I have spirited you away; a passage leads back from my home to Bromigos's hall."

A frisson of something akin to fear passed through me at the words "what I require of you," and I found myself grudgingly admitting that maybe Mab had been right. It would have been wiser for us to have avoided the High Council. On the other hand, perhaps I was overreacting. He could have left me among the fixed stars, my soul fled. Shaking off my surge of panic, I let the joy and wonder of our flight again wash over me.

Wrapping my arms about the thick neck of the great black swan, I peered downward. Below us lay a palace shaped like a windrose. The domes and spires of the airy palace formed its center, the eight tall towers rising around it marking the cardinal directions, while the circular outer wall delineated the circumference. The eternal dawn-light gleamed off the silver roofs, dyeing them rose and cherry red, except for the spire of the palace dome, which glowed a peachy gold, as if it rose high enough to be struck by the first ray of the rising sun.

The beauty of it took my breath away.

Leaning over the side of the black swan, one hand upon the base of the wing, Astreus pointed toward one of the towers. "Rightfully, that belongs to Caekias. Before your father stole them from me, he, Caurus, and Boreas were my right hand, the weapon with which I smote my enemies." It took me a moment to realize he was referring to Mab.

I had been here once before, I realized suddenly, during the early days of the Great Wind Hunt, the time we chased the North Wind across the Russian steppe and over the Rhipaean Mountains to Hyperborea. We had been within sight of this palace when we finally captured Boreas, by sneaking up on him from behind.

"What was he like?" I asked. "Caekias, I mean."

"Wild and free and as fierce as the Northeast Wind should be," he replied. "Come!"

Astreus offered me his hand. I did not know what he wanted, but I took it, rising unsteadily. As I did so, he yanked me toward him, caught me up into his arms as if I were a bride, and leapt from the black swan's back.

Downward we plunged.

We fell through the rosy glow of the eternal early morning, the wind whistling around us. Astreus dropped feet-first, holding himself as calmly as if he were back in the feast hall. His silvery-gray eyes upon me, he leaned forward, until his face was only a little distance from mine.

"Mortal maid," he said. I could hear him clearly despite the whistling of the wind. "I have but to release you now, and you will fall and break apart upon the spires, speeding your way to Heaven. Is this your desire?"

"No," I cried, clinging to him with all my strength. His laughter rang out about me, both mocking and joyous.

As I clung to him, breathing his crisp cool scent, a heady sensation of dreaminess enveloped me. Though still awake, I dreamt I flew, surrounded by icy cutting winds. As we dove, screaming with joy, towers tumbled before our might; cities crashed into the sea; fleets of ships were blown against the rocks, splitting like kindling. Dead bodies washed up upon the shores until they lay in stacks. Somewhere nearby, Astreus laughed with glee, his eyes as dark as a tempest.

"All those people! Dead!" I cried, my throat dry.

"It is their fate to die. Does not an early death speed them to Heaven's Gate?"

"Are you crazy?" I cried, not even finding it odd that he could see my dream.

His brows drew together, surprised, and I realized that his question had been serious. I struggled to find words that would convey to him the horror of what he was suggesting. Appeals to human sympathy would avail nothing. Elves had none.

Gritting my teeth, I said with what restraint I could muster, "Any man you kill who has not yet made his peace with his Maker goes straight to Hell!"

Astreus's eyes turned white with shock. "Have I sent men to Hell?"

"Does it matter?" I asked, curious.

"All things regarding the Infernal are weighty. I would not, of my own doing, swell Hell's ranks by a single soul, not again!" He glanced down at me with eyes that blazed with a scarlet fire. "What of you, Maid? Do you fear Hell? Is that why you cling to this mortal coil?"

"No," I said truthfully. I had commended my soul to Heaven long ago.

"Then, why do you not wish to die? Why stay here, in these dreary Shadowlands, when the true beauty of Heaven could be yours?"

"I like it here!" I snapped, clinging to him harder, for I feared I felt his hands loosening about me.

Astreus stared at me, as if thunderstruck. "Do you? Can such a thing be? Are not all souls homesick for High Heaven? I saw how the celestial choir drew you. Why do you deny its lure?"

"Why do you?"

"It is denied to me."

"Oh!" I whispered, biting my lip. "Oh . . . how sad."

"Were I able, I would weep tears of blood."

We fell in silence for a time. Now that my fear had ebbed, the exhilaration of our fall delighted me. I laid my head against his shoulder. The wolverine fur trimming his garments tickled my nose. I luxuriated in the wind and motion. As if in a daze, I dreamt the elf lord leaned over me, brushing his mouth across mine and licking the stardew from my lips. But it was a dream only. When I looked up, I saw Astreus gazed off into the distance, his eyes clouded.

We landed softly upon a high silvery balcony adrip with hoarfrost. He placed me upon my feet, and I stood shakily, trying to get my bearings. He laughed.

"Poor mortal maid, as shaky as a newborn fawn. Was it our fall that spooked you so?" His eyes gleamed a brilliant green with humor and mockery. "Or does your sudden weakness blow from another quarter? 'Tis said that mortal maids find elven lords captivating, and cannot but become enamored of our charms, weaving elaborate dreams in which we come unbidden to their marriage bowers. Have you such dreams, Miranda? If so, shake them from you, like old cobwebs, for they shall not come to pass. Mortal maids are puny things compared to our elven ladies, and hold no allure."

"I am fine," I snapped, steadying myself, but the memory of the stolen dream-kiss suffused my cheeks with heat.

Astreus led me into the tower, down a pearly spiral staircase, to a doorway made of ivory.

"Wait here," he said. "I shall be back presently."

He was gone but a moment, returning with a smile to lead me through the ivory door. Almost immediately, I recognized the pine-bedecked cedar halls of Father Christmas's mansion. Turning a corner, we entered a small nook in the hallway, in which stood a silver samovar heated by a cheery blue flame. Silver goblets rested on a tray beside it. A Douglas fir decorated with lit candles stood to one side, and the pungent scent of its needles mingled with the cinnamon and clove of mulling spices. The garlands of pine boughs strung along the walls were hung with bells.

The elf lord stopped to pour us both goblets of mulled wine. He seemed so tall and elegant as he poured. I gazed at the enameled blue leather that covered his back and wondered whether he, too, had scars over his shoulder blades, where once wings had sprouted. Astreus handed me a cup, which I quaffed gratefully, relieved to see that I was still capable of drinking mortal draughts.

"What was this thing you said you required of me?" I asked presently.

"I have a gift for you," Astreus said.

Unbidden, the thought came to wonder what he could possibly offer me that could improve upon this glorious ride, the like of which I had never experienced in all my long years, but I held my tongue. Admitting I had received a gift from an elf might give him power over me. Instead, I laughed aloud.

"Do you take me for a child, Lord Stormwind? I know better than to accept gifts from elves."

Astreus's eyes, now blue as sapphires, danced. "My heart tells me you will accept this one."

"Mine tells me I shall not," I replied firmly.

"We shall see. . . ."

"Is that so?" I murmured under my breath.

"Do you propose a wager, then?" Astreus laughed, delighted. "The promptings of my heart against those of yours? I accept!"

"I said nothing about a wager. . . ."

"But a wager has been proposed. You cannot back out now. What shall we wager? A boon, perhaps?

"No!" I cried, but he would not be dissuaded. Better to take the wager and define the terms, than to find myself trapped in the classic fairy-tale blunder of having offered an open-ended boon. That way lay only madness.

"Very well," I said, "but we must agree on something ahead of time. Something simple, and easy to accomplish."

"If you insist. How about: if I triumph in our wager, you will . . ." Astreus leaned his head back, thinking, "make a coat of arms for me such as the one Mephisto once described that you made for your deadly brother in centuries past."

"You mean the embroidered one?" I asked, amazed. "This is not some kind of trick, is it? Where I'll find out too late your coat of arms is infinite? Or must include colors not found on Earth?"

"No trickery. It is a heraldic image such as any coat of arms."

"Then why ask me?" I asked. "Surely you could have a much finer version if you asked some elven seamstress?"

"True, but such a piece would lack the quaint imperfections of a coat of arms made by mortal hands. Besides, what else could you offer me?" he asked, the inflection of his voice making clear I had little else of worth.

Great, I was to be the butt of elven jokes for all eternity. I sighed. At least, he had not asked me to kill a family member or eat the moon.

"And if you should win, which you will not," he continued, "what will you ask of me? Shall I tie up a rainbow for you? Or, draw down a star from the night sky? Would you prefer I cast a befuddlement over some enemy? Or, shall I sing to you a song never heard by mortal ears? Mind that you choose something I can complete quickly, for I shall soon be away about the queen's dread work again, and my time will not be my own."

"What is it like in the Void?" I asked curiously.

Astreus's eyes darkened. " 'Tis not a fit subject for such a fair house."

I nodded, chastened, and considered. Setting him upon the Three Shadowed Ones was tempting, but the trouble with elves was they tended to solve problems to their satisfaction—which would not necessarily be mine. No, I needed something simple and straightforward, something he could not turn awry.

I crossed my arms. "I would like an apology."

"For my treatment of you before the court during the Christmas feast?"

When I nodded, he stared off into the distance, twirling his goblet between his fingers and sipping the sweet scented wine. Finally, he gave a shake of his head.

"Nay, that price is too high."

"What!" I cried. "You want me to embroider you a coat of arms, which will take me weeks, if not months, but you won't apologize for insulting me before the entire elven council and Father Christmas? You don't have to apologize publicly," I decided, "just to me."

"It is too high."

"Forget it," I cried, exasperated. "I don't even want to see this gift of yours. Go back and dance with that poor elven lady you spurned. She seemed quite disappointed."

Astreus gave an amused snort. "Lady Sylvie? She cares naught for me. She came at the elf queen's urging, her mission being but to keep us apart."

I arched an eyebrow. "Because I'm an 'Aftercomer'?"

Astreus's eyes were as silvery as mirrors and disturbing, for in them, I looked far more delicate and frail than mundane looking-glasses reported. "Because you represent all that Her Majesty despises.

"Back to our wager!" He leaned forward, eyes suddenly aglow. "You have been to the Well from which the Water of Life flows, have you ever looked over the World's End, where the Eridanus plunges off the edge of the world, and wondered what was beyond the brink?"

"No," I replied stuffily, though of course I had. I have stared into the darkness, watching the beautiful cascade of silvery light with its stardust spray and wondered what lay beyond.

"Only seven have passed over that brink and returned." Astreus touched his chest. "I am one of the seven. If you win, I shall tell you of the wonders I saw, and the secret of how to pass over the brink and come back again."

I recalled the siren call of the eerie quiet Void and was sorely tempted. Just because a particular technique worked for Astreus, however, did not mean it would work for me. And while I would love to hear tales of his journey, I did not want to hear them more than I wanted an apology.

"No."

Astreus cocked his head, his eyes dark and starry. "Did you enjoy our flight among the stars?"

I would have answered demurely, but I could tell by his laughter that the joy shining in my face had betrayed me.

"It was wonderful!" I admitted softly. "Everything I could have desired."

"If you win, I shall whisper in your ear the name of that fair black swan. By uttering it, you shall be able to call her from the night sky and fly about upon her back whenever you please."

I pictured soaring among the stars, taking my siblings on rides to share with them the glory and marvel of it all. How fast did that beautiful bird fly? Was it limited to mortal speeds? We had just lost the Lear. Could I switch to a more magical form of transportation?

But this was foolishness, of course. Much of my traveling was for mundane business. I could just imagine the confusion of air traffic control when I tried to land the giant swan at SeaTac or LAX. Besides, just because Astreus gave me the creature's name did not mean that it would obey me, or that it would not carry me away only to strand me in some foreign sky.

Sadly, I shook my head. "No."

Astreus leaned toward me, his eyes a sparkling violet. "Tonight you heard the Music of the Spheres. Few mortals can say the same. So compelling was its music to you that it drew your soul out of your mortal flesh. Do you want to hear it again?"

My mouth had gone dry. Flying filled me with joy, but this music had transported me beyond myself, beyond the mortal world. Compared to that, what did anything else matter?

Astreus continued, "I will give you a flask of stardew. If you sip it on clear nights from a tower balcony or a mountaintop, you shall be able to hear the Celestial Choir. I shall even throw in a vial of mothan juice, so your servants can call you back to your body again."

Of all his offers, this one was the most tempting. I had already experienced the effects of stardew and mothan juice, so I did not fear that his offer was somehow a cheat. The very strength of my desire, however, warned me of the dangers of this course. If I had a flask of the milky stardew and heard the Celestial Choir again, would I ever elect to return? I could not accept and run the risk that I might leave Father's work undone.

"Thrice asked and thrice refused," I said. "I am excused and need not consider your gift."

"Wait, Miranda! I shall agree! If you do not take my gift, I will give you the apology you seek." His eyes went an eerie violet. "For if you do not accept my gift, you are not the woman I take you to be. Nor shall it matter whether I apologize or no."

I frowned, uncertain what to make of this last speech. "Show me this mysterious gift, then, but keep in mind, I want an apology very much. Even were I tempted to take the gift, I would refuse it, thanks to this wager."

"We shall see," Astreus replied, smiling enigmatically. He refilled the two goblets, handing me one and raising the other. I shook my head to clear it of strange sensations, my heart beating rapidly. Elves were not good companions for men, regardless of their intent.

"To our wager: may fortune smile upon us both!"

"I do not see how she can," I replied, touching my cup against his. The silver goblets rang like bells. "That is the nature of wagers."

"If you are pleased with the present, and I gain a coat of arms, we both prosper," he said. When I continued to frown, he said, "You do not approve of that toast. I will propose a new one: To freedom!"

"To freedom," I agreed.

Lifting his cup, Astreus drained it in a single draught. I sipped mine cautiously and wondered anxiously how well elves held their liquor.

"May we elves be released from the tithe, that terrible curse laid upon us by the Powers of Hell," he finished.

"I have heard Hell once excused the seven-year tithe, and you were given the credit for having orchestrated it," I said. "Perhaps, the same thing could be done again?"

A haunting shadow passed across Astreus's face, contorting his handsome features. His eyes grew the horrible red-brown of old blood.

"The price was too high," he whispered grimly. Then, as quickly as it had come, the shadow was gone. "But let us speak of joyful things, such as Christmas tidings and the gift I have for you."

"Astreus, why are you even bothering?" I asked wearily. "You know as well as I—better, I am sure—what sorts of things elves do to unsuspecting mortals. How could I trust a gift from an elf, even if I wanted to?"

The wine had turned his eyes a warm azure blue. "How cautious is wise Miranda," he laughed, "a gentle dove, fearful of sharp elven talons. You are wise not to trust my people, for we are capricious and would do you mischief in the blink of an eye. Such mischief is not my purpose here. By my troth, I swear it.

"Besides," he added, "I am bestowing it in Bromigos's house, the Mansion of Gifts. Were it not wholesome, he would not have allowed it."

This last thought cheered me, and I felt mildly less foolish. For the first time, I found myself curious. Was this the same present Father Christmas had promised me? What might this creature, who offered me rainbows and stardew, expect me to want? Did he believe he knew enough about me, from a single dance on one star-studded night, to guess what my heart desired?

"Behold," he said, "the gift I have been keeping for you these three hundred years, for I had intended to gift you with it when we met beneath the willow by the Avon. Nor was it an easy task to find it. It is this we journeyed to my stronghold to fetch." He held out the little package to me. The green paper sparkled. "Open it, sweet Miranda, and you shall not regret it. Refuse it, and you shall regret evermore."

An eerie premonition came upon me. What if he were telling the truth? Elves sometimes did. What if all chance of future happiness lay within this fey gift? I closed my eyes to pray, and felt the warm steady calm of my Lady's presence.

"You unwrap it," I insisted. Had he really gone to so much trouble, or was that just the elven version of poetic license?

"That is not how things are done within the House of Christmas," he replied, extending it again.

Slowly, I untied the ribbon and opened the wrapping paper. The green foil rustled and fell away. I breathed in the pleasant odor of leather. Inside, lay a small black volume, no thicker than a pamphlet, unblemished by any title or ornament. From the style of the binding, I judged it to be from the fifteenth or sixteenth century, about the time I first met Astreus. A shiver of anticipation tingled along my spine.

"What is it?" I whispered, as my fingers touched the soft supple leather. As I lifted the cover, a strange tremor danced skittishly through my limbs. Startled, I tried to jerk away, but it was too late. My eyes had lit upon the first page. All the apologies in the universe could not have torn that book from my hands. Written there, in a beautiful looping script, were the words:

I, Deiphobe of the Seven Hills, Sibyl of Eurynome, herein do record the secrets of my order.

Here ends Part One.

To be continued in Part Two:

PROSPERO IN HELL

In which we meet the remaining Prospero siblings,
and many secrets are revealed.

ABOUT THE AUTHOR

This is L. Jagi Lamplighter's first novel. She lives with her husband and children in northern Virginia, where she's working on *Prospero in Hell*, book two of Prospero's Daughter. For more information, visit her website at www.sff.net/people/lamplighter.